SOME WILDFLOWER IN MY HEART

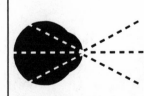

This Large Print Book carries the
Seal of Approval of N.A.V.H.

SOME WILDFLOWER
IN MY HEART

JAMIE LANGSTON TURNER

THORNDIKE PRESS

An imprint of Thomson Gale, a part of The Thomson Corporation

THOMSON
GALE

Detroit • New York • San Francisco • New Haven, Conn. • Waterville, Maine • London

THOMSON

™

GALE

Thomson Gale is part of The Thomson Corporation.

Thomson and Star Logo and Thorndike are trademarks and Gale is a registered trademark used herein under license.

ALL RIGHTS RESERVED

Thorndike Press® Large Print Christian Fiction.

The text of this Large Print edition is unabridged.

Other aspects of the book may vary from the original edition.

Set in 16 pt. Plantin.

LIBRARY OF CONGRESS CATALOGING-IN-PUBLICATION DATA

Turner, Jamie L.
    Some wildflower in my heart / by Jamie Langston Turner.
        p. cm. — (Thorndike Press large print Christian fiction)
    ISBN-13: 978-0-7862-9667-5 (alk. paper)
    ISBN-10: 0-7862-9667-4 (alk. paper)
    1. Large type books. I. Title.
PS3570.U717S66 2007
813'.54—dc22   2007011428

Published in 2007 by arrangement with Bethany House Publishers.

Printed in the United States of America on permanent paper
10 9 8 7 6 5 4 3 2 1

For my parents
James Tyndall Langston
and
Carolyn Louise Thomas Langston
who planted and watered my garden
with faith, hope, and love.

*The Lord shall open unto thee his good
treasure, the heaven to give the rain unto thy
land in its season, and to bless all the work of
thine hand.*
DEUTERONOMY 28:12

■ ■ ■ ■

PART ONE:
SOMETHING FROM
OAK & PINE

■ ■ ■ ■

SECRET CHAMBERS
1

I first saw Birdie Freeman at a funeral one hard winter day more than a year ago, but I did not meet her then. When she arrived in my life some months later, I had not the vaguest notion that I would one day write a book about her. Had someone suggested such a thing, I would have dismissed him as a fool.

Had I known that Birdie Freeman was to bring into my life drastic changes, I would have fled to a distant land. But I did not know. How misleading were her plainness and smallness, her quick smile and ready touch. When my eyes first lighted upon her face that January day, I could not begin to know the wrenching pain I was to undergo because of her.

"Love sought is good but given unsought is better." Thus says Olivia in Shakespeare's *Twelfth Night.* Mine is a story of love unsought.

My passion is reading. I am haunted by phrases from things I have read and by things

I have seen and done as well, though I prefer by far the haunting from things I have read. Many years ago I read a story by a German author named Heinrich Böll that began with the words "One of the strangest interludes in my life." I do not recall the particulars of the story from which I extracted this single, rather unremarkable phrase, but I have kept it these many years as a memento of the story and have thought of it upon several occasions, for I have had many strange interludes in my life.

Yesterday, while I was in my office cubicle in the cafeteria at Emma Weldy Elementary School, clearing off the top of my desk for the much-anticipated summer hiatus, it came to me that the phrase was a fitting summary of the past nine months. Indeed, it was one of the strangest interludes in my life, perhaps *the* strangest, and I must now take the summer before me to sort it out, to write it down as it comes to me. It is a story that demands a spare, straightforward telling, yet it cannot be rushed.

I am a great keeper of secrets and have many to keep, but the time is right for the sharing of them. I have no doubt that I can tell my story in such a way that will catch a publisher's eye. I feel prepared for my mission, as if my whole life of reading has been aimed toward this summer of writing. The fact that I am fifty-one and writing something of this magnitude for the first time does not give me pause except for a brief, encouraging reflection that many fine works of literature have been composed by writers much older than I. If it is true, as they say, that a man must walk through darkness before he can become a writer, then I am well qualified.

Perhaps I shall someday offer my finished manuscript to my husband, Thomas, who will likely stare at it in bewilderment — so many words! — before attempting to read it. Though he respects the written word highly, the spoken word via television is more to his liking. Indeed, it has been many years since Thomas has read the complete text of any work, excluding our local newspaper, which some imaginative soul in the early days of the township titled the Filbert *Nutshell,* a witticism that is lost upon the present generation, most of whom know only the peanut.

My thoughts are at sixes and sevens. Such is not usually the case. I made the decision yesterday upon arriving home from school that this summer I would undertake to write the story of the past nine months, and last night I purchased ten red spiral-bound notebooks at Kmart for this purpose. I find now, however, that writing a book requires a far greater leap than I had supposed, for I have no provocative opening.

From my many years of reading, I know that there are questions to be answered when one enters a story. A reader wants a speedy orientation as to the main character, conflict, and setting.

I shall therefore plunge in. The main character of my story is Birdie Freeman, a gentle and beautiful woman. I am not Birdie Freeman. I am Margaret Bryce Tuttle, and I am telling the story. The conflict, I suppose, occurs between Birdie and me, although the collision is one of will and philosophy more than of literal combat. You, the reader, must care about Birdie because what you conclude about her may very well change your life as it has changed my own. In truth, she may impact me in ways I have yet to discover. The story takes place in Filbert, South Carolina, five miles south of Derby and ten miles west of Berea.

You no doubt will object to the setting, for you already hear my voice, and it is not the voice of a native southerner. You are accustomed to drawls and affected twangs in southern literature, to gangling, loose-jointed sentences and quaint colloquialisms. An immigrant to the South from northern and midwestern cities, I do not speak in such a manner. Though I have grown to love the melody and pulse of the speech around me, I do not mimic it.

The truth is that for most of my adult life I have spoken aloud as infrequently as possible, although I have always possessed what my

14

mother once called "a rich, voluble inner dialogue." When I was twelve, my mother described my speech patterns as one part King James, one part William Shakespeare, one part Jane Austen, and one part Theodore Geisel, whose rhythmic cadences entranced me as a child and who was to become increasingly popular over my lifetime as a writer of versified children's stories under his pseudonym, Dr. Seuss.

But I must not stray from my purpose. Mine is truly a southern story through and through. Birdie Freeman is a southern woman, and Filbert is a southern town. As I said, I first saw Birdie Freeman at a funeral. It occurs to me now that the funeral may serve well as an entry into my story.

Though I have no living blood relations of whom I am aware, my husband, Thomas, has an intricate genealogy, and it was his elderly uncle Mayfield Spalding who bore the misfortune of dying on New Year's Day a year and a half ago. It was Thomas, in fact, who found his uncle collapsed on the floor of his bathroom on New Year's Eve and who called to tell Mayfield's only daughter, Joan, and Joan's three brothers that their father had suffered a severe stroke and was not expected to live. He did, in fact, die in the early hours of the next morning. Joan lives in Berea, only ten miles away, yet she had not spoken to her father for over six years and had been at odds with him for most of her life. Her brothers, grown men now, live in various locations of the Southeast.

Joan and her brothers asked Thomas to arrange the funeral since he lived in Filbert and, unlike the rest of the family, had always been on speaking terms with Mayfield. The arrangements proved easy enough, for on top of his uncle's desk, Thomas found a typed sheet of instructions with the heading *My Funeral,* signed and dated a few months earlier.

It was clear that death had not taken Mayfield Spalding unawares. Indeed, he seemed to have been expecting its arrival. He had purchased a burial plot eight years ago at the cemetery located halfway between Derby and Filbert, a large green acreage known as Shepherd's Valley, though it is no valley at all but rather a flat, level expanse with a grassy knoll at the entrance. We further discovered that in December, only four weeks before his death, Mayfield had driven to the Mortland Funeral Home in Derby and chosen his casket, an excursion that could hardly stimulate one's holiday spirit, although it had not appeared that Mayfield was more melancholy than usual that Christmas. He had prepaid all expenses, including what is referred to as the "family wreath" to adorn the top of the casket.

Listed first on the typed instructions, which

were numbered from one to twenty-three, was *Call Brother Theodore Hawthorne at the Church of the Open Door in Derby.* Thomas did so immediately, and Mr. Hawthorne drove over from Derby to pay a consolation call. I told Thomas I would not be present under the same roof with a preacher, and for the first time in his life, he said to me quite sternly, "Margaret, you got to put all that baggage behind you for now and think about Uncle Mayfield." I was so astounded by both his tone and his remark that I did not answer, and when Mr. Hawthorne arrived twenty minutes later, I was present.

I watched the preacher shake Thomas's hand at the door and then approach me with a look of sympathy. I was sitting in my rocking chair, where I had been reading the last chapter of a book titled *Beloved* by Toni Morrison, an eerie story in which the ghost of a dead baby girl comes back as a young woman to live with her mother. I did not rise or extend my hand for shaking, and Mr. Hawthorne was not the pressuring, grinning kind, for which I was grateful. He spoke to me briefly, saying, "I'm sorry about your husband's uncle, Mrs. Tuttle," and I replied with a nod.

Theodore Hawthorne was not a tall man, perhaps five feet seven. Thomas showed him Mayfield's sheet of instructions, and the two of them sat down on the sofa to talk. They were a study in contrasts: Thomas, seventy years old, tall and straight-haired, dressed in paint-stained overalls, and the young preacher, small and curly-haired, wearing a very white, very starched shirt, dark trousers, and a deep maroon paisley necktie. As they talked, Mr. Hawthorne wrote on a note pad. He stayed only fifteen minutes, during which time I pretended to read. As he took his leave, he apologized for his haste, informing us that he was to officiate at a wedding that afternoon and would contact Thomas the next day.

On the following Monday evening, Thomas felt that he should be in attendance during the entire three-hour visitation at the funeral home and again during the painfully long funeral ceremony on Tuesday. Since Mayfield's family had rejected him in his lifetime, Thomas feared that they would not be gracious enough to rise above their grudges and rally around their father in his death. I suppose he saw himself in the role of mediator, though the dead hardly need a representative. As it turned out, Mayfield's children were all present and behaved themselves with reasonable decorum.

Both the viewing on Monday and the funeral on Tuesday took place at Mortland Funeral Home on Holcombe Avenue in Derby. I doubt that anyone else in Filbert or Derby realizes the irony of a funeral home bearing the name of Mortland, the root of which is the Latin *mors,* meaning death. The owners and operators of the funeral home for the past three decades have been the Haskins brothers. I do not know who originally named it Mortland, but perhaps it was the same wag who named our local newspaper the Filbert *Nutshell.*

I was present only during the first five minutes of the viewing. Thomas had driven over earlier in his truck, but I waited until precisely five o'clock and then walked into the viewing parlor, as they call it. I stopped about eight feet from Mayfield's casket, an inexpensive gray model that he himself had selected, and seeing Mayfield's gaunt, waxy face clearly enough from my vantage, I had no desire to move nearer. I caught Thomas's eye momentarily, then left and drove back home, where I spent the rest of the evening reading.

By now I had started *Bailey's Cafe* by Gloria Naylor and was deeply moved that night when I read the story of Sadie and Iceman Jones. After one of my cafeteria workers at school, Algeria, had declared in my hearing — for my benefit largely — that white people had no idea what black people were "forced to go through," I had set out to read all I could about what is referred to as "the African-American experience." After I finished *Bailey's Cafe,* I sat in my rocker and considered writing to Gloria Naylor and telling her another story to include in her next book. I would not tell her that I was a white woman and that the story of sorrow was my own. But I am getting ahead of myself. And I did admire the book, you must understand that.

The funeral on Tuesday was "something else," to borrow the words of Francine, another one of my cafeteria workers. Whatever deviates in the smallest degree from the ordinary is, in Francine's way of thinking, "something else." The service was set for three o'clock, a convenient time for me since my lunchroom duties are finished by then.

For several years before his death, Mayfield had been attending a so-called "independent" church over in Derby — the Church of the Open Door — pastored by Mr. Hawthorne. During that time Mayfield had often attempted to proselytize Thomas and me, but without success. I had seen firsthand the dark underside of religion as a teenager, and even now I feel a churning of physical revulsion at the memory of certain phrases repeatedly intoned by my grandfather — "he that refraineth his lips is wise" being among those I heard most often. But I was a child. How could I have known the emptiness of my grandfather's implied threats? By securing my lips, I granted him an awful freedom.

The reader must forgive me for wandering. I shall tighten the reins. It surprises me to find that in the telling of my tale, my thoughts, which are usually quite orderly, run to and fro as the eyes of the Lord. Strangely, *that* verse from the Old Testament Chronicles was not among those that my grandfather quoted to me, though he would have done well for his own sake, and surely for mine, to do so. But again I digress from my course. I am not being deliberately cryptic. Everything will be set forth in its time. Should I succeed someday in getting my manuscript published, perhaps an editor will repair the disarray of thought.

The funeral chapel was crowded. I must admit my surprise at seeing so many in attendance, for Mayfield was not known as a genial, popular man. Before his religious transformation five years ago, he had endured many personal failures, the most devastating of which had occurred more than thirty years earlier when his young wife had taken her own life after having given birth to twin boys, thus leaving him a middle-aged man with a four-year-old daughter, a two-year-old son, and infant twin sons. Grief had stamped its indelible mark upon the face of Mayfield Spalding long before I had met him. Even when he had tried to evangelize Thomas and me in recent years, reciting the numerous rewards of being "born again," his jowls and eyes sagged mournfully. It was always a marvel to me that so thin a man could have jowls.

My initial response was that perhaps it was his sad history that drew people to his funeral, as a final act of human sympathy for one so beset by misery. Once the funeral was underway, however, an unknowing observer would have deduced that Mayfield's life had been on an entirely different order, for the spirit of the service can be described only as abundantly joyous.

There were a number of testimonials from church members vouching for Mayfield's integrity and generosity — I heard his daughter, Joan, snort softly at the word *generous* — his love of truth and righteousness, his faithfulness, and his assurance of a "royal palace up in glory," as one elderly woman described it. This large and homely woman, who introduced herself as Eldeen Rafferty, had all the hallmarks of a raconteur. She warmed up the audience with a story of Mayfield's anonymous donation of one thousand dollars to her family several years earlier at the death of her son-in-law and told, quite humorously, of the method by which she had divined his identity. When she had gone to Mayfield privately to confront him with the fact and to thank him for his gift, he had answered gruffly, "Inasmuch as ye have done it unto one of the least of these" and had walked away.

Eldeen Rafferty ended her story with these words, which I remember well: "Mayfield Spalding wasn't one to laugh and cut up, but that doesn't matter one jot or whittle in the Book of the Lamb, 'cause I know as sure as I'm standing here on my own two feet" — here she pointed down to her large feet, over which she wore black rubber boots — "that that man yonder in that casket" — here she pointed with the other hand directly to Mayfield's lifeless form — "is a'sittin' at the blessed banquet table of Jesus right this very minute and has got hisself a royal palace up in glory that'll be for everlasting and everlasting, amen." As she sat down, the chapel reverberated with a rousing chorus of her final word: "Amen!"

But I have not yet brought my main character into the scene. Birdie Freeman, though at the time I did not know her name, was playing the organ intermittently during the entire funeral. I had noticed her upon first entering the chapel, for she was playing a prelude of familiar gospel hymns that I had not heard for over thirty-four years, though I knew them all: "The Old Rugged Cross," "Shall We Gather at the River," "What a Friend We Have in Jesus," "Rock of Ages."

The organ was in front, and Birdie sat at it somberly, wearing a brown dress and small brown hat. I had not seen such a hat since the early 1960s. My prompt assessment was that she was plain. The reader no doubt recalls my earlier description of her as beautiful, but my change of perception did not come until much later in our acquaintance. First she was plain. She immediately brought to my mind the image of the common sparrow, though I was unaware at this time that her name was Birdie. I watched her during the next hour and a half and wished that I could see her hands and feet as she played. In addition to books, music is another of my passions, and although I had taken no formal training at the time, I recognized that the woman had a gifted touch.

Besides the prelude, Birdie accompanied a vocal solo, a small choral ensemble, a vocal duet, and most peculiar of all, a tuba solo played by a young teenaged boy. These numbers were performed at varying levels of skill. The vocal duet — "I've Got a Mansion Just Over the Hilltop" — was comically mawkish, but the tubist proved to be quite proficient, I thought, for one so young. I also recognized the song that the young man played: "He Hideth My Soul."

Before Mr. Hawthorne preached, a woman read a lengthy, amateurish poem from a large red book, which she held aloft in a theatrical pose so that the title stamped on the cover — *A Harvest of Inspirational Poems* — was plainly visible to the audience. The poem spoke often of "that blissful yonder shore," and the last line of each stanza of the poem repeated the phrase "Crossing the raging Jordan 'twixt earth and heav'n." Mr. Hawthorne's "charge," as he called it — the portions of it that I heard — was quite eloquent in comparison to the speech of the others that day. I heard from him no grammatical gaffes, no ill-chosen diction. In contrast, a man who had delivered one of the brief eulogies earlier had spoken of the "tempestulent waters of life's sea that buffer and batter us" and of "crossing the portholes of heaven."

As Mr. Hawthorne spoke, I tried to distance myself from his words. Thomas was seated in the front row with the other pallbearers, and from my seat in the sixth row, I stared at the wisps of hair on the back of his neck, noting that his latest visit to Pate's Barber Shop — another example of the creative nomenclature of our local businesses — had obviously been many weeks ago. I do not wish, however, to paint a picture of Thomas as a slovenly man. The stained overalls mentioned earlier had nevertheless been newly washed and pressed, and in spite of his untrimmed neck on the day of the funeral, Thomas looked properly dignified in his black suit. He has broad shoulders for a man of his age and a full head of thick gray hair.

To occupy my mind during the lengthy service, I began recalling books I had read that included funeral scenes. I believe I may have even smiled when I thought of the chapter in *The Adventures of Huckleberry Finn* in which a dog raises a mighty disturbance in the basement while a funeral ceremony is underway in the parlor of the home of the deceased. If I remember correctly, the undertaker slithers out of the room to investigate and returns a few minutes later, having stilled the commotion. By way of explanation, he whispers loudly to the mourners, "He had a *rat!*" But between my mental diversions, I heard enough of Mr. Hawthorne's words to know that I did not want to hear more. Many of the words were agonizingly familiar, bringing back memories I had labored for many years to suppress.

As I studied the people around me, I noted their raptness of expression, their readiness to respond audibly to the preacher's words, their glances one to another by which they signified their concord.

My eyes kept returning to Birdie Freeman, still seated at the organ, her small face turned attentively to the preacher. I tried to recollect where I had seen a face like hers before, and near the end of the funeral service it suddenly came to me. It was in a book titled *Pioneer Women: Voices from the Kansas Frontier,* by Joanna L. Stratton, which I had read a few years earlier. I looked it up at home later and confirmed the fact. Should the reader want to see for himself what Birdie

Freeman looked like, secure a copy of the book and find the photograph of a woman named Sarah Jayne Oliver. The brown hat that Birdie wore at the funeral, conforming snugly to her small head, gave the same effect as Sarah Jayne Oliver's closely combed, neatly pinned hair. As for the faces, the two women could have been twins had they not been separated in time by more than a hundred years. They had the same ordinary brown eyes, the same white forehead, the same high cheekbones, the same suggestion of an overbite around prim, cautious lips.

As I studied Birdie Freeman's face that day of the funeral, I could not rid myself of the idea that there existed within her a core of uncommon mettle, that she knew secrets I did not know, that she had witnessed great mysteries. While I was curious on the one hand about these secrets and mysteries, I nevertheless suspected that they were matters against which I would close my ears. It was strange to me that from my first sight of Birdie Freeman, I felt both desirous and unwilling to know her. As I seldom engage in idle speculation concerning the lives of others, I knew not what to think of my sudden arousal of interest in this woman whom I had never before seen. Perhaps some inchoate instinct suggested to me that she, like me, possessed a singular personal history that she would not readily yield.

My beginning chapter has grown more protracted than I had planned, and I find that writing is far more exhausting than I had imagined. Furthermore, though I had intended a more cheerful beginning, I see already the pall of death upon my book. And though I know that the time is right, I fear the thought of filling the empty pages that follow, for I know that to do so will demand the opening of my own secret chambers.

WEAK AND BEGGARLY ELEMENTS

2

It is early June, and Thomas has made no sign of noticing the change in my nightly occupation. I still sit in my rocker after our evening meal, but instead of reading, I now write. Perhaps Thomas has noticed but remembers how strongly I dislike being asked what I'm doing. He posed this question to me one night sixteen years ago after we had been married only a week, and I replied, "When and if I wish to yield my privacy to the scrutiny of others, you will be the first to be invited to the exhibition." He laughed good-naturedly, his brow creased with puzzlement, but he never again asked what I was doing.

I cannot say why Birdie Freeman's face lingered in my mind in the months following Mayfield's funeral, nor why I asked Mr. Hawthorne, when he called on us again two weeks later, "Who was the woman who played the organ at the funeral?" That was when I learned her name. Thomas and I were civil to

Mr. Hawthorne during this visit, Thomas's manner perhaps even approaching cordiality, but we informed him unequivocally that we were not interested in finding a "home church," as he referred to it.

When the preacher asked if we had considered our dwelling place for eternity, Thomas answered, "Naw, I can't say as I've given it more than a passin' thought, and even that might be stretchin' it." When ill at ease, Thomas often assumes a slightly more ignorant, countrified style of speech than is his wont.

To this Mr. Hawthorne soberly replied, "Well, you should. You will have to spend eternity somewhere, and eternity is a long, long time." He went on to describe the two options open to all men.

So vivid was his portrayal of hell that Thomas told me later, "I was starting to feel like the seat of my John-Brown britches was on fire."

As Mr. Hawthorne discussed the pleasures of heaven, I tried to imagine his look of astonishment were I to begin quoting the entire fourteenth chapter of the gospel according to John, which my grandfather had required me to memorize as punishment for what he called my "unwavering willfulness" one Saturday when, at the age of thirteen, I had balked at his suggestion that I attend a teen singspiration at church. Though I had lived with my grandparents only a few months, my doubts about the Bible were already well planted by this time, and the fourteenth verse of John 14 served to water my skepticism, for I had repeatedly asked that my grandfather die, in the name of Jesus as the verse stipulated, but to no avail. With the thinnest thread of hope, I tried to cling to verse eighteen, in which I was promised comfort, but once again fulfillment was denied.

I have laid aside a number of novels — dismissing them as unworthy of my time — for their overuse of coincidence at critical points in the plot. I must tell the events of my story as they happened, however, and I will neither omit nor apologize for what is to follow.

The memory of Birdie Freeman's firm lips and steady gaze as she sat at the organ remained with me during the months to come. I cannot explain this. I even reread the entire book *Pioneer Women: Voices from the Kansas Frontier,* something I rarely do, in an effort to rid myself of her ghost, though perhaps subconsciously I was hoping to acquaint myself with her more intimately. I was reminded in this second reading that Sarah Jayne Oliver, the nineteenth-century kinswoman I had appropriated for Birdie, was a wife and mother of sturdy character who had adapted herself to the rigors of frontier life with uncomplaining gallantry. She was noted for her careful planning of the family's menu, shunning heavy fried foods and pastries. She also played a small reed organ called the melodeon, a fact that, in addition to the physical similarities between her and Birdie, provided another striking parallel — though this is not the coincidence to which I alluded. Let me continue.

Mayfield's funeral was on the fourth day of January. Five months later at the beginning of June, almost exactly a year ago now, Vonnie Lee, another of my lunchroom workers at Emma Weldy Elementary School, told me she would not be returning to her job the following fall. Actually, her exact words to me were, "Buddy says he's sick and tired of me having to come to work so blasted early an' says I gotta quit and try to get me a job at the R. C. Cola plant, same shift he works." Buddy was her husband, whom Vonnie Lee both liberally praised and maligned in the cafeteria kitchen.

I met this news of her leaving us with outward stoicism but inward distress. In spite of her infuriating loquacity, Vonnie Lee was a fast and careful worker, possessing an artistic flair with institutional food, which, although adding little in nutritional value or actual palatability, nevertheless contributed enormously to its appeal in the eyes of the children. It was Vonnie Lee's idea, for example, to toss a boxful of raisins, cornstarch, honey, and brown sugar into a simmering pot of water and ladle a small portion over each serving of ham. The results were such that I felt the additional expense to be justified. Later she even experimented with chopping instead of slicing the ham so that the younger children could eat it more easily with spoons. Vonnie Lee was a culinary innovator.

It was with no small degree of pessimism, therefore, that I awaited the opening of school at the end of that summer and the arrival of a new employee. In my twenty-two years at Emma Weldy Elementary School, I had suffered my share of unsuitable cafeteria workers, several of whom had failed even to complete the opening preparatory week before resigning. Three of them had tried to lay the blame at my feet, calling me various unflattering names and complaining of my demands for perfection. I have no use for whiners, though I am always fair with a worker who shows stamina and a modicum of intelligence.

The reader can well imagine my astonishment when I walked into the cafeteria at 7:50 on Monday morning, the twenty-eighth of August, and found seated in one of the bright orange plastic chairs none other than Birdie Freeman. She looked at me pleasantly, her child-sized hands folded gently over a large tan purse in her lap. She wore a green cotton jumper, a white blouse, black canvas sneakers, and white socks. Her hair appeared to be quite long, but it was neatly braided, coiled, and pinned to her small head. As I noted this, I felt a sudden chill run through me, for I recalled that Sarah Jayne Oliver, pictured in my book about pioneer women, had worn her hair in much the same arrangement. I recognized Birdie instantly but of course refrained from acknowledging the fact.

"May I help you?" I asked. She informed me later that I was frowning when I said this. Besides the surprise of recognizing her, perhaps I was a bit chagrined by her excessive punctuality, for I was always the first of the cafeteria crew to arrive.

"Yes, thank you, I'm here to work," Birdie replied, smiling but remaining seated. As I was her superior, I felt that she should have stood to talk to me.

"Let me direct you to the office in that case, and the secretary will escort you to the proper location," I said.

"Oh, I've already checked in at the office," she said, "and Mrs. Cameron brought me on down here."

"Am I to assume then that you are our new cafeteria employee?" I asked. She claimed later that I spoke these words in a tone that conveyed a total absence of faith in her aptitude for kitchen work.

"That's right," she said, still smiling and

standing now, at last, to offer her hand. "My name is Bernadetta Freeman, but my friends all call me Birdie. And you must be . . . ?"

"Good morning, Bernadetta," I said, keeping my distance. I do not make a habit of shaking hands with people. Even as I do not imitate the speech of southerners, I do not participate in their loose frequency of physical touch. Though I do not consider myself *rude* in the strict sense, I do not deny that I am highly reserved, a characteristic that others most often translate as rudeness. However, if the general public understood the degree to which germs are transferred by means of casual contact, I believe that the custom of handshaking would be allowed to die out. Birdie took a quick step toward me nonetheless and clasped my hand in a firm hold that I neither expected nor desired. Her hands were much smaller than mine, but they were surprisingly strong.

"Oh, please — it's Birdie," she said.

As her smile broadened, I saw the severe extent of her overbite.

"I know we're not friends *yet,* but I sure didn't mean you couldn't call me by my nickname. I'd feel a lot more at home if you would call me Birdie."

She laughed, for no reason that I could see, and I noted that all of her teeth were unusually large for the size of her mouth. It was hard to imagine what she would look like without the conspicuous dental defects, for her smile completely overtook her features. It was as if a weed had suddenly produced a grotesque bloom. I nodded and pulled my hand from hers, quite forcefully, she told me later. Just then Francine burst into the cafeteria whistling. She stopped when she saw Birdie and me.

"Hey, hey, hey, everybody," she said. Then she saluted me and spoke in the staccato fashion of a serviceman to his officer. "Here's Francine, reporting to duty, *sir!* Ready to fill up the bellies of all the little starvin' children of Filbert, *sir!* Forward, march!" Francine's attempts at humor are invariably weak and ill-timed.

Birdie smiled at her, however, and said, "How do you do," at which point Algeria wandered in, silent and surly as is her morning custom.

"Let us begin the preliminaries," I said, turning to lead the way from the lunchroom into the kitchen. I went into my office cubicle and picked up from my desk a folder, the tab of which bore the label *Opening Staff Meeting,* then went back out into the kitchen, seated myself on a tall stool at the big stainless steel worktable, and waited for the other three women to do the same.

Birdie pulled up a stool next to Algeria, who glowered darkly at her before flinging her keys onto the metal tabletop with a fierce clatter. Francine, smiling blithely, sat down heavily next to me and began picking from her black T-shirt what looked like hairs from a white feline. I leaned over to her and said, "Let me remind you, Francine, that a floor strewn with animal hair is not a clean floor. I will conduct my standard fall inspection on Friday."

Francine looked at me blankly for a brief second, then carefully, with thumb and forefinger, pulled another white hair from her sleeve, stretched open the top of her T-shirt with her other hand, dropped the hair inside, patted her chest, and grinned at me. Francine has a vulgar streak. "There," she said. She and Algeria exchanged glances, and Algeria grunted — a sound she often intends as a form of laughter. I chose to ignore Francine's small act of rebellion.

"As we all know, Vonnie Lee is no longer with us," I said, addressing all three women. "Bernadetta Freeman will be serving in her place." I paused and looked at Birdie, whose face wore the expectant look of a six-year-old. Her torso swayed slightly, and it occurred to me that she must be swinging her feet. Pointing to myself, I said, "I am Margaret Tuttle, the lunchroom supervisor. Next to me is Francine Perkins, and across from me is Algeria Simms."

Algeria's mother had consulted a map of Africa in the naming of her children, eight altogether. I had once overhead Algeria listing for Vonnie Lee the names of her siblings: Cairo, Sahara, Kwando, Nyasa, Karisimbi, Cameroon, and Gomera. Algeria's mother had evidently used no system of selection, for the names she had chosen included names of countries, cities, a river, a mountain, a desert, and an island. Furthermore, it was impossible to identify the sex of the child by the name. For example, Sahara — a name with a decidedly feminine ending — was Algeria's youngest brother, though Gomera was a sister, as was Kwando.

As I took a breath to continue, Birdie spoke up. "I'm so pleased to meet all three of you," she said, "and I'd like to ask you all to call me Birdie instead of Bernadetta, if you don't mind." She looked at me and smiled sweetly, giving no indication that I had pointedly disregarded her earlier request to use her nickname.

"Birdie as in tweet-tweet?" asked Francine, raising her hands and flapping them.

Birdie nodded happily. "When I was just a girl, there was a little boy where I lived one time who couldn't say Bernadetta, so he called me Birdie — and it stuck." She laughed again, making no effort to conceal her oversized teeth. Algeria flashed her a suspicious look and grunted again.

"You ever worked in a lunchroom before?" asked Francine.

Birdie shook her head. "Not in a lunch-room, really," she said, "but I did work in a restaurant kitchen in Tuscaloosa for seven years after I was first married."

She looked down at her lap then, and I could hear her unsnapping and snapping her purse. It is my purpose in our opening meeting to keep our attention squarely focused on business rather than personal concerns and to discourage an atmosphere of time-wasting chitchat. I therefore could not understand, and still cannot, my hesitance at this point to direct our attention back to the agenda inside the open folder before me. In the silence that followed, I realized that Francine, Algeria, and I were staring at Birdie, who continued to snap and unsnap her purse. In retrospect, I know that it could not have been a lengthy pause, but it was a moment full of import as we sought to delineate this new player upon our stage.

Still I did not speak, though barely able to stifle the impulse to slap her hands away from her purse. Birdie looked up at last, swept her eyes around the table, and locked her gaze with mine.

"My husband's out of work," she said. "That's why I applied for a job here."

Still no one spoke. Then Algeria, without turning her head, said to Birdie, "Where'd he work at?" This was a historic occasion, for in the ten years during which Algeria had been

39

at Emma Weldy Elementary School, I could not recall her making an intelligible utterance before ten o'clock in the morning.

"At the textile bleaching plant just outside Derby," Birdie said, placing her purse on the table now and pushing it back away from her. "He'd worked there for twenty-one years, ever since we moved here from Tuscaloosa. But they got a new plant manager a few months ago and changed everything, cutting out lots of jobs. Mickey's was one of them. 'Corporate restructuring' was what they called it — that and 'downsizing.' " She clasped her small hands together tightly and set them on the shiny table in front of her. Her nails were neat, tiny ovals, I noted.

Algeria grunted again, but her inflection this time did not signify laughter.

"Maybe he can get on at the new BMW over in Greenville," Francine said. "That place is something else. My cousin put in there, and he got him a job on the assembly line. Had to go through lots of tests and stuff, and it took *forever,* but he finally got hired. I say who cares if it's German cars putting food on your table. Your kids sure can't taste the difference. Everybody's got to make a living somehow."

Birdie smiled at Francine. "Why, thank you, Francine. BMW is one of the places where he's applied, as a matter of fact, and we're praying something will open up. I sure ap-

40

preciate all of you caring. That's real nice."
She leaned over and patted Algeria's dark,
gnarled hand as if Algeria had done something more than ask where her husband had
worked, though Algeria had said or done
nothing, as far as I could see, to communicate
sympathy.

During Birdie's patting of Algeria's hand, I
found my tongue. Fearing that the format of
our opening meeting was degenerating into
that of a talk show, I spoke vigorously. "I have
received the menus for our first month and
will be consulting our May inventory as I
place my first orders for the new school year.
I certainly hope the inventory count was
performed accurately last spring." I had no
reason to say this, for I had meticulously
recounted most of the foodstuffs in the
storeroom and freezer the previous spring,
verifying the numbers on the inventory sheet.
In so doing I had found that Vonnie Lee,
Algeria, and Francine had apparently submitted a precise count in spite of the continuous
flow of chatter among them. However, I
thought it beneficial from time to time to
make indirect references to a mistake made
three years earlier concerning a miscount of
boxes of confectioners' sugar.

I could sense Francine pulling a face and
exchanging glances with Algeria again, but I
had learned long ago to take no outward note
of these puerile expressions. "As you know,

41

one of our primary functions during the coming week," I said, "will be to clean the kitchen thoroughly." I paused so that the word *thoroughly* might linger in the minds of the three women.

Then I continued in the third-person mode that I had adopted many years ago in my role as moderator for staff meetings of this nature. "Over the past few years" — it was actually ten, and I knew it — "the supervisor has permitted Francine, Algeria, and Vonnie Lee the privilege of deciding upon a division of labor agreeable to all in the cleaning of the kitchen. She sees no reason to alter this arrangement now that Vonnie Lee has resigned. Francine and Algeria know the procedure well, and they will serve as mentors for . . ." Here I paused, not for effect but for guidance from my instincts. "For Birdie," I concluded. I did not look at Birdie as I said her name, but I clearly heard her emit a soft, pleased murmur.

"Both Francine and Algeria no doubt recall the importance placed upon details," I continued. "It is no accident that the cafeteria of Emma Weldy has been selected by the county superintendent as the blue-ribbon winner for the past twenty years. It has been accomplished through hard work and assiduous supervision. As in years past, the supervisor will conduct a white-glove inspection of the kitchen on Friday of this week, and it is her sincere hope that every square inch will meet with her approval. She would not want to discover on hidden surfaces of certain pieces of equipment, for instance, a residue of grease." Five years earlier I had run my index finger along the underside of the receiving tray on our large Hobart slicer and found such a residue.

I looked up to find Francine staring at me wide-eyed, with a "face as broad and innocent as a cabbage," to borrow Flannery O'Connor's fine simile from her story "A Good Man Is Hard to Find," and Algeria studying me mutinously with "little hard shoe-button eyes," in the words of William Faulkner in *Go Down, Moses.* Turning my gaze to Birdie, I saw in her eyes something kind and gracious, something akin to mercy or devotion, something that spawned in my memory another quotation from my reading, this one from Tennyson: "Her eyes are homes of silent prayer."

Momentarily discomfited and unable to recall the next item of business, I turned my attention back to my folder. After a lengthy pause, I continued my opening remarks, reviewing the dress regulations for cafeteria employees, the procedures for sanitary handling of food, and so forth. I then rose from my stool and said, "Well, I suppose we all know our duties. Let us commence. Francine, you may want to begin by sweeping the floor." I let my eyes travel meaningfully to the tiles under her.

Francine looked swiftly at Algeria, then at me. Without a trace of ill will, she said, "Well, now, that's a dandy idea, Margaret. I think I'll just do that. Just get all that hairy *trash* outta here!" She looked down at the floor and wagged her finger. "Vamoose! You gonna be *history,* you little nasty boogers, you!" Then she slid off her stool and pivoted toward the custodial closet, as much as a woman of her bulk could be said to pivot, and went marching off, chanting, "Left, right, left, right, left," though stepping at each word with the opposite foot. There was the faintest of smiles in Algeria's dark eyes.

Birdie's face held an expression of pleasant neutrality. "Well, I can tell I'm going to like working here just fine," she said to me. "Just fine."

Though excessive emotional voltage can destroy a work of literature, I must inject here a word about my feelings at the time. I have long disdained the emphasis on emotions in modern society — in every area from advertising to politics — and though I have held my own emotions in check throughout my life, I cannot deny the fact that I was flooded at that moment with sensations that can be called by no other name, the most puzzling of which was shame. *What cause have I to feel ashamed?* I asked myself but heard no answer. All I knew for certain was that in the presence of Birdie Freeman I felt the unmistakable power of goodness, whereas when I turned away from her, I was painfully pricked by the knowledge of weak and beggarly elements within my own soul.

Birdie dismounted her stool with a little hop, and as I turned and walked toward my glass-enclosed cubicle, I heard her say to Algeria, "Well, if you'll show me where to keep my pocketbook, Algeria, I'll be ready to do whatever it is you want me to do first."

A Continual
Dropping
3

Although my aim throughout most of my adult life has been to operate with what Henry James called a "perfect presence of mind, unconfused, unhurried by emotion," I know that my own emotions have been steadily thawing over the past months. While I feel in a sense more fully alive than ever before, I am finding that feelings complicate the ordinary business of life. Common, daily occurrences that I once observed impassively have begun to affect me in significant ways.

For example, as I was sitting in my rocking chair last night, my pen still poised above the last word I had written, there came a quiet knock at the front door. Thomas had been dozing in his recliner, rousing himself periodically to check the score of the baseball game on television and to scan the other twenty channels by means of the remote control. Upon hearing the knock, he started from his nap and went to open the door. It was Joan, Mayfield's daughter, of whom I wrote earlier.

I closed my notebook and laid it aside before she entered.

She was driving home from a business dinner in Greenville, she explained, and had bought strawberries at a roadside market. She offered us two pints, which Thomas quickly accepted and took to the kitchen. Joan left almost immediately afterward. This is one of Joan's most attractive qualities, in my opinion: She does not tarry. As I stood at the door and watched her walk to her car, however, I felt a strong tug of emotion. I wanted to summon her back and prolong her visit. I suddenly yearned to talk and feel the warmth of her companionship. Without intending to, I called out her name. When she turned back, however, I fell back upon the old cliché, "How are you doing?" to which she gave a similarly mindless reply: "Fine." I thanked her again for the strawberries, and she left.

I believe Joan would agree with me that we are fond of each other — we have never stated our feelings aloud, of course — and that our affection springs in part from the fact that each of us sees something of herself in the other. The reticence of some people is mellow and sweet. In the case of Joan and me, our reserve has been allowed to grow hard and bitter, like the pit of an unripened fruit. Though we have gradually begun to extend ourselves to each other over the past months, Joan and I are still working our way into the clearing, so to speak.

Before I return to my narrative, I believe that the time is right to supply a cursory autobiographical sketch. This was not in my original plan, for as I stated in chapter one, the main character of my story is Birdie Freeman, not myself. Moreover, I believe that background information in a story should be doled out sparingly, bit by bit, as the action of the base time continues so that the story line does not become impeded and ultimately flounder by excursions into the past. I am a great admirer of a shapely story, one that unfolds in an orderly fashion. In addition, my past is a source of great pain to me — an understatement of tremendous degree — and I would prefer to keep it hidden. These arguments aside, however, I realize that the reader must understand certain facts about my life in order to see Birdie in a proper light. These facts I will dispatch quickly in order that I may return to Birdie.

First, a word about my education. I did not officially graduate from high school, although I am well educated and widely read due to an unquenchable zeal for knowledge and a love of literature passed on to me by my mother, who died the summer of my thirteenth birthday. Before my mother died, I had never sat in a traditional classroom. My mother had been my teacher as we moved from city to city. To my knowledge, no truant officer ever accosted her concerning the matter of compulsory school attendance, and no landlord or neighbor ever raised questions. Our frequent moves and the fact that we kept to ourselves very likely protected us. I stayed indoors all day while my mother worked.

On a bus somewhere between Akron and Terre Haute I read a book by myself for the first time. I was not yet five years old. In Fort Wayne I began to write. My mother taught me both printing and cursive simultaneously. In Saginaw I spent happy hours adding and subtracting, setting my numbers down in neat columns, and in La Crosse I mastered the multiplication tables. In Peoria I concentrated on long division and the history of America, and I went through stacks of science books in Cedar Rapids, studying everything from asteroids to zooplankton. In Huntington Mother bought a used set of the *Encyclopaedia Britannica Junior,* which I read voraciously. I remember reading straight through most of the *P* volume on our next move to Muncie, losing myself during the long miles as I absorbed facts about partridges, Pearl Harbor, photoelectricity, polo, and so forth.

And always, always there was literature. Mother and I read together in the evenings — a great variety of works in all genres — and so cloistered was I that I truly believed that every child knew Hawthorne, Shakespeare, Melville, Tolstoy, and the King James

Bible as intimately as I. I knew that other children attended schools, of course, and I merely assumed — indeed, my mother explained it thus to me — that I did not do so because she was a capable teacher herself, therefore eliminating the need to seek additional instruction from strangers. I took it as a sign of privilege. My learning was so important to my mother that she wanted to oversee the process herself.

Further, I assumed that all the other children of the world were ingesting knowledge in the same enormous doses as I. I was truly sheltered, for we had no television and did not subscribe to newspapers or magazines. We frequented public libraries, however, and listened to my mother's box radio when we could tune in to stations that programmed classical music.

The summer that Mother died and my world changed forever, we were living in Dayton, Ohio, and I was computing algebraic logarithms and studying Latin. For my thirteenth birthday a few weeks earlier, we had ridden a bus to Cincinnati and attended the opera *Tosca*. My birthday gift had been a copy of Charlotte Brontë's *Jane Eyre,* which I had already finished by the time Mother died.

I think of my years in school after Mother's death, from the ages of thirteen to seventeen, as a vast black hole into which I fell. It was a great shock to find such abysmal ignorance on every hand. Even my teachers were failures in my eyes. Yet I longed for morning to come so that I could leave my grandparents' house and walk — more often I ran — the seven blocks to L. K. Drake Junior High School and later the twelve blocks to Latham County High School. My grandparents lived in a small town near Corning, New York, called Marshland. I feel a constriction in my throat at the very mention of the town. I left Latham County High School the fall of my senior year and never graduated, though much later I took the GED examination, parts of which I thought to be almost insultingly elementary, and passed it, thus earning a high school diploma. Circumstances did not allow me to attend college, but more of this later.

Second, I will speak briefly of my marriage, which at times has astounded even me, for I am certain that a more unlikely match than that between Thomas Tuttle and me has never been legalized. One day eleven years ago, in the fall of 1984, Thomas appeared in the school cafeteria to borrow my house key, for he had locked himself out of our duplex. Francine, Vonnie Lee, and Algeria gaped openly at him, and after he left Vonnie Lee said, "Don't tell us *that* man's your *husband.*" I looked at her evenly and replied, "As it is none of your concern, I would prefer to tell you nothing at all about the man. However,

51

lest your speculation distract you further from your work, I will tell you that he is indeed my husband."

Francine threw up her hands and said, "Now, if that's not something else! Here we been wondering all this time what in the world your husband's like, and here he is just a plain man in overalls." Algeria asked how long we had been married, a question I chose not to answer, though it had been almost six years at the time, and Francine asked if he repaired vacuum cleaners, a question no doubt inspired by the hand-painted words *Tuttle's Vacuum Cleaner Service* on the side of his pickup truck, which he had parked directly outside the large rear windows of the cafeteria. Vonnie Lee remarked, "He sure looks a whole lot older than you," an observation to which I did not reply.

Indeed, my three co-workers were in such an agitated state of curiosity that they whispered among themselves and cast sidelong glances at me the rest of the day. I might have been a carnival exhibit. From the pantry I overheard Vonnie Lee say later that day, "Don't you just wonder if Margaret *loves* that man?"

The truth was that I had been clear with Thomas on this fact from the beginning. I had told him that I would not marry him for love, that I was not seeking a romantic liaison, that indeed I did not want such a relationship with any man. He had pinched his chin several times before inhaling deeply and releasing his breath slowly and audibly. At last he had responded, "Well, all right, then, Rosie, if you'll just keep up with the main course of washin' and cookin', I reckon I can forgo some of the side dishes." Thomas has a colorful style of speech. I have often wondered whether he thought that I really meant what I said or whether he was gambling on the notion popular among men that what a woman says and what she means are often strangers one to the other. Whatever he thought, he was soon to discover that my word was good.

And now I have raised another question, have I not? You are likely wondering why Thomas called me Rosie when my name is Margaret. Again, I will settle the matter quickly. When Thomas and I first met over sixteen years ago, I had a hammer in my hand and was making my way down an aisle toward the cash register of Norman's Hardware Store where Thomas rented space for his vacuum repair service. He paused from what he was doing — restocking nails of various sizes — and stared at me openly, then laughed and pointed at the hammer in my hand. "Well, now, ma'am, I think you got the wrong thing there in your hand," he said. "Don't you mean to be buying you a riveter?"

I stared at him coolly and replied, "I beg

your pardon?"

He slapped his knee and said, "Oh, 'course you wouldn't get it. You're not old enough to remember them posters of Rosie. She was the home-front gal that rolled up her shirt-sleeves and went off to work in the factories back during wartime. Rosie the Riveter they called her. Not a real woman" (he pronounced it WOE-man), " 'course, just a picture, like Uncle Sam."

I said, "Of course I know of Rosie the Riveter. I have read of her. But she was more than just a picture. She was based on a real woman named Rose Monroe, who was a riveter in a war munitions factory. Not only was she featured in films supporting the war effort, but her picture appeared on countless posters promoting the themes of sacrifice and heroism during World War II." I paused, and Thomas looked at me as if struck dumb. He then pulled a red handkerchief out of the back pocket of his overalls and began rubbing his face vigorously.

Normally I would not have said more, but during the silence I recalled from a book I had read a specific picture of Rosie flexing her arm, with the caption *We Can Do It!* printed beneath. "Rosie wore coveralls and tied up her hair with a bandanna," I added, and Thomas lifted his face and studied me gravely as he stuffed the handkerchief back into his pocket. "Poster art was a very persuasive patriotic stimulant during World War II, and Rosie was a noble heroine," I concluded before turning to continue my way down the aisle. I heard him clear his throat behind me, but he made no reply.

No one was at the cash register, but Thomas ambled up the aisle behind me and walked behind the counter. "Norm's gone off to his granddaughter's wedding," he said, "so I'm filling in." He silently entered the correct figures on a small adding machine, then took my money and handed me the change, placing the coins in my palm first before handing me the bills. I found his manner as a cashier satisfactory. I dislike listening to a chatty cashier who feels compelled to wish me "a nice day," and then lays down my change in the wrong order, bills on the bottom and coins piled on top, thus forcing me the inconvenience of sliding the coins off the bills, sometimes dropping one or more in the process, in order to transfer them into safe-keeping. Coins should be deposited into the customer's palm first, then bills. I have instructed more than one cashier concerning this point.

Thomas slipped my hammer and the adding machine receipt into a brown paper bag and handed it to me, clearing his throat again. "You always talk that way?" he asked, smiling.

"What do you mean?" I asked.

"Oh, I don't know. So . . . you know . . . like it's written in a book."

"I suppose my speech is rather bookish," I replied. "It is not, however, a style that I affect. For me it is natural." I paused and added, "I did not grow up here."

Thomas was not the first to be taken back by my manner of speech. I can still clearly visualize the astonished expression that formed upon the face of my homeroom teacher when my grandmother enrolled me in the eighth grade in Marshland, New York, the fall after Mother died. My teacher, a young woman in her twenties named Mrs. Hartwell, asked me, in a tone that fell upon my ears as callow and indifferent, if this were my first year at L. K. Drake Junior High School, to which I replied, "Not only is it my first year at L. K. Drake, Mrs. Hartwell, it is my first year of formal schooling at any institution." Several of my classmates laughed outright, and Mrs. Hartwell, who very likely interpreted my words as insubordinate, assigned me to a desk in the back corner. She was to be my English teacher as well as my homeroom teacher, and our relationship was not a happy one.

The smile faded from Thomas's lips and settled in his eyes. "You *do* favor Rosie, you know. Anybody else ever said that to you before?"

I shook my head. "No," I said. We stared at

each other briefly before I turned to leave. He had a kind yet friendly, inquisitive look, though not intrusive. I had grown accustomed to avoiding the eyes of men.

"I meant it as a compliment," he called as I walked toward the door. "I always looked on Rosie as a real fine lady with a lot of grit and gumption. Pretty gal, too. Don't think she had curls in her hair like you, though."

His words found favor with me, for as a child I had studied pictures of Rosie the Riveter in books and had admired her both as an American icon of wartime fortitude and as a handsome specimen of womanhood, being tall, with strong, well-sculpted features and thick dark hair.

I stopped beside a display of gardening spades and turned around. I had thought of something. "Did you serve in the armed forces during the Second World War?" I asked.

He nodded. "Sure did, ma'am. Sure did."

"Where and when?" I asked.

If his answer had been different, I am quite certain that our conversation would have ended there and would never have led, as it did three months later, to our marriage.

"I was in the second wave of forces that invaded Normandy," he said. "June the eighth, nineteen and forty-four."

"I see," I said. "My father was there two days earlier on Omaha Beach."

He inhaled sharply, a mannerism that he continues to this day. "Did he . . . I mean, is he . . . ?" His brow was furrowed, and his gray eyes were the color of morning fog.

I shook my head. "He was killed exiting the landing craft — before his foot touched the sand." I opened the door and walked out.

He followed me out to the car. "I'm sorry about that, ma'am. Your daddy died a hero's death. Him and all those others like him led the way for the rest of us to get in." He looked off sorrowfully toward a row of shiny green wheelbarrows lined up on end against the front window, as if seeing a phalanx of small armored tanks. As I opened my car door, he said, "You live here in Filbert, Rosie?"

"I do," I said.

Three months later I repeated these same two words in the office of a justice of the peace in Berea. At the age of thirty-five, I knew full well that no human could ever fulfill such grand, sweeping vows, and now sixteen years later, I am still stung by the thought of my cowardly acquiescence. I should have spoken aloud my honest intention: "No, I do not assent to these awesomely abstract promises, but I will be Thomas Tuttle's wife. I will keep his house clean and decent. I will mend and launder his clothes. I will cook his meals and sit with him in the evenings. Do not ask more of me, for I cannot pledge what these vows demand." Instead, I answered, "I do."

If the reader has never seen a picture of Rosie the Riveter, he may find one on the cover of the March 1994 issue of *The Smithsonian,* one of the two magazines to which I subscribe, the other being the *Atlantic Monthly.* I remember clearly the day last year when Thomas met the mailman beside the curb. It was a Saturday, and I was inside hemming a panel of draperies that hung too close to the baseboard heater. I heard Thomas give a whoop and looked out the window to see him hurrying toward the front door waving the new issue of *The Smithsonian* and shouting, "You're a cover girl, Rosie! You're a cover girl!" Of course, the picture of Rosie never ages. She is a much younger woman than I am now. She has no gray in her dark hair. It pleases me nonetheless that I have been compared to her — evidence, I suppose, of a vanity that, if accused of possessing, I would very likely deny.

In our prenuptial conversations, I made no pretense of marrying Thomas for love, as I said earlier. My conscience is clear upon that. I cannot say why I married, given my history and the premium I placed upon privacy. I have often thought that perhaps I was still searching for the father I had never known. Too, Thomas was not a man of drink and was handy with tools and repairs. I had an eye toward the maintenance of my duplex, having recently paid what I considered an outrageous sum for a new roof and gutters.

His manner of proposing marriage struck my fancy also. One evening, two months following our meeting at the hardware store, he brought me a largemouth bass that he had caught. He filleted, breaded, and cooked it in a small deep fryer outside in my carport ("or else your house'd smell to high heaven," he said), and after we had eaten the fish along with the lima beans, corn on the cob, and fresh tomatoes he had brought from his garden, he looked me in the eye and said, "Barkis is willin'."

I was nonplused — not by the allusion, for I identified it instantly, but by the unprecedented phenomenon of Thomas's having made reference to a work of literature. Surely this distinctive quotation from *David Copperfield* was not the sort of thing one could utter accidentally.

He laughed heartily at my puzzled silence and said, "I sure hope it's not gonna take as long for you to answer me as it did for Peggotty to answer poor old Barkis." He went on to explain that his great-aunt Prissy, who had lived with his family for a time when he was a boy, had been a devoted admirer of Charles Dickens and over the course of several months had read aloud all sixty-four chapters of *David Copperfield* at the kitchen table after supper, regardless of whether anyone stayed to listen on a given evening. I believe it to be the only novel that Thomas is familiar with. If a person were limited to a single choice, however, he could do worse than to choose a work by Dickens, an author whom I deeply respect in spite of his penchant for sentimentality.

At any rate, Thomas's proposal pleased me for its brevity and droll indirectness, and whatever my motivation, I married a man old enough to be my father: Thomas Alva Tuttle, named after the famous inventor. Thomas did not pry into my background, and I divulged very little. In fact, we had been married almost a year, a very quiet year, when I said to him one morning at breakfast, "Today is my thirty-sixth birthday."

He looked surprised. "Today, right now? *This* day?" He had looked down at the date on the Filbert *Nutshell,* which he was in the process of reading at the moment. "You was born on June the sixth?" he asked. He looked up and frowned out the kitchen window. "Thirty-six years ago? That means you was born in 1944." I removed a piece of toast from the oven, which produces a crisper piece of toast than an electric toaster, and began spreading plum jelly on it. Thomas was still staring at me. "Margaret, you mean to tell me you was born *on* D-day — the original, real McCoy D-day?"

I nodded, cut my piece of toast in half, and

61

set the knife down. I spoke as if reading a report. "I was born just before midnight. My mother did not know that my father had died early that morning. She would not know for weeks."

Thomas took a long drink of his strong black coffee. "How long was they married, your folks?" he asked.

"They married in September of 1943 after my father had completed flight training," I said. "He met her on a Friday, asked her to marry him on a Monday, and on Tuesday they had a small wedding in a preacher's living room. My father left for the war two days later on Thursday. He and my mother had known each other less than a week and never saw each other again."

I believe that Thomas was overwhelmed by this sudden spate of information, for I rarely spoke of my past. I said no more, and he did not press me further. I did not tell him that throughout my life I had suffered recurring dreams in which I heard the roar of the ocean and saw white-crested waves rushing toward the beach, turning to red as they washed over my father's dying body. He was twenty-three years old when he died. I did not tell Thomas that the only male relative whom I had known in my entire life was my mother's father — actually her stepfather, I learned later — from whom my mother had fled at the age of twenty-two and whom I did not meet for the first time until I was thirteen. I did not tell him of the mighty waves of nausea that washed over me at the thought of my grandfather.

As I said earlier, Thomas has an extensive network of relatives, most of whom live in North Carolina. He had been married before, and his first wife had died in 1970. When I met him, Thomas had lived alone for almost nine years. When we married, all that I knew of his first wife was that her name was Rita and that she had borne him one daughter, who had lived only two days. To Thomas, *family* is a word of many pleasant associations, though I know now that some are darkened with grief. In spite of small tiffs and even a significant rift or two, as among Mayfield and his children, enough loyalty and goodwill exist to make the annual family reunion a robustly convivial affair.

To my mind, *family* is a word of small dimensions and ambivalent connotations. My mother, of course, was a genius and an angel. The only other blood relatives I have known were my grandparents: my grandmother, weak and fearful, puppetlike and willfully blind to things that she chose not to see; and my step-grandfather, fiendish arch-hypocrite and upstanding elder of the First Unified Bible Missionary Church in Marshland, New York. I never knew my father's parents. I do not believe that my mother ever established contact with them.

The journey backward has become quite lengthy, one fact being linked as it is to so many others. I must therefore close this chapter and begin anew tomorrow. I find myself waking early each morning, for my story is like a continual dropping on a rainy day, and I must rise in haste and set pails to catch it.

A Shadow of
Things to Come
4

From the moment I first saw her at the funeral, Birdie had the look of an earlier era about her, an anachronistic countenance and bearing. Each time my eyes came to rest on her, I felt a slight jolt, as if I were passing a 1950 Studebaker on the freeway. She had the kind of face to fit a name such as Lavinia, Adelaide, or perhaps Hepzibah. During that first week in the cafeteria kitchen, I set about measuring her character and intellect, a project that was to continue over the following months.

Vonnie Lee, Francine, Algeria, and I had worked together for ten years, a long time for a school lunchroom crew to remain intact. I myself had served in the cafeteria at Emma Weldy for twenty-two years but had been the supervisor for only fifteen. Through our cafeteria doors, I had seen many women come and go, and once a man named Dexter Bright was employed in the kitchen for five months. Another employee at the time —

Sally Sue Slater — openly called him "Not-very." Sally Sue had a wicked tongue to which she gave free rein. She left after a year to marry a race car driver, and I was not sorry to see her go.

Before the fall of 1984, our school district boundaries were hastily enlarged due to a fire that summer which destroyed the elementary school in Berea. As a result, the enrollment at Emma Weldy, a large school that had been built in 1941, almost doubled. The empty classrooms upstairs were reopened and aired out, and new teachers were hired or transferred from the Berea school. The cafeteria underwent staffing changes also, the result being that my two part-time workers moved to the high school in Derby, and Vonnie Lee, Francine, and Algeria came to Emma Weldy as my new crew.

I soon discovered that each of the women had her own gifts. Vonnie Lee, in spite of her incessant chatter, was quick-witted and resourceful. She could prepare 235 serving portions of any menu item with negligible excess and could accurately gauge the multiplying of ingredients if we were adapting recipes intended for small groups. She added salt by hand, tossing it into the pot as if it were grass seed. Vonnie Lee, in her early thirties when she first arrived at Emma Weldy, took pride in knowing all the words to every popular song from the years 1964 to 1973.

Francine was several years younger than Vonnie Lee. Though annoyingly silly, she was nevertheless industrious and consistently good-natured. Not overly keen of intellect, she was certainly smarter than she acted. Francine often retorted with remarks irrelevant to the situation. Considerably overweight, she frequently made self-deprecating comments about her size, although she had, and still has, a soft, lovely face. Only twenty-six years old, she already had four children but no husband when she first began working in the cafeteria ten years ago. Her oldest child, a daughter named Gala, graduated from Derby High School this past year. As a lover of talk, Francine distinguished herself from the outset by her excitability, exclaiming extravagantly over the most trivial of circumstances, and even now she freely and cheerfully discusses embarrassing or inappropriate topics, such as surgical procedures, bodily functions, and gruesome crimes, savoring and repeating each detail.

Compared to Francine's general bonhomie, Algeria's temperament fell at the opposite end of the spectrum. In spite of her smoldering surliness, however, and her distrust of the white population in general, she and Francine developed a peculiar friendship, exchanging conspiratorial glances and sotto voce comments when I had to reprimand one or the other of them. These I pretended not to notice, then even as now. Algeria was forty-one when she came to Emma Weldy, she and I being only a few months apart in age. Tall, lanky, and powerful, she observed the world through heavy-lidded eyes and generally curled her lip at what she saw. These characteristics still apply to Algeria ten years later. She never married and to my knowledge has never participated in a romantic partnership, although she is unfailingly interested in those of others.

Far brighter than Francine, Algeria has displayed upon many occasions an uncanny ability to perceive attitudes behind spoken words or facial expressions. She can quickly dissect a situation, lay it open, and label causes and effects. She foretold the termination of our principal's marriage six months before it took place and cited as a contributing factor a romantic involvement between Mr. Solomon and the special education aide at the high school. No one else, including Mr. Solomon's longtime secretary, had any inkling of the relationship.

Unstintingly outspoken when she chooses to unleash her opinions, Algeria displays relentless argumentative talents, though she lacks the grace of speech and breadth of vocabulary to promote her views winsomely and therefore convincingly. She and Vonnie Lee often debated warmly, generally concerning the issues of civil rights and the welfare system, and many times the two of them left the cafeteria in the afternoons hurling last words at each other.

Their wrangling aside, I saw numerous evidences that Vonnie Lee and Algeria regarded each other with a degree of affection. Once when I intervened and demanded that they stop their arguing and concentrate on their work, Vonnie Lee said, "Arguing? What's that you're calling arguing, Margaret? We call it *discussing*." To which Algeria added, "And looks like to me we gettin' our work done just fine." At this point Francine contributed the following: "Did I tell y'all our dog's gone into heat? You ought to see the crowd of boy dogs hanging around our trailer!" I suppose Vonnie Lee and Algeria were more like men than women in their ability to disagree one minute and stand together as a team the next.

These brief portraits of my co-workers represent only a small fraction of what I know about them. One can discover many things by listening. If I were to be quizzed on such minutiae as Francine's average monthly electric bill, the name of Algeria's junior high track coach, or the color and model of the first car Vonnie Lee ever drove, I could answer them all. Of their personal lives, I never inquired, nor did they share with me their family concerns. When they broke off in the middle of sentences upon my approach, I was grateful, for I shunned the airing of private troubles.

All three women had proved over the ten years to be dependable workers with only occasional minor lapses in efficiency — lapses that, I admit, I greatly exaggerated so as to make a lasting impression. I believe I can fairly assert that they all respected me as their superior, though our relationship never evolved into anything resembling friendship. Whereas the three of them talked freely among themselves throughout the day, I maintained a wall around myself that none of them ever attempted to scale. They never included me in their conversation, and I never offered to join.

This, then, is the background of the group to which Birdie Freeman found herself a newcomer nine months ago. Having lost Vonnie Lee from our crew, I was somewhat anxious about Birdie's capabilities and performance.

A substitute had been foisted upon us a few years earlier when Francine had taken a leave to assist her mother following surgery, and it had been a most horrendous month for the other three of us. The woman, named Larkin Depp, had possessed not the smallest spark of initiative and could not remember the simplest procedure once she had performed it. For example, Vonnie Lee had demonstrated the preparation of rice five times before Larkin could do it alone, and one morning the dull-witted woman had dropped and broken an eight-pound jar of mayonnaise on the floor of the pantry, then stepped in it and left greasy white tracks all over the kitchen as she slowly plodded after me to report the accident. I was in the rest room off the kitchen at the time, but rather than wait until I emerged, she pounded on the door and called to me, "We got us a mess to clean up!" Algeria had made Larkin remove her sneakers and run them through the dishwasher.

Happily, I discovered early that I had no cause to worry, for Birdie stepped into her new position with ease and competence. When I emerged from my cubicle two hours after our brief meeting that first morning, I saw Birdie at one of the large sinks with a bottle of Clorox, scrubbing between the white tiles of the backsplash with a toothbrush. She had tied a vivid purple scarf over her hair and had donned a white plastic apron. She smiled at me brightly as I walked past her into the pantry.

"Now, doesn't that look just a whole lot better?" she asked, waving the toothbrush toward the area that she had finished scrubbing.

I stopped and studied the backsplash, noting the stark contrast between the scrubbed and unscrubbed tiles. "Whose toothbrush are you dipping into bleach?" I asked.

"Oh, it was under the sink in the bathroom," Birdie replied. "Francine said it was Vonnie Lee's."

Algeria appeared at Birdie's side and scowled at me. "No way Vonnie Lee gonna be comin' back askin' after her toothbrush," she said.

I turned sharply and continued on my way into the pantry. I heard Algeria say, and I am certain that she intended for me to hear, "You be findin' out real soon that don't none of us here sit around waitin' for Margaret to brag on us. If she don't say nothin', then it's prob'ly good. If it's just medium, she make you feel like it's bad, and if it's bad, she jump on you hard."

And I heard Birdie laugh lightly and say, "Oh well, we're all old enough not to need a lot of praise the way little children do." I had to stand in the center of the pantry a moment in order to recall my mission. During this moment I admit to feeling peeved over two matters: first, Algeria's frank and uncomplimentary summary of my supervisory manner, and second, the fact that the condition of the tile grout had escaped my notice, for I was certain that the discoloration had not occurred just over the past summer.

Remembering why I had come to the pantry, I opened the large sealed tin of flour from the previous school year and began checking carefully for meal bugs. As I did so, I heard Birdie humming. I stopped and listened, and within a few moments she began singing softly, her voice light and high, with a trembling vibrato. I could barely discern the words, but I knew them from many years ago. "So precious is Jesus, my Savior, my King," the song began.

Had it been Vonnie Lee singing "You've Lost That Lovin' Feelin' " — one of her favorites, always performed while holding as her microphone a large beater from the Sunbeam mixer — I would have put a speedy end to it. Looking back on Birdie's first song, I have often wondered whether I could have prevented many of the subsequent changes in our kitchen milieu had I responded decisively at that single moment. Had I charged forth and pronounced a ban on all singing, or at least on all singing of religious songs, maybe I could have held Birdie at bay indefinitely. But perhaps I am only deluding myself. Birdie's singing was, in truth, only a small accessory of her person. Upon reflection, however, I am quite convinced of the incomprehensible fact that something within me that day perversely craved a reminder of some aspect of my earlier life. It was as if a small seed planted long ago had begun to stir.

At lunchtime that first day, Francine, Algeria, and Birdie sat down together at the large stainless steel worktable around which we had met that morning. I could see them from my cubicle, but because of the combined din of the two large window fans and the dishwasher, which Algeria had loaded with all the pots, pans, and utensils that hung from large hooks above the worktable, I could not hear them.

My own lunch that day, which I ate at my desk, consisted of a pimento cheese sandwich, a pear (which unfortunately was too hard and green to be satisfying), a small bag of pretzels, and a thermos of iced tea. As I ate, I pretended to read a sheaf of papers in a large envelope labeled *Current Regulations for School Cafeteria Employees* that had been in the stack of mail on my desk. I found it difficult to concentrate, however.

Birdie had removed her apron for her lunch break, but she still wore the purple scarf. It was tied with a small bow on top after the fashion of housewives in the forties — very much, in fact, as Rosie the Riveter had worn her bandanna. As I studied a page from my packet titled *Percentage of Fat in New Dietary Standards,* I looked over the top of the sheet to see Birdie remove a few wrapped items from a small brown paper sack, lay them in a neat row before her, and then bow her head.

Francine and Algeria glanced at each other, but when Birdie finished and raised her eyes, they were staring at their sandwiches, eating mutely. The dietary notification I was reading was a duplicate of one that I had received in the spring, stating that over the course of the next three years our menus would be reexamined and revised to eliminate approximately twelve percent of the fat. I skimmed through the page, assured that the changes would not affect our operation this year, and set it aside to be filed.

Birdie was laughing gaily when I looked back at her. She had unwrapped something from her lunch and was pointing to it. Francine was laughing also, and Algeria was shaking her head, her eyelids half-closed, her expression inscrutable. As I watched, Birdie turned to my cubicle, still laughing. I quickly averted my eyes and, bending to open the bottom file drawer of my desk, pretended to be searching for something.

A moment later I looked up to see Birdie standing in the doorway of my office. "Look at this, Margaret." She was smiling broadly, her large front teeth overlapping her lower lip, and she held before her what appeared to be a sandwich. I said nothing. I saw no cause to smile and certainly not to laugh. Slowly Birdie separated the two pieces of bread to reveal — nothing. I sensed that Francine and Algeria were watching us, waiting for my reaction.

"Yes?" I said, looking up at Birdie with what I considered a sensible, steady gaze.

In her other hand Birdie held up a slip of white paper and stepped closer to me. In small, neat letters, a combination of printing and cursive, someone had written these words: *you said just make it something plain and simple did'nt you?*

"What do you think I ought to do to a husband who'd pull something like this on me?" Birdie asked, her brown eyes twinkling.

I said what immediately came to my mind. "Tell him that he failed to capitalize the first word of his sentence, that he omitted a comma after the word *simple,* and that he misplaced the apostrophe in the contraction *didn't.*"

Birdie looked again at the note and burst out laughing. "Oh, now that's a good idea, Margaret! I think I'll do just that. Not say a word about the sandwich but just talk about the note instead." She turned and left, and I heard her call eagerly to Francine and Algeria, "Margaret's got a good idea! She says I should . . ." Then her words were lost to me. I turned my chair to face the opposite direction, and as I drank the last of my tea, I faintly heard the sounds of her laughter still wafting through my doorway.

A minute later Birdie was back. "Just so you won't worry, Mickey had a slice of ham and some lettuce wrapped up for me in *another* little package. So I've got me a real sandwich after all."

I nodded at her and said, "Very well."

"But I'm still going to tell him that thing you said about his note." She bobbed her head happily, and one end of the bow on top of her scarf flopped over her brow. She turned to go, then immediately swung back around. "Oh, Margaret, do you like oatmeal cookies?" she asked.

"Not particularly," I replied.

"Oh, that's all right," she said, waving a hand. "I just thought you might like to have a couple of mine. I don't know what Mickey was thinking of — he put *eight* in my lunch sack!"

She returned to Algeria and Francine, leaving me to ponder the strangeness of a woman Birdie's age having a husband who packed her lunch and played practical jokes on her. I suddenly felt an ardent conviction that I wanted nothing to do with this woman who wore a scarf and jumper, who plaited and pinned her hair, whose small hands were so ready to touch, whose feet moved so quickly and softly. I told myself I wanted no part of someone who sang hymns and prayed before eating her lunch and who offered to share her oatmeal cookies. These idiosyncrasies, if allowed to go unchecked, could conceivably bring about a dangerous permutation of the working environment that we had all grown accustomed to. They could chafe and choke.

Though she had been at Emma Weldy only four brief hours, something deep within me could not imagine our kitchen now without the presence of Birdie Freeman.

On that first day, had I been granted the use of a single word to describe Birdie Freeman, I would most likely have chosen the word *innocent.* I realized, of course, that at her age, which I judged to be close to that of Algeria and myself — that is, around fifty — she had undoubtedly seen enough of life to have shattered any rosy ideals about human nature, hope, or the ultimate fulfillment of dreams. Nevertheless, her shining brown eyes were innocent.

My earliest assumption was that from childhood Birdie Freeman had been shielded from all worldly corruption by protective, religious parents. Further, I could not imagine that she had borne children, for she was so childlike herself. If the relationship between Thomas and me excluded the usual conjugal practices, I reasoned, no doubt there were other couples who, for various reasons, lived under similar terms of cohabitation. Perhaps Birdie and her husband were such a couple.

At the end of the day, a small, high-spirited man appeared at the kitchen doorway, produced a piercing series of whistles and trills such as one might hear in an aviary, and called to Birdie from the doorway, "Birdie, treasure, you about done?" He was wearing brown pants and a green plaid shirt, and though he was not a tall man, he held his shoulders erect. (I detest a drooping posture.) His ears, somewhat too large for his head, seemed to be angled forward as if to enhance his hearing. The effect was that of an adolescent boy.

At the time of his arrival, I was posting sheets of safety regulations on the bulletin board beside the rear door. Algeria and Francine were finished for the day and were removing their aprons. Francine was telling Algeria of a serial killer featured on *Unsolved Mysteries*. Birdie, still scouring the knobs on our large grill with a Brillo pad, was the last to note her husband's arrival, and by the time she saw him standing in the doorway, the other three of us were staring at him as though viewing a Martian. Perhaps we were all attempting to reconcile this small, nondescript man before us with the mischievous one who had packed two plain pieces of bread and eight cookies in Birdie's lunch. For the benefit of those familiar with politics in the nineties, Mickey Freeman could be said to resemble Ross Perot.

Mickey smiled at us, bowed comically as if ending a vaudeville act, then raised his voice and repeated his question. "Birdie, treasure, you about done?" His words brought to mind a book I had read soon after its publication in 1991. I had seen an interview of the author, Kaye Gibbons, on a television program featuring southern writers. Her voice had enchanted me, and I had immediately secured copies of her three novels: *Ellen Foster, A Virtuous Woman,* and *A Cure for Dreams.* She has since written others. In *A Cure for Dreams,* the young narrator and her mother discuss men and their manner of addressing their wives in public. The mother informs her daughter that the most polite mode of address includes the woman's name, spoken in a respectful tone, and she warns the girl to reject a man who uses honeyed, insincere pet names such as *dear* or, even more detestable, one who merely commands "Come on!" without any accompanying noun of address.

I believe that there is a great deal of truth in this mother's observation. If such were possible, a woman would do well to listen to her prospective husband — without his knowing it, of course — for many years before marrying him in order to project his voice to a time when the newly spun threads of courtship have been anchored into the loom of marriage. During the television interview with Kaye Gibbons, she was asked why most of the positive characters in her books were women and why the men usually vanished from the plot through a variety of unheroic means. She smiled briefly, I recall, and then said that she had "never been overly impressed with southern men in general."

For my part, I would not have limited the generalization to southern men.

Mickey Freeman's address of Birdie passed the test set forth in Kaye Gibbons' novel. He spoke his wife's name, followed by a rather quaint term of endearment, then asked a brief question. His tone of voice was patient and respectful. When Birdie looked up to see her husband in the doorway, she smiled and beckoned him to come into the kitchen.

"I'm just finishing this one last thing," she said, sponging the knobs with clean water. She began polishing them quickly with a rag, then spun around and said, "Oh, wait a minute. I'm forgetting my manners!" She laid her rag aside and steered Mickey in my direction. Motioning to Algeria and Francine, she called, "Can you come over here just a minute and meet my husband?" Birdie made the introductions in perfect accordance with the rules of etiquette. We all seemed to be transfixed, as if Emily Post were in our presence. Even Algeria extended her hand to Mickey and muttered, "Nice meetin' you." Mickey shook our hands in turn and had a polite word for each of us. Mine was "Margaret — I've always been partial to that name. My favorite cousin growing up was named Margaret."

Then, lowering his eyebrows, he looked at all of us and said, "I sure hope Birdie can keep this job. I guess she told you it's her first one since she's been out on parole."

Before he had finished, Birdie was reaching out to try to cover his mouth with both of her hands, laughing as she did so and saying, "Stop it, Mickey! Stop it! They're going to believe you!"

Though Francine let out a great yap of laughter, Algeria looked as if she wanted to pick Mickey Freeman up and wrench his neck. She could easily have done so.

After she ceased laughing, Birdie looked around at us and said, "He's hopeless. I can't do a thing with him!" Then she looked at her husband and shook her head in mock reproof. "Now, you be good, Mickey. These ladies have been so nice to me today." She beamed at each of us within the small circle before I turned and retreated into my cubicle. Behind me, I heard her say good-bye to Algeria and Francine. Then she called to me, "Thank you, Margaret! I'll see you in the morning," and Mickey said, "Adios, adieu, and catch you later, as they say in Nepal!" They laughed as they left, and I heard Birdie say, "Oh yes, it was a delicious sandwich once I got it all put together."

I tidied my desk and turned out the lights before exiting. It had been an uneventful day, free of accidents or mistakes, yet strangely troubling also. In past years, Vonnie Lee had filled up time and space with constant motion and with a swift, endless flow of words. Today had seemed quiet in comparison, almost leisurely, although I felt sure that the women had accomplished a great deal of cleaning. It was as though I had lifted the phonograph needle from the "1812 Overture" and set it down on "Prelude to the Afternoon of a Faun."

Driving home that day, I saw Birdie's homely face before me, and I knew for a certainty that her many gentle words of the day were but a shadow of things to come.

My fingers now ache from the labors of my pen. My spirit is heavy, and my mind divested. I shall pause for the renewal that only sleep can bring. In looking over the novel referred to earlier, *A Cure for Dreams,* I am struck with the fluidity of the narrator's voice. The colloquial style, the comic insights, and the stunning appeal of finely created characters — so delightful to me when I first read the book — are somewhat discouraging upon closer inspection, for now that I have embarked upon a written narrative of my own, my confidence is shaken.

I fear that my story, so rich and solid in its reality, is but a pale, trembling phantom of itself. By the time my tale is told, I fear that I will have wrung my soul dry, dispossessing myself of the energy to repair the stylistic slackness of these early chapters. Some books are published with the notation *Unabridged* beneath the title. Perhaps mine shall bear the label *Unrevised.*

TUTORS AND
GOVERNORS
5

When I disembarked from a Greyhound bus in Filbert, South Carolina, more than twenty years ago, I was twenty-nine years old. Though well acquainted with sorrow and exceedingly disillusioned by the people, places, and things in my life, I sought sympathy from no one. Even now I despise the person who publicizes his misfortunes and promotes himself as a victim. It is my unshakable belief that martyrs should be burned at the stake and thus permanently eliminated.

Vowing to conceal my past grief, to fold it away like stained linen and set it upon a high shelf, I prepared myself to start afresh in this small town where no one knew me. I had chosen Filbert a week earlier from a United States atlas at the public library in Marshland, New York, the day after I had overseen my grandfather's burial, an occasion that I shall treat more fully in a later chapter.

It was an early fall day in 1973 when I emerged from the bus station, suitcase in hand, and turned right to follow wherever the sidewalk might lead. The trees in Filbert, South Carolina, had just begun to change their colors, though they would not reach their peak for several more weeks. As I passed the local fire station — a small wooden edifice that itself appeared to be a fire hazard — I avoided the eyes of the man (a fireman, I assumed) who was seated upon an unstable bench beside the gaping maw of the fire station, inside which was parked a single glossy red fire engine, and who was engaged in what appeared to be whittling. I also passed a residence bearing the shingle *Notary Public* and a drugstore with a sign above its door that read *Health-2-U.*

Beyond the drugstore, the sidewalk led me past a small grocery named The Convenient and then along streets lined with houses, all of them modest in size and varying in degrees of upkeep from immaculate to slipshod. I passed a bakery, The Rolling Pin, its window case displaying only five rather deflated doughnuts (and one fly), and a neighborhood park, deserted in the afternoon heat. Though my description of Filbert may create images in the reader's mind of turn-of-the-century quaintness, such was not the impression in reality. Many of the buildings were indeed old, but the townspeople's dress, the automobiles, and the common public equipage such as parking meters, stoplights, and overflowing trash receptacles modernized the overall visual effect. Moreover, there was a certain indefinable smell of fried foods and accumulated grime congruous with more recent decades.

Since my mind was filled that day with the pressing needs of employment, housing, and a car, I was alert. My purse held a sum of cash — the liquidation of my grandfather's assets — and in the suitcase were a few personal possessions.

Presently the sidewalk led past Emma Weldy Elementary School, a low construction of yellow brick, where I viewed a host of children at play. They paid me no heed, for I was beyond the periphery of their fenced playground. Had I been a child, perhaps I would have gained their notice, but, being an adult, I was as a tree or post. I halted and gazed at the seething mass, listening to their childish shouts and noting the vivid patchwork of the many colors of their clothing. Colors affect me to such an extent that I have often wondered whether, with training, I might have succeeded as an artist.

It was the boys I sought most earnestly, their strong, wiry legs pumping in games of tag, their untiring arms in ceaseless motion. I saw a group of older ones in a far corner of the play yard engaged in a game of kickball. The sidewalk led me in that direction, and as I approached I heard a slim, well-built boy positioned near third base shout, "Here, Skeet! Throw it! He's goin' home!" A stocky outfielder hurled the ball to the speaker, who caught it cleanly, then smoothly whirled and launched it toward the runner.

I marveled at the boy. He wore green denim jeans, I recall, and his hair was a shock of dark auburn. He could not have been more than ten or eleven, yet he had the graceful coordination and power of a natural athlete. The ball hit the runner squarely behind the knees a few feet from home plate, and the entire outfield erupted into cheers of triumph. The boy who had thrown the ball received the congratulatory thumps of his teammates appreciatively but, it seemed to me, without self-importance. I heard them call him Bennet. Whether his first or last name, I could not tell, but it further endeared the boy to me, for it called to mind the main characters of Jane Austen's *Pride and Prejudice,* the Bennet family.

Jane Austen is perhaps the author whose works I love best, although I personally favor *Emma* over *Pride and Prejudice.* I have long admired Austen's unmatched genius for transforming the small business of everyday life into memorable scenes for her readers, painting detailed character cameos with her fine brush of words. As a young woman, I had entered the world of the Woodhouses, the Dashwoods, the Bennets, and the Elliots as a means of escaping my grandfather, and for the periodic sanctuary they afforded, I remain grateful. Austen's orderly world was a balm, the temporary domestic troubles of her characters a respite.

But I must return to the boys on the playground at Emma Weldy Elementary School. There is little else in my opinion as completely satisfying and fascinating as a boy — not a man, but a boy. The potential for tenderness balanced against the unfolding of physical might, the unflinching frankness, the lightness of emotional baggage, the unerring instinct for fairness and truth — in sum, when he reaches adulthood, a man is well past his peak, for this was reached between the ages of three and twelve.

I watched the boys at play until the shriek of a whistle marked the end of their liberation and they were herded inside. The auburn-haired boy, Bennet, loped along ahead of the others as if eager now for other challenges inside the yellow brick building.

Instead of continuing on my way through town as I had intended, I turned in at the school gate and found my way to the principal's office to inquire concerning staff employment. Until the moment that I had seen Bennet and the other boys at play, it had never occurred to me to seek employment at this or any other school. My brief experience with schools had left me no fond sentiments.

On my way into the office, a harried young woman in a white uniform almost bowled me over as she stormed through the doorway, pushed past me, and ran down the corridor in the direction from which I had come. The secretary, who was occupied on the telephone, cast a quizzical glance toward the momentary hubbub at the doorway but continued nodding into the receiver. I set my suitcase down beside a potted plant, and running my hand down the buttons of my dark suit jacket, which was too warm for a September day in South Carolina, I walked directly into the principal's office to state my business.

"I have come to ask about a position of employment at your school," I said.

The principal of Emma Weldy at that time was a portly woman in her late forties named Mrs. Edgecombe, who stood up from behind her large oak desk and tilted her head backward until her spectacles had apparently brought me into focus. She wore an expression of impatience, though taking time to study me thoroughly from head to toe. I would have been only mildly surprised had she requested me to turn around slowly or to open my mouth so she could examine my teeth.

"One of my third-grade teachers just this minute went home with chills and a fever," she said, "and my librarian is lying in the teachers' lounge with a migraine headache. And besides all this, one of our lunchroom workers just now flounced in and quit without a word of explanation." The combination of her deep, resonant voice and her unique, delicate southern inflections (*teachers* was pronounced "teach-uhs," for example, *lounge* was "lou-wunge," and *librarian* was "luh-BRAIR-yun") struck me as comedic, though I made no outward show of such.

I took her statement to mean that she had no time at present to answer my inquiry. "I will wait," I said and turned to exit her office. Outside her door there was a small alcove furnished with an unattractive brown Naugahyde sofa and two gold plaid chairs, and I meant to sit here. One of the chairs, I had noted earlier, was occupied by a young boy of a scowling and pugnacious countenance, whom I assumed to be a troublemaker awaiting his own private consultation with Mrs. Edgecombe.

Before I had taken two steps, however, Mrs. Edgecombe cried out, "Stop!" I wheeled around to see the woman advancing on me, one hand raised as if halting traffic and the other laid gently across her breast. "I can use your help for the next hour if you will be so kind," she said, passing me at the doorway. "Please follow me." For so large a woman, she moved with surprising lightness. The word *trippingly* came to mind. Her feet were quite small, I noticed, and her hands white and eloquent as they floated beside her. She wore an olive green dress, dotted with a print of white stars, and she was shaped like a small stout bureau.

She led me down a hallway, around a corner, and up a short flight of stairs, which she negotiated quite nimbly. We entered a large sunny room with many low shelves of books, toward which Mrs. Edgecombe made a wide, sweeping motion with her hands, and in a drawl as soft as velvet though paced with urgency, she said, "Choose one to read to the third-grade class. I'm going now to bring them in. They usually have a thirty-minute library time, but we're going to stretch it to an hour today and shift the fourth-graders to tomorrow." As she turned to leave, she fixed me with a stern look. "This is *not* the way we normally handle things around here, miss . . . now please tell me your name again."

"Margaret Bryce," I said.

"Yes, well, there's only a little of the school day left, and I haven't been able to get hold of a substitute. I'd do this myself except that I have an appointment with two parents in five minutes, and the assistant principal also needs to sit in on it. This is *not* a meeting we can postpone, unfortunately. You stepped into my office at just the right minute, it seems." She shook her head briefly, as though recalling with dismay some imminent, unavoidable unpleasantness, and added, "I have no idea who you are, Miss Bryce, but I'm risking my position on your integrity. Something tells me you won't let me down." She wavered just a moment as if reconsidering, then turned swiftly and left. Her low black pumps made dainty, rapid echoes as she retreated down the hallway.

Thus was my introduction to Emma Weldy Elementary School. Though I had never supervised a group of children in my life, I was undaunted by the prospect. I felt completely fortified in the comfortable old library, having spent countless happy hours in such rooms during my early childhood, and I set about quickly to select a book. Almost instantly my eyes lighted on a book titled *Charlie and the Chocolate Factory,* which, upon cursory inspection, seemed appropriate for reading aloud to third-graders, whom I calculated to be eight or nine years of age. I recognized the name of the author, Roald Dahl, for I had read his collection of stories titled *Somebody Like You* some ten years earlier.

Mrs. Edgecombe returned presently and stood beside me at the library door, both index fingers held to her lips as if to ensure a double measure of quiet, while a line of children filed into the room. The children seated themselves immediately in the metal chairs that were arranged in two semicircles around a large blue wing chair, where I assumed I was to sit. Twenty-five heads were turned in my direction and as many pairs of large eyes studied me curiously.

"You may let them browse through the shelves after you read to them awhile," Mrs. Edgecombe whispered. "Remember," she added, placing the palms of her hands together and tapping her fingertips lightly, "you need to keep them here for an hour. If I'm not back by two-thirty, take them back to their classroom so they can get their things ready to go home. Ask Jessica March to help you if you need to know anything. She's a very dependable little girl. My meeting should be over by then, though." A weary look crossed her pink face. "I certainly hope it is."

I nodded.

Mrs. Edgecombe glanced quickly at the large clock on the wall. "Thank you, Miss Bryce. Come by my office at the end of the day." She left, and I closed the door.

"Miz Gardner always leaves the door open," stated a red-haired boy.

"What's wrong with Miz Gardner?" asked a pudgy girl, who then whispered something at which several children snickered.

"Who're *you?*" asked a pale boy, rising to his knees and pointing at me. The folding chair almost buckled, but he averted a spill and quickly sat back down with a loud thump. The other children laughed raucously. There was a great scraping of metal chairs as the children twisted in their seats.

I walked slowly to the blue wing chair and sat down without speaking. I set my purse on the floor beside my chair and placed both hands on top of the book in my lap. My instincts told me that silence was a powerful tool with children. Indeed, it seemed to be so, for the group soon fell quiet and observed me with a look of great wonder. Although I was but twenty-nine years old at the time, I had often observed families in public places and had by now concluded that the primary fault of parents was an excess of talk, much of it redundant, irrelevant, and lacking conviction. I believed a reserved and somber demeanor to be of great value in all interpersonal exchanges, and I still believe this to be true, although my acquaintance with Birdie Freeman has revealed to me certain benefits of open and friendly discourse.

I opened the book, raised my eyes, and moved my gaze slowly across the group, looking briefly into the eyes of each child before reading from the author's introduction the names of the characters in the story. " 'The five children in this book are Augustus Gloop, Veruca Salt, Violet Beauregarde, Mike Teavee, and Charlie Bucket, who is the hero.' " I was instantly encouraged by the thought that any writer who would bestow upon his characters such splendid names surely would not disappoint his readers in the invention of a plot.

"Aw, yeah. That's a good book!" the red-haired boy said. There was an immediate eruption of questions and comments, which quickly subsided under my mirthless eye.

After thirty minutes I had read to the end of chapter five. "Would you like for me to stop now so that you may find your own books to read?" I asked.

As one, the children cried, "No!"

By the end of the hour, four of the five golden ticket winners in the story had come forward, and Charlie Bucket had just discovered a dollar bill in the snow beside a curb. I knew the faces of the third-graders well by this time, having watched their responses for the past hour. As a child, I had read aloud to my mother each evening, and she to me. I had always admired and tried to mimic my mother's style of oral reading. I now discovered, happily, that I still possessed the ability to read ahead and retain lengthy phrases to speak aloud as I lifted my head to look into the eyes of my audience. Thus, I appeared to be telling the story rather than merely reading it. I am not boasting, for I do not know to what extent this played a part in the children's attentiveness. I rather think it was the story itself that captivated them.

At exactly two-thirty Mrs. Edgecombe opened the door and entered. Her round face was drained of color, as if she had been sorely tested during the previous hour. A sprig of her faded brown hair drooped over her forehead. I read, " 'Carefully, Charlie pulled it out from under the snow. It was damp and dirty but otherwise perfect.' " Then I paused and addressed the children. "Mrs. Edgecombe has come to take you back to your classroom, but perhaps she will agree to our finishing this page, which concludes chapter ten." I held the book up toward Mrs. Edgecombe and pointed to the sentence I had just read, which was midway down the page.

The children emitted groans of disappointment and cries of supplication, to which Mrs. Edgecombe responded by stepping forward and clapping her hands lightly. "It's almost dismissal time, children, but it won't hurt to finish the page." She looked at me and said, "Go ahead. I'll wait." And she sat in a wooden armchair near the door.

I resumed reading. Though bordering on starvation, Charlie Bucket displayed admirable self-restraint in the use of his dollar, deciding to purchase a single bar of candy and then to take the rest of the money home to his mother. I closed the book when I had read the last sentence on the page but made a mental note to resume with page fifty if by some improbable development I were asked again at a later time to take the librarian's place with the third-graders.

Six days later, having acquired a position in the school cafeteria, I borrowed *Charlie and the Chocolate Factory* from Mrs. Gardner, who had recovered and returned to her duties in the library, and I read the remaining chapters one evening, not only because the thought of the book weighed upon me as unfinished business but also because I truly desired to know the conclusion of Mr. Roald Dahl's clever morality tale. I recall that when I read of the glass elevator bearing Charlie's entire family upward through the roof of the Buckets' house and out into a clear winter sky, I felt that Mr. Dahl had hit upon a very suitable ending.

But I have jumped ahead of my story and must return to the events of that first day at Emma Weldy Elementary School.

"Line up at the door, children," Mrs. Edgecombe said briskly, clapping her hands again. I was to discover in the months to follow that Mrs. Edgecombe clapped her hands habitually, oftentimes even when addressing teachers and parents. The children rose obediently and straggled toward the door.

"You gonna finish it next time?" a boy asked me. His hair was a tangle of blond curls, and his cheeks were cherry red.

Mrs. Edgecombe answered for me. "We'll tell Mrs. Gardner where the story left off so she can pick up there next week. Now, let's all give a big thank-you to your substitute for today."

All the children chorused a loud, drawn-out "Thank you!"

I nodded and said, "You are most welcome," then stood and watched them as they departed the room.

The pale boy who had almost upset his chair earlier said to no one in particular, "She reads lots better'n Miz Gardner," and another boy said, "I betcha Charlie gets a ticket." As the last child exited — a tiny girl with an ethereal face — she turned and waved to me, her fingers bunched together in a half fist, just the tips of them moving ever so slightly. I nodded to her and said, "Good-bye." As the sound of the children's footsteps grew fainter, I realized that neither I nor Mrs. Edgecombe had told them my name.

In my subsequent conversation with Mrs. Edgecombe in her office that afternoon, I noted that she appeared to be quite distracted, yet having been in her presence only briefly by this time, I was not certain whether this was her usual state or whether the events of the afternoon had overtaxed her. She asked me a number of questions that day about my past employment, my education, and my interests and seemed to be putting forth considerable effort to listen to my answers, which were succinct and unembellished. Before I left, she told me somewhat apologetically that she could offer me no monetary compensation for the assistance I had given that day, but that she would be happy to recommend me for a position in the lunch-room, to replace, I presumed, the distraught young woman whom I had encountered at the office door earlier.

"Of course everyone has to be approved officially through the superintendent's office," she said, "but Mr. Parker has always taken my recommendations before. You'll have to fill out an application, then go to the county office for an interview, but really, I don't foresee any problems." She gave me a feeble smile, lifted her eyeglasses with one hand, and pinched the bridge of her nose with the other.

The processing of my application was amazingly simple and my interview with Mr. Parker satisfactory. Though he seemed to me inordinately, but I must admit understandably, curious about my reasons for coming to Filbert, he waived the requirement of personal references after a prolonged silence, which had been preceded by my statement that for private reasons I sincerely wished all ties with my former life to remain severed. "We will hire you on a provisionary basis," he said at last, and I merely nodded, choosing not to press him concerning the exact nature of the provisions.

Within a week — an exceedingly busy week,

during which I made arrangements to purchase a duplex in a neighborhood outside the city limits of Filbert — I was employed in the lunchroom of Emma Weldy Elementary School under the supervision of an aging woman named Mrs. Lola Tyler, whose hands shook so badly that she could not operate the meat slicer, pour liquids, or write legibly. She spent most of her time watching the others of us perform our work while she circled the kitchen, conversing with herself. Mrs. Tyler was relieved of her duties the following January.

Mrs. Edgecombe remained grateful to me for my small contribution in her time of need and never failed to greet me courteously during the ensuing months. Our acquaintance was limited, however, not only in depth but also in length, for she resigned at the close of that school year. It was rumored that a certain parent had complained about her treatment of his son, a boy with severe learning disabilities, and had circulated a petition among other parents, finally taking his grievances to the board of education. I wondered later if the meeting in her office on the afternoon of my service in the library was in any way related to the trouble that led to her resignation. I do not know the particulars of Mrs. Edgecombe's reassignment to another school and her eventual departure from South Carolina, but I shall always remember her warmly. She extended to me her trust at a time in my life when mistrust could have been especially damaging.

During my first year at Emma Weldy, I saw the auburn-haired boy of the playground daily as he came through the cafeteria line with his classmates, and while I always felt an initial surge of delight at the sight of him, my pleasure was invariably clouded by a scrim of sadness as I imagined his life snuffed out and his mother bowed with grief. I had learned early in my life that conceiving of the worst was one means of preparing myself for its frequent arrival. I nevertheless watched for the boy each day. I learned from the lunchroom roster that Bennet was his first name, Caldwell being his last, and I wonder even today what became of young Bennet Caldwell. I am certain that he stands tall among his peers.

I must stop here. Once again I am aware of the inadequacies of my story as I hold it against professional standards of writing, for I know that it is riddled with flaws of implausibility. The coincidental timing of my arrival at Emma Weldy Elementary School at the very moment that Mrs. Edgecombe was faced with the sudden loss of a cafeteria worker and the prospect of an unattended class during the last hour of the school day seems unlikely even to me, to whom it happened. Had my bus arrived ten minutes earlier, my inquiry concerning a position at the school might have played out quite differently, and I might never have secured employment among the tutors and governors of children. Consequently, I might never have met Birdie Freeman.

THE VOICE OF DOVES
6

Had Birdie Freeman been a flintier woman, producing friction within her small world, her story would more actively and instantly spark the reader's interest. If I could report that Birdie's quiet, religious fervor and virtuous conduct rankled us all, that Algeria held out against her first friendly overtures with her usual wary cynicism, that Francine found her primness laughable, that I hated the very sight of her, then my story would hold the valued appeal of conflict that lies at the heart of drama.

Such claims about Birdie Freeman, however, would be patently false. I cannot alter the truth, and the truth is that we all regarded her favorably, though for the first three months of our acquaintance my own regard took the outward form of hostility, and that most convincingly. And perhaps I was not pretending altogether. As I recall, my feelings during those early months were dichotomous. On the one hand, I was powerfully drawn to

Birdie, while on the other, I resisted her intensely.

At the end of Birdie's first week, it seemed that she had been with us for years. On Wednesday morning of the following week, after school had officially begun, I was on my way to work at 6:10. The sky was dark yet, with a faint glow of sherbet orange seeping over the eastern horizon. I was sitting in my Ford Fairlane at the stoplight on the outskirts of Filbert, at an intersection anchored by a Winn Dixie Grocery Store, the Mirror Brite Car Wash, Sonny's Pizza Shack, and Lackey's Grass-Is-Greener Nursery.

At the sight of the nursery, Birdie's earnest face came to mind, for she had presented me with a tiny bonsai the day before, a plant that she had nurtured from a cutting that Mervin Lackey, the owner of the Grass-Is-Greener Nursery, had given her. Mervin Lackey was Birdie's neighbor. "His yard looks like the Garden of Eden!" she had told me. She did not know the name of the little tree, which struck me as careless. I learned later its name is Serissa, and it is also known as Tree of a Thousand Stars.

Though I had accepted her gift without comment other than the requisite thank-you and had asked Birdie to set it on top of my file cabinet so that it would be out of my way, I had taken the bonsai home that afternoon and examined it at length. Including its jade

105

green four-inch square ceramic planter, the miniature tree stood only seven inches high, its tiny trunk the girth of a pencil, its branches fanned out to one side in the asymmetrical contour of a candle flame near an open window. Upon the branches sprouted a delicate profusion of emerald leaves the shape of teardrops, and interspersed among these were fourteen — I counted them three times — pearl white blossoms, no larger than the buttons on a baby's dress, and as many unopened buds.

"I just trimmed its roots a couple of months ago," Birdie had said when she gave it to me, "and I was fixing to shape up the branches, but Mickey said to leave it out of balance like it was. Mickey's got a good eye for things like that, so I left it alone. I was going to cut it back a little over here" — she cupped her hands to form a canopy over one side of the bonsai — "but then when I stood back and looked at it, I could see Mickey's point. It's kind of interesting and . . . *Oriental-looking* the way it floats out sideways, isn't it?"

She pressed an index finger gently into the loose, pebbly soil and smiled up at me. "I hope you'll get to liking it as much as we do, Margaret," she said. "Mickey gets real attached to my plants. At night he'll pat their little branches and say, 'Bedtime for Bonsai.' " She paused, then added, "It's real pretty in its blooming stage, isn't it?" Without waiting for me to answer, she continued, "But it doesn't bloom all the time, of course. That's the way it goes with everything, isn't it?" She went on to tell me the name of a soil treatment I could use to prevent the leaves from yellowing, and then she left my office, humming as always.

Sitting at the traffic light by Lackey's Grass-Is-Greener Nursery that Wednesday morning, I reminded myself to stop there on the way home. The thought of the bonsai leaves turning yellow was not a happy one. Looking back on Birdie's first gift to me — there were many others to follow — I realize now that it touched me far more deeply than I was capable of understanding or was willing to admit at the time. Thomas had given me gifts, of course, and even now frequently brings me things from the hardware store, which he leaves for me on the kitchen counter (household gadgets and supplies: a dust mop, a jar of silver polish, a watering can, a wire whisk, and so forth). But besides Thomas's offerings, Birdie's was the first gift I had received since my seventeenth birthday, when my grandmother had bought me a pair of new saddle oxfords at JCPenney's in Marshland, New York. She generally purchased my clothes and shoes secondhand from a Salvation Army store.

These thoughts were going through my mind as the light turned green, and I had just formed a picture of the prized saddle oxfords when, strangely, I saw an object hurled from the back window of the compact car in front of mine. I caught only a momentary glimpse of it flying through the air before it hit the pavement, bounced a few feet, and landed beside my car door. It was a child's rubber-soled sneaker. The car from which it had been launched sped off with a squeal of tires, and I saw the driver, a woman with long hair, leaning to the right as if groping inside the glove compartment. In the back seat I could see a small head above the top of a child's safety seat and two little hands waving erratically after the fashion of very young children.

A car had just pulled up behind me at the traffic light, and the driver honked his horn. I remained stationary, however, as I considered the situation. If I retrieved the shoe, would I not be accepting an obligation to try to locate its owner? Surely such a project was doomed to failure. To leave the shoe where it had fallen, however, would be irresponsible, for it would very likely be flattened and battered by the daily traffic. The car behind me honked again. The child's mother might discover the missing shoe within the next few minutes, deduce what had happened, and retrace her path in search of it. If I took it now, she would not find it and would be forced to buy the child a new pair of shoes or have him go barefoot.

It would be of no use to take it to the Berea Police Station, for locating the owner of a lost shoe would hardly be a priority for those charged with upholding the law. I looked into my rearview mirror. The driver in the car behind me, a large man whose silhouette dwarfed the steering wheel, backed up and, swerving around my car, cast me a look of undisguised contempt. No doubt he was muttering uncomplimentary remarks also, for his lips were moving.

I hit upon a compromise. Activating the emergency flashers, I got out of my car. By this time the stoplight had turned red again, and because there was very little traffic at this early hour, I had no fear of posing a traffic hazard. Picking up the little shoe, I studied it briefly. It showed signs of heavy play, the canvas having worn through at the toe, leaving a frayed hole the size of a nailhead. The broken lace had been secured with a make-shift knot. Clearly, the child needed a new pair of shoes. Would I not be doing him a service to leave the shoe in the road and thus complete its ruination?

It appeared to be a boy's shoe, for the faded blue canvas was imprinted with tiny pictures of footballs, football helmets, and goalposts. The rubber sole was wearing smooth but was still intact. The shoe felt warm as I held it in my palm, and the rubber strip around the edge of the sole was slightly sticky. I imagined the owner, right foot shoeless now, kicking and prattling happily in the backseat with no recollection of what he had so recently done. He was probably no more than two. I wondered how his mother would respond when she noticed the missing shoe. Perhaps she would vent her anger in a harmful way. I felt a sudden, tight pressure within me.

A red Volkswagen stopped in the lane next to mine, evil black fumes curling from its exhaust pipe, and the teenager behind the steering wheel looked at me with the churlish expression of one long accustomed to doing battle with adults. Next to my car was a narrow, raised concrete median, separating the two northbound lanes from the two southbound. A metal pole, painted in black and yellow stripes, rose about four feet from the center of the median, serving as a warning marker. The pole was capped with a rounded metal cone, and upon this cap I upended the little canvas shoe. If the child's mother frequently drove this route, I reasoned, she would certainly spot the missing shoe — unless someone else took it first.

The teenager was still watching me furtively, but when the light turned green, his car sprang forward. I returned to my own car, the thoughts of loss and waste troubling me, and continued on my way, trying not to think about the possibility of the teenager in the Volkswagen returning to take the shoe, perhaps to dangle from his rearview mirror as a trophy of yet another victory over the impotent adult world.

I sincerely endeavored that day to erase from my mind the image of the child's shoe. One reason is that the thought of the tiny canvas sneaker evoked memories from which I must take constant care to distance myself. Even today I can close my eyes and feel the weight of a small foot within the palm of my hand and can recall the frequent tying of laces as if it were yesterday. Another reason is that my solution to the dilemma — the transfer of the shoe from the road to the top of the pole — filled me with great unrest, for it reminded me again of the many unsatisfying choices in life.

I had long been resigned to the fact that life held very few grand, well-marked crossroads at which the signposts of *Good* or *Evil* flashed unmistakably. There were a few of them, of course; diverging roads at which point the traveler had to make a single, life-altering choice. My decision to leave my grandfather's house at the age of seventeen was one such choice. I know now, however, that even these momentous choices rarely, if ever, lead to either unalloyed happiness or to abject misery of soul. Life's choices, I learned long ago, are difficult and unrewarding, even in so small a matter as what to do with a child's lost shoe. Even right decisions bring doubts and twinges of regret.

As I drove on my way that day, the phrase "Traveling through the dark" preyed upon my mind, the words coming from the title and opening line of a poem by William Stafford, in which a driver must decide whether to leave a dead doe on the road or push her over the mountainside into the canyon below. The speaker's dilemma is complicated when he realizes that within the doe lies an unborn fawn; he can see its movement. Now, as I thought of the poem and of the narrator's decision to sacrifice the fawn for the safety of other motorists, my spirits were dampened by the reminder of life's dark, cramped corners. I set about presently, however, to put these thoughts out of my mind, disturbed at myself for overreacting to an event of so little consequence as a boy's lost sneaker.

When I arrived at school, though I still felt unsettled, I determined to immerse myself at once in the simple, familiar tasks before me. Birdie arrived at a quarter of seven, and Algeria and Francine walked in together only seconds later. Because the children who qualified for the government's Start-Off-Right program began arriving at the cafeteria at 7:50 for their free breakfast, we had no idle time in the mornings. By 6:53 all three women were busy with their kitchen duties.

When I came out of my office at 7:20, Birdie was standing beside the heavy aluminum cauldron that we used for heating water. The water was steaming, on the verge of boiling, small silver bubbles sliding up the sides to bob at the surface, then vanish quickly. I could hear the muted rumbling and gurgling within the cauldron, the ticking sound of the electric burner that presaged the full, roiling eruption. Even today I find it difficult to sit at my desk when I sense this prelude to boiling. I often come out to be on hand when the boiling commences. In her left hand Birdie held a large Pyrex measuring bowl of oatmeal and in her right our largest wooden spoon with the longest handle.

She flashed me a smile. "I guess it's true what they say about a watched pot, isn't it?" She clutched the handle of the measuring bowl tightly. The spout was poised above the rim of the cauldron, ready to release the contents at the proper moment.

As I gazed into the pot, the bubbles grew larger and gradually began swirling and foaming, then rapidly accelerated into a turbulent boil. I watched Birdie slowly pour the dry oats into the cauldron, stirring all the while. The steam rose toward her, but she did not retreat. Nor did she throw resentful glances toward me in the manner of Algeria and Francine when they felt intruded upon. Once when I was standing behind Algeria, she had

113

inquired huffily, "Here — you wantin' to do this yo'self?" and had even thrust the stirring spoon toward me. Instead, Birdie said, "I don't think I've ever seen such a big pot of oatmeal as this, and I know for sure I've never *made* one!"

No one knew, nor did I reveal, the cause of my extreme solicitousness in the boiling of water. The narrator of Poe's story "The Tell-Tale Heart" speaks of the heightened awareness of his senses, especially of his hearing, as a result of a peculiar disease. "I heard all things in the heaven and in the earth," he says. "I heard many things in hell." I, too, have suffered the hearing of many hideous sounds, among them the hiss of boiling water, the tremendous clatter of an upset pot, and the tortured screams that ensued.

Birdie continued to stir the oatmeal, reducing the heat until the mixture merely simmered. "Algeria told me how to do this to make the amount come out right," she said, looking up at me jubilantly as if she had perfected a great art. I moved away without speaking to correct an error that I noted in Francine's preparation of cheese toast. She had taken from the refrigerator a new box of sliced cheese rather than finishing the box that we had opened on Monday for cheeseburgers.

It has occurred to me that the way a writer acquaints his readers with a character in his story should be no different from the way we come to know someone in ordinary life. Since I began writing my story, I have wrestled with the insurmountable obstacle of describing on paper the enormous composite reality of Birdie Freeman. I see the task more clearly as my tale grows, for I understand that though it is a painstaking process, the drawing of her portrait must be accomplished through "minutely organized particulars," to borrow the words of William Blake, a poet whose words I seldom find cause to borrow, for I have always felt that Blake was too conscious of himself as he composed his verse. I would have liked him more as a poet had he been less of a mystic. The point, however, is that by piling up specific evidence, I shall eventually succeed, and you shall know Birdie as I knew her.

Twenty-five minutes after Birdie had emptied the oats into the boiling water, the children began filing in for breakfast. Each morning I stood at the end of the line to mark my forms for the government. I watched the children receive their trays in the kitchen and then exit into the cafeteria to sit at the three tables nearest the door.

This morning I observed Birdie as she set the bowls of oatmeal onto each tray. Francine stood to her left, adding a piece of cheese toast, an orange, and a carton of milk. Algeria was at the stove ladling oatmeal into bowls.

These she placed, a dozen at a time, onto a large tray, which she then carried over to the serving line. As Birdie emptied each tray of its twelve bowls, Algeria took an empty tray back to resupply it with full bowls.

The children chattered freely, laughing and shoving one another playfully, but the women did not talk among themselves during the time they were serving. I watched this morning, however, as Birdie spoke directly to each child, something Francine and Algeria never did when they served unless asked a question.

Vonnie Lee had been fond of teasing the children, though not individually, and they had liked her despite the fact that they rarely understood what she was saying when she tossed out bits of nonsense such as "Hey, it's the little old lady from Pasadena!" or "It's my party and I'll cry if I want to!" Although Francine had children of her own, she seemed, for the most part, uninterested in those of other people. Algeria, though I often saw her quick eyes scanning their faces with something akin to hunger, held herself aloof from the children. We were in many ways, I suppose, an odd lot to be working in the cafeteria of an elementary school.

I had always strongly recommended that my workers refrain from fraternizing with the pupils in order not to interfere with the efficiency of our serving, and this had become a tacit regulation. I realized this morning, however, that I had failed to repeat the injunction in our opening meeting this year, and now as Birdie encircled the rim of each bowl with her small hands and lifted it onto every tray in turn, she addressed each child. "It's hot, honey," she said, or "Blow on it a little before you eat it, sweetie." She looked at every child as she spoke, and I saw that she had already learned the names of several. "Good morning there, Maria, here's some nice hot breakfast" or "This here will make those bright eyes even shinier — Lamont, isn't that your name, sweetheart?"

After all 130 children were served, I observed Birdie as she went out into the cafeteria and bent over a fifth-grade girl sitting at the end of a table. I knew who the child was and understood well why she always sat alone. Mrs. Triplett, the school nurse, had attempted at one time to intervene but had been rudely rebuffed by both the girl, whose name was Jasmine Finney, and her grandmother, with whom she lived.

Birdie spoke to Jasmine only a moment, then stooped down and appeared to look at the child's feet. When she returned to the kitchen, I called her into my office. I stood behind my desk to address her. "Here at Emma Weldy, your duties are to be confined to the kitchen," I said. Even as I spoke, I was

117

aware that my words sounded cold and sodden.

"Oh, I understand that, Margaret," Birdie said with a sprightly nod. "I was just saying a word to little Jasmine." I had never thought of the child as "little Jasmine," considering her hefty size and her malicious temperament.

"You were hired to prepare and serve the meals here," I said, "and anything that distracts you from those duties will be a detriment to the success of your employment." Birdie looked up at me quizzically, turning her head slightly as if straining to hear an inflection by which she would know that my words were in jest.

I continued. "Each pupil here at Emma Weldy has ready access to a teacher, a counselor, and a principal, all of whom are professionally equipped to deal with the problems of children. Your concern must be in the refining of your kitchen skills. When serving the children, you will no doubt see the wisdom of keeping silent so that we can all make better use of our time."

I stopped and looked past Birdie into the kitchen. Algeria and Francine, though pretending to be busy, were casting surreptitious glances in our direction.

At the same moment that I saw Algeria lift the cauldron from the stove, I realized that Birdie was shaking her head. "Oh, Margaret," she said, and she continued to shake her head quite briskly. "My heart would just shrivel up inside of me if I couldn't talk to the children."

"Nevertheless," I said, averting my eyes.

She reached out and touched the cuff of my blouse. "You don't mean this as strict as it sounds. I know you don't. I can see it in your eyes, Margaret. You just mean for me to be sure to put my work first, and I understand that. I really do — and I will, too. You can count on that."

"I do not say things that I do not mean," I said. I took one step back, and her hand fell from my wrist.

Birdie's expression tightened, and as her front teeth clamped over her lower lip, two deep, dimplelike indentations formed on either side of her mouth, though she was not smiling. She glanced down at her shoes — she had exchanged the black canvas sneakers that she had worn the first day for white ones — then again brought her eyes to mine, lifting her chin just slightly. With astonishment I saw that her eyes were rimmed with tears.

"If you want me to leave my job, I will," she said. Her voice did not quaver, but from the corner of one eye a tear overflowed messily.

"I was not suggesting that you resign," I said. Acutely peeved over her show of emotion, I am sure that I must have raised my voice.

"Oh, but I'll have to if I can't be friendly with the children," she said, wiping her cheek with the flat of her hand. She spoke softly, but her tone was resolute. I knew that she was not staging a performance merely to get her way. I was certain that, if pressed, Birdie Freeman would remove her hairnet and white plastic apron at this very moment and take her leave.

"Your primary duties here at our school are to be confined to the kitchen," I repeated firmly, yet I realized that I had added what amounted to a qualifier.

"I know that, Margaret." The pool of tears had already begun to recede, I noticed. Only the one had spilled over. The two of us gazed at each other for several moments, during which time I noted that one of her brown eyes contained a fleck of amber, like a tiny shard of bottle glass embedded into the iris. Birdie spoke at last. "I give you my word that I won't let my interest in the boys and girls get in the way of doing my job."

"Take care that it does not," I said, and turning my back on her, I picked up the weekly menu and studied it, though I knew it by heart.

I waited for her to leave my office cubicle, but when I turned my head I could see that she was still there. "You are free to go," I said.

Behind me her voice was low and mournful. "There's just so many problems, aren't there?" I did not answer. "Some of these poor babies break my heart — but I needed your reminder, Margaret, and I truly will try not to let myself get too wrapped up in their little lives. I'm a *kitchen* worker."

"Very well," I said, and I turned abruptly, brushed past her, and left her standing in my office.

The next morning I saw that Birdie had come to school with a large brown paper bag, and when she reached inside and removed a shoe box I knew at once what she had done. After the children filed through for breakfast, I retreated to the pantry to open a large box containing eight-pound cans of pinto beans. These I began arranging on a shelf. From the pantry I heard Birdie speaking to the children who came back for second helpings. "There you are, sweetheart." "I bet you just love pancakes, don't you, honey?" "That sure is a pretty barrette, Lindy." I afterward busied myself straightening the boxes of gelatin and pudding mix, then checked to see how many packages of paper napkins were on the shelf.

By the time I returned to the kitchen, Birdie was helping Francine prepare the apple cobbler to be served at lunch. I noticed that the shoe box was still sitting in the cupboard where the workers stored their personal belongings, but the lid had been removed, and the box was now empty. Later, when the classes passed through for lunch, I made a point of looking at Jasmine Finney's feet. As I had suspected, the girl wore a brand-new pair of sneakers, huge white ones with purple and pink stripes stitched down the sides. She wore the same malignant expression on her face, however, and as she passed me, I heard the echo of Birdie's gentle, sorrowful words from the day before, like the voice of doves. *"There's just so many problems, aren't there? Some of these poor babies break my heart."*

It struck me as a curious coincidence that the inadequate footwear of a child had recently been brought to the attention of both Birdie and me. I could not help wondering that day what course Birdie would have taken had she been in my place at the traffic light the morning before.

The shoe was still on the striped pole when I drove past the intersection the following two days but was gone by Monday of the next week. I never pass that way now without visions of shoes filling my mind — my own saddle oxfords of long ago, which I had recalled that day as I considered the matter of gifts; the ragged shoe flung from a car window by an anonymous toddler; the large white sneakers on the feet of Jasmine Finney; Birdie's canvas Keds. And each time I pass the intersection, I pause to contemplate the quiet aggressiveness of one small woman against the problems of the world, then to question the lasting consequence of her good deeds.

A TINKLING CYMBAL
7

I am no longer writing my story by longhand in my red spiral notebooks. Let me explain how this change came about.

Two days ago Thomas came home at one-thirty in the afternoon to search for a receipt verifying the recent purchase of two new tires for his pickup truck, one of which was proving unsatisfactory. He entered through the kitchen door, as he typically does, and made his way directly to his bedroom. I heard him rummaging about noisily, as I suppose all men do, and after many thumps and exclamations I heard him cry, "There she is, by jings!" Had I known what he sought, I would have instructed him to look *first* in the pockets of his overalls, which is precisely where he had located the missing receipt. I never wash a pair of his overalls without checking the pockets, and my search invariably yields candy wrappers, nuts and bolts, loose change, and the like. In many ways Thomas is simply a very tall little boy.

As he passed through the hallway on his way back to the kitchen, he must have glanced into the living room, for he stopped abruptly. I did not look up but was aware of his presence. He inhaled sharply and stood there for several moments before speaking.

"Margaret." It was not a question but a statement of moderate surprise.

"Yes." I continued writing, though I later had to delete the entire ungainly sentence and reconstruct the thought more gracefully.

"You mean to say you're sittin' here writin' in those red books of yours *all day long* and nights, too?" His tone was not accusatory; rather, he seemed to be awed by the fact. To this point, Thomas had made no outward sign of noticing my nightly occupation.

I looked up. Thomas was wearing his oldest pair of overalls and a faded but well-pressed red shirt. On the wall behind his head hung a large handmade clock with a triangular wooden frame and hands comprised of flattened nails. Norman Lang, the owner of the hardware store where Thomas rents the space for his vacuum repair business, had custom-designed it for our wedding gift in 1979. Though it violated all principles of aesthetics, I had watched without comment on the day before our marriage as Thomas proudly hung it on a prominent wall in my duplex, where we were to live.

Thomas stood now in the small hallway

gazing at me, his hands clasped behind his back, his neck extended forward, his head tilted as though examining an encased museum relic. The triangular clock, positioned as it was behind him, made him appear to be wearing a colonial hat such as those worn in the days of George Washington. The effect could have been comical had I not been annoyed by the interruption.

"Is it somethin' that *needs* to be put down on paper so bad you gotta spend all day and night doin' it?" he asked.

His questioning me thus struck me with sudden force as further evidence of his increasing boldness. A year ago he would not have dared interrogate me so. One of the side effects of a large steady dose of Birdie Freeman has been, I suppose, a diminishing of my customary brusqueness toward Thomas. As a result, he now approaches me more frequently and unabashedly with direct questions and opinions. Of my evolving relationship with Thomas, more will come later.

Though I have tolerated his gradually expanding inquisitiveness, yesterday I was suddenly moved to wrath by his encroachment.

"My time is my own, is it not?" I said irritably. "You see no dust upon the furniture, do you? Your clothes, which you simply drop into the hamper, continue to be returned to your bureau washed and ironed, do they not?

You have not yet come home to find your table empty at mealtimes, have you?" My words sounded harsh even to me, and I could not look Thomas in the eye as I spoke them.

The air between us was still, though the small air conditioning unit in the window labored continuously. Thomas took a step forward as if to attempt pacification, then apparently reconsidered. He turned slowly into the kitchen and exited through the back door, closing it quietly behind him.

Feeling chastened by his mildness, as I often do, I tried to continue writing but found my thoughts resistant to molding. At the time, I was endeavoring to recreate my conversation with Birdie concerning her excessive communication with the children in the serving line. For the first time since I began writing my story two weeks ago, I found myself groping for words, or rather, desperately pursuing them. The sentences would form themselves in my mind, appropriately worded, but in the brief moment between the flash of thought and the applying of my pencil to the paper, they would begin to dissipate. I would quickly snatch the ones I could recall but upon rereading a passage would deplore its hollowness.

I struggled on for the better part of an hour before giving it over. If Thomas had not broken my thought, I am quite certain that I could have finished the chapter that afternoon. I suppose this was my first experience with what I have heard labeled as "writer's block," a term I had previously suspected to be merely a weak excuse invented by slothful writers.

As I recall, I abandoned my writing for a time and spent the next hour in the kitchen making preparations for supper. I do not assemble meals in the hasty, slapdash manner shown on television commercials. My suppers never consist of an indistinguishable sauce poured from a jar over heaps of rice or noodles. Though it was only midafternoon, I prepared the chicken for baking, placed it in a covered dish for the time being, and then set it in the refrigerator. That done, I mixed the batter for a cake of which Thomas was especially fond. Several years ago I had experimented with a recipe for fresh strawberry cake, adapting it from my best recipe for white cake, and Thomas had eaten three pieces the first night I served it.

I was not making the cake, I told myself, as penance for my curt response to him earlier that afternoon; rather, I needed to use some of the strawberries that he had brought home the day before. By now we had already eaten the two pints that Joan had brought us. I placed the cake in the oven to bake, set the timer, and began peeling carrots.

As I worked in the kitchen, my mind returned to my story, and gradually finding myself once again in calm possession of my thoughts, I sat down and opened my notebook around four o'clock to resume my writing but was interrupted shortly thereafter by a telephone call from a representative of Bellaire Marketing Research. It was a woman's voice, inarticulate and poorly modulated. She mumbled her first name — Doris — and then immediately launched into quite a lengthy introduction of the organization's services, stumbling over a number of words and mispronouncing *subsidiary* and *cyclical.*

When she finally paused and asked if I had three or four minutes to answer a few questions for a survey, I replied, "No, I do not, Doris, and in the future, you would do well to polish your speaking skills before imposing upon the time of busy people. Take your paragraph home tonight and practice it. Get your dictionary out and look up the pronunciation of each word. Record your voice on an audiotape and critique it. When you have perfected your script, you may call me back and perhaps then I will participate in your survey, though this is not a commitment. You might also suggest to your superiors that they simplify the script for the sake of reaching the general public." I believe in speaking the truth and find myself to be especially frank and sometimes garrulous with telephone solicitors.

I tried again to return to my writing, but

within five minutes I was interrupted once more by a telephone call, this one from Thelma Purdue, who occupies the other side of our duplex. She was calling to inform me that the Jansens' dog was in our front yard. "He's done relieved hisself again right by our mailboxes," she said.

As soon as I hung up, the oven timer sounded. I transferred the cake to a cooling rack, then set the chicken in the oven to bake before I went outside with the intention of driving the Jansens' dog across the street to his own yard, at which time I found that he was already being dragged home by Mrs. Jansen, who was scolding him like a termagant. "You get outta our yard one more time, Pedro, and it's curtains! I mean it! Curtains! The end! Last chapter — all she wrote! I'm sick and tired of chasing all over creation for you! I never wanted to get you in the first place." I quickly surmised that her harangue was for my benefit, for she undoubtedly knew that I was within earshot. Phyllis Jansen and I had exchanged words on more than one occasion concerning the perambulations of Pedro.

As I was already outdoors, I checked the mailbox and found a telephone bill, an envelope bearing the notation *Open Immediately! You Could Already Be a Millionaire!* (which would be deposited into the trash can unopened), and a mail order catalogue from a company called Just What You've Always Wanted. I flipped through it and saw nothing whatsoever that I wanted.

There was also a new issue of *Field and Stream,* to which Thomas subscribes. One of the lead articles was "Seeking Out the Sweet Spots for Summer Smallmouth." I paused for a moment to wonder about the writer of such an article. Who was this man? His name was printed below the title: Dallas Kincaid. Were articles such as this one the sole source of his income? Did he have a family to support?

Immediately following these thoughts, I was again struck by my burgeoning interest in the lives of others — of an obscure writer of an article about smallmouth bass, for instance. I know not to what cause to lay this development except to Birdie Freeman's unrelenting *nearness,* both physical and otherwise.

Clutching the mail in one hand, I stooped to pull several tall blades of grass from around the mailbox post and then turned back to the house. Thelma Purdue accosted me as I mounted the three steps to our front door. I would have groaned aloud had it been of any use. Thelma Purdue is a person whose company I find it difficult to endure. As Thomas says, "That woman can talk the horns off a billy goat." She opened her door, which is only five or six feet from our own, and hissed at me. Yes, she hissed.

Thelma Purdue never initiates a conversation in a polite, conventional manner. Her customary greeting is a series of sharp, sibilant whistles: "Sss! Sss! Sss!" This is the closest approximation of the sound she makes, although at times she provides variety with "Shh! Shh! Shh!" or "Psst! Psst! Psst!" It is a vile sound and never fails to bring to my mind the sinister character of Gollum in J. R. R. Tolkien's book *The Hobbit,* which, though fantasy has never been my first love in fiction, I read with relish a few weeks after my arrival in Filbert in 1973. Tolkien had died in England only weeks earlier, and as I had never read any of his works, I paid posthumous tribute to him in this way.

I stopped and looked at Thelma, refusing to speak until she did.

"I done told Phyllis that that dog can unlatch the gate hisself. I watched him lots of times just go over and jump up and bat at it with his paws till it flips up. Pokes at it with his snout, too. She don't believe me, I don't guess, or else they'd fix it up with something stronger. Tie it with a rope or something."

"Yes, I suppose so," I replied.

"You having yourself a nice summer now school's out?" she asked. "I don't see much of you like I do other summers. You not doing a garden this time?"

"Thomas may plant some late limas and corn," I said. I glanced down at the pieces of mail in my hand as if to suggest that I had business to which I must attend.

"Mmm . . . I wisht I could get Nick to do that," Thelma said. "I sure like limas. Corn, too, if it's sweet." She paused and breathed heavily, each exhalation a soft hiss. Like Gollum, Thelma has "pale, lamplike eyes," though hers are magnified by the thick lenses of her eyeglasses. I took two steps toward my front door.

"My sister's coming next week from Sumter to see me," she continued. "You met her once when she come after Nick had that 'pendicitis attack that time, you remember?"

"Yes."

"Name's Arlene. She lives in Sumter. Be here next week."

"Yes." I reached forward and opened my screen door.

"You ever put limas and corn both together and make succotash?" Thelma asked, speaking louder and leaning out a bit farther. She was wearing a red-striped housecoat with dark stains down the front.

"Rarely," I said.

"Mmm. Phyllis sure ought to get that gate fixed, else that dog's gonna keep poppin' it open. Chain or wire or something. Maybe a rope."

"Yes, she should. Good day, Thelma." I pushed the front door open and stepped into my living room. I must be kinder to Thelma.

I have asked myself more than once, "How would Birdie treat her?" When weighed in such a balance, I am found wanting.

As I stepped inside, the smell of baking met me, a mingling of confection and meat, not unpleasant but curious. I set the mail on the small table beside the door, then moved to my rocker and closed my notebook, transferring the paper clip to mark the page where I had stopped writing. I then returned to the kitchen, for Thomas would be home from the hardware store within the next hour. As I continued with supper preparations, my thoughts turned once again to my story, and sentences began to shape themselves in my mind. I have found that it is possible to write without pencil or paper. My memory is such that I can reposit within it a considerable quantity of text to be retrieved and committed to paper at a later time.

Much of my composing in the kitchen that day, two days ago now, was simply recalling and storing the dialogue that had passed between Birdie and myself concerning her fraternization with the children, though I was also providing transitions between our spoken words. Thus engaged, I continued my kitchen work and was cutting out the last of the biscuits as the words "a fleck of amber, like a tiny shard of bottle glass embedded into her iris" were linking themselves together in my mind. At that moment the back door opened, and Thomas entered the kitchen.

I had not heard his truck in the driveway and was therefore startled, though I maintained my composure. I did not look up but continued lifting biscuits from the floured cloth and placing them onto the baking sheet. In my peripheral vision I could see that Thomas was carrying something, and when he set it down at the end of the counter to the right of where I was standing, I said, "Not there. I will be using this space." Still I did not look up.

Thomas picked up the object again — which appeared to be a box, quite large — and took it into the living room. I heard him exit through the front door and come back in, then repeat the process two more times. As the biscuits baked, I quickly frosted the cake, covered it, and set it on the lower shelf of the utility cart beside the stove. I heard Thomas in the living room, moving things about with a great deal of audible exertion. He was clearly "up to something," as the idiom goes, but I chose not to investigate.

I will not belabor the following events more than is necessary. We ate our supper a few minutes later, during which Thomas talked of the day's work. That day he had repaired an old Filter Queen vacuum cleaner that had been kept in immaculate condition. "Lady's had it since she married," he said, "and she's got to be eighty if she's a day. Told her I didn't see many like hers. Called it a one-owner classic, and she got a real kick out of that." He went on talking of various customers throughout the entire meal, with only occasional lapses, and I listened with only minimal comment.

After the meal Thomas cleared the table while I wrapped the leftover biscuits in foil, emptied the remaining peas and carrots into a freezer container — I save all leftover vegetables to be used in vegetable soup, which I make at the end of each month — and disposed of the chicken bones. I then began running hot, soapy water into one side of the sink in preparation for washing the dishes. We have no dishwasher, as I have never wanted one. By this time Thomas had left the kitchen, but he suddenly reappeared in the doorway between the kitchen and small hallway.

"John-Brown-it, Rosie, don't you ever *wonder* 'bout *nothin'?*" he asked.

I turned my head to look at him. "I wonder about a great many things, Thomas Tuttle," I replied.

"Well . . . if you just . . . why don't you . . ." He did not seem to know what it was that he wanted to say, but I saw him look over his left shoulder into the living room.

Placing the stopper in the other side of the sink, I began filling it with hot water for rinsing. Thomas remained in the doorway. He rested one of his hands against the doorjamb, and I could sense that he was studying me. I set the silverware in the sudsy water and then reached for the plates and glasses.

"Come out here, Margaret," Thomas said abruptly, straightening and again looking back over his left shoulder. "Quit your washing a minute and just come on in here." It was not a request.

My face must have registered instant opposition, for he said quickly, "Now, don't go gettin' that way on me. I brought somethin' home, Rosie, and I want you to come on and see it before I get so agitated I bust a gut."

Not wanting to seem too compliant, I finished arranging all the soiled dishes in the sink so that they could soak, then slowly dried my hands. He watched my every movement as if fearful that I might break for the back door. When he saw that I meant to follow him into the living room, he extended one hand in the manner of a parent to a reluctant child, and I took it. Thomas and I have held hands three times: once during our marriage ceremony at the direction of the justice of the peace; another time a few years ago when I lost my footing as I stepped onto the escalator at the JCPenney store and reached out toward him to stabilize myself, at which time he came to my aid most readily and tenderly; and this time, two days ago, as he led me from the kitchen into the living room.

Following Thomas into the living room, I saw a portable metal carrel sitting beside my rocker, and upon it was what appeared to be a computer. I took it all in before I spoke. The carrel had two shelves: a lower one at lap height on which rested the computer, and a higher shelf on which sat a piece of equipment that I knew to be a printer. For several years I have firmly declined Mr. Solomon's offer to furnish my office cubicle at Emma Weldy with a computer, though I have seen the machines crop up throughout the school — in the main office, the library, even the classrooms. Perhaps this fall I shall tell Mr. Solomon that I have reconsidered the matter.

"Did you buy this for yourself?" I asked, though I knew he had not.

He made an impatient, dismissive gesture and emitted what can only be described as a growl from deep in his throat. Then, "Naw, this ain't for me. What in tarnation would I do with such a contraption?"

"And what do you propose that I do with it?" I asked. I folded my arms and glared at the small Apple logogram, horizontally striped in the colors of the spectrum, below the screen of the computer.

He answered at once. "Whatever it is you're writin' in them books of yours can be put in here lots faster. Norm's got one in the store office now, just like this. He's showed me how to work it, and it's easy as eatin' pie."

"These cost a great deal of money," I said. I knew that Thomas would never buy anything on credit; therefore, he must have purchased the equipment with cash. The truth is that we seldom discuss finances. We have separate checking accounts. With my salary I pay for our groceries. With his social security check and the modest income from his repair business, Thomas sees to all other expenses.

"Naah. Maybe I got a bargain anyways. Far as that goes, maybe I found it settin' 'longside the curb somewhere for the trash man to pick up." He kicked a cardboard box aside and bent down to straighten a cord.

"That is not humorous," I said. He did not respond but leaned forward and turned the computer on. "I do not need this," I stated, raising my voice.

"Maybe not, but you sure as shootin' *got* it," he said.

"I will not permit you to spend your money on something nonessential and extravagant," I said. "I do not want this machine, Thomas."

The screen was now a bright rectangle of light, a small square with a question mark flashing in the center. Thomas manipulated a small control with his right hand and began typing with two fingers: *Rosie has got a cumputor. It is real nice. Rosie will like it.*

"You misspelled *computer,*" I said.

He grinned at me and said, "Yep, well, so I

did. Okay, now, watch this." I knew by his response that he had misspelled the word purposely, and I had played into his hand. He again moved the control, clicked it once, and changed the first *u* to an *o*. "See?" he said. "What'd I say? Easy as eatin' pie. There you go, it's all fixed now."

"No, it is not," I said. "The word ends with *er,* not *or.*"

He narrowed his eyes and glared at the screen. "That so?" he said. "Well, I'd sure never argue with you when it comes to spellin'," and he quickly corrected the remaining spelling error. "Norm showed me lots of things," he said, "like how to take a whole paragraph outta one spot on a page and stick it somewhere else" — he snapped his fingers — "just like that!"

"It defies belief," I said dryly.

I stood behind him and watched as he slowly pecked several more sentences. *The computer can go fast. Rosie will write on it. She will not have to sharpen her pencil.* Then he moved the control again, clicked it, and slid it across the pad. The three sentences that he had just typed were set off within a dark block. In only seconds he had transferred the three sentences so that they now came between the first two sentences that he had typed: *Rosie has got a computer* and *It is real nice.*

Though I took care to keep my countenance unyielding, I began to consider what the ownership of a machine with such capabilities could mean. I was not a writer whose handwritten manuscripts were marred by corrections, erasures, deletions, and cramped insertions, for I take care to fashion my thoughts before committing them to paper, yet I quickly recognized the advantage of a computer in the project that I had undertaken. Already I had begun to realize that though I knew my story from beginning to end, the physical act of setting it down in words was to consume an inordinate number of hours. It had taken me four weeks to write six chapters, and although I had begun to gain speed more recently, I was not deluded into believing that I could finish the manuscript to my satisfaction in the remaining eight weeks of summer.

I had studied typewriting during my sophomore year at Latham County High School some thirty-five years earlier and had quickly developed into a remarkably fast, accurate typist. "You have keyboard fingers," the teacher had said. Her name was Mrs. Cowger, and these are the only words that I recall her speaking to me individually. Her teaching tools were a series of wall charts and a long, slim pointer with a black rubber tip. We did a great deal of chanting as we typed through the alphabet, and she wrote our daily assignments on the chalkboard in a frail script with a backward slant.

Having been employed a number of times as a typist after fleeing my grandfather's house, I had maintained my speed and level of skill over the years. Even now I can type all the numerals on my forms at Emma Weldy without having to look at the keys. Thomas and I have never had a typewriter in our home, however, as we have seldom needed one. At the outset of my project this summer, I assumed that to write a book one must first work with paper and pencil, after which at some point one might type the entire manuscript if one wished.

Studying the computer, however, a question presented itself to me. Why could I not write my story directly into the machine? I had no doubt that I could learn to use it quickly, and if it were as efficient as Thomas testified, perhaps I could finish my project before school took up again.

Thus I relented in the matter of the computer and am now using electronic technology to record my memories. I have written this chapter in only three hours and twelve minutes, which includes another telephone call, this one requesting donations for the Lung Disease Research Foundation. I declined after recommending to the solicitor that she contact the tobacco industrialists for contributions.

Before I conclude this chapter, I will again regress in time some ten months and reconnect the reader with my narrative of Birdie. The following event took place on the same afternoon that the new shoes appeared upon the feet of Jasmine Finney. The words of Mrs. Cowger, my typewriting teacher in Marshland, New York, provide a solid and timely bridge, for they were very similar to the words that Birdie uttered that day, which eventually led me to a new venture in the period that I have heretofore termed "one of the strangest interludes in my life."

It was around one o'clock as I recall, and I was at my desk counting out the tickets taken in that day when Birdie entered my office cubicle. I could see her at my side, swaying to and fro like a nervous schoolgirl as I continued my work. I finished counting, recorded the figure, and then looked up at her.

Before I had time to recoil, she reached forward and took one of my hands in hers, examining it closely, turning it over and lightly tracing the length of each finger. I must have been frozen with horror, for I did not withdraw my hand, though I sincerely wished to do so. I stared, transfixed, at her small mouth with its overabundance of teeth, at her downcast eyes, and her plait of hair pinned atop her head. She looked into my face at last, smiled, and said, "I just know you must play the piano with hands like this. And they're so pretty and *white,* not like mine with all these old brown spots starting to show up."

I eased my hand out of hers and laid it palm down beside my other one on the desktop. "Do you have a question to ask me?" I said.

"Do you?" she countered.

"I beg your pardon," I said. "Do I what?"

"Play the piano."

"No, I do not."

"Well, now, that's a shame with hands like yours. I noticed them the first day I was here." She was still rocking back and forth like a child.

"Do you have a question that pertains to your work?" I asked.

She placed both of her hands on the sides of her head with an expression of mild dismay. This was a gesture that I was to see many times. "I almost forgot," she said. "I *do* get sidetracked sometimes. I wanted to tell you that Mickey's found him a job, the seven to three shift, and is going to be starting next week. It's over in Spartanburg, though, so he'll have to leave home a little past six every morning. It's at a place called the Barker Bag Company, which I think is the funniest name for a company, don't you? They sell nothing but bags — all kinds of them. Little plastic zipper bags and mailing bags and drawstring trash bags and brown paper bags and —"

I interrupted her. "Are you informing me that you will not be returning to work next week since your husband has found employment?" I distinctly recall feeling a peculiar blend of dread and relief at this prospect.

Birdie laughed. "Oh my, no! I'm not quitting already! I just wanted to tell you that since Mickey's got to be there by seven, I'll have to be coming in to work a little earlier starting next week. I can just sit on that little bench out by the bike rack, though, if nobody's here yet. I can read or write letters or watch the traffic, if nothing else."

"I arrive at a quarter past six," I said.

"Well, now, that'll work out fine," she said. She leaned forward and touched my thumbnail with her index finger. "I used to wish I had hands like yours." I didn't reply but slid my hands into my lap and pushed my chair back.

She laughed. "Speaking of hands, I've got to go help scrub up. French fries sure can make a mess." She turned to the doorway, then stopped. "I could teach you, Margaret."

I must have looked puzzled, which I was, for she quickly added, "The piano, I mean. We could set up a lesson time. I've got some beginner books, and I know you'd go through them in no time. I probably wouldn't be so much teaching as just watching, but I'd love to help you get started. I've got a piano at my house."

I stood up decisively. "We both have a great deal of work to do." Because I could not bring myself to address her directly by the name Birdie during the early weeks of her employment, I used no name at all. The sound of my voice filled the glass enclosure of my office and sounded to me as a tinkling cymbal.

Birdie smiled and waved her fingertips at me. "Well, let me know if you want to take me up on my offer sometime. I wouldn't charge you, of course. I'd just consider it a real privilege." When I saw her next, she was hanging the clean spatulas and large slotted spoons on the hooks above the steel work-table, humming "Jesu, Joy of Man's Desiring" and smiling as if fitting holes to hooks were the culmination of her life's work. The words from Robert Browning's "My Last Duchess" sprang to my mind as I passed by her: "She had a heart too soon made glad."

A Live Coal
8

Birdie's offer of piano instruction created a restless stirring within me for almost a week. I spoke earlier of my love of music, which I inherited from my mother, who, given her natural gift and her rigorous self-discipline, could doubtless have made a name for herself in professional music had she not spent her few adult years taking care that her stepfather did not discover her whereabouts. I know now that her deepest fear was not for herself but for me. Before she left her stepfather's house at the age of twenty-two, she had studied piano and voice at a private college near New York City, though to my knowledge, all of the jobs that she subsequently held were unrelated to music.

As a young woman she had played the piano quite proficiently, I believe, but later, due to our frequent moves and our limited monetary resources, she was unable to advance her skills. She spoke of music reverently, however, and often sang to me in what

I remember as a beautiful contralto. We listened mostly to operas and symphonic concerts on our radio, though her range of musical interests was wide and varied. She knew many spirituals by heart, as well as German tone poems, medieval plainsongs, Italian arias, Broadway musical tunes, hymns, and American folk songs. Many of these she taught to me, and we sang them together in the evenings.

In Akron, Ohio, we lived in an old hotel that had been converted into an apartment building. The lobby was dank and dim, I recall, but against one wall an old piano was ensconced like an aged and neglected matriarch amid an array of dusty artificial potted plants and an inoperative Coca-Cola machine. One day my mother stepped in among the large plastic planters and lifted the lid of the piano. Many of the ivory plates were missing from the keys, leaving a hard residue of glue, but when my mother leaned forward and played a series of chords, the fullness of the sound delighted me. There was no bench for the piano; she stood as she played.

I requested that she play a song for me, and thereafter I remembered what she had played as clearly as if it were but moments before. That is, I remembered the tune and character of the piece, although it was many years before I knew it by name. I have no doubt that my mother properly identified it on the day she played it for me, but I was very young, not quite five years of age, and I believe I must have confused the title with the novelty of the occasion, for I later discovered that the piece, one of Robert Schumann's *Kinderscenen,* was titled "An Important Event."

From that day I nursed a secret yearning to play the piano as my mother did. It was not to be, however, for we left Akron only days after her brief recital in the old hotel lobby and never again to my knowledge had access to a piano. When I went to live with my grandparents after my mother's death, no mention was made of music lessons, and my life was so fraught with confusing developments from that point that learning to play the piano drifted far from my immediate concerns.

I continued to listen to classical music on the box radio after my mother died, however, and rarely missed an evening program broadcast from Faraday, New York, called *An Hour with the Masters.* Though I heard my fellow students at L. K. Drake Junior High and later at Latham County High waxing enraptured over the popular singers of that day, such as Bill Haley and the Comets, the Platters, and Little Richard, I was never interested in what was known as rock and roll. The first time I saw a picture of Elvis Presley on a magazine cover, the thought that sprang to my mind was this: *He should be exiled to an uninhabited island.* Though my response to music has been strong and ready from my earliest recollection, I have always regretted the absence of opportunity for formal study. Reading and listening, though invaluable, are not adequate substitutes for firsthand instruction.

Six days after Birdie said to me, "I could teach you, Margaret," I beckoned her into my office as she was sitting down to eat her lunch. The workers eat between the completion of their lunch preparations, which is generally a few minutes before eleven o'clock, and the arrival of the first class of children at 11:20. A dish called beef-a-roni was the day's entree, I recall, and Birdie had spooned a portion for herself into a Styrofoam cup. When I tapped on the glass of my office cubicle and motioned to her, she cheerfully dismounted her stool and came to me at once with the Styrofoam cup of beef-a-roni in one hand and a plastic spoon in the other.

"This is really tasty!" she said, pointing into the cup with her spoon. "Have you had some?"

"No," I said. "I do not care for it." I was standing beside my desk, and she was just inside the doorway. Positioned thus, we were only three feet apart. My office, as I have said, is quite small.

"The biscuits are good, too," Birdie said. "Algeria put some of the beef-a-roni on a

150

biscuit, and she's eating it like a sandwich. Maybe you'd like it that way." She smiled hopefully, as if eager to please.

"I seldom eat the beef casseroles," I said firmly, and then without pausing for her to reply I added, "I would like to engage you as a piano instructor if your recent offer still stands."

She opened her mouth and stared at me, then quickly recovered herself. "Why, Margaret . . ." she said, implanting her spoon into her beef-a-roni with a swift jab and laying her right hand over her heart, "that would just thrill me to pieces. Just absolutely to pieces."

"I will inquire about the availability of the pianos in the music room or the auditorium," I said, speaking quickly and avoiding her eyes. "I believe that the last music class ends at two o'clock. We could perhaps have our lessons then."

"Well, we could do that if you'd like," she said. "The time would be fine since we're done in the kitchen about then." She removed her hand from over her heart and let it fall toward me palm upward. "I was just thinking, though," she continued, "that it might work better for you to come to my house. I live about four miles from here, but it's right on Highway 11 going to Derby. That way we wouldn't have to worry about being in anybody's way or any of the children interrupting us or anything like that." I started to

151

reply, but she winked at me and continued. "And besides that, if you came to my house, you could give me a ride home after school those days so I wouldn't have to wait for Mickey."

The thought of entering this woman's home filled me with alarm. One did not visit another person's home lightly. Such a visit invariably expanded the dimensions of a relationship, I felt, regardless of how casual or businesslike the connection might be in its initial stages. It has always been my custom to enter the homes of others only vicariously, through the media of books and an occasional television program. When I choose to attend the summer gatherings of Thomas's clan in North Carolina, I generally station myself outdoors in a folding chair on the fringes of the crowd.

Birdie was smiling up at me sweetly, awaiting my response. She took another small bite of her beef-a-roni and chewed in silence. As I quickly considered the options, I thought of the dark, cavernous interior of the old school auditorium, its musty smell, its narrow rows of squeaky seats, and the ancient upright piano near the stage. I imagined the sound of a piano lesson in progress and thought of the tremendous echo that would resound inside the large, empty room.

The music room would provide a more pleasant atmosphere; it was cozy and cheerful, with large windows along its length. I knew, however, that the room was frequently occupied even after school hours. Our music teacher, Miss Lorraine Grissom, held rehearsals with the Emma Weldy Singers two afternoons a week, and I had heard, upon passing the room from time to time in the afternoons, the sounds of a small ensemble of recorders, which often caused me to wince. It was a busy room along a well-traveled passageway. The prospect of pupils and teachers overhearing my piano lessons was not to my liking.

"Very well," I said. "Seeing that it will be a convenience for you, I will take the lessons at your home."

Birdie smiled and said, "Well, now, that'll be just perfect."

We settled upon a schedule to begin the following week. Each Tuesday and Friday, I would take Birdie to her home and stay for a forty-five minute lesson. She gave me the names of two piano books I might want to purchase for what she called "supplementary exercises once we get past the basics," and she asked me to bring to each lesson a notebook of some type in which to write assignments.

"This is going to be so much fun!" Birdie said. "We can make lots of headway with two lessons a week. You know, I've given lessons to little boys and girls off and on for years and years, but I've never had a grown-up interested in learning to play." She reached forward and patted my arm. "With those hands you can't help but be a natural. We'll have us a real nice time, Margaret."

"Yes, well, it is arranged, then." As I turned my back to her and opened a drawer of the file cabinet, I added firmly, "I do not care to have others know about this. Please do not discuss the lessons with Algeria or Francine."

Behind me, she was quiet for a moment before replying. "Well, now, that's perfectly understandable. I don't guess I'd necessarily want people knowing I was taking up something for the first time at my age, either, especially something most people learn early in life, like swimming, maybe, or roller skating or even piano. Or learning to read — I know a man at my church who just learned to read last year, and he's in his late sixties! Although, when you really stop to think about it, you have to admire anybody who decides it's never too late to make a dream come true. It's a credit to you to want to take piano lessons, Margaret! It's nothing to be ashamed of."

I turned around and fixed her with an icy glare. "No one is talking about learning to swim or skate or read," I said. "And I do not need your admiration, your cheerful encouragement, or your sermonizing. I simply value my privacy and request that you not speak of my business in front of the other women."

The expression on her face changed in an instant. She opened her mouth as if preparing to yelp in pain, but no sound came. Her forehead puckered in distress, and her nostrils flared. Neither of us spoke for several long moments, but her face gradually cleared and her lips relaxed into an uncertain smile. "I sure didn't mean to offend, Margaret. Please forgive me. I do have a way of going on and on sometimes. I promise you I won't tell the others about our piano lessons. You can count on me for that." She looked down into her Styrofoam cup, sadly, it seemed, stirred the spoon about slowly, then turned and left my office.

I thought at once, uncomfortably, of the incident at Box Hill in Jane Austen's novel *Emma* in which Emma Woodhouse speaks with caustic wit at the expense of the tedious Miss Bates. I thought of Mr. Knightley's gentle yet unmincing reproach of Emma after her unkind words. I could almost hear him saying to me, "It was badly done, indeed!"

I would not tolerate an invasion upon my private affairs, however, and the thought of the lunchroom women discussing my piano lessons, pitying me for not having had the opportunity as a child, commenting on my spunk, and charting my progress filled me with loathing. I had had every right to speak sternly to Birdie, I told myself as I returned to the work on my desk.

We conversed very little on our way to Birdie's home the following Tuesday afternoon. Birdie made several attempts to probe into my past with questions such as "You haven't always lived in the South, have you?" "Where were you born?" and "How long have you worked at Emma Weldy?" to which I answered respectively, "No," "In Indiana," and "Twenty-one years." She soon ceased asking questions and contented herself with aimless comments calling for no response. "Those little maple trees will be turning the most beautiful color in October," "I believe that's the same mail truck that delivers out to our house," and "It's been so handy since the Rite-Aid out here on this end of town started selling milk."

She remarked at some length about my car — a black 1967 Ford Fairlane that Thomas had bought and reconditioned for me the year after our marriage — informing me that she and Mickey had owned a yellow Ford of the same year and model when they lived in Tuscaloosa but had sold it after an ice cream truck had sideswiped it. "Yours is in tip-top shape," she said, and leaning in my direction, she added, "Eighty-two thousand miles — is that all it has on it?" to which I nodded and replied, "Yes."

If I had stopped to map out the location of Birdie's house according to her earlier description of "about four miles from here, right on Highway 11 going to Derby," I would have known precisely which house it was. I had passed it many times over the years of traveling from Filbert to Derby. Derby boasts a modest mall, a thriving Wal-Mart, an excellent dentist, and a well-appointed library for so small a town.

"You'll need to turn left at the driveway up here past this," Birdie said, waving toward the large brick marker for the Shepherd's Valley Cemetery. A small stone statue of a shepherd holding a lamb stood on a concrete base beside the marker. I recalled distinctly the cold January day some eight months earlier when I had attended the interment of Thomas's uncle Mayfield, the day I had, in fact, first observed Birdie Freeman playing the organ at the Mortland Funeral Home. I remembered thinking as we drove slowly through the cemetery entrance that winter day that the statue was disproportionately small, that it looked like something a religious devotee might place in his flower garden rather than a focal image suitable for marking so large and solemn a field as the Shepherd's Valley Cemetery.

I could have told anyone that there was a small white frame house to the north of the cemetery, set well off the road at the end of a long gravel driveway, though I suppose I had always presumed it to be the home of the Shepherd's Valley groundskeeper. As I followed the narrow driveway toward the house, I took in the details. Beside me, Birdie had begun rustling about, refolding her brown paper lunch bag and pressing it against her large tan purse, then clutching them both to her chest with one hand as she smoothed her white skirt. She lifted both feet off the floor of the car and lightly tapped them together.

"I just love coming home!" she proclaimed at last. "There's nothing like that feeling of knowing your day's work is done and you're back *home*."

If I had been asked to draw a picture of the kind of home in which Birdie and Mickey Freeman would live, I am certain that I would have produced something very similar to what stood before me at the end of the driveway. I suppose the absence of contrapuntal elements between the main character and her habitat only adds to the unfortunate predictability of my story. I cannot change the facts to make my story more engaging, however. Birdie's house must stand as it is.

It was a white house, exceedingly white, so white that it had a slightly bluish cast. In fact, there was a great deal of white to be seen everywhere, from the billows of cumulus clouds overhead to the white sheets on the clothesline alongside the house. Indeed, it could have been the setting for a television commercial for laundry detergent. I thought it most imprudent, however, that Birdie had left sheets on the line while she had been away from home for nearly eight hours, especially as there had been a thirty percent chance of rain showers that morning, which, fortunately for her, had not materialized.

There were black shutters at each window; the front windows consisted of small panes of beveled glass. Ruffled curtains, two planters of white chrysanthemums beside the front steps, and a black wrought iron railing around the tiny porch completed the quaint effect of Birdie's house. A stand of tall pine trees behind the house made the house appear even smaller. A whimsical thought came to me. It would be easy to imagine Snow White inside this house awaiting the arrival of the seven dwarfs.

The house beside the cemetery brought to mind a novel that I had read, the first work of fiction, I believe, by the talented journalist Anna Quindlen, a book titled *Object Lessons*. As I recall, the father of the main character lived in the caretaker's cottage within a cemetery. The main character herself had lived there before her marriage. Sharply delineated impressions remain in my mind of the lush, brilliant foliage surrounding the cottage.

As I have said, Birdie's house was not within the confines of the cemetery, however, and as I looked more closely I could see the dim outlines of at least two other houses beyond the pine trees. Since I saw no direct access to the houses from this side, I assumed that they faced McKinney Bridge Road, which runs parallel to Highway 11 on the other side of the cemetery. I concluded that the neighbors to which Birdie frequently alluded must reside in these houses, for I observed no others nearby.

The long driveway led eventually to a carport, the free-standing type, with a trim aluminum roof painted black. Dark flagstones provided a walkway from the carport to the front sidewalk. I did not drive under the carport, which sheltered no car at present, but stopped my Ford about six feet away from it.

"Come on in," Birdie said before I had even turned off the ignition. "I know you must be ready to get started, and so am I."

My heart was strangely unsettled as I walked behind her up the stone walkway and then to the sidewalk. I kept my eyes upon her small white sneakers, and as I watched her mount the front steps, I could not decide which I desired more: to return to the safety of my Ford in the driveway — that is, to start the car and put it in reverse, to undo this awful mistake by canceling all future piano lessons — or to follow Birdie Freeman's steps across the threshold of the white door that she was preparing to unlock.

Of course I followed her.

That first day I wanted to see nothing inside her house, yet I saw everything. My desire was only to have the first lesson finished so that from that day onward a routine free from distractions could be established. I wished for the setting to become irrelevant, invisible for all practical purposes. I wanted to view my piano lessons as a visit to a clinic. Birdie was merely a doctor who would diagnose my condition, prescribe a semiweekly remediation, and chart my progress. I might as easily have leapt into Niagara Falls and tried to imagine myself sitting beneath a lawn sprinkler.

Birdie's home was as tidy inside as it was outside, yet while the blacks and whites of the exterior gave forth an air of subdued conservativism, the interior was a riot of color. In an earlier chapter I mentioned my sensitivity to color. A multitude of strong, intense colors affects me on a visceral level.

After stepping across the threshold into Birdie's house, I stood very still. The brightness of the room assaulted me. Though in perfect order, it was clear to me that the living room was used a great deal. The two recliners, one upholstered in peach and the other in royal blue, appeared comfortably "broken in," as they say. The sofa fabric was yellow, with startling designs of white prisms woven into it. Imprinted bands of bold, rich colors fanned from each small white pyramid.

It was what is referred to as a busy pattern, one which, if stared at too long, begins to writhe or jerk.

There were several multicolored braided rugs of varying sizes positioned over the hardwood floors, and upon the coffee table was arranged — although the effect was more informal than the word *arranged* suggests — an assortment of ceramic figurines, which Thomas would refer to as "gimcracks and doodads." The table also held three house-plants (an African violet, an ivy, and a bonsai similar to the one that Birdie had given me), framed photographs, and a few magazines. I noted in particular two issues of *National Geographic* and one of *Reader's Digest.*

A rectangular cabinet of blond wood occupied one corner, its lid raised to reveal a phonograph player. Leaning against it on the floor were a number of phonograph albums. The one facing outward featured the smiling visage of Jim Nabors. Other miscellaneous furnishings included a low bookcase, an old dictionary stand — displaying what I assumed at first to be a huge dictionary but that I later discovered to be a family Bible — and two floor lamps. The curtains were striped in yellow, green, and navy.

The walls were covered with a plethora of art: original paintings, including everything from a watercolor of a red schoolhouse in the style of folk art to a convincing impressionistic oil rendering of trees along a shore-line at sunset; two cross-stitched samplers; framed quilt squares; floral prints; several large photographs of nature scenes such as one might see on wall calendars; two wreaths; and an old metal Nehi Soda sign. Right above the piano was a hand-stitched poem with an embroidered forest scene in the background. This poem, to which I will return later, was titled "Gifts from the Wildwood," and I was to memorize it over the course of the next several weeks as I sat at Birdie's piano each Tuesday and Friday afternoon.

As I absorbed the blow of finding myself inside the fastidiously kept yet madly kaleido-scopic living room of Birdie Freeman, I heard her offer me a glass of ginger ale. Resting my gaze at last upon the piano, beside which sat a small rocking chair with a red gingham seat pad, I declined with a brief shake of my head. For a moment I felt that the room was in mo-tion.

"Well, then, let's come on over and sit down here," she said, pointing to the piano stool. "You'll probably need it lower." She spun it around a few times as if she were steering a ride at an amusement park. It was an old-fashioned stool of dark mahogany, with a needlepoint design of dusky pink roses upon the round seat. It was small but sturdy.

"These are what we'll start out with," she said, picking up four books of different colors titled THE MUSIC TREE series. "This first one is just real basic," she said, choosing the gold book, which bore the subtitle *Time to Begin,* and setting the others aside. "But since you said you've never had any music lessons at all, I guess we'll just go through the whole series from the beginning like I do with all my new pupils." She smiled at me, then flipped through the gold book from back to front. As she did so, I saw the titles of several songs: "Trapeze Artist," "Noisy Neighbors," "Goldfish," "Naptime," "Inchworm."

When she reached the front of the book, she stopped and folded it back with great deliberation. "Well, here we go," she said. She set the book on the music rack in front of me and traced with her small forefinger as she read aloud the words at the top of the page. "Unit One. Discoveries. Learning about Higher." Then she leaned down by my side, her hands on her knees, and said, "You're so quiet, Margaret. Is anything the matter?"

"No," I replied. "I simply want to get about our business."

Her face broke into a smile at once, uncomely for its dental defects yet radiant for its spontaneity. "Yes, let's do that," she said, her eyes sparkling. "Let's get about our business. I like that." She straightened up and, pointing again to the page, said, "Now, first of all, when a note goes up higher on these five lines called the staff, it sounds" — here she raised the pitch of her voice — "*higher,* and you use one of these higher keys up here on the keyboard to play it." I watched as she applied a finger to keys of successively higher pitches, striking lightly and quickly as if each key were a live coal, hot to the touch.

NIGHT SEASONS
9

One Saturday evening in late September, after I had completed four piano lessons at Birdie's house, I accompanied Thomas's cousin Joan to a play, or a "play trilogy" as it was billed, in Greenville. Though Joan's salaried career is in advertising and publicity, she also writes a weekly freelance column for the Berea *Bugler* and the Filbert *Nutshell* called "Arts in the Upstate" in which she highlights the work of various regional artists, musicians, and writers. As an ancillary of the news media, she receives two free tickets to all area arts events, and when serving as reviewer, she frequently invites me to share the evening with her.

For me these evenings are charged with a mental stimulation that can only be described as electric. A live performance naturally produces a powerful current of response, but the evenings with Joan are further intensified by the knowledge that she is compelled to formulate a balanced, well-focused, succinct judgment for immediate publication. After each performance, we generally stop at the Second Cup Coffee Shoppe, though I do not drink coffee, where Joan reads her notes to me, and we discuss the performance.

The program that we attended that September evening was staged in a small theater known as the Factory Floor, located in what had once been a leading textile factory in Greenville. Although the building itself was enormous, the factory had ceased production in the early sixties, the owners claiming that there was no room for expansion at the present site.

Several enterprising businessmen had subsequently purchased the vacated factory and transformed it into a so-called "art and trades center," which they named Marva-Loom Marketplace, Marva-Loom being the name of the original textile factory. Besides a host of upscale specialty shops, the Marva-Loom Marketplace houses the Candy Corner, an art gallery called the Signet Studio, the Yogurt Yacht, and, as I said, the Factory Floor, the theater where a troupe of aspiring young dramatists take to the stage.

The director of the Factory Floor, an outspoken woman named Ramona Hull Chadwick, has during her tenure been touted as "a gutsy crusader of the avant-garde" and has received great publicity throughout the Southeast for her use of the stage to "proclaim unorthodoxy" — an unpopular activity among the large conservative element in this region — and to champion the causes of minorities. I read an interview of Miss Chadwick recently in which she was quoted as saying, "Rich, educated, elitist, white Anglo-Saxon Protestant males are the scourge of society." Some of the wind is taken out of this statement, however, when one considers the fact that Ramona Hull Chadwick herself is a rich, educated, elitist, white Anglo-Saxon female.

"Did you say you've seen these plays?" Joan asked after we had found our seats.

"No, I have read two of them," I replied. "Reading a play on the printed page and seeing it performed are two different experiences, however."

"You can say that again," Joan said. "Did you go with me that time over to Spartanburg to see *Hamlet*?"

"No," I replied.

"That's right. I went with this man from work. How could I have forgotten? Dumbest thing I've ever done. The guy wore a *toupee*. Anyway, I must have studied *Hamlet* at least a dozen times in different classes, but I'd never seen it. So this man asks me to go with him, right? And it was like I'd never even heard this story before! They decided to be real creative and change the setting to a South Pacific island. What a hoot! Everybody in the cast wore Polynesian garb and ate pineapples and coconuts. When Hamlet told Ophelia to 'get thee to a nunnery,' I laughed right out loud all by myself. There she was, wearing a grass skirt and a lei and being told to go to a *nunnery.* Where do you suppose the nearest one of those was? Bora Bora?"

Without turning to face her, I saw Joan shake her head and then open her purse, rummage through it, and at last remove a piece of Doublemint chewing gum. As I wondered whether she had written a review of *Hamlet* that night and, if so, whether her sarcasm had been veiled or blatant, I saw that she was unwrapping the gum and folding it into her mouth.

I could not recollect ever having seen Joan chew gum before, and it struck me then that her behavior this evening was out of the ordinary in a number of respects. She had arrived ten minutes late to pick me up, though I knew well her preference for claiming her seats for a performance at least twenty minutes in advance and preferably thirty; she had talked far more than usual on the trip into Greenville, much of what she said being disconnected and incomplete; she had missed the turn to the Marva-Loom Marketplace and had taken an inefficient detour through several winding residential streets; and now she was masticating a stick of gum as if she had a vast surplus of nervous energy.

You would not call Joan "pretty" if you passed her on the street. You would, however, immediately perceive an expression of intelligent skepticism in her dark blue eyes. If you were to spend an afternoon with her, no doubt her physical appearance would steadily improve to the point that you might describe her as "arresting" or speak of her "mystique." Her widely spaced eyes, which she often closes in thought, the patina of her fine dark hair, her habit of smiling with only half of her mouth (the right side), and her tasteful but unstudied manner of dress combine to produce an aura of detachment and nonchalance, which I believe generally attracts the interest of others.

On this night Joan wore a dark green dress of raw silk and a single strand of pearls. As she opened the stenographer's pad she always carries with her on occasions such as this, she asked me, "So which two have you read?"

"*Trifles* and *The Twelve-Pound Look*," I replied. Though I believe that my company is not onerous to Joan, I also understand that she values my extensive knowledge of literature and places confidence in my assessment of a given performance. I admit to feelings of gratification upon reading her newspaper reviews, not only because I think highly of Joan but also because I recognize in what she has written certain phrases of my own invention.

"I looked all three of them up at the library last week and read them," Joan said. "I was surprised at how tame they are. From what I can tell, tonight's going to be pretty unusual for the daring Ramona."

"Yes," I replied.

Joan's energetic and unprecedented gum chewing produced a distinct snap. As if I did not understand, she continued. "You know what I mean. She normally uses such way-out stuff that everybody pretty much equates the Factory Floor with weirdness as far as drama goes."

I nodded. In the past three years Ramona Hull Chadwick had directed performances of classic absurdist drama such as Elmer Rice's *The Adding Machine,* in which the main character is a cipher named Mr. Zero, and Eugene Ionesco's *The Chairs,* which tracks a couple's unsuccessful search for the meaning of life as they exchange aimless dialogue in a castle in the middle of an ocean.

I glanced to the rows behind us and saw that the theater appeared to be filled to capacity. My watch revealed that the performance should begin in one minute.

"So we can safely say that these three plays have a pretty strong feminist agenda, right?" asked Joan, uncapping her pen.

"Undoubtedly strong," I said, "though admirably subtle." I went on to comment on the wisdom of Miss Chadwick in including

171

the work of a male playwright in her trilogy, for J. M. Barrie, whose name is so fondly linked with such beloved books as *Peter Pan* and *The Little Minister,* also wrote the play *The Twelve-Pound Look.*

The lights were dimming as Joan whispered, "It's interesting how the play that's from the furthest back is really the newest." Joan's spoken words are often characterized by a lack of clarity, although her writing is quite lucid and precise. I understood her meaning, however. *The Man in a Case,* though set in the late 1800s — and based, incidentally, upon a story by Anton Chekhov — was published quite recently, in 1986, whereas the other two plays were both set and published, I believe, during the first half of the twentieth century.

The actors and actresses were capable, the costumes appropriate, and the sets adequate though not elaborate. As these were all one-act works, there were scene changes only between plays, during which time many members of the audience took a brief leave from the theater to the Yogurt Yacht next door. The man seated next to me returned after the first intermission with a large, damp stain on his light blue necktie.

The three plays — *The Man in a Case, The Twelve-Pound Look,* and *Trifles* — were set, respectively, in an outdoor park, an elegant English parlor, and the kitchen of a midwestern farmhouse, and for their speedy transformation of the stage between plays, the stage crew earned a word of commendation in Joan's review.

Briefly, Wendy Wasserstein's *The Man in a Case* presented a brisk scene between an impetuous young Russian girl and the dignified schoolmaster to whom she is betrothed. Miss Chadwick's interpretation of the work made the schoolmaster out to be even more of a dolt, in my opinion, than the script suggests. For my part, I feel that the girl in the story is not the only one to benefit from the termination of the engagement.

As the schoolmaster tore up the note in the closing moments of the play, thus implying that the relationship had ended, I was relieved that he had extricated himself in a timely fashion from what was destined to be a miserable union. I sympathized with the man — something I rarely do in works of literature — as I contemplated the intrusion of such a flighty, undisciplined girl upon his well-ordered life. Furthermore, I felt that his character had been misrepresented in the drama, that he had been made a caricature, while the girl had been granted undeserved favor simply for being gaily youthful.

The Twelve-Pound Look impressed me as adhering faithfully to the playwright's intent. I believe that J. M. Barrie meant to evoke scorn and contempt for the arrogant, heavy-handed husband who had driven away his first wife and was clearly in the process of doing the same with his second.

Susan Glaspell's play *Trifles* was, in my opinion, the strongest work performed that night, the title summarizing ironic truths: that small acts can lead to tumult, that what seems to be a mere triviality may hold the key to a great mystery, that while the slenderest thread of hope is often enough to sustain life, the snapping of that thread can wreak sudden and total destruction. The play examines what can happen when a lonely woman lives with a hard man. It explores on a very human level the struggle between emotion and reason, between compassion and duty, between love and law. Though afterward I heatedly stated to Joan my objections to the conclusion that grows out of this play, I acknowledge the truth that when the human soul is wrung dry of hope, normal standards of decency are often abandoned. I do not say that this is right; I say that it is so. I know a great deal about hopelessness.

At the Second Cup Coffee Shoppe, where Joan ordered espresso and I a cup of hot raspberry tea, we exchanged our opinions of the three plays. She removed her chewing gum from her mouth and set it on a paper napkin, which she then wadded into a ball. As we talked, Joan wrote copiously in her stenographer's pad, expanding the notes she had taken during the program, striking through certain lines, drawing arrows, and at one point even rotating her pad as she wrote around the perimeter of a page. From time to time she tidied her bangs, starting at her left temple and running a forefinger in an arc across her brow and down to her right temple. It is a mindless habit that she performs often, and it is a wonder that her finger has not worn a curved groove into her forehead. At last she looked at her watch and slid out of the booth. I followed.

As we started home, I noted that Joan seemed less edgy than earlier. No doubt the plays had taken her mind off whatever had been troubling her. We traveled in silence for several minutes after leaving Greenville. It was a dark night, I recall, with a waxing moon of butter yellow. That night it was "just a big old lopsided beach ball," as Thomas describes the stage just prior to its reaching maximum fullness.

Suddenly, Joan blurted out a most amazing question, one for which I was totally unprepared. I must clarify that before this point she had never trespassed into my personal life, nor I into hers. Though I knew sketchy details of her family background, she knew almost nothing of mine except that I had married her cousin more than fifteen years ago.

"What do you think of men in general,

Margaret?" That was her question. I was stunned.

In the silence that followed, I quickly considered why she might ask me such a question. Hoping that it was merely a stray thought resulting from the three plays that we had attended that evening, I framed a cautious, oblique response. "As we agreed earlier, I believe the three plays can be seen as a collective statement that men often undervalue women."

She lifted one hand from the steering wheel in a weary gesture. "Oh, I know *that,*" she said, "but I'm talking about the men *you* know. Do you have faith in them? Or can you really have faith in anybody these days? Is marriage just the ultimate gamble, or is there some way to know if it's going to hold up? I keep thinking of all the men in history, all the way from Adam — if there ever really was such a man — on through the pharaohs of Egypt and the Greek philosophers and the Roman generals and the pilgrim fathers and the explorers and inventors and log-cabin politicians and all the rest. Were any of them really *great men* of history? Or forget the history part — were they as great in private as everybody thought they were in public?"

A line from *Montana 1948,* a novel by Larry Watson and the winner of the 1993 Milkweed National Fiction Prize, sprang to my mind, and I spoke it aloud. " 'I find history endlessly amusing.' "

She replied immediately. "Why's that?"

I went on to paraphrase the narrator of Mr. Watson's story. "No one ever knows the true story of a man's life. Behind the records of public history lies a dung heap of shameful, private deeds."

Joan's low, breathy laugh gave no evidence of amusement. "I guess that answers my question. So you think those men in history weren't great at all?" With hardly a pause she continued. "And are you making a blanket statement about all men?"

"Because of his physical power and rampant ego, a man is predisposed to violate the trust of helpless, dependent women. And I am not using the noun *man* in a generic sense to include all of humankind. I am speaking of the male of our species." The caustic nature of my reply must have shocked Joan, for I saw that she glanced at me sharply.

Neither of us spoke again for a full minute. I did not want to talk further, wishing already that I had responded with less venom. Joan seemed wary of questioning me more, but at last she said quietly, "I hope you're not saying that Thomas mistreats you, Margaret."

At that I emitted a short, derisive laugh. "Thomas is the ideal man, for he leaves me alone."

She seemed to relax. "Well, I guess I should be relieved. I was sitting here trying to imagine such a thing, and I couldn't. I mean, I couldn't see Thomas hurting a flea, for one thing, but I also couldn't see you putting up with it for a second if anybody did try something like that."

Ready to clear the air, I saw an opportunity to lay the cause for my sudden vehemence upon Larry Watson's novel, referred to earlier, and thus divert Joan's attention from myself. "Have you read *Montana 1948*?" I asked. Had I prudently considered my question, I certainly would have foreseen its potential danger of opening up a risky line of conversation. The book's initial effect upon me had been painful, as of the salting of deep wounds. Why did I think that I could now discuss it casually? I was later to chastise myself soundly for speaking in haste rather than holding my tongue.

Joan was immediately interested, for we often recommended books to each other. "No, what is it?"

"A novel."

"Is it good?"

"It is both simple and complex, vividly specific yet profoundly universal. It is a good story, yet a horrible one."

Joan laughed. "Well, you've sure grabbed my attention. What's it about?"

Again, without thinking ahead, I answered. "A white doctor and an Indian woman who is his patient."

She nodded, frowning thoughtfully. "Oh, I think I can predict that one. The doctor abuses the Indian woman, right?" Joan's mind is quick and nearly always accurate in making connections.

"I do not want to spoil the book for you," I replied.

Joan pointed to a billboard on Highway 11 advertising the Dairy Queen in Filbert. "They're open till midnight on weekends, I think. Do you mind if I stop for a shake? I'm about to faint for something sweet."

I was tempted to request that she drive me home first, but I merely shook my head.

Unfortunately, she had no intention of changing the subject. "So you think the doctor in this book represents men in general? If given half a chance, any man would do the same?"

"The evil of which men are capable is boundless," I said.

She sighed. "I know some pretty lousy women, too," she said. "In fact, did you ever take a look at that book by Margaret Atwood I told you about? *The Robber Bride*?"

I nodded.

"That was her point, remember?" Joan continued. "She summed it all up in that character Zenia. See, if I'm going to be a feminist, I've got to be ready to admit that women can be just as mean and ratty as men. At least I *think* that was one of her points.

179

And that means we're every bit as morally responsible as men for the mean, ratty things we do."

"I care not one whit for feminism," I said.

"Well, you can say that all you want, but I think the feminist movement was created by and for women who are angry, truly *angry* at a deep level. And that anger is *always* directed at men." She paused. "Not that we don't have good reason to be angry — some of us."

When I remained silent, she sighed again. "How did we get off on this? Margaret, you sure aren't helping me any." She pounded the steering wheel lightly with the heel of one hand and added, "I'm trying to sort out my feelings right now, and they all seem to revolve around two men. Here I am, almost forty years old, and I just can't reconcile things."

I felt myself go cold. I had no desire to serve as confidante or counselor. I had nothing to say to Joan concerning the men in her personal life. I turned my head to the right and studied the scattered houses that we were passing on the outskirts of Filbert, most of which were dark. Those in the working class of Filbert were not given to late-night carousing.

"I can't quit thinking about the last three years of Daddy's life," Joan said. "I was awful." I thought at first that she must have meant to say, "It was awful," but she clearly said, "I was awful." No doubt the reader will remember that it was Joan's father and Thomas's uncle Mayfield Spalding whose funeral I described at the beginning of my narrative.

When I did not respond, she continued. "You know, he'd started going to that church in Derby and had turned religious. Then he started on a campaign to 'mend our relationship,' he called it. He started calling me on the phone and sending me cards and leaving all kinds of *gifts* on my back porch — strange stuff you wouldn't think of, like a brass door knocker with a *J* monogrammed on it and an umbrella with pictures of jungle birds all over it. Once it was a two-pound box of imported Dutch cocoa, and — oh, here we are."

Joan pulled into the Dairy Queen and turned off the ignition, then reached for her purse on the seat between us. As she removed her billfold, she laughed dryly. "I always hung up when he called, and I tore up the cards as soon as I read them. I didn't want to read them, but I always did. I kept the gifts and even used some of them, believe it or not." She took out a five-dollar bill. "You want anything?"

"No," I said, as she got out of the car.

I watched Joan speak to the young man behind the order window, then throw her head back and close her eyes. She reached

181

back with one hand, gathered a clump of her dark shiny hair near the crown of her head and crushed it, then slowly released it, letting it sift through her fingers. She repeated this action several times, then shook her head vigorously and ran her finger around the fringe of her bangs.

It was clear by now that one of the two men to whom she had alluded was her deceased father. Though I do not intrude into matters that are none of my concern, I could not help wondering who the other man was. I had known Joan only as a single woman and had difficulty now trying to imagine her otherwise.

When she returned to the car with her milk shake, I was disappointed to see that she made no move to put the car in motion. Furthermore, she had not lost her train of thought.

She dipped her spoon into her milk shake, filled it, and then slowly, pensively placed the spoon in her mouth. I looked at my watch, hoping to signal my wish to be taken home, but she appeared not to notice.

"That poor man tried and tried," she said after a few moments, "but I never let him get to first base. I didn't have a chip on my shoulder — I had a boulder. I think I always meant to give in sooner or later and start patching things up, but then he died. There I was, getting my jollies out of holding a grudge, and all of a sudden he was gone. I tried to stay mad at him. I even went to the funeral mad. But I know now that I was mad at myself and at my brothers because I knew Daddy had tried to settle things with them, too. We were all in cahoots against him. We'd call one another and compare notes on everything he did. At the funeral I was ticked off, I guess, that we wouldn't have him to kick around anymore. He'd gone and pulled a fast one on us. But underneath it all, of course, was this huge load of guilt. I was mad at myself for not giving him a chance, and I was mad at my brothers for their part in our little conspiracy."

Though I did not want to hear Joan's confession, I was thankful that her thoughts had turned inward and that she was no longer quizzing me; therefore, I said nothing. She continued, as if finding great comfort in the outpouring. "And he thought of us even in planning his funeral. That preacher at his church said Daddy had asked to have the funeral at Mortland's since he thought we kids would be more likely to come to it than if they had it in a church, and he wanted to make it easier for us." She broke off with a brittle laugh. "*Daddy* — I can't believe I'm calling him that after all these years. It doesn't fit, does it, for somebody you spent your life hating?"

She stirred her milk shake and then turned

to me. "Margaret . . ."

I knew that she wanted me to look at her, and after her pause grew uncomfortably lengthy, I relented.

"Margaret, I was awful. I wanted to make him suffer for all those years I didn't have a mother, for not ever noticing I was alive unless I burned the toast or didn't have his shirts starched just right. As if punishing him now was going to erase it all."

Turning my eyes from hers, I realized that I was breathing more heavily than usual.

She continued. "Every day I'd think of something I'd almost forgotten from my childhood, and I'd get a little harder. I remembered the way he'd watch my brothers gang up on me for trying to make them behave. He'd just watch them punch at me or pull my hair, all three of them at the same time, yelling and poking me from all sides, and he'd walk out of the room."

She stopped and took several furious draws on her striped straw. "Of course, I was bigger than they were and could defend myself pretty well, but the point was he never showed me that he cared about what happened to me. He never came to school and talked with my teachers. He never let me sign up for any kind of team or club or any of those things kids do. We could never have a dog or cat, not even a sorry little goldfish. The first time I went to the dentist was when

I was ten years old, and my aunt Geri took me then. I was just like a piece of furniture to him. He never talked to us. He was always wrapped up in a hard little knot when he came home. When I was fifteen — *fifteen* — I took some money out of his wallet one day and bought myself a bra at Woolworth's. He'd never even noticed I needed one."

Still, I made no reply.

"He never once hugged me, Margaret. He never kissed me. He never even *touched* me."

Though I take pride in my self-control, at that moment my composure was straightway shattered, and I cried out passionately, "And for *that* you should count yourself among the blessed, Joan Spalding!"

Joan gasped audibly and sat motionless. I looked down at my hands and saw them balled into fists. I willed myself to loosen them and lay them flat, palms downward, in my lap. I concentrated on taking slow, regular breaths.

As I said, Joan is smart; she infers accurately from the barest clues. When she spoke again, I could hardly hear her words. "I'm sorry, Margaret. I never dreamed . . . who did it to you, Margaret? Your father?"

I could not answer. I looked out the car window and saw the teenaged boy inside the Dairy Queen close the order window and lower an interior shade over it, then turn off the fluorescent light that illuminated the large menu board.

"And that's why the book you were talking about upset you so much," Joan said. "You must just want to choke me, blubbering on and on about a father who wouldn't let me join Girl Scouts or have a puppy, and you're carrying something like *that* around inside you." She exhaled slowly. "I can't think of anything to say except I'm sorry. And that's pretty weak." She lifted her milk shake, then stopped. She opened the car door and walked slowly to the trash bin, where she deposited the cup. When she returned, she started the engine, and as we pulled out of the Dairy Queen, she asked, "Have you ever told anybody about your father?"

"It was not my father," I stated flatly. "And telling people neither alters the facts nor repairs the damage. At any rate, my grandfather was a pillar of the community. No one would have believed me."

As we rode toward my house, Joan fell silent. She seemed to be done with questions. I gazed through the window at the countryside, aglow under the yellow moon, and I felt again the utter darkness of my night seasons as a girl when a great black cloud hid the moon.

THE FRAGMENTS
THAT REMAIN
10

I must return now to Birdie, but first a final word about the disclosure of my grandfather's sordid deeds. As indicated to Joan, I had indeed read parts of Margaret Atwood's novel *The Robber Bride*. Of the three interwoven stories in the book, I lost myself most thoroughly in the life of Karis, who as a girl had been misused by her uncle Vernon.

It is a fact, I believe, that incidents of particular distress to an individual may continually repeat themselves forever afterward as one reads or hears of similar occurrences in the lives of others and thus experiences again and again his own personal tragedy. I say *may* continually repeat themselves, for I have read many accounts of the mind's unique means of protecting itself by obliterating the memory of such unspeakable suffering. My mind did not perform this merciful feat, however, and every day of my life I have lived with the dark knowledge of my grandfather's heinous acts upon me.

I clearly recall feeling a flash of envy, and of something akin to wistfulness, upon reading in *The Robber Bride* that Karis's uncle had ceased to abuse her when she reached puberty, for he feared the possibility of pregnancy. Had my grandfather been of the same mind, my torment, though inalterably devastating and unforgivable, would have been short-lived, for I was already thirteen when my mother died and I went to live with my grandparents.

Though I detest laying forth so bluntly such a despicable fact as that which I am about to reveal, I feel strongly compelled to do so, to set down the whole truth in words that my eyes can see. My grandfather developed a methodical system for the scheduling of his nocturnal visits to my bedroom; he kept a chart, actually a small calendar, with certain dates circled.

On the Sunday following my Saturday evening with Joan, during which I had let slip the black secret of my past, I felt as if something had gnawed itself free from my soul, some vile and voracious rodent perhaps, leaving a ragged hole but a welcome vacancy. It puzzled me at the time that the mere process of verbalizing a disaster could serve a purgative function, and I suspected it to be only temporary. It puzzles me now that the recording of such facts in writing, as I am presently doing, has a further cleansing effect. *This happened to me, I am saying. I ask no pity; it is merely a fact of my life that cannot be changed or forgotten.*

I had slept more heavily than usual on Saturday night and awoke late that Sunday morning to the sounds of Thomas singing "The Riddle Song." At seventy, Thomas still has a strong voice, true to pitch, though he rarely sings at home in my hearing. More often he whistles. However, he is still pressed to sing at his family reunions each summer. The words of the song that he was singing that morning were these:

I gave my love a cherry that has no stone.
I gave my love a chicken that has no bone.
I gave my love a ring that has no end.
I gave my love a baby with no cryin'.

I lay in bed and listened as verse by verse he unraveled the riddle. The cherry without a stone was a cherry blossom; the boneless chicken was one hatching from its shell; the ring was endless because it was rolling; and the quiet baby was asleep. It was a soothing song that I had known for many years. My mother had often sung it to me. I was only five or six when I recall her first singing it, at which time I felt a presentiment of fear instead of comfort. Coupled with the somewhat mournful tune, the last line suggested calamity to my childish mind; I believed the baby to be dead. I remember my mother holding me in her lap when I told her this. "No, no, Margaret, the baby is *sleeping,*" she said over and over.

When I put on my robe and walked into the kitchen a few minutes later, Thomas was standing at the counter eating a bologna sandwich. On weekends he often eats sandwiches in lieu of traditional breakfast foods. He appeared startled upon seeing me. "What . . . ? Why, I thought you was out on one of your walks. You been sleepin' all this time? I never thought to peek in your room."

"I was tired," I said. "Joan brought me home at twelve o'clock last night." I removed the small pork loin from the refrigerator, where I had set it to thaw the day before, and began preparing it for roasting.

I remember that September Sunday as a mellow day. Thomas and I spoke very little, and we both lay down to rest after our mid-afternoon dinner. Thomas rested by sleeping on the sofa. My rest consisted of reading in my bed. I was currently reading a book by two elderly black women, Sarah and Elizabeth Delany — or Sadie and Bessie, as they call themselves — titled *Having Our Say.*

As I reported earlier, I had taken on the project over the past months of reading books featuring African-Americans as the main characters, and by September I was still interspersing these books regularly among others whenever I heard of one that interested me. In August I had read *The Women of Brewster Place* by Gloria Naylor and *I Been in Sorrow's Kitchen and Licked Out All the Pots* by Susan Straight, both of which I consider worthy fiction. *Having Our Say* is different in that it is nonfiction, a collection of memories and observations rather than a novel.

I mention my reading on Sunday only because it became relevant on the following Monday in the lunchroom at Emma Weldy. It was a few minutes past 10:30 that Monday morning when Algeria was mixing the mashed potatoes for the children's lunch. Birdie had just returned from the kindergarten rooms, to which she had delivered the morning snack of cheese and crackers, and Francine was removing a large pan of baked chicken legs from the oven and transferring it to the warmer. I was filling out the Production Sheet for the day's breakfast items. These forms and scores of others must be completed and filed daily by all lunchroom supervisors. Much of my time is taken up with such paper work.

Birdie stopped at my office door and called out cheerily, "Oh, those little children sure enjoyed their snack this morning! I think they were hoping for cookies, but they got over it real fast and dug into those crackers lickety-split. They're so cute. One little boy told me that the round crackers make him think of faces with freckles."

I placed my finger under the line upon which I had just written *106 4-ounce cartons Vita-Fresh apple juice* and lifted my head. As I opened my mouth to suggest that she busy herself with lunch preparations, Birdie laughed and said, "The little fellow went on to explain that the little holes were the freckles. And then another little boy said maybe they weren't freckles, maybe the cracker had the chicken pox." Before I could speak, she added quickly, "Well, I've got to wipe off these trays, then finish up the last two pans of biscuits for lunch," and she swiftly left.

It could not have been more than ten seconds later when I heard a tremendous clatter and a loud outcry in the kitchen. Springing from my chair, I looked through the side of my Plexiglas cubicle and saw Algeria half-sitting, half-lying on the floor with great clumps of mashed potatoes splattered across the bib of her plastic apron and her white T-shirt beneath. Her face was frozen in disbelief, and from her chin hung a pasty white goatee of mashed potatoes. In an instant I took in the large pan that lay overturned beside her and the small bog of mashed potatoes on the tiled floor.

Her hands clutching either side of her head,

Birdie stood speechless in front of Algeria, and Francine looked on, her mouth agape. As I hurried out into the kitchen, all three women began to talk and move at once. Algeria, who is muscular and tall, began struggling to arise, and as Francine stepped forward, Birdie reached down and took Algeria's hand, apparently believing that she possessed the strength to assist a woman of Algeria's size to her feet. The whole time Birdie was crying, "Oh, Algeria, honey, what have I done to you? What *have* I gone and done? Oh, *honey!*"

Could I have halted the action and given warning, I would have told Birdie to let Algeria rise from the floor on her own. As it was, a great flailing of arms and legs ensued, with ill-fated results. In her attempt to help Algeria, Birdie stepped into a dollop of potatoes and lost her footing. Algeria extended her hands to break Birdie's fall, and the two of them fell together on the floor, this time with Birdie seated squarely in Algeria's lap. At some point in her fall, Birdie's head had evidently been pressed against Algeria's apron so that half of her face was now covered with a sticky poultice of mashed potatoes.

For a moment there was complete silence except for the hum of the ventilators. I hastened toward the scene and stood in front of Birdie and Algeria with my arms folded.

Birdie informed me later that I looked exceedingly angry. The truth was that I was torn between sympathy and annoyance. That it was an accident was evident, yet there was the waste of food and time to consider, not to mention the soiled floor. The first class of children would be arriving in less than thirty minutes.

Birdie spoke first. Tugging her dress down over her knees, she looked up at me and boldly stated, "It was all my fault, Margaret, every single bit of it. Algeria is not to blame one iota. I was the cause of the whole thing." Then she turned to Algeria and looked directly into her eyes. "I don't know how in the world you're ever going to forgive me for this, Algeria, but I'm just so sorry I don't know what to do. I wasn't watching where I was going!" She bowed her head and shook it remorsefully. Francine was still standing behind the two of them, and she had by now covered her mouth with the hand on which she wore a large, padded oven mitt. I should have told her that such contact of the mitt with her mouth undermined our standards concerning the sanitary handling of food and equipment, but I did not.

It was an embarrassing moment for all of us. I believe that we were all taken back by Birdie's prompt and unqualified apology. I had not witnessed the prelude to the accident, of course, and Francine, if she had seen it, seemed presently incapable of speech. Algeria's face registered a conflicting blend of distrust and bewilderment, as if she were trying both to decode the words she was hearing and to reconstruct the steps by which she had come to be sitting on the floor with Birdie Freeman in her lap.

As Birdie had been the first to speak, so she was the first to laugh. Carefully she eased herself out of Algeria's lap and stood to her feet. She reached up and touched her own face, then shook her head in mock exasperation. "Well, at least if I was going to be the cause of all this mess, I got some of it on myself, too!" She chuckled at her sticky hand. "I've heard of those facial masks women use for pretty complexions, but this is a new one."

Algeria, still seated on the floor, said nothing. She was wiping potatoes off her apron and slinging them into the pan, her brow deeply furrowed. "I guess we can be thankful these were going *to* the oven instead of *from* it," Birdie continued. "They could've been hot!" She took another swipe at her cheek and said, "I bet I'm a sight!" Then she laughed again, but lightly, tentatively.

Knowing Algeria's volatile nature when riled or offended, I could not predict her response. I had once seen her wrench apart a pair of tongs during an argument with Vonnie Lee about Martin Luther King. She had stoically and sullenly endured a severe reprimand from me afterward and had subsequently purchased a new and better pair of tongs, which she brought to work the next day. She had always been quick to imagine injustice, to interpret innocent remarks or actions as insults to her or her race. But now as I stood watching, Algeria's face slowly relaxed, and though she puckered her lips and thrust them forward, her expression was closer to a smile than a frown. "We both of us in a sorry fix," she grumbled.

"Here, Algeria, let me help," said Francine, removing her oven mitt and coming around in front of them. "And for goodness' sake, let's watch what we're doing. No, Birdie, you stand back. I sure don't want all three of us to end up down there in all that mush." She laughed and extended both hands. "Y'all are something else, you know it?" Although Algeria tensed and attempted to shrug her off, Francine finally succeeded in helping her to her feet. "Now, flex yourselves, both of you, to see if anything's broke!" Francine said. "I knew a boy once who walked around for a week with a cracked tailbone before he went to the doctor to see why his rear end was hurting so bad."

For a moment neither Birdie nor Algeria moved. Very likely they knew they were not injured in any serious way. But Francine had found her tongue and seemed bent on exercising it. "Come on, check yourselves! See if everything still works right." To demonstrate, she flapped her hands as if shaking off water. "Y'all sure need baths!" she added. "You got that mess all over your clothes and face, both of you. Birdie, you'd have it all in your hair, too, if it wasn't for your cap." Then she doubled over with laughter, slapping her knees in exaggerated fashion and pointing at both of them. "Oh, I wish y'all could just see yourself!" As I have said before, Francine is inclined to overreact.

It was at this juncture that I spoke. "There is a great deal to be done, ladies. May I suggest that you reserve your jollity for a more convenient time and set about at once making things right?" For some reason, this remark set Francine off afresh, and as I wheeled about to return to my office, her laughter was punctuated with shrieks. I heard her gasp, "You just landed right smack in her lap, Birdie! That was something else!"

In reporting the details of the accident and its aftermath, perhaps it may seem to have happened slowly. The truth is that it passed with such speed that I was again seated in my office not more than five minutes after my alarmed exit. Five minutes is hardly worth noting, one might think. It was, however, a radically significant five minutes in our lunchroom, for within that small space of time the last arm's length of distance between Algeria and Birdie closed. Though Algeria had treated Birdie with a certain measure of politeness during the previous four weeks, she had nevertheless maintained an aloofness from her, an attitude almost of suspicion, as of waiting for inevitable proof of falseness.

I pretended to be busy with my paper work when I returned to my desk, but I frequently glanced out into the kitchen to see whether my help might be required. I was ready to give it but did not want to appear eager to do so, for I feel strongly that my workers must accept responsibility for their errors. Algeria disappeared for a few minutes into the rest room, and while Birdie stood at one of the big double sinks and wiped her face with a wet cloth, Francine posted herself by her side and attempted to scrape the potatoes off her white polyester jumper with a spatula. I had heard Birdie tell Francine earlier that morning that she had made the jumper over the weekend "to give me another uniform for work." Though some supervisors now allow a great variety of colors, I always make a point in our opening meeting of stressing my preference for white uniforms.

The next time I looked out, Birdie was down on the floor with two large spoons, nimbly scooping up the potatoes and depositing them into the pan from which they had spilled. When she finished, Francine emptied a bucket of water over the area and together they washed the residue toward the drain, then laid down towels and rags and set about mixing more potatoes.

Algeria joined them, and I watched the three of them work as a team around the large mixer, adding pitchers of water, potato flakes, dippers of melted oleo, then more water and potato flakes until the consistency pleased them. Algeria spooned the mixture into a large roasting pan and then brushed it with melted oleo while Birdie wiped off the mixer and took the beaters to the sink. Francine tore off a length of waxed paper and one of aluminum foil, which Algeria then placed over the potato mixture before setting the pan in the smaller oven to warm. With relief I noted that three other pans of the same size were already in the warmer. The accident, therefore, had fortunately occurred with the last batch.

By the time the children arrived, the only signs of the morning's impeded schedule were the towels on the floor and the damp, starchy stains on Algeria's and Birdie's clothing. After the final class was served, Birdie took on the task of giving the floor a thorough scrubbing to remove the last traces of the spill, and I heard her say to Francine, "I'll take these towels home tonight and give them a good washing."

As I counted the ticket stubs, clipped them to the register tape, and then totaled the money from the children who had paid with cash, I was aware of the usual postlunch activity in the kitchen. I heard Algeria call, "That pizza dough's gotta come out the freezer 'fore we leave!" I heard the squeaky wheels on the cart of dirty pots and pans that Francine wheeled past my door, as well as the swish of fabric between her ample thighs with every step that she took, and I heard the later clunking and spraying from her work at the dishwasher. Birdie was everywhere, wiping down surfaces, tying up garbage bags, stacking empty boxes by the service door.

Francine left first, a few minutes before two o'clock. I had just placed the cash in the bank deposit pouch and zipped it when I saw Birdie disappear into the walk-in pantry with the leftover box of potato flakes.

I saw Algeria quickly gather up the unused packets of salad dressing and follow Birdie into the pantry, ducking her head to clear the low entrance. Though I do not, as I have said before, consider myself a meddlesome person as regarding the affairs of others, I could see that Algeria had business on her mind other than the returning of the packets of dressing, and I could not suppress my curiosity.

The refrigerator, which is actually the size of a large closet, occupies one corner of the kitchen, next to which is the pantry. I took a pen from my desk drawer, walked out of my cubicle, and approached the refrigerator door, on which is posted a chart for notating the temperature of the unit. Twice each day I must check and record the temperatures for each of the two freezers, the large refrigerated storage room, and the smaller cooler. Standing before the chart, my pen poised as if to write, I could distinctly hear the voices of Birdie and Algeria in the pantry a few feet away.

". . . the blame for it all?" Algeria was saying. Her tone was gruff but not hostile.

"Well, now, no. I don't remember it that way at all," Birdie said. "I was in such a hurry to get my little jobs done that I wasn't remembering there were two other people working just as hard, and I whirled around and scooted off without even checking to make sure the way was clear."

"Don't matter what you say, you know we was both of us whirlin' 'round at the same minute headin' off different ways. Wasn't you any more'n it was me. We had us a head-on what wasn't nobody's fault, or else was both of us's." I heard a soft scraping like boxes moving on a shelf. Algeria continued. "No need you going on that way to Margaret like you just come over and push me down or somethin'. Wasn't that way 'n you know it."

Hearing Birdie talk but being spared the distraction of seeing her, I realized what a gentle, agreeable voice she had; it could be called melodious. She replied pleasantly but firmly, "Well, it seems funny, doesn't it, that you were the one who ended up on the floor? If we both ran into each other, it looks like I would have been the one to get knocked down. You're a whole lot stronger and taller than me, Algeria. No, you see, *I* was the one who took off pell-mell and had time to work up a little steam, and you just innocently turned around when I" — I heard a clapping of hands, which I assumed to be Birdie's — "ran right into you. And *that's* the way it was."

"Wasn't neither," said Algeria, "but you got your mind made up, don't do no good arguin' with somebody stubborn like you." Her tone had changed, though, and I could detect the shift to bantering.

"And the funny thing about it," Birdie resumed, taking up Algeria's playful tone, "was that I could almost *declare* that you pulled that pan of potatoes in toward yourself on purpose, like you were trying to protect *me.* Oh yes, there's no doubt in my mind that I was the culprit from start to finish. It's awfully nice of you to try to take part of the blame, but I just won't let you do it."

"You don't make no sense," Algeria said. "How come you doin' it?"

"Doing what?" Birdie said.

"Bein' so nice like that all the time. Like everybody else so good and nice you can't think nothin' bad 'bout 'em. People *mean,* 'n you know it. You always talkin' nice — how Francine so funny 'n Margaret so smart 'n

202

somebody else so purty. And you always goin' 'round givin' people stuff." (Birdie had brought Algeria a tin of homemade divinity that very morning.) "People *mean,* girl," she repeated.

"Oh well, I know we're not all saints and angels," said Birdie. "I know I'm not, that's for sure. But God's been so good to me, and the way I see it, Algeria, I'm not going to be here on earth very long. Nobody is. So I can either make up my mind to be happy and kind and show the love of Jesus, or I can be a negative sort of person and miss out on . . . well, on *everything.*"

"You crazy, girl, plum crazy," Algeria said, and as I saw her exiting the pantry, I put my pen to the chart and recorded beside the date the numeral 40, though to be honest, I had not yet looked at the thermometer inside the refrigerator.

After overhearing the conversation between Birdie and Algeria, I returned to my desk in a state of agitation and prepared to leave, these being the thoughts that filled my mind: First, Birdie's moralistic sermonizing concerning one's years on earth brought to my mind a similar statement by Sarah, or "Sadie," Delany in the aforementioned book *Having Our Say,* the book I was, in fact, currently reading at home. At the end of chapter eighteen, Sadie proclaims, "Life is short, and it's up to you to make it sweet."

I have no reason, I suppose, to doubt the sincerity of either Birdie or Sadie, but I admit to feeling a flush of impatience toward them both. What narrow, tidy, untroubled lives they must have lived to be able to cling to such a philosophy, I thought. I would like to have presented them with a variety of scenarios and asked them both how they would propose making such a life "sweet" or "happy."

I would like to have invited them both for a private reading of selected chapters from some of the books I had read. *Gal: A True Story* by Ruthie Bolton could have served well. After reading several chapters to them, I would have asked, "Would the mere act of *making up her mind to be happy* have transformed Gal's life into a good, sweet one?" Although Gal's grandfather did not approach my own in the degree of his moral degradation, happiness and sweetness were out of the realm of possibility for her, given the indisputable *reality* of her circumstances.

Though I meant at this time never again to share my own dark memories with anyone else, after having unintentionally divulged the truth to Joan, I could not help wondering how Birdie Freeman and Sadie Delany — one a white woman and the other black — would have stretched their shared ideology, pat and rosy, to accommodate a past such as mine.

I did not think only of myself, however.

Knowing very little of Algeria's personal life, I nevertheless felt reasonably confident from her general saturnine demeanor and occasional verbal flares that she had been allotted a generous portion of sorrow. As I left the kitchen, walked through the lunchroom, and approached my car in the minutes that followed, I indulged in a few moments of speculation concerning Algeria.

Was she presently ruminating, as was I? Was she privately arguing with the idealistic preachments of Birdie Freeman, a woman whose life had apparently borne no blemish of shame or cruelty? These thoughts perhaps marked for me a turning point of sorts, for until this time I had rarely wondered about the lives of real individuals within my circle of acquaintance. If asked to name those whom I knew most intimately, my list would have been composed largely of the names of characters in books.

Had Birdie's world been destroyed as mine had been following my thirteenth birthday, would she have grown up to be happy and kind? Had she, or I, been born black and underprivileged — two conditions not invariably paired, of course, as illustrated in the case of the Delany sisters, though Algeria would surely argue otherwise — would we have achieved lives of sweetness and joy? After a life breaks apart like a tree ripped asunder by a violent storm, can it take root again? After one's heart crumbles, can one gather up the fragments that remain and make them whole again? Can debris be re-assembled into beauty? It was the last Monday of September when I posed these questions to myself in that order, and I answered each of them without hesitation: *No.*

It is now more than nine months later, however, and I am reinvestigating the matter. In the process of laying out on paper the past months, I mean to discover the clue to another riddle song, that of Birdie Freeman. Of a certainty there is something in one's soul, in the heartwood of his being, that is imperishable. When one leaves the wildwood, does he not carry with him *something from oak and pine* that is indestructible, that remembers the promise of spring?

■ ■ ■ ■

PART TWO:
TO BE FOREVER MINE

■ ■ ■ ■

THE HANDWRITING
OF ORDINANCES
11

Birdie was a formidable opponent. One can see what I was up against. As the weeks wore on, she made herself indispensable at Emma Weldy by virtue of her tireless generosity. I cannot begin to chronicle the sum of her dealings with others, each interaction giving evidence of her fundamental and unceasing kindness. I realize as my chapters mount that I cannot tell it all, that by the end I must be prepared to admit, as the Queen of Sheba, that the half has not been told. I must therefore carefully choose the events to include, those that will best define the essence of Birdie Freeman.

From the beginning she rarely appeared at work without a gift for someone, and I believe it is accurate to say that before six weeks had passed, that is by the first of October, everyone at the school knew Birdie by name and everyone loved her, though for my part I continued to behave outwardly as if I could scarcely tolerate her presence. Her ministrations extended beyond the kitchen walls. By October she had volunteered to help the music teacher, Miss Grissom, with the Emma Weldy Singers on Monday and Thursday afternoons.

While waiting for Mickey to pick her up after school one day, Birdie had sat in the back of the music room during one of Miss Grissom's rehearsals, after which she had inquired of Miss Grissom concerning the possibility of putting her time to use by helping to pass out books, file music, prepare bulletin board materials, and so forth. When Miss Grissom discovered that Birdie played the piano, she had asked whether she would consent to serve as accompanist so that Miss Grissom could devote her full attention to conducting the group. Heretofore Miss Grissom's conducting technique had consisted primarily of bobbing her head and shouting instructions as she herself played the piano score for each number.

Moreover, by October Birdie had further endeared herself to the entire school by offering to type up what she called "our very own school newspaper with samples of all the little children's stories." The inception of the idea had taken place one afternoon near dismissal time when she had gone to Mrs. Tina Lowry's second-grade classroom to return a child's lunch box that had been left on one of the cafeteria tables. As Birdie told it, the pupils were reading stories they had written about autumn, and she reported, "They were just the cutest things!"

I heard her talking to Algeria and Francine about the experience in the days that followed. "You know, it's too bad all the other children and teachers couldn't hear those stories" and "I wonder if the children in other grades are writing stories like that, too" and "To see that little ragamuffin of a boy looking so proud and cheerful reading that story of his about the little twirly-pods, he called them, blowing down from the trees. Why, it just reminded me of how simple and precious little children are." I could imagine Birdie standing in the back of Miss Lowry's classroom, her hands laid to her cheeks, her mouth opened wide, her eyes sparkling as she listened.

The following week she asked Mr. Solomon, the principal, if he would allow her to solicit from the teachers samples of their students' stories so that she could compile a collection and type a master copy to be duplicated for distribution to all the children. Before talking with Mr. Solomon, Birdie had calculated the exact cost of the paper and staples needed and made it clear that she would donate her time to do the typing, duplicating, and collating. At that first meeting with Mr. Solomon, she had even suggested a few names for the "newspaper," as

211

she called it, which I felt to be a misnomer.

As the mascot of the school was a sheep — purportedly designated by the first principal of Emma Weldy in 1940, who pointed out that the school's initials spelled EWES, though I felt the choice to be an unfortunate one, for the sheep is not a bright animal — Birdie proposed the name *EWES-ful News* and suggested that an art contest be held among the students for an appropriate picture to serve as the newspaper mascot: a sheep reading a newspaper, perhaps. As other choices, she offered the titles *The Ram's Horn,* featuring a picture of a sheep blowing a horn, *Bo-Peep's Treasures,* and *Sheep Tales,* the last being Algeria's contribution.

The plan was approved, presented to the teachers at one of their weekly meetings, and set into motion in mid-October. From that time forth, as the teachers escorted their students through the lunch line, they spoke to Birdie as to a personal friend, frequently handing her sets of papers, which she put into a large canvas bag to read at home. It was Birdie's desire to surprise the children with each issue of *Sheep Tales,* which was the title subsequently selected by a school-wide vote. She did not want them to know beforehand whose stories would appear in print. I overheard her explaining to Francine that she was "keeping a written record with tally marks by each child's name so that lots of *different* children can have their stories in the paper."

Our piano lessons continued on Tuesdays and Fridays, and as I have said, on Mondays and Thursdays Birdie assisted Miss Grissom with the choir. This left her with but one weekday afternoon, Wednesday, to fill as she waited for Mickey's arrival at about three-thirty from his job in Spartanburg. Because I generally made my departure an hour before she left, my desk was unoccupied during her wait.

The Tuesday after Mr. Solomon granted his permission for the school paper, Birdie walked with me to my car following my piano lesson at her home. I was progressing "like a house on fire," according to Birdie, and she had just told me before we exited the house that I "ought to think about giving a little recital in a month or two for a few friends," to which I replied that I had absolutely no intention of ever doing such a thing.

"Margaret," she said hesitantly as we neared the car, and I steeled myself to resist what I expected to be a listing of gentle arguments in favor of a piano recital. But her mind was on a different subject now. "Margaret, I've been wondering," she said, "if you'd let me use your desk at work on Wednesday after-noons for about an hour after you leave." This was characteristic of Birdie, at times, to drop a matter without remonstrance yet immediately take up another.

I disapproved of the idea at once. I suppose I am in many ways a territorial person, and the thought of someone else sitting at my desk was disagreeable to me. "I leave my desk in order at the end of the day, and I want to find it undisturbed when I return each morning," I said. By this I meant to communicate a negative response to her request. I opened the car door and seated myself behind the steering wheel.

Smiling, she closed the door and gestured with a swiveling of her wrist for me to lower my window. "Well, I can sure promise you I won't touch a *thing*," she said with grateful mien. "Why, you won't find so much as a paper clip out of place!" I understood then that she had interpreted my words to be the stipulation for her using my desk rather than a clear statement of opposition.

I tried again. "I do not want others to work at my desk."

Again she misunderstood. "Oh, don't worry, I'll be the only one. I won't open your office up for general use! Nobody else even has to know about it. And I'll keep your desk so neat you'll never even know I was there."

She placed both hands over the top of the car window, bent down — though she was so small she did not have far to bend — and smiled joyously at me. I knew that in order to make her understand I would have to be brutally direct. *"No, Birdie,"* I would have to say, *"you may not seat yourself at my desk, not on Wednesday afternoon or any other after-noon. The answer again is no."*

However, glancing at her guileless face, I knew that the time for refusal was past. I could not correct her misconception. I believe that I could have done so two weeks, or perhaps even one week, earlier, but I could not do it now. Because she herself was so genuinely magnanimous and selfless, she found it easy, I suppose, to assume the same of others. More than once she took my words and translated them into saintly utterances.

"Thank you, Margaret," she said now. "I won't be a bit of trouble, I promise. I thought I could read some of the children's stories or maybe write letters and notes while I wait for Mickey. I sure appreciate it, and you can count on me to keep it nice the way you like it."

I inserted the key into the ignition and began rolling up the window. "Margaret," she said, raising her voice over the sound of the engine, "I wish you wouldn't keep leaving that money on the piano after every lesson. It sure makes me feel bad that you won't let me do it without pay. That was my offer, remem-ber?"

Through the half-closed window I replied, "I will not accept the lessons free of charge. I

215

have told you this before. It can be no other way."

"You're just really something else, Margaret," she said. I suppose she had picked up the expression from Francine. "It's so hard for you to take —" but she stopped and appeared to give a small sigh. She tipped her head to one side and smiled at me again.

"I know you've got to know this already," she said, "but I'm going to say it anyway. You're an awfully pretty woman, Margaret. You carry yourself so tall and dignified, and you're just . . . well, *pretty*." I felt myself stiffen as she continued. "You've got such a pretty complexion and such pretty eyes. And your beautiful curly hair and your hands — but I guess people must tell you this all the time. It's one thing to be smart like you are, but when you're smart *and* pretty — well, that's just a real special combination."

The top half of Birdie's face was framed by the narrow open rectangle above the car window. Her eyes, the color of strong tea, shone with simple goodness. She was wrong, of course. People did not tell me such things all the time, although in high school someone had once said that I looked like the girl in *National Velvet.* Before we were married, Thomas had told me that I was a "looker," and, of course, I will not pretend to be blind to what my own eyes tell me when I stand before a mirror. As a girl, however, I viewed pulchritude as a handicap, my mind continuously playing back the dreaded sound of my grandfather's sonorous nighttime murmurings: *Be still, Marg, shhh . . . you're such a beautiful girl . . . a beautiful girl,* always spoken menacingly as if it were a curse. Perhaps if I were ugly, I had often thought, I would be free from his horrible acts.

I shifted my gaze past Birdie's face to the fence some distance behind her, the fence that apparently marked the boundary between her yard and the Shepherd's Valley Cemetery. "Fences taut as the lines on sheet music." Annie Proulx had described such a fence in her novel *Postcards,* which I had recently finished reading, a book full of startling descriptions in a hardy, spare, energetic style. Miss Proulx's *Shipping News* is also a marvel of brilliant, laconic prose. Beyond the cemetery fence I saw the rows of headstones and bright clusters of artificial flowers. A green Mortland Funeral Home tent stood at the site of a new grave.

"Well, good day," I said, glancing briefly at Birdie and then shifting my car into reverse gear. Though I felt in that moment a peculiar void that I knew could most likely be filled only by verbalizing some measure of gratitude to Birdie, I could not form the words. What could I say? *"Your praise of my physical attributes is most kind"? "Your piano instruction is most helpful"? "Your employment at Emma*

Weldy is proving beneficial in ways which I had not anticipated"? All of these were true, of course, but I could not say such things. It did not occur to me simply to say, "Thank you."

Birdie stepped back from the car and waved. "I'll see you at work tomorrow!" she called. "Thank you again for saying I can use your desk!"

Perpendicular to the driveway was a gravel extension suitable for the turning around of a vehicle. This I did. As I drove slowly down Birdie's narrow driveway, I saw her through the rearview mirror. She stood in the same place and continued waving, not a great flapping of the hand but rather a small circular gesture like the wiping of a smudged pane.

As I drove home that day and as I went about my housekeeping duties, I recall musing over what manner of woman I might have been had my mother not died and left me in the hands of my ignoble grandfather. Not that it was my mother's wish that I be consigned, upon her death, to the home of my grandparents. Indeed, she would have moved heaven and earth to prohibit such an arrangement had she foreseen her untimely death.

I do not know by what means my grandparents were identified and contacted following the death of my mother. I only remember that a neighbor in Dayton, Ohio — a large, friendly woman, soft and loose of flesh, named Mrs. Gault — knocked on our apartment door one afternoon in mid-June and called to me, "Margaret! Margaret, are you there? Come to the door! It's about your mother!" Mrs. Gault was the only neighbor whom Mother had ever invited into our home. The two of them frequently played Scrabble and drank hot tea together on Saturdays, and I had been allowed to join them upon a few occasions.

It had been so deeply ingrained within me never to open the door while Mother was at work that I would not give entrance even to Mrs. Gault, a trusted neighbor. I would not even talk to her through the keyhole. "I know you're there, Margaret!" she continued to shout. "Your mother sent word to me to come get you. She's been hurt and wants you at the hospital!" Something told me that Mrs. Gault was telling the truth, but still I would not respond. Since we had no telephone, Mother's contacting me through Mrs. Gault was perfectly plausible.

I suppose a thirteen-year-old might be excused for hiding herself away in the face of a tragedy, for believing that the truth could be avoided or perhaps altered if she denied it, particularly when the tragedy involved the only person in the world whom she loved. I screamed when a key turned in the lock and Mrs. Gault entered with the landlord, a pale, thin-lipped man with purplish folds of skin sagging beneath his eyes. Though Mrs.

Gault's face was full of compassion, I fled from her and locked myself in the bathroom.

Eventually, of course, I could not escape the news that she bore, and as I rode to the hospital beside Mrs. Gault in the backseat of the landlord's car on June 13, 1957, I am certain that I knew my life was forever changed. Had we reached the hospital sooner, had I been cooperative with Mrs. Gault from the beginning, perhaps I could have seen my mother alive one last time. As it was, I saw her lying white and still beneath a sheet, having been stricken by a heavy blow, a gauze headband over her brow and a crimson abrasion upon her chin.

They told me that it had been a mishap at work, a horrible freak accident. She was working at the time as a secretary for a pipeline company in Dayton, and she had ventured into the warehouse that afternoon in search of her supervisor, who was needed on the telephone. The intercom system by which she usually conveyed such messages had just that morning developed a malfunction, rendering it inoperative. I was too dazed to listen well, but my mother's death, they explained to me, was the result of a faulty forklift, an enormous load of heavy-gauge pipes, and unlucky timing.

In the days that followed, I stayed with Mrs. Gault while people I did not know questioned me and examined my mother's personal effects. It was through her papers, I suppose, that they were able to trace the name and address of her parents, who were soon notified of her death and of my existence.

As my mother had never spoken to me of her parents, I did not know that I had a grandmother and grandfather. I had asked her once as a much younger child whether I had aunts and cousins and grandparents such as I read about, and she had replied, "You have only me, Margaret." At first, the knowledge that I had grandparents and that I would go to live with them afforded me some small degree of comfort, but it soon came to me that my mother's reticence on the subject was perhaps, or most likely, inauspicious.

I cried when I left Mrs. Gault. She was wearing a navy-and-white polka-dot dress the day she took me to the train station — a comforting, motherly dress — and I left dark, splotchy teardrops upon it. At the other end of the train ride, my grandmother was wearing a black dress of sinister sheen, and my grandfather was clothed in dark gray trousers with a flamboyant green and gold necktie. When I stepped from the train, I shuddered to see his white shirt stretched over his great, broad belly.

As I say, I pondered on the way home from my piano lesson that day whether under different circumstances I might have become a woman who, like Birdie, could easily praise others, from whose lips words of simple thanks could fall naturally, whose spirit toward others could be open and artless, the type of woman who could present bonsai plants — mine was and is still thriving — to people she hardly knew, who could accept blame with effortless grace and sincerity, who could stand in the driveway waving until her company was out of view.

I believe I could have, for my mother had the capacity for warmth and liberality in her speech and manner. Though never offering unreserved friendship to other adults (I know now that she feared the discovery of her family ties), she was nevertheless a cordial and ready conversationalist, operating freely within safe limits of acquaintance. She was witty, vibrant, and highly intelligent, though she once told me she had been mortally shy as a child.

I do not know to what extent my grandfather victimized my mother, but the fact that she never spoke of him and that she spent her life making certain he could never track her down is, in my opinion, full of meaning. I cannot, however, reconcile the memory of my mother as I knew her — charming, cerebral, and in my youthful judgment, perfectly stable — with the possibility of a traumatized childhood. Perhaps her mind had done her the favor of obliterating from her memory the nightmare. This I see as the only possibility, for surely no mere human could rise above such a perversion of the father-daughter relationship.

The fact that my mother had a quiet, steady respect for the Bible further mystifies me. In my childhood we read the Bible morning and evening and discussed it at length. How could she believe in something that my grandfather claimed to revere by day yet by his behavior he so flagrantly desecrated by night? It defies comprehension. The question plagues me yet, and still it has no answer. Such a duality cannot exist. Perhaps he did not abuse her. Yet why did she deny his existence? I am certain that I will never fit together the pieces of this puzzle, for many are missing, the greatest of which is my mother herself.

For thirteen years at the beginning of my life, there was my mother. After fifty years there was Birdie. But sandwiched between were the vile and abhorrent years of my grandfather with their residue of ghastly memories. Though I had lived in his house only four years, it was because of him that I had rejected the Bible. I had been abandoned. For me the love of God was fiction. Birdie Freeman could retain her illogical faith in a loving God. She could go on worldwide tours of mercy, drawing from her bottomless well of charity to ease the suffering of untold millions. She could even, perhaps someday, gain a toehold in my own fortress of affections —

this, if I were honest with myself, I knew her to be already in the process of doing — but she could never begin to lift me from the chasm of faithlessness into which my grandfather had thrown me.

These unhappy thoughts were still on my mind on the evening of that same October Tuesday. I was washing the supper dishes in the kitchen when the telephone rang. Thomas answered it. So many events, small and large, crowded together during those autumn weeks that I must take care now in recalling them and setting them down in order. I am positive, however, that the phone call from Joan occurred on the same day that I spent a great deal of time, all of it admittedly unprofitable, considering the woman I might have become had I been spared the horrible years with my grandfather.

I dried my hands when Thomas summoned me to the telephone. Since Joan seldom calls unless extending an invitation to a concert or play, I assumed that this was the purpose for her call. But it was not.

"I wasn't going to tell anybody this," Joan began, "but I can't get it off my mind. I've got to talk about it."

"Yes?" I said. I could hear the tightness in my tone. It came to me suddenly that she might want to resume our conversation from a few weeks ago, and I was resolved that this would not be.

"You won't believe what I did on Sunday, Margaret," she said.

I knew what I was expected to say and complied. "What?" I asked.

She laughed, a heavy, joyless single syllable. "Ha!" Then she paused. "I got up that morning and went to church."

I did not reply to this astonishing news.

"Put on my blue suit and went to *church,* Margaret!"

Still I remained silent.

"And not just any church," she continued. "I mean, you can halfway understand a person going to some huge, gorgeous church just for an aesthetic high or a little shot of righteousness to ease your conscience after a wild weekend or something, but that's not the kind of church I went to."

"Yes?" I prodded when she paused again.

Another sharp laugh. "I went to Daddy's church. I went to that little white church over in Derby — the Church of the Open Door. I just marched in and sat in the back row."

"Why?" I asked.

"I knew you'd ask that," she said. "And I even asked it myself the whole time. *What am I doing here?* And you know what? I have no idea what the answer is. I've just been so . . . well, I've been thinking about so many things, like I told you the other night, and it just seemed like this was something I could do as a kind of starting place in all this."

"In all of what?" I asked.

"Oh, you know . . . about Daddy, and then I haven't even told you the other part of my big dilemma right now, but that's not the point. The point is I went to that church, and it was the weirdest experience, Margaret."

"In what way?"

"I don't mean crazy and wild, like they picked up rattlesnakes or anything, but I just mean the feeling of sitting there with all those people right where Daddy had sat all those Sundays. And after the service I was practically mauled to death by everybody wanting to shake my hand and welcome me and invite me back and all that. And do you know that when I told one woman my name, she asked if I was related in any way to *Mayfield* Spalding. Come to find out, I had been sitting in the exact spot where Daddy used to sit every Sunday morning. Same pew, right on the end. Weird."

"A coincidence, to be sure," I said.

"Margaret, I have a favor to ask. That's part of why I called. You know how you go with me to concerts and plays and then we talk afterward and figure out all the angles and then I write it all up and they send me a check for doing it because they think I did it all by myself? Well, I was wondering . . ."

I knew where this was leading, and I headed her off. "I will never step inside another church as long as I live, Joan."

"But it could be just like going to another play. We could even drive over to the Second Cup afterward, and —"

"I feel quite sure that the Second Cup is not open on Sundays," I said, "but that does not matter. Nothing could persuade me to attend a church."

"Nothing?" Joan's tone was jocular as if I were speaking playfully.

"Nothing," I replied in a tone that removed all possibility of jest.

After a pause of intense silence, Joan spoke tersely. "Well, all right then. I'll just . . . get through all this by myself, I guess. I'll let you go, Margaret. Bye." And she hung up.

To say that I returned to the dishes undisturbed and free of regret would be an untruth. I did not like the feeling that I was responsible for another's distress, some small portion of which had been within my power to relieve. I was an avid proponent of the slogan To Each His Own, especially as it applied to the bearing of burdens, and nothing could shake my unremitting antipathy toward all things religious.

To be sure, I knew of the words *mercy, grace, love, forgiveness, benevolence.* I had even begun to see these abstracts played out daily in the small, kindly words and deeds of Birdie Freeman. But for me, no amount of grace could blot out the handwriting of ordinances penned so darkly upon my heart as a young girl, the first of which spelled out "The Innocent Shall Suffer."

A SOLEMN SOUND
12

I telephoned Joan the following evening, of course. This fact alone is noteworthy, for though I have always had great respect for Mr. Alexander Graham Bell's invention, it is my custom to use it only for business purposes. I cannot remember making what is termed a "personal call" to anyone before this point, excluding my telephone calls to Thomas at the hardware store concerning household needs, the kinds of calls to inform him, for instance, that a large oak branch had fallen against a window and broken the glass.

Perhaps someday I will ask Joan why, after more than fifteen years of casual family acquaintance, she so suddenly chose to confide in me, to seek my counsel in a private matter, to petition my emotional involvement in her life. Though I was quite certain that neither Joan nor Birdie knew each other, their coincident openness toward me was peculiar. Had Birdie's persistent gentleness begun to bring about gradual changes in me, I wondered, so that others found me more approachable? Could this softening have begun unbeknownst to me and in so short a time? After all, Birdie had been at Emma Weldy only seven or eight weeks by this time.

In examining the events of the past year, I have been forced to aim the light of truth upon myself. Since the age of thirteen, I have masked my emotions. This I cannot disavow. I have read that three common defenses developed by survivors of childhood abuse are memory repression, denial, and withdrawal. The memories are ever with me, and I have never denied that the terror was real. My protective response, thus, was emotional withdrawal.

To endure my grandfather's ongoing attacks, I dissociated myself from my feelings, both on a short- and long-term basis. My short-term withdrawal, I believe, rendered me emotionally numb during the actual experiences, as if surveying the scenes from a distance, while my long-term withdrawal blocked the exercise of all but three emotions: fear, anger, and hatred, each of which fed upon the others, and combined, very nearly erased all vestiges of my former self. Indeed, from the time I moved to Marshland, New York, to live with my grandparents, I became a different person. On more than one occasion I heard myself described as a "hostile child," though when my mother was living, I was of a mild and peaceable temperament.

I am not, may I repeat, submitting an application for pity, nor am I offering excuses for my personal foibles. I am simply setting down what I see to be true, all in the ultimate endeavor of clarifying and magnifying the impact of Birdie Freeman upon my life. Because a major part of her impact includes the unlocking, or perhaps the reconstitution, the exhumation, the emancipation — I know not what to call it — of my feelings, I must present some small history of their arrested development.

I offer these facts to make the point that for thirty-seven years, from the age of thirteen until the advent of Birdie in my life, I had succeeded in shutting out the world insofar as my emotions were concerned. I detached myself from others — both from caring about them and from hoping that they would care about me. The quickness with which all positive emotions such as love and trust can be expunged from the heart of a child is astounding. The berth that others will give upon being made aware of one's desire to be left to oneself is wide. The tunnel of escape by means of books can be deep, the gulf of separation from fellowmen immense, the hardness of a scarred heart very nearly impenetrable.

A Birdie Freeman, however, may shatter such generalizations. Since my mother's death, I had made of myself a stronghold of obdurate self-control and total independence. Then Birdie appeared and set about gaining entrance. For thirty-seven years I had forcefully fended off the occasional overture of friendliness; no one had tried more than once. Then Birdie came into the kitchen of Emma Weldy Elementary School and daily besieged me with small acts of affection. And in the midst of Birdie's campaign against me, my husband's cousin unveiled to me her secret pain.

Very well, enough talking. I know that a story needs specific scenes. And here is a scene that springs to my mind at present: a baby enfolded in his mother's arms. I see the young mother gaze upon her newborn son with an awe approaching stupefaction. I see her smile as she has not smiled in a very long time. But the time is not right for this part of my story. Were I preparing my manuscript for publication, I would strike through this paragraph — or rather, merely delete it by means of the speedy process that Thomas demonstrated to me on my computer. I will let it remain for now, however, for I want an unaltered record of my first thoughts.

As I said, I telephoned Joan last October on a Wednesday evening. As I also said, I was unaccustomed to placing calls of this nature. I will even admit that I felt somewhat nervous.

Joan answered the telephone after the fourth ring. Once I had identified myself, I said, "What is the other part of your dilemma to which you referred last night?"

Although I have reason to believe that Joan was taken by surprise, she answered without delay.

"Oh, Margaret, it's not anything you need to worry about. I'm sorry I even mentioned that stuff about Daddy. It's okay. I'm a big girl. I can handle it by myself." When I did not immediately reply, she added, though somewhat perfunctorily, "But it's nice of you to call anyway."

"I am not calling to be nice," I said. "You spoke earlier of two men and of trying to reconcile your thoughts concerning them." I paused, then continued. "I felt that perhaps you considered me unwilling to listen after our conversation last night, but that is not the case."

"Oh, I guess I was a little . . . hurt or miffed or *something* last night when you cut me off," Joan said. "But honestly, Margaret, when I hung up I gave myself a good scolding. Anybody who went through what you did as a kid must want to slap somebody for pouting about a daddy who didn't pay enough attention to her. And I sure don't have any right to get mad because the idea of going to some little backward church doesn't strike you as very exciting."

I realized how little I knew of Joan. I would not have expected her to make allowances for the curtness of others. By nature, she was highly critical, ready to scoff at weakness or stupidity. The thought came to me that perhaps she now considered me emotionally fragile in the wake of the revelation concerning my grandfather's wicked indiscretions and perhaps — unhappy thought — she pitied me. This would not do.

A line from William Wordsworth came to me, and I spoke it. " 'Suffering is permanent.' " By this I suppose I meant to imply a great many things: that Joan's suffering, though different from mine, was nevertheless authentic, that it could not be discounted; that one's deepest pain does not evaporate with the mere passage of time; that trying to understand one's suffering does little or nothing to lessen its severity, for suffering cannot be reasoned away; that suffering must be accepted and must be permitted its quarter in the heart; and more specifically, that visiting the church her father had attended would in no way cancel the effects of his inattentiveness to her as a child.

How Joan interpreted the quotation I cannot tell, for she answered bluntly and irrelevantly, "You ought to write it all down, Margaret."

"I have no idea what you mean," I replied sternly. "I telephoned you tonight concerning your dilemma."

"I've got a book about the therapeutic value of writing," Joan continued as if she had not heard me. "The woman says it helps to get your feelings down on paper and face them head on. I think she's got a point. It might be good for you to just put it all down on paper — the whole thing about your grandfather. This book says —"

"I am not interested in the book," I interrupted.

"Margaret, you need to *talk* about it!" I believe Joan was shocked by her own show of passion, for she fell silent.

At this point Thomas entered the kitchen through the back door with a bag of groceries. He often goes to the supermarket in the evening after supper. He looked at me curiously, for as I have said, I rarely use the telephone at home. He must have thought I was listening to a telemarketing speech because he said, "Want me to take over?" I wondered later how he and Joan would have recovered from the surprise had I complied and handed him the receiver.

I shook my head, however, and said to Joan, "If people could only understand that neither talking nor writing about adversity can ever change the thing that happened, we would not be plagued today with such a surfeit of shoddy television programs and books."

Joan laughed as if ill at ease but did not

speak for several seconds. "How do you do it, Margaret?" she said at last. "How do those words just roll out of your mouth like that? What was that again? 'Plagued with a surfeit of . . .' what was it? Oh, never mind, let's just forget it all."

"I never said that one could forget."

Thomas began removing items from the paper bag and setting them on the countertop.

"Well, thanks for calling," Joan said.

"Yes, well, I wanted to . . ." I groped for words. "I wanted you to finish what you began."

"And I appreciate that a lot, Margaret. I really do." Joan's voice was calm and steady. "Maybe I will sometime. Maybe we can both do that sometime . . . when the time's right."

It was a few minutes after eight o'clock when I hung up the receiver. The conversation itself was not important for its substance except to document the fact that it was Joan who first planted the idea in my mind of the value of writing my story on paper. Of course, she would have me focus on the four years with my grandfather, while it is my purpose to divine the effect of Birdie Freeman upon my life and the lives of others.

Of greater consequence than the content of the telephone call, however, is the stimulus behind it. Never before in my recollection had I ventured to this level of personal

236

interaction, initiating a conversation in which I expressed an interest in the affairs of another. I cannot account for my arousal, but as it occurred at the same time as my expanding familiarity — it was not yet truly friendship — with Birdie, I feel certain that much of the credit somehow belongs to her. Her influence upon me was warm and constant, like an ocean current.

As I write this, the calendar tells me that it is now June 30. Though I have been writing every weekday since June 8, I have not completed even a dozen chapters of my narrative. I must therefore urge myself forward. Certain details must be sacrificed, I acknowledge, though I feel every particular to be pertinent to the telling of Birdie's story.

From the moment I met Birdie she was *with me,* truly an omnipresent complication in my life. Before she came I had drifted, or rather fled, into a dim corner of life, backed myself tightly against the walls, and kept the world at bay. Nursing my conviction that no one could be fully trusted, I took no risks.

October was a critical month in the timeline of my story, for as I have stated, several events of import took place. As Birdie daily interjected herself into my life, I could actually feel my resistance weakening against my will. I began to behave, at times, in an uncharacteristic manner.

For example, one day in late October I

brought a dozen homemade doughnuts to the school kitchen and placed them on the stainless steel worktable. When Birdie came to my office door and said, "Do you know anything about these doughnuts out here, Margaret?" I replied stiffly, "Yes, I know about them. I made them and brought them to . . . share with you and the others." She, of course, effervesced to an embarrassing degree about my act of generosity and went flittering from my office into the kitchen to continue her laudatory remarks to Algeria and Francine, both of whom cast skeptical sidelong glances toward my office. Francine's lower jaw appeared to be unhinged, and Algeria's eyes had contracted to slits.

On October 26, 1995, a Wednesday, a strange thing happened. I was driving home from work at 2:40 in the afternoon, listening to an audiocassette recording of Annie Dillard's *An American Childhood.* The day before, on my monthly visit to the Derby Public Library, I had examined the shelf of new acquisitions in the audiovisual room and had discovered the set of cassette tapes. Having already read Annie Dillard's *Pilgrim at Tinker Creek,* I readily checked out the set of tapes of *An American Childhood.*

Since Thomas had recently installed a tape player in my car, I had begun to consider the drive to and from work a pleasurable experience, often decreasing my speed as I neared my destination and once even taking a deliberate detour in order to finish a tape. I listened to both music and literature as I traveled, grateful to be relieved of the inferior early morning and afternoon radio fare. At times I sang along softly, adding my voice to the Cambridge Singers or harmonizing with some of the best: Beverly Sills, Kiri Te Kanawa, Frederica Von Stade, and the like.

On this October afternoon I recall being struck by the remarkable sense of place exuding from Annie Dillard's work. Her American childhood was rooted in Pittsburgh, and every chapter of her book bears the signature of that locale. Indeed, in the prologue of her work, she declares topology to be the last thought of a dying man: "The dreaming memory of land as it lay this way and that." If this is so, I shall envision in my dying moments a vast, disorderly montage of hills and valleys, plateaus and shores, for my childhood was spent in more than a dozen cities, hundreds of miles apart.

I had just finished listening to the chapter in which Annie Dillard extols the virtues of baseball and had just begun the next chapter, which describes a broken power line spitting fireworks along Penn Avenue following a tornado, when simultaneously I came to a stoplight and I heard a siren.

Though I am not a person who looks for a crisis in every deviation from routine, I felt at that moment a distinct and palpable surge of live fear, as if the violent cable in Annie Dillard's book was thrashing about within me. I had read of such premonitions of danger and had even experienced one myself many years ago, of which I will speak later. I turned the tape player off and depressed the accelerator urgently as soon as the traffic light was green. I saw the ambulance speeding toward me, traveling in the opposite direction. The driver strained forward, and the vehicle passed in an instant, the caterwaul of its siren fading quickly.

"Thomas," I said aloud. I cannot say why I thought that Thomas was inside the ambulance, but suddenly I strongly believed it to be so. I briefly considered turning around and following the ambulance to Dickson County Hospital but decided against it. Perhaps there was word awaiting me at home, although I knew that in the event of an emergency, Thomas would not have had opportunity to write a note, such as *Rosie, had me a silly old heart attack. Called 9-1-1. Sincerely, T. T.* or *Cut off my John-Brown arm with the new saw. Gone to hospital. Your clumsy, bleeding husband, T. T.*

I was now only four blocks from our duplex. Passing Pate's Barber Shop, I saw Lyle Pate sitting in a ladder-back chair by the front door staring down the road in the direction that the ambulance had taken, a newspaper spread across his lap and the stripes of the barber pole above his head spiraling lazily.

When I turned off Trident Street onto our street, Cadbury, I saw Thelma Purdue, Phyllis Jansen, and two other neighbors — an elderly man with the preposterous name of Ivan Zix, and Ruby Hamrick, a widow who occupies one side of the duplex next to ours — at the curb in front of the Jansens' house casting distraught glances across the street toward our duplex. I also noted that the Jansens' gate was open again and that Pedro was in the Beltons' yard, next door to the Jansens', investigating the trunk of a young apple tree.

Phyllis Jansen, upon seeing my car, began waving her arms in a hysterical fashion. She was wearing lime green knit slacks that clung unbecomingly to her ample hips and thighs. Thelma Purdue stood beside her, a look of consternation in her eyes, clutching the sleeve of Phyllis's sweat shirt.

I did not pull into our driveway but rolled down the window and spoke before Phyllis Jansen could seize the moment for herself. "Thomas was in the ambulance, was he not?"

Phyllis Jansen's mouth fell open, and she nodded blankly.

As I rolled up the window and sped off, a sharp shriek of tires punctuating my departure, I heard Phyllis Jansen shout something, whether to me, Thelma Purdue, Ruby Hamrick, Ivan Zix, or Pedro, I knew not. I made a hard turn from Cadbury onto Becker Street, honked my horn repeatedly at a brown UPS truck slowly wending its way down the middle of Becker, and finally circled back to Trident.

Dickson County Hospital is the only facility of its kind within a radius of twenty miles, and I felt certain Thomas would be taken there rather than to one of the hospitals in Greenville. As I look back on it, I realize that the drive from Cadbury Street to Dickson County Hospital was, in an elemental way, life changing. I have heard others speak of the distortion of time during critical moments, of the replaying of an entire lifetime in an instant, of the hallucinatory sensation of spinning off into an orbit separated from reality, of functioning as an automaton. All of these I experienced during my drive to the hospital.

Though panic had unsettled my mind, I can still recall with perfect clarity the startling comprehension that descended upon me that autumn day. The drive actually passed quite swiftly, unlike the movement in dreams in which one's feet turn to great blocks of lead or one is beset by numerous obstacles in the haste to flee. My car seemed to be racing to keep pace with my thoughts. The distortion of time in my case, therefore, was that of acceleration rather than deceleration.

Here is the progression of my thoughts as I remember them: First, I tried to conceive of Thomas in an invalid state but could not do so. Though he was seventy years old at the time, I had never known him to be gravely ill. He still worked at Norman Lang's hardware store five days a week, repairing vacuum cleaners in his rented space at the rear of the store and frequently ringing up sales when Norm was unavailable. Thomas showed every sign of a strong constitution. Nothing beyond an occasional head cold or inflamed knee interrupted his otherwise excellent health. Both of his parents, though deceased now, had lived past the age of ninety. As I tried to grasp the concept of Thomas on a stretcher in an ambulance, I realized not only the extent to which I would miss his help at home in the event of serious illness, but more importantly, the degree to which his own enjoyment of life would be reduced. That is, I deplored the possibility of his physical impairment *for his own sake,* and for me this line of thought was a novelty.

Second, the images of his many gifts to me suddenly glutted my thoughts: the frequent kitchen items from the hardware store — the potato peelers, the canning jars, the sponge mops, the rubber gloves, the paring knives, the spatulas that were set upon the kitchen counter without comment — and the costlier items such as the recent tape player for my car, a compact disc player, and his grandest offering only three weeks earlier — a gleaming black studio piano. The knowledge, undeniably selfish, suddenly overwhelmed me that if he were truly sick, I would miss his gifts.

Third, I could not help considering the possible conclusion of such an emergency as we now faced. What if Thomas died? All at once the thoughts of utter solitude and silence at home, conditions that I had always imagined myself to covet, became undesirable to me. A dreadful vision of Shepherd's Valley Cemetery rose in my mind. I did not want to see Thomas's name engraved upon a white headstone. I did not want to lie awake at night and ponder the concept of eternal life.

I was only vaguely aware of passing familiar places along the route. However, when I came to the corner on which was located Two Guys Auto Parts, owned and operated by twin brothers named Winston and Churchill Guy, I realized I was only two blocks from Dickson County Hospital. In the two blocks between Two Guys Auto Parts and the hospital parking lot, two alarming realizations burst upon me: First, I was quite sure that Thomas *loved* me — though I had never heard him speak the words; indeed, I would not have stood for it — and second, though I could not take my feelings for him to such length at this time, something within me ached unbearably at the thought of losing him.

I parked my car and walked quickly toward a short flight of concrete steps. Though the temperature that October day was moderate, I felt my face aflush with heat. As I approached the entrance, I heard a solemn sound, that of the hospital doors parting, a high-pitched electronic whirring, as if the doors themselves were wailing empathetically for the human sufferers within.

NO PLEASANT BREAD
13

Thomas had once told me of a puppy that had crept from under his family's front porch one day when he was nine years old. Its mother had apparently given birth in the cool darkness beneath the porch, and the pup had eventually sought daylight. Within a few days it was discovered that the mother had died under the house, along with four of her puppies. This event came as a disagreeable inconvenience, especially to Thomas's older brother, who was assigned the task of extracting the lifeless bodies from their birthplace.

The surviving pup miraculously thrived, being possessed of a feisty and indomitable nature, and attached himself to Thomas's family, and to Thomas in particular. Permitted to choose a name for the pup, Thomas immediately struck upon the name Flipster.

"That was the first name that popped into my head," Thomas had told me. "He was the playfulest little rascal you ever seen, always turnin' flips and runnin' thisaway and that-away. There wasn't any stoppin' his shenanigans." He had spoken often of Flipster, who became a loyal friend and fearless hunter, all the while retaining his penchant for mischief.

When Flipster had later become embroiled in a fight with two bulldogs, he had been so severely injured that Thomas's father had been forced to relieve the dog's misery by shooting him. "I cried like a baby," Thomas said, describing the experience. "I was near 'bout sixteen years old by then, but I sobbed my heart out. I remember settin' on the ground holdin' Flipster in my lap after Daddy shot 'im. I knew he was dead, but I kept beggin', 'Git up, Flipster! Git up!' His fur was all matted down with blood and tears; the blood was his, the tears was mine."

As I entered Dickson County Hospital that October day, I could not account for the vividness of these memories of a dog that I never knew. I am not overly fond of animals in general. As I imagined a boyish Thomas cradling the dead body of his beloved Flipster, I heard the words clearly and repeatedly: *"The blood was his, the tears was mine."* With each step my fear intensified. Was this vision a presage of disaster? Was I to find Thomas bleeding to death? Would it be I who would shed tears over a wounded and lifeless body?

"Please direct me to the emergency room," I said to the woman behind the desk in the lobby. Her lips were darkly outlined in wine red lipstick but filled in with a garish shade of ripe persimmon. I cannot explain why the sight of this woman's lips filled me with such ire, but I felt that I could have throttled her without compunction or observed with satisfaction while someone else did so. I suppose her lips were merely a representation to me of wasted minutes, of *time,* which at present seemed a commodity of short supply.

The woman toyed with one of her gold hoop earrings as she peered up at me. "Beg pardon?" she said. Her enameled fingernails gave further evidence of time carelessly frittered away, as well as of a disregard for efficiency on the job. It is my opinion that a woman with long fingernails should not be allowed to draw a paycheck and certainly not to hold a position of responsibility.

"The emergency room," I said again, articulating each syllable with exaggerated clarity. "Where is it?"

"Do you have somebody in there?" the woman asked, batting her thickly frosted eyelashes three times in rapid succession.

"I have good reason to believe so," I replied.

She stood up at once and pointed, her armful of copper bracelets jangling as she did so. "Down that hall, turn right, all the way to the end, and you'll see the doors marked," she said. "There's a nurse at the desk in there," she called as I left. "She'll help you find your person."

Your person. Though I felt a fleeting twinge of perturbation over her generic word choice, I had no desire to stop and apprise her of the name and relationship of *my person,* and as I hastened down the hallway, I once again heard Thomas's words: *"The blood was his, the tears was mine."* A scene took shape in my mind of myself weeping over Thomas's blood-soaked, outstretched form, a ridiculous scene in which I urged, "Git up, Person, git up!" Actually, I could not recall the last time I had shed tears. It was something that I had stopped doing many years ago.

I quickly erased the scene from my mind, and though I once again scolded myself for the untimely humor, I realized I was merely seeking refuge in what dramatists call comic relief — a jolt of amusement to lighten an oppressively heavy moment. It was, of course, a means of staving off my fears, for if I could imagine so wildly implausible and horrible a situation, I would perhaps be less shaken by the reality.

With such a prelude as I have described, you may well imagine my confusion when, upon entering the emergency waiting room, I saw Thomas, from all appearances unscathed and in full possession of his faculties, seated in a chair upholstered with gold velour. His ball cap was resting on one knee, and a thick sprig of gray hair behind his left ear had been disarranged and was stiffly angled upward like the stub of a small antler. He was calmly leafing through a *Popular Mechanics* magazine in the midst of a great hubbub of noise and motion.

Though a profound relief swept over me, I also felt the outrage of having been duped. While I had been flying toward the hospital, my heart filled with uncertainty and dread, Thomas had been browsing through a magazine in a padded chair. The tender thoughts spawned by what I had taken to be an endangerment of his life — the illumination I had witnessed en route of our feelings for each other — were pushed aside as I now surveyed him in the velour chair scratching the back of his neck. I bore down upon him.

"Thomas Tuttle, what are you doing here?" I asked, halting directly in front of him.

A young child curled in a chair nearby stirred and cried out. At the same time I heard a woman's voice behind me. "Is there a Farley Whitcomb in here? You have a phone call, Farley Whitcomb."

Thomas was looking up at me in great perplexity. He inhaled quickly and said, "Well, Margaret, how come *you're* here?" He closed the *Popular Mechanics,* took up his baseball cap, and stood to his feet. I stepped back, almost overturning a Styrofoam cup of coffee that someone had carelessly left on the floor.

"I came to . . ." I paused, suddenly unsure of how to state my purpose for coming. "I came because I thought my help might be required."

He shook his head. "Naw, not now, I don't guess. Nurse said they'd git things settled down with 'im, then come tell me how he's doin'."

As Thomas continued to speak, I soon came to understand what had transpired. Thomas had been in the ambulance, as I had suspected, but only as a neighborly escort to Nick Purdue, Thelma's husband, who lived in the other side of our duplex.

As Thomas told it, he had come home that afternoon around 1:30 to meet with a man he had contacted about cutting down two pine trees in our backyard. As the two of them were talking in the yard, Thelma Purdue had suddenly "screamed bloody murder," as Thomas put it, and had hobbled down her back steps to "sputter and hiss a bunch of nonsense" that neither Thomas nor the other man could comprehend. Thomas had rushed to her assistance, however, and discovered Nick Purdue inside at the kitchen table, slumped over a piece of sweet potato pie.

"All Thelma could do was gabble and cry," Thomas said. "I don't see how Nick's put up with her all these years. The tree man, he come on in Thelma's house, too, and took over with Thelma, tryin' to keep her from goin' off the deep end while I checked on Nick and called the ambulance. Looked like to us he'd had him some kind of attack right in the middle of eatin' his pie. The whole side of his face was smashed right into that pie, and the fork was still in his hand." He paused and shook his head, lifting his own hand to stare at it.

Behind me I heard a nurse call out, "Mrs. Cordell? Wait a minute, please. I need you to fill out some information." Somewhere in the room someone was crying, a shrill gasping and sputtering.

"When Thelma heard the siren comin'," Thomas continued, "she got all riled again and started hissin' like a steam valve and shakin' all over. So I called Phyllis Jansen, and she come over and said she'd stay with Thelma if somebody'd go in the ambulance with Nick, which I naturally said I'd do since the tree man had his work to get back to. I called Thelma after we got here and told her Nick was bein' tended to now and they'd be tellin' us somethin' before long. She said Phyllis was still there and was helpin' her get dressed and was gonna bring her on up here to the hospital. Poor Phyllis, she's got her hands full. I bet Thelma's runnin' 'round there like a chicken with its head cut off."

"Thelma was standing quietly outdoors with Phyllis Jansen, Ivan Zix, and Ruby Hamrick a few minutes ago," I said. I suppose

252

Phyllis Jansen was the ideal companion in this time of crisis, for her ready flow of speech would have allowed Thelma little opportunity for hysterics.

Nick Purdue came home from the hospital three days later, having recovered from what was diagnosed as a mild stroke. The event itself had few permanent repercussions, except for a new prescription of medication "to add to the truckload I'm already takin'," as Nick himself put it.

As for myself, however, the eleven-minute drive to Dickson County Hospital that day was an emotional benchmark. For many years prior to that October day, I had allowed myself no tide of feelings. They had ebbed long ago, and I took care to keep them low and distant. On the day of Nick Purdue's stroke, Birdie had already begun her patient work on me, of course, but it was the threat of losing Thomas that suddenly impelled me to care about something with absolute fervor. Had my emotions been quantifiable, as on a thermometer, the mercury would have soared during my ride to the hospital that day. I *felt,* irrationally and eruptively.

This is not to say that I outwardly became a changed woman from that moment onward. To be honest, I believe I concealed any trace of my emotional enlightenment as I spoke with Thomas in the waiting room and as we resumed our daily routine at home following the incident. Even as I write this some nine months later, I have not as yet told Thomas of the change of heart I felt that day. I do not believe he suspected for a moment that my sudden appearance at the hospital was motivated by a trepidation that harm had befallen *him.* There was no tearful expression of devotion to him on my part. There were no overt gestures of appreciation for what he meant to me.

In fact, I perversely altered my plans to prepare lasagna for our supper that evening, for it was one of Thomas's favorite meals. Instead, I made Mexican rice and served corn bread muffins reheated from a previous meal in order that I might give no signal of tenderness. I do not know why I quashed any impulse toward the display of my feelings except that it was out of habit, a habit that had been nurtured by a deep-seated conviction that no one was to be trusted. And, of course, this was a habit born and bred of fear.

The awareness had triggered something within me, however, and ever afterward I was to remember my ride to the emergency room as evidence that I was capable of feeling and of reentering life as a participant. And ever afterward I was to observe Thomas more closely. For eleven minutes I had lost him — in a sense — and finding myself repossessed of him, I began to take careful and daily note of his . . . *person* is the only appropriate word that comes to mind.

I am quite certain now as I write this that Thomas must know I have begun to contemplate the possibility that I may feel for him, if not love, at least a supreme measure of gratitude for his companionship. Such knowledge has brought into our home certain changes of which we do not speak openly. Since Thomas is seventy years old, and I am now fifty-one, the prospect of openly declaimed love is daunting. Romantic simpering is a garment befitting only the young.

The day following Nick Purdue's stroke was Thursday, October 27. When Birdie came to school that morning, she appeared to have been crying. Ironically, however, she brought with her three bookmarks inscribed with the words *Joy Cometh in the Morning,* which she presented in the meekest of manners to Francine, Algeria, and me. I accepted my glossy, betasseled bookmark, which in addition to the verse also bore a picture of a pale violet sunrise streaked with gold, and put it in my purse.

The day's work went smoothly, as I remember. The menu called for boiled eggs and French toast for breakfast and chicken nuggets for lunch. While passing through the lunch line, several teachers offered comments to Birdie concerning the church that she attended, for Birdie had invited the entire faculty and staff of Emma Weldy to what she called "Fill-a-Pew Night" at the Church of the Open Door in Derby the previous night. A visiting evangelist named Jesse Goodyear from Memphis, Tennessee, was "holding a week of special meetings," as she explained it in the written invitations that she had distributed on Monday. When she had delivered an invitation to me at my desk and asked if I would be able to attend, I had replied in a single, resolute syllable: *No.* I did not elaborate, nor did she press me.

In addition to teachers, a number of staff members — Ed Silvester, the janitor, for instance, as well as Merle Cameron, one of the secretaries, and Blanche Triplett, the school nurse — offered remarks concerning the church service. Ed Silvester told her he hadn't heard such "celestial organ playing" since he was six years old. "Of course, I've not cast my shadow across the threshold of a church since I was a young tyke knee-high to a grasshopper, either," he said, grinning. In his conversation with others, Ed Silvester seems to be searching for a style that suits him, one minute affecting the speech of a scholar and the next sounding like an un-learned rustic.

From all indications, Birdie had succeeded splendidly in the campaign to fill a pew. It would not have surprised me to hear that she had lent some of her visitors to the sparsely occupied pews of other church members.

Francine had been among those who attended the meeting, for I overheard her describing Jesse Goodyear to Algeria. "I never heard a preacher who could make me *laugh* like that. He was something else! And then he'd hit you with something so serious you couldn't believe you'd been laughing a second earlier. And he didn't preach long, either, was the other thing I couldn't believe. He started off making a joke about his name. Said something about him traveling lots of miles but still having lots of tread and said people feed him so much he's afraid he's gonna turn into a *blimp.* Then pointed to his belly and said, 'See, I already got me a spare tire around my middle.'"

When Francine gave a jolly hoot, Algeria pinched in the corners of her mouth and shook her head. "Huh! Can't stand preachers that tries to be funny," she said.

Though Birdie accepted everyone's kind words about the church service with a gracious smile, she nevertheless remained subdued the entire day. She spoke sweetly to the children, of course, but without her usual spark of gaiety. After all the classes had been served lunch, Birdie went into the pantry, and when she emerged I saw her wipe her eyes with a tissue. Minutes later when I went into the kitchen to check on the quantity of leftover pineapple slices — for as I have said, we often serve the leftover fruit or cookies to the kindergartners as their morning snack the following day — I distinctly heard Birdie sniffle.

"May I speak to you in my office?" I said to her. I saw Algeria whip around as though ready to take up Birdie's defense, but I shot her a warning glance and she remained silent. Francine began humming off key but continued rinsing a large aluminum baking pan at the sink, producing drumlike clunks as she turned it over.

I led the way into my office and positioned myself behind my desk, though I did not sit down. Birdie stood across from me, her small hands resting motionless upon the surface of my desk, fingers splayed as if sounding a chord on the piano. She fixed her brown eyes upon me, two worried seams running parallel between her eyebrows. Her hair was braided more tightly than usual, I noted, and pinned, as always, close against her head, thus giving her face a stark, unrelieved homeliness.

"Are you ill?" I asked.

She shook her head briskly. "No, Margaret, I'm feeling just fine — physically, I mean."

"Because if you were feeling ill," I continued, "I was going to suggest that you make arrangements to go home."

"I'm fine," Birdie repeated, shaking her head. "I appreciate it, though, Margaret."

"For we cannot run the risk of contaminating our kitchen environment with the coughing and such that typically accompany the common cold. The transfer of germs from the hands to the serving areas or to the food itself could of course be . . . deleterious."

It seemed to me that Birdie colored slightly. She lifted her hands and laid them against her cheeks, her movements producing a faint crackling of her white plastic apron. "I always try to be extra careful about keeping my hands washed," she said, "and I'll try not to —" She broke off and closed her eyes. Her voice fell to a whisper. "I just can't get over those poor babies!" Her face was a pale oval of sorrow.

I did not reply at once, for her meaning was unclear, but at last I did speak, hesitantly and perhaps even softly, though emitting a sigh of impatience. "As I have said before, you must not allow yourself to bear the collective burden of our students at Emma Weldy, for no amount of agonizing on your part will alleviate the difficulties that exist in the homes of many of these children. You must learn, as I have emphasized repeatedly, to lay aside your feelings at work or they will adversely affect the quality of your performance."

She opened her eyes and looked at me. Dropping her hands from her face, she began nodding her head. "You're right, Margaret. I know I can't fix everybody's problems." She smiled sadly and added, "But it's not our own little children I'm upset about today. It's those two little babies in Union."

I suppose I already knew, though at that moment I understood it more fully, that Birdie Freeman's heartfelt anxieties on behalf of others were not restricted to individuals within her immediate circle of acquaintances. Indeed, I was beginning to discover that Birdie's concerns pertained not to a simple circle at all, but rather to a sphere — that is, to the entire planet Earth. She was referring, of course, to the recent news report that I had first heard two days earlier, on the evening of October 25, of the disappearance of two young boys in an alleged car-jacking in Union, South Carolina. Susan Smith, the mother of the two boys, aged three and fourteen months, told authorities that she had been accosted at a deserted intersection and forced from her car, after which the thief, purportedly a black man, had driven away with her two children in the backseat.

Birdie went on to explain, pausing at intervals to compose herself, that a co-worker of Mickey's at the Barker Bag Company in Spartanburg lived in the same neighborhood as the two little boys and their mother. "He told Mickey that the whole family's just torn apart over it, wondering if those two babies will come home alive," she said. "And I can't quit thinking about what they're going through — especially that poor mother. She must be nearly out of her mind!"

Over the following week, although she carried out her kitchen duties conscientiously, Birdie bore the Smith family's grief as if it were her own. She looked as though she had been struck when Algeria cast aspersions on Susan Smith. "Huh! Ain't no mama gonna look like a blank wall the way that woman look when she talk 'bout her babies on the TV, and I *still* say she know somethin' she ain't wantin' nobody to find out."

"Oh, Algeria, honey, *please* don't say something like that. Nobody knows how they'll act when hard times hit. People take trouble in so many different ways. Why, that woman is probably so numb by now from the shock of it all that she doesn't even know what she's saying. Let's don't be harsh with her. She needs our prayers."

But Algeria was intractable. "Can't help it. Don't trust her. Her eyes don't look right. Oughta pray for her babies, not *her.*" However, Algeria did not state her suspicions in Birdie's hearing again.

Many readers remember the outcome of this sordid saga. When the truth came out — that is, when the woman admitted to sending her two sons to their deaths in John D. Long Lake — the entire school was abuzz with disbelief and anger. When Birdie walked into the kitchen on the morning of November 3, the morning after the news of the confession

261

had been made public, I saw that her aspect was drained. I was in my office cubicle filling out a form.

Paper work, as I said earlier, constitutes the bulk of my duties as lunchroom supervisor, and because the particular form on which I was working at the time — one that bears the heading of *Free and Reduced Meals* — is confidential, I had closed the door to my office. Aside from the principal, I am the only person at Emma Weldy who is privy to the names of the children whose meals are subsidized by government funding.

As Algeria and Francine had not yet arrived, Birdie set about her breakfast duties alone, counting out the miniature boxes of cereal and packets of jelly in the pantry and transferring them by tray to the serving line. She was spreading melted oleo onto slices of bread with a pastry brush when Algeria walked into the kitchen. Thermos in hand, I left my office, first turning the form face down on my desk and then closing the door securely, and approached the ice machine. As Algeria donned her apron, I heard Birdie speak. "Well, Algeria, honey, I guess I owe you an apology." I slowly filled my thermos with ice cubes. I could see them both in my peripheral vision. Algeria did not reply audibly, but I could well imagine her typical response, that of shrugging her shoulders.

Birdie continued. "You saw right through it

all, but not me. No, sir. I just went along so foolishly, thinking that little mother was telling the truth and *insisting* that everybody else think the same thing. You turned out to be right, and I was wrong. I sure wish I was quick enough to see things like you can. I feel just completely empty inside. Not that it matters about me being wrong. That's sure not the first time that's happened. But I just can't figure it all out — how she could *do* what she did."

I walked to the sink and turned on the faucet. Allowing the water to run for a few moments until at its maximum coolness, I then decreased the water flow and slowly filled my thermos. Appearing beside me at the other side of the large double sink where I stood, Algeria turned on the hot water to wash her hands. She replied with her back turned to Birdie, slowly and ponderously as if wishing it were not necessary to formulate sentences so early in the day. "She *bad*, Birdie. No way to figure that out. Can't nobody figure out liars 'n killers."

"I'm always so *gullible*," Birdie said, then again added, heatedly this time, "but that sure doesn't matter at a time like this!"

"You just used to thinkin' everybody good like you," Algeria replied.

Birdie made a choking noise, a mixture of self-deprecation and scorn. I held my thermos aloft and began wiping off the sides with a brown paper towel. Algeria scrubbed her large hands violently, sudsing them generously, and the discussion appeared to be finished, though I knew it would be resumed and extended ad infinitum in the hours, days, weeks, and months to follow.

As I deposited the paper towel into the trash can and turned to walk back to my office, I glanced at Birdie's face, bent over the large tray of bread slices while she methodically brushed them one by one. Her features were set in lines at once mournful and indignant, and I knew that the taking in of the horrible truth concerning Susan Smith was to require excruciating effort on Birdie Freeman's part. Though she did not look at me when I passed her, she addressed me. "How a mother could do that, Margaret — it just doesn't make sense, does it? There's got to be something more to it than we've heard on the news." Clearly, she was still giving Susan Smith the benefit of the doubt.

No, I thought, though I did not speak aloud, *wanton cruelty and deception make no sense whatsoever in your safe and orderly world, Birdie Freeman. Had you sojourned in a strange land as I have, you would know that evil needs nothing, certainly nothing as cold and fixed as logic, to grow and thrive. Evil breeds upon itself and multiplies to horrific proportions.*

Had Birdie Freeman eaten at the same table with me, she would have expected from others no pleasant bread, no cup to quench her thirst, no strong hand to shield her from injury, no *reason* to explain corruption. Had her eyes seen what mine have seen, she could have easily envisioned manifold scenes of human depravity, including that of a young mother watching her innocent children, utterly dependent upon her, roll down a ramp into the dark waters of a lake.

It is the helplessness of the two boys — and all victims of all crimes — that incites me not to compassion but to anger. I recently read parts of Joyce Carol Oates's novel *Foxfire* and was drawn to its premise of *protection* by a society of friends. Although I put the book aside for its disturbing coarseness, I could not help contemplating the direction my life might have taken had such a society been available to me after my mother's death, had there been even one person to love and defend me, to seek retribution against my grandfather on my behalf.

But I seek no pity. There is security in having known the worst.

EVERY EVIL WORK
14

I shrink from the chapter at hand. While I
have been viewing it with dread from afar, as
if through a spyglass, I have been powerless
to stay its inexorable approach. Now that it
has arrived, I wish to skirt around it, if not to
flee from it altogether, at least to fend it off
while I grasp for other material to place
before it. Yet I know that my tale will fall
short of its mark if I guard this secret. It must
be told.

For years I have striven, on the one hand,
to eradicate from my mind the memories that
I am preparing to divulge, yet on the other,
to shelter them from such expunction. Such
ambivalence is common in cases of tragedy, I
suppose, and quite simple to strip to its
cause, for while the yearning to forget origi-
nates from the final tragedy itself — that
relatively brief moment in literal time of
inexpressible anguish — the pleasure of
remembering finds its source further back
and over a greater expanse of measurable

time. To forget the tragedy, one would have to erase from his mind all things relevant to it, for the ending is fused with the context. To divorce the tragedy from the prior happiness, therefore, becomes impossible, and in a sense, I believe, undesirable.

I admit, even as the reader must recognize, that these ramblings are merely additional tactics of postponement, but the reader must permit me to creep forth at my own pace.

Four years ago I read a novel by Mary Mc-Garry Morris titled *A Dangerous Woman.* The protagonist, a pathetic figure named Martha Horgan, was the dangerous woman. I was puzzled by the title at the outset of the story, for though Martha Horgan was many things — feeble-minded, clumsy, inept, despised, stubborn, unlovely — she did not seem in the least dangerous, that is, not at first. However, in the course of my reading, I soon understood that *because no one loved her,* Martha Horgan's final act in life could be nothing but destructive, to herself certainly but most likely to others as well. (One is not labeled "dangerous" if he brings harm only to himself.)

My predictions proved true, for by the end of the book Martha Horgan did indeed inflict severe and irreversible damage upon others. The thesis of Mary McGarry Morris's novel, as I see, is this: A person who knows no love is dangerous; that is, he is ripe for the carrying out of indefinably malicious and despicable acts against his fellowman. It matters not whether the mental faculties of the unloved individual are acute or sluggish. The potential danger is equally grave.

Miss Morris's book left its mark upon my mind, not only for its superlative integration of life and art but also for the posing of a timely question. Is one truly and perpetually accountable for his conduct? Was Martha Horgan's culminating crime to be laid at her feet, or was it the fault of others — her callous-hearted aunt, the man who gently but nonetheless knowingly misused her, the coworker who pointedly spurned her friendship, the great whole of society who should have taken note of her loveless state but did not?

Freedom from personal accountability is busily promoted in today's media, the word *victim* being bandied about at every turn. Lawyers for confessed murderers routinely dredge up and exhibit the unhappy circumstances of a client's past in an attempt to obscure the truth that a life was taken at the killer's hand. Was Martha Horgan guilty? Was Susan Smith guilty? Yes, I vehemently reply. An individual must bear the responsibility for his own actions.

Yet one could question — indeed one *has* questioned — whether my principles are consistent in matters closer to my own heart.

In recent months I have given considerable thought to my personal responsibility. To clarify, am *I* guilty? Though certainly I have not committed a capital offense, am I to be held culpable for lesser peccadilloes — for instance, my misanthropic spirit toward my fellowman? Or, given my history, am I not justified in withholding from others my faith and affection? I have Birdie Freeman to thank for reducing the question of grand-scale guilt to the daily allowances I make for myself — that is for my inhospitable, though harmless, behavior toward others — for it was she who put the point to me one day in February. But I shall come to this later.

Unlike Martha Horgan, I am not a dangerous woman, for I have known love. In fact, were she a living human instead of a fictional character, Martha Horgan would surely deem me a child of fortune, for I knew love two times before I reached the age of twenty.

My mother, were she living, would wish me to increase the number to three. "God loves you, Margaret," she whispered to me as a child each night at bedtime. Mother's favorite Bible passage was Psalm 103, a chapter that I had memorized in its entirety by the time I was six years old and that we frequently quoted together after supper in the evenings. When Mother died and left me alone, however, I grew to hate the words of the psalm, for I felt they mocked me and made light of the misery into which I was so suddenly pitched. Oftentimes in the deep of night at my grandfather's house, phrases from the passage would come to me, and I would rail against them. *"Forget not all his benefits! Who redeemeth thy life from destruction! Who satisfieth thy mouth with good things! So that thy youth is renewed like the eagle's! The Lord executeth righteousness and judgment for all who are oppressed! For as the heavens are high above the earth, so great is his mercy toward them that fear him! Bless the Lord, O my soul!"* I pulled the bedclothes over my head as I spat out the words and pronounced them lies.

At nighttime during those black years there festered within me a deep resentment toward my mother for having taught me such untruths and for having abandoned me. How could she have schooled me in empty promises, I reasoned, if she truly loved me? How could she have presented the canards of the Bible as facts? How could she have died and left me defenseless? At a level beyond my anger, however, I knew that she had loved me past all telling, and in the daytime I knew that she would have died to protect me, though ironically, it was her dying that left me vulnerable.

Concerning the Bible, many of its words are firmly rooted in my mind. Though I reject their message, I nevertheless value them for their style. I often borrow phrases from this trove of biblical language, at times unwittingly. For instance, I had completed three chapters of the manuscript that I am presently writing when I realized that the titles I had chosen for all three were phrases from various books of the Bible — Matthew, Galatians, and Proverbs, to name them specifically. The idea appealed to me as a unifying device, and I purposed to continue selecting chapter titles from the Bible. Concerning chapter titles in general, I have noted in recent years their regrettable absence in contemporary works. I suppose some editors may consider them to be an inessential, perhaps even adolescent, heralding of the material to come. *Nota Bene:* It is my wish, however, should my manuscript ever make its way to a professional editor, that the chapter titles be retained.

I must delay the advancement of my story no longer. Before I had reached my twentieth birthday, as I said, I had known love twice. My first love, of course, was that of my mother. This was a mutual love, both received and given in unstinting abundance.

Now for the second. The previous chapter, in which I reported Birdie's conduct during the shameful ordeal imposed upon the American public by Susan Smith, segues quite smoothly into the revelation that I am now at last ready to make known, for both include mother, child, and death by water.

I will state it now. Besides the love of a child for her mother, I have also known the love of a mother for her child. When I was eighteen years of age, I gave birth to a baby. Not having spoken of this in many years, I feel a shortness of breath; I smell the musty scent of fear; I hear the scrabbling of demons and the moaning of ghosts; I see the eerie flickering of uncertain lights as I enter the haunted house of my memories.

I was terrified for many reasons upon discovering that I was with child. Imagine yourself, if you will, as a girl of seventeen, utterly devoid of friendships with peers, teachers, neighbors, or relatives. Though required to attend church with oppressive regularity in the company of my grandparents and to present myself at various functions of the young people, I did not mingle well. The youth leader, an overeager man by the name of Lester Kirby, with the soft pink features of a toddler, told my grandparents that I seemed to intimidate the others with my standoffish attitude. I detested the church, I suspect, because of its high esteem of my grandfather, who was the elder in charge of financial disbursements. I viewed it as an altogether ignoble institution because of its failure to see and judge him for what he was.

At school I was shunned by teachers and fellow students alike, largely because of my supercilious manner toward the inferior instruction being passed off as education, but partly, I know now, because I had no idea how to go about making friends. I told myself that I did not *need* friends, but I would have given all that I had, including my considerable intellect — perhaps *especially* my intellect — to have had a single true friend to claim as my own. I often read of friendships, of course, and they seemed to me an exceedingly precious but elusive possession. I suppose my only friends were my books.

I was terrified, then, because I had no ally in my trouble, and I knew for a certainty that I had fallen headlong into trouble. I had learned by now that my grandmother was merely an extension of my grandfather, not as actively evil, but let us say willfully and adamantly ignorant. As a girl of thirteen, I had attempted one day to stammer out the truth to her about my grandfather's offenses toward me, only to have her pummel my ears soundly and at great length and then order me never again to open my foul lips against "such a man of God," as she called him.

She went on to impress upon me the debt of gratitude that I had accrued. "Your grandfather took me and your mother in when we didn't have hardly a shoestring between us," she said. "And he never once complained about having to support a child that wasn't his own — not once! And he didn't blame me, not ever, not a single time, for not being able to bear him any children to carry on his bloodline. He's a *Christian,* Margaret! You know that! Ask anybody! He's never once darkened the door of a saloon or so much as lit a cigarette! And here you are trying to soil his good name. You're a wretched child, Margaret, stubborn just like your mother. She broke your grandfather's heart when she sneaked away from home against his will, and I wouldn't have blamed him a bit if he'd refused to take you in when they tracked us down after the accident."

"I wish that he had refused," I whispered, and she struck me again.

"You don't deserve the good home we've given you!" she cried. "When they called us after the accident, your grandfather never even hesitated for a minute to think about taking you in! He welcomed you like you were his own flesh and blood. You better just fix whatever's wrong with you to make you so mean and ungrateful, Margaret. I won't have you spreading lies. Not one person would believe a little castoff like you anyway. You'd be taken away and locked up for libel and slander!"

The speech went on in this vein for some ten or fifteen minutes, after which my grandmother ordered me to the bathroom, where she placed in my palm a bar of soap and instructed me to "wash out your filthy mouth." She stood by grimly to oversee the procedure, and as I choked and frothed, she commanded that I rinse and repeat the process.

The only person at Latham County High who smiled at me upon occasion was Mr. Wadworth, my chemistry teacher. He was the only teacher, I might add, whose knowledge of his subject seemed to me sufficiently thorough to be beyond challenge. Perhaps I could have gone to Mr. Wadworth had I known how to initiate a conversation in anything other than a confrontational manner, but even then there existed the inalterable difficulty of his being a man. How did I know whether he could be trusted? In 1961 teen pregnancy was not the common occurrence of today. And one certainly did not confide in a male teacher concerning such a delicate matter. Yet I have often wondered how he would have responded.

After realizing with an appalling shock that I was carrying a child, I endured a day — November 7, 1961 — that I shall always equate with the word *panic.* I cringed to imagine the response of my grandparents upon learning of my condition. I could anticipate only two courses of action that they might take, and I could bear the thought of neither. Perhaps they would seek to terminate my pregnancy, after which time my life would resume as it had been, save perhaps for a more scrupulous monthly record keeping on my grandfather's part. As I had an indescribable phobia of medical procedures and had read frightening stories of the particular procedure required to destroy a fetus, I was terrified of this possibility. Or perhaps my grandparents would choose for me to bear the child. If so, I was certain that they would portray me to the community as a promiscuous rebel to whom they continued, in their great kindness and unrequited charity, to offer refuge and material aid. Were I to identify the father of the child, no one would believe me. If I did not, I would become the object of scorn and eventually pity as, Hester Prynne-like, I would bear my shame alone.

The reader of today must wish to ask me this: "Why did you stay in a place where you were so grossly and repeatedly mistreated?" In today's society of public assistance for abused women and children, of shelters for runaways, of hot lines for unwed mothers, it is perhaps easy to forget that these provisions were not available to the same degree some thirty or forty years ago.

Besides, I had no place to go. My grandparents had left their home in West Falls, Oregon, in 1925, a month after my grandfather had so mercifully taken to his bosom my grandmother and her four-year-old daughter — my mother — and had traveled by train to Marshland, New York, where they had settled, my grandfather having secured a position with a company that manufactured elevators. They had no relatives except those in Oregon, with whom they never corresponded and of whom I never heard them speak. When I asked my grandmother about her parents one day, I recall a clearly discernible cloud descending upon her spirit as she said faintly, "Oh, Margaret, all that was so long ago."

As for returning to one of the cities where I myself had lived as a child and trying to establish contact with a sympathetic acquaintance, this prospect appeared hopeless. I had, in fact, once written a letter to the motherly Mrs. Gault, my former neighbor in Ohio, but had never received an answer. Whether my grandfather intercepted the letter, I do not know, though I suspect this to be true. Or perhaps Mrs. Gault had moved by then, or my letter was misdirected by the postal service. Perhaps the missive, in which my pleas for rescue were polite though quite direct, is even today wedged under the rubber conveyor belt of an antiquated letter sorter in some distant city.

I suppose my story gives testimony to the sense of total entrapment that one feels in an incestuous home, for in spite of my superior academic prowess, I had never seen fleeing my grandparents' home as an option until November 8, 1961, at the age of seventeen years and five months. After the previous day of mad reckoning, however, my panic subsided and my course became plain. All at once I saw that I *must* flee. I suppose I do not fit the profile of the typical victim of incest, for what must become for many the nadir of disgrace — that is, the bearing of a child as a result of the sin — was for me the redeeming of my life from destruction, promised (but heretofore undelivered) in Psalm 103, of which I spoke earlier.

For two days after my decision to leave my grandfather's house, I feigned illness, both to employ my time during the day in the laying of my plans and to keep my grandfather from my bed at night. I had tried the pretense of various maladies many times before, but to no avail. Either my grandfather did not care that he might be causing me additional discomfort as well as exposing himself to illness, or he saw through my deception. This time, however, I threw off all inhibitions and staged a drama that was persuasive enough to drive him from my room.

Let me hasten to the conclusion of this chapter. What is yet to come is horrible to remember but essential to the revelation of my history, which impinges upon the larger story I am telling, that of Birdie Freeman. I will not recount the details of my departure and flight from Marshland, New York, but I came at last by an elaborately circuitous route to the city of Evansville, Indiana. I had chosen Evansville for its size. It was not so small as to invite close inspection by snooping neighbors, I reasoned, nor so large as to be the typical hiding place for a runaway and the target of police investigations in the event that a search for me were conducted.

By the age of seventeen, though slender as a birch withe, I had grown to a height of five feet nine inches. My grandfather, however, stood six inches taller than I and, although decidedly corpulent, was massively powerful even in his sixties. My facial features, though fair in the sense of classical symmetry, were customarily drawn down into lines of despondency and rage, my hatred being directed not only at my grandfather and the church but also, more aggressively, toward myself for my powerlessness; therefore, my youth was, I believe, well concealed. Binding and pinning my thick dark curls, I donned a scarf — that most naive of disguises — and thus passed for an adult woman.

My life for the following eight months is shameful to recall, for it was of necessity characterized by deceit. Having stolen from my grandparents the sum of three hundred dollars, I rented a single room in a boarding-house along the Ohio River in Evansville, Indiana. By day I found honest though menial work, which provided an adequate income for my few needs. By night I read, having located a public library even before I sought lodging, and listened to radio programs on the old box radio I had brought with me. Thus I regressed to the solitary life I had known as a child during my mother's daytime absences. For some time I called myself by mother's and father's middle names: Paula Andrew.

Whether my grandparents cried an alarm or attempted to trace my whereabouts following my departure, I never discovered. Pictures of missing children did not appear on milk cartons in 1961. Perhaps my grandfather sensed the risk of scandal if he set the law on my heels. Perhaps he thought after my years of silence that I would suddenly and publicly unburden myself of evidence too convincing to be dismissed.

I imagined, however, a throbbing network of interstate communication concerning my flight, and because I lived in continuous fear of being apprehended by uniformed authorities, I could not sleep well. Nevertheless, as I preferred the fear of being stalked and located to that of being routinely molested, I felt an odd sense of liberation in spite of the strictures of my new life.

Concerning the baby that I was carrying, I was, of course, frightened, not only by the process of childbirth but also by deep misgivings about the child itself. I often grew inutterably distressed as I reflected upon the genetic makeup of a child sired by my grandfather. As he was my step-grandfather, I had no cause to fear the idiocies caused by inbreeding, yet surely, I thought, it was folly to think that one conceived by an act of brutality would be untouched by the flaws of its heredity.

If it were a boy, would I not see in him certain bestial likenesses of my grandfather and thus abhor him? If it were a girl, would I not see her as a symbol of my own ill luck and victimization and thus loathe her as I often loathed myself? I saw the child within me as both savior and nemesis. I could not destroy it, yet I could not imagine loving it. I could not decide whether it would be better to abandon the infant after its birth or to clutch it possessively. Could a mother *hate* her own child? Was the child evermore to serve as an instrument of torture? My thoughts during these months were a vortex of confusion.

I am certain that in the vast span of history I was not the only seventeen-year-old girl to endure such circumstances. Surely somewhere in the records of mankind another young woman — strong, intelligent, comely — has been despoiled as rapaciously and unremittingly as was I, has subsequently found herself with child and, friendless, has made her own way of escape, subsisting by her wits, earnest toil, and subterfuge. Surely I was not the only young woman to be governed by a strange antinomy: to regard her unborn progeny with fear and bewilderment, oftentimes with a full measure of ill will and horror over what she was nurturing within herself, yet to consider the bond of mother and child sacrosanct and thus to reject any thought of severing the tie.

Except for the necessary business of housing and employment, I rarely spoke during these months. Others kept their distance, asking few questions. In that my work was always exemplary — I ironed, mended, typed, and cleaned — my reticence was overlooked and perhaps even appreciated by many who hired me. As the weeks passed and my condition became apparent, I was no doubt accounted worthless by many — a "lost cause" as they say — since unmarried mothers-to-be were more severely censured during the sixties than at present.

The only acquaintance I made during these bleak days was that of a solitary middle-aged Hispanic woman who occupied the room next to mine in the boardinghouse and with whom I shared the bathroom at the end of the hall, along with another woman whose racking, chronic cough could be heard all night. In the beginning the Hispanic woman was as wary of me as I of her, but as the days passed she began speaking to me gruffly in the hallway. "Good day this morning" or "Outside is not warm today." Her name, I learned from seeing her mail on the hall table, was Lucita Orozco. She was a large woman, nearly as tall as I, and broad of hip. One front tooth was missing; somewhat flat of face, she was not what one would call an attractive woman.

The landlord of the boardinghouse spoke to me one day in May, after my condition was made known to him, informing me that he allowed no tenants with children in his establishment. Though I had no plans at the time to do so, I told him that I would move before the baby was born. I did not, however, set about to make other arrangements, for as I had not seen a doctor during my pregnancy, I could make only a reasonable guess as to when the baby was due to be born. As it turned out, my guess was wrong by three weeks.

I will proceed quickly. The child was born at 3:55 a.m. on July 2, 1962. I had turned eighteen in June. At a quarter past ten the night before, I knocked on the wall between my room and Lucita's and cried out her name. Though I had not asked her earlier for help in my time of need, I believe that she was expecting my summons, for she appeared at my door within a minute's time, carrying in her arms two thin blankets and several towels. Lying on top of the stack of towels was a pair of scissors. Strangely, I still remember the scissors. They had painted handles of red and a curiously large square bolt that fastened the two blades together.

I had expected discomfort, of course, but was completely overcome by the intensity of the pain. Lucita was efficient and surprisingly gentle. Looking back upon the hours of my labor, I recall her black eyes above me. The only thing I remember her saying over the next six hours is this: "Baby will come, baby will come." For a while she held my hand so tightly that it ached. I was dimly aware of sounds: coughs from the woman at the end of the hall; the slamming of a car door outside; a muffled squeal that could have been laughter or fright; a faraway siren. In an age-old play Lucita and I were the only actors — no, not the only actors, for by the end another had made his entrance.

Though too weak for such a journey, I fled Evansville three days later, taking a bus to Bowling Green, Kentucky. I had been greatly frightened by a vivid dream of the landlord coming to my room, accompanied by my grandfather and the police. The taxi driver who transported me to the bus station carried my suitcase to the ticket window for me, and I carried Tyndall in a large canvas satchel. Miraculously, as if sensing the danger in attracting attention, Tyndall did not utter a cry.

It shames me today to remember that I never thanked Lucita for her comfort and aid. I did not even tell her good-bye. Six years after I left, however, I returned to Evansville for the brief space of ten months. I attempted to find Lucita, but she had moved away from the boardinghouse as had the former land-lord. The idea has suddenly come to me while typing these words that, though the likelihood is small, the possibility does exist that Lucita, who would now be in her seventies, could someday read what I am writing and understand it was my fear and youth that pushed all thoughts of gratitude from my mind. Perhaps, I tell myself, she has always understood this.

Thus was my child brought into the world. My apprehensions concerning my feelings for him were laid to rest the moment he was born. I was anointed with love for him. To say that I loved my baby instantaneously and profoundly seems but a pale shadow of the truth. The thought that branded itself upon my mind when Lucita placed him in my arms was this: *He is beautiful and innocent.* I named him for my father: Tyndall Andrew Bryce. From a department store in Bowling Green I purchased a blue album called *Baby's Firsts* and set about recording within its vellum pages the many wonders I observed daily. I bought a Kodak camera and interspersed my written account with snapshots, which I glued onto the pages.

It is a terrible mystery to me that the same

language, the same letters of the alphabet that I have used to report the marvel of his birth, must now be utilized to set on paper the pain of his death. On October 22, 1966, Tyndall died at the age of four.

I find it intolerable at this time to review the details of his death as if reciting a newspaper account — he was my son! — but to provide a conclusion for this chapter, I will record the barest of facts. Tyndall died two days after overturning upon himself a large cauldron of boiling water. He suffered unspeakably. He died, and I, too, truly wanted to die. For many months afterward I felt that every evil work had descended upon me to crush my heart and to siphon from my soul every drop of humanity.

A Far Country
15

"The abused child, not understanding the cruelty of his abuser, can only make sense of it by blaming himself. Since he must somehow be the cause of the abuse and since it continues, he becomes self-destructive and comes to think of himself as an unworthy person — doomed and stupid." This is the theoretical stuff of which self-help books are made.

Some years ago I read parts of two books on the subject of sexual abuse, though I have not admitted this to Joan, and in so doing saw glimpses of myself and my past. Though I did not need a book to tell me that my emotional rigidity, my wholesale distrust of others, my cynicism regarding religion, my perfectionism, my escape into the land of fiction, and the like were the direct results of my grandfather's lustful exploitation of me, I suppose it was some small consolation to read that the manifestations of my suffering were somewhat normal, if such a word may be used.

In other ways, however, I saw myself as atypical. For example, I did not deny what had been done to me. I had never pushed from my consciousness the dreadful knowledge of my grandfather's sins against me, though one of the books stated that "children who are victims of frequent sexual abuse refuse to accept the truth, setting up a blockade about their memories so that they can survive." My memory had no such blockade.

The other book claimed that "sadly, a child often continues to love the abusive adult, seeking ever more earnestly to win his favor." This, too, was untrue for me. Not for the briefest particle of time did I ever feel for my grandfather anything approaching love.

On the other hand, much of what I read in the two books to which I have referred rang of truth. However, I did not complete the reading of either book, most likely not because I disagreed with the authors on so many points but because the closeness and heat of the truth stifled me. Denial? Perhaps some would term it thus. I prefer to think of it as maintaining a sensible distance from danger.

I must return to Birdie Freeman, however. But first, to review: I lost my mother when I was thirteen. I was the victim of my grandfather's perversions between the ages of thirteen and seventeen. I fled from my grandparents' home at seventeen. I bore a son out of wedlock at eighteen, and I lost my son when I was twenty-two. A clinical summary of human damage, to be sure, but the tone is what I wish it to be, for as I have said, I am issuing no plea for sympathy. These are facts necessary to the understanding of Birdie's effect upon me.

Between the ages of twenty-two and the recent past (I turned fifty-one on June 6), I ceased to feel by an act of my will. After the death of my son, I lay on my bed one night and formed a picture of myself in my mind. I imagined that there ascended from my body a tattered apparition of sorts that I knew to be my heart, frail and wounded, which took the form of a limp gossamer garment as it hovered above my bed. I saw myself rise and reach for it, lay it flat upon the bed, and begin folding it with care. With each fold, the thickness of the fabric remained the same, however; that is, though its length and width decreased, there was no compensatory increase in the third dimension of depth. I continued to fold it until there lay upon the bed a tiny diaphanous square of a single layer.

In my vision I then opened a large wooden chest, placed the square of fabric within it, and closed the lid. I pushed the chest into a dark closet, the door of which I then locked with an iron key. Grasping the key within my fist, I applied upon it such superhuman force that when I released it, there fell to the floor, compacted and transmogrified, a small but heavy lump of ironstone. I then saw myself recline once again upon the bed, at which time the stone rose from the floor, began a slow, searching orbit about the room, picking up speed until at last, bulletlike, it found its mark within my bosom.

Thus was my heart locked away and the key buried, so to speak. I had cut off all access and raised the drawbridge to my castle, for having been savagely attacked and irreparably injured, I intended to see that it would never happen again.

However, I had not counted on Birdie Freeman's assault upon my citadel. There is a lovely poem by X. J. Kennedy titled "On a Child Who Lived One Minute," which, though mourning death, gives voice in its closing line to the great wonder of life as the narrator marvels that "so much could stay a moment in so little." I only recently came across the poem, and I shuddered with the thrill of an idea well put, for of course it brought to mind first my son "so little," whose four years of life were "so much," and second, my friend Birdie Freeman, from whose small frame emanated such quiet and far-reaching explosions of kindness. "How far that little candle throws his beams!" cries

Portia in Shakespeare's *Merchant of Venice.*

Now to resume the chronicle of my acquaintance with Birdie. It was in November, perhaps two weeks following the drowning of the two young boys in Union, South Carolina, that Birdie latched upon the idea of hostessing a tea party for the lunchroom staff. She spoke of it frequently over a period of many days, discussing with us the particulars of time and place. Her ardor was so touchingly childlike that, although the prospect of spending an hour socializing with my three co-workers filled me with dread, I could not find it within me to dampen her joy by declining the invitation.

"I want all three of you to be guests in my house at the *same time,*" she told us early in the planning stages. "And I've decided that the best time for it would be in the early afternoon before Francine's children will be needing her at home. If we could find a day when the cleanup after lunch wouldn't take as long, we could try to leave here at one-thirty, if we *could,* and then get to my house and have our little party between then and three or so. Would that work for you, Francine, honey? Or would it be better on a Saturday?"

Francine pinched her nostrils together and replied in a clownish, high-pitched voice. "Any day's hunky-dory. I'll come for food anytime!" In a more sober tone she added,

291

"But I guess a weekday would really be better 'cause our house is a zoo on Saturdays. Some weekends I think our trailer's gonna tip right off those cement blocks! It wouldn't really matter if I wasn't there right when the kids got home from school 'cause Champ knows where the key is and can ride herd for a little bit if I warn him ahead of time." Francine's children have unusual names: Gala, Champ, BoBo, and Watts.

Birdie nodded thoughtfully and, with all the deliberation of a parliamentarian, asked if Wednesday, November 16, would be suitable to our schedules. "Since I help out with the school choir on Mondays and Thursdays," she said, "and then give a piano lesson every Tuesday and Friday, I guess that leaves just Wednesday for me, unless I switched my schedule around some, which I sure *could* do if we needed to." True to her promise, Birdie had never spoken of my piano lessons in the presence of Algeria and Francine, and even now she did not break faith either by word or glance.

As it turned out, the lunch menu for November 16 specified hot dogs, tater tots, and fruit cocktail — a meal requiring less time for cleanup than others — and thus the date for Birdie's tea party was set. When Francine suggested that we all ride together in her car, I immediately spoke up. "I will drive my own car." For Birdie's sake I would undergo the ceremony at her house, but I knew that I could not endure confinement as a passenger in Francine's car. I had seen the backseat of her car littered with pop cans and Hardee's sacks and had witnessed her erratic driving on a number of occasions.

On the appointed day I purposely lagged behind, telling Birdie that I would follow as soon as I cleared my desk and deposited the day's cash in the bank. By shaving ten minutes off the beginning of the party, I reasoned, and perhaps taking my leave before the others at the end, I would fulfill my duty to attend yet spare myself some degree of discomfort, of feeling hedged about and scrutinized at close range.

After my stop at the bank that day, the drive to Birdie's house seemed shorter than usual, most likely because I longed to forestall my arrival. I recall the rich late-autumn blue of the sky above the treetops, as if layered thickly with tempera, and the lingering color of the leaves, though for the most part muted russets by now, as I slowly drove through the streets of Filbert and turned onto Highway 11 toward Birdie's house.

I was well aware of the fact that the familiar route was altered this day by the absence of Birdie herself in the front seat of my car. I had grown so accustomed to her affable chatter every Tuesday and Friday as we drove to her house for my piano lesson that the silence seemed chill and foreboding, thus magnifying my reluctance concerning the tea party. I could muster no interest this afternoon in listening to an audiotape, in spite of the fact that I had recently borrowed from the Derby Public Library a recorded reading of the essays of Virginia Woolf, which I had found most intriguing.

As I passed Shepherd's Valley Cemetery and turned into the narrow driveway leading to Birdie's house, I glanced toward the rows of headstones to my left, thinking as I did so of the blessed serenity afforded by burial plots: no obligations of communal festivity, certainly, but even more enticing, no futile regrets, no corrosive memories. At this very moment Birdie's voice came to mind, for scarcely a week earlier she herself had gazed toward the cemetery and had said in soft, lubricated tones, "It sure is peaceful around here." Though it seemed to me that such a remark was an invitation to jest, I did not reply. Had Thomas heard her, he would have retorted with a clever, though outworn, quip, "Yessiree, I betcha folks are *just dyin'* to buy a lot next door to you!"

I parked my car behind Francine's maroon Pontiac, the muffler of which I noted appeared to be not only insecurely affixed but also riddled with ragged perforations. Girding myself for the trial of sociability before me, I approached Birdie's front door, which was standing open as if awaiting my arrival. I heard from within a harmonic chord of combined laughter, followed by an exclamation of delight from Birdie.

"Oh, good, here's Margaret! Now we can start!"

She appeared at the screen door, beaming euphorically, and as I entered she crooked her elbow through mine as if we were partners in a square dance and escorted me to the royal blue recliner. Her action must have given rise to the same comparison in Francine's mind, for Francine, who was sitting next to Algeria on the yellow sofa, began to clap her hands and chant, "Swing your lady round and round, do-si-do and promenade!" Though I ignored her, or possibly *because* I ignored her, Francine continued clapping after I was seated and even attempted singing a snatch of "Turkey in the Straw," off key, of course. Algeria sat stiffly, I noted, glaring at the Nehi Soda sign on the wall above the bookcase. From all appearances she was as ill at ease as I at the thought of a tea party.

Birdie took a small, framed picture from Algeria's lap and brought it over to me. "We were just having ourselves a laugh over my wedding picture," she said. "See what Mickey did?" The youthful bride in the picture was unmistakably Birdie; though there were notable differences — a slightly fuller face, for instance, and loose, midlength hair in a tumble of curls — the pronounced malocclusion of the front teeth set to rest any question concerning her identity. A similarity struck me upon studying the photo. In her homeliness Birdie resembled a diminutive Eleanor Roosevelt.

In the picture Birdie wore a floor-length white gown as befitting a bride but with no adornment of lace, seed pearls, or the like. It appeared to be made of plain cotton, for it had no sheen. Upon her head was a laurel of entwined ivy and flowers, and in her left hand she clasped what looked to be a small white Bible. The expression upon her face was one of exquisite triumph at having won a prize of great worth. Her *prize* in this case — the man wearing a black suit and standing next to her in the photo, whose dark hair rose above his forehead in a slick crest, whose countenance betokened the same victorious attainment as her own — was holding his right hand aloft in the pose of one taking an oath. Very clearly imprinted across his palm was the message *Help! She Snagged Me!*

I made no comment, and Birdie took the picture from me again and set it upon the coffee table. "My husband's a real cutup sometimes," she said, sitting down on the edge of the other recliner and looking directly at me. "I never know what he's got up his sleeve. I was telling Francine and Algeria that on our honeymoon he just *insisted* that I

296

order the lobster at this seafood restaurant in Mobile. Then he got up to go to the lavatory — I *thought* — but really he went back to the kitchen and talked them into putting a *live* lobster on a plate with one of those fancy silver covers on it. A little later, here came the waiter bringing it out."

She looked up at the ceiling and laughed with abandon, laying her hands upon her cheeks. "I don't think he expected me to react like I did!" she said at last. "I *screamed* right out loud and threw that lid straight back over my shoulder and pushed my chair back so hard I lost my balance and landed on the floor! The waiter felt just awful, and Mickey did, too, really, except when he jumped up to help me off the floor, he *stepped* on the lobster, which I had knocked clean off the plate, and you could hear its shell *crack!*"

She began fanning her face with both hands, adding, "It was sure a circus there for a while! The lid I had slung landed on somebody else's table and knocked some lady's plate of spaghetti right in her lap. When we finally got settled down again and everything was cleaned up and set straight, Mickey looked at me across the table, and we just burst out laughing. I'm surprised the manager of that restaurant didn't throw us out! There's no telling what all those other people thought about us. And Mickey didn't help any when he stood up and said, 'You'll have to excuse my wife, folks. This is the first time she's been out in public since they let her out of the asylum.' "

Francine hooted and slapped her knee. "Now *that's* the funniest part of the whole thing! Didn't you just want to choke him?"

Birdie smiled and shook her head. "No, not really. I knew for sure I'd never have to complain about life being boring with Mickey around. And it sure hasn't been one bit boring, not in the whole twenty-eight years." As if recalling the purpose of our gathering, she stood up. "Well, I better quit talking or we're going to run out of time. Now, does anybody want coffee?"

When Birdie left the room, the three of us sat silently for several moments before Francine said, "She's something else, isn't she?"

"She crazy," Algeria said. "Any man do that to me, I'd kill 'im." They both glanced at me as if it were my turn to advance the conversation, but I said nothing. By means of a swift mathematical calculation, it had suddenly struck me that while Birdie Freeman had been good-naturedly contending with the adolescent pranks of her new husband twenty-eight years ago, I had been moving through my days joylessly benumbed, having locked away the blue book in which I had stored the written treasures of Tyndall's short life and having sealed my heart from communion with others.

This line of thought brought to mind an observation recorded in William Styron's lengthy novel *Sophie's Choice,* during which Stingo, the young narrator, pauses to reflect upon the cruel absurdity of *time,* that incomprehensible dimension that can simultaneously accommodate both the sublime and the sordid, the divine and the damnable.

I, too, have pondered this same mystery many times, the most memorable of which occurred in 1966 on the day I returned to my apartment after having left the newly dug grave of my son. By some monstrous coincidence, as I approached the entrance of the building, there exited a woman whom I had never seen and in whose arms was cradled an infant. Behind her, holding the door open for me to enter, a man, her husband presumably, called to her, "Hadn't you better cover up his head, Brenda? Wouldn't want him to catch his death, you know. He's the only one we've got." Indeed, the same millisecond of time can give birth to acts both poisonous and regenerative, both craven and noble, both trivial and momentous, as well as all gradations between.

Incidentally, although Styron's novel was marred with what I judged to be gratuitous vulgarity and unrealistic excesses of behavior, I felt a powerful kinship with Sophie, especially so when she pointed to her heart and declared, "It has been hurt so much, it has turned to stone." Furthermore, like myself, Sophie had given up on the idea of God.

A few minutes later Birdie reentered the living room, slowly pushing a serving cart. We all watched her as if stupefied. Perhaps none of us had seen such a cart put to its intended use. I admit that I had not. When she encountered the raised edge of the blue braided rug positioned in front of the recliner in which I sat, causing the tea in the glass pitcher to slosh wildly, Algeria rose to her feet and said, "Wheel's caught. Here, push it back." When the cart had come to rest in the middle of the room, Birdie laid her hands together, patted them lightly in a series of small circular motions as if flattening a round of dough, and smiled at us all. "All right, ladies," she said, "I think I have it all here, and if nobody minds, I'll say a blessing on our refreshments and our time together."

I did not close my eyes but only lowered my gaze. Though I did not look at Birdie, I heard her words clearly and have retained them in my memory since they were uttered, with perhaps minor alterations in phrasing. "My Father, you see us gathered here and you know what's in our hearts and minds. Thank you for this food and thank you for my friends. Thank you for Francine and her sweet, happy way and for Algeria and her big, kind heart and for Margaret — she's such a good, strong leader, Father, and so smart and talented. Please give us all a nice time today and help us to grow closer to each other as we work together this year and to learn to love each other more and more."

At this point in my text, I must interpolate that Birdie's method of evangelization — it was no secret to me that such was her life's objective — was seductive, whether by design or timidity I knew not. She spun a silvery web of crafty, ingratiating kindnesses in which to catch her prey unawares. No sermons by way of speech, not in the early stages of beguilement, at least, but only strand after sticky strand of ensnaring good works, beautiful and shining, especially to those whose lives were sullied and worn with defeat. I was wary, however, and saw her tricks for what they were. Though gradually and ineluctably she began in the early days of our acquaintance to bore an aperture into my "box," as she later termed it, I was nevertheless most vigilant. I believe I sensed from the beginning that she would stop at nothing, that roadblocks would only spur her to search for back alleys by which to insinuate herself into the lives of others.

The menu of refreshments on the serving cart was meager, though appealing in both appearance and taste. Birdie first offered to each of us a small crystal plate, a dessert fork, and a white linen luncheon napkin embroidered with clusters of lavender grapes. We all sat mutely, as if the formality of her actions and the accouterments of the tea service had deposited us in a foreign land. She moved about with a sacramental air.

We served ourselves as Birdie circulated among us, proffering each platter of refreshments and keeping up a steady patter of polite talk. First she said, "These little cookies are called cream wafers, and Mickey said to tell you that you *ought* to at least try one because even if they look a little washed out and underdone, they'll just melt in your mouth. But if you don't like them after just one, he said not to worry because he'll eat your share after he gets home from work. They're his favorite cookie of all the ones I've ever made."

Then, "This is praline candy. I sure hope you all like pecans. That's fine, Francine, take as many as you like, honey. Mickey got the pecans from somebody at church who has trees in his yard but doesn't like to fool with them. Mickey cracks them all for me and shells them so I can put them in the freezer and use them all year. He just got these and shelled them last week, though, so they're not the frozen ones."

And finally, "These are little squares of raspberry jam cake, and I've got some Cool Whip for the top if anybody wants it. Here, Margaret, take a bigger one than that. You don't have enough on your plate to even *taste*.

One of our neighbors behind us started trying to grow some raspberries in his yard a
few summers ago, and he had a real nice little
crop this past summer and gave us several
pints. You might know who he is — Mervin
Lackey, the owner of the plant nursery. That
man can make anything grow! Mickey keeps
telling him he needs to work on developing a
money tree so we can all quit work."

Algeria was the only one who drank coffee,
and we all watched as Birdie poured it from
a green ceramic teapot into a pale pink china
cup. Birdie, Francine, and I drank iced tea
poured into small cobalt blue glasses from a
clear glass pitcher. In spite of the fact that
few of Birdie's dishes seemed to match, the
appearance of the tea cart and Birdie's dainty
ministrations had created an ambiance of
elegance far removed from the lunchroom
kitchen at Emma Weldy. Even Francine, the
only guest who appeared to be capable of
speech, had now shed her jester's guise and
was behaving somewhat decorously.

"I'd sure like to hear you play something
for us on your piano before we have to go,"
Francine said to Birdie. "I took lessons when
I was a little girl but hated 'em like everything. Never could keep the notes straight
and about made my teacher pull her hair out.
I think she must've begged my mother to let
me quit." Francine opened her mouth and
inserted an entire cream wafer as if it were a

large coin in a wide slot.

"Well, I guess I can play something in a little bit," Birdie said. She took a small bite of the praline candy and chewed quietly for a moment, as if lost in speculation. "But maybe somebody else would like to play, too," she suggested, smiling innocently at all three of us. "Or sing?"

"Not me!" stated Francine. "Not on your life! I already told you how bad I was. I don't want to make a fool out of myself!" Francine looked over at Algeria, who was staring into her cup of coffee. "You don't play the piano, do you, Algeria?"

Algeria jerked her head sideways and said, "Nuh-uh!"

"How 'bout you, Margaret?" asked Francine, addressing me. "You play the piano any?"

I spoke with even tones, looking straight at Birdie. "I am certain that Birdie is the only proficient recitalist among us," I said.

"We could all sing something," Birdie said brightly. "I have a little book of favorite songs that's a lot of fun. Mickey and I sing straight through it sometimes."

Francine forgot her manners and laughed in a braying sort of way, her mouth full of jam cake. "Now *that* would be a sight, for all four of us to *sing* something together!" How characteristic of Francine to confuse the senses; though I feel confident in asserting that she had never heard the term *synesthesia,* she often inadvertently put the poetic technique to use in her speech with such ejaculations as "That color of orange stinks to high heaven!" or "Mr. Solomon was yellin' like a hot pepper!" or, as just mentioned, describing the singing of a song as a "sight."

"Do you sing, Algeria?" Birdie asked. "I imagine you have one of those real low, smooth singing voices. I don't know what it is about women like Ella Fitzgerald and Mahalia Jackson and that woman who used to sing 'When the Moon Comes over the Mountain,' but they're just so rich and full of *feeling.* White people can't usually hold a candle to them."

No one responded immediately, for I believe we were stunned, living as we do in an era in which racial differences are minimized. Algeria took a long sip of coffee and then said, "Lots of ways white people can't hold a candle to us."

Though Algeria's face was empty of expression, somehow Birdie knew that the remark was undergirded with humor, and she boldly picked up the challenge and shot back a playful rejoinder. "Well, now, just listen to you cutting down white people, and here all this time I thought you were so nice and fair minded." She laughed and shook her finger at Algeria. "But I'll tell you one thing, Algeria. I sure wouldn't want to get into any contests with *you*. You could show me up in almost everything!"

Turning to me, she said, "Margaret, I don't think we ever told you, did we, about that day last week when everything just stopped all of a sudden. I was using the meat slicer, and Francine was heating up soup, I believe, and we had rolls in the warmer, and all kinds of things going. You were standing out back talking to one of the deliverymen about that late order, and Algeria went to run something through the dishwasher when all of a sudden . . . pop! Everything shut down. And without so much as an uh-oh, Algeria walks over to the fuse box just as calm as if she was strolling to the park and opens it up and takes care of the problem like it was one plus one equals two." Francine was nodding in agreement as she bit into a praline candy and then examined it appreciatively.

Birdie exhaled a sigh of admiration and looked at Francine. "Remember how *we* just froze in our tracks when everything stopped working? I thought it was some big catastrophe and was wondering how we'd ever get lunch ready on time. I never even thought of it being just a *fuse!* But Algeria had it fixed before we even had time to say, 'Oh, my goodness.' "

Though Algeria grunted and said, "Wadn't nothin'," it was plain to me that Birdie had won yet another crumb of Algeria's hoarded affections.

An odd assortment we were in our white uniforms that day, seated around Birdie's tea cart in her living room, partaking of her cream wafers, praline candy, and jam cake, all of us but Birdie feeling removed from our element while she labored with felicity toward her self-appointed goal, not only of drawing us one by one to her heart but also of fusing the four of us into a unit, like the leaves of a lucky clover.

Before we left, Birdie seated herself at the piano, first adjusting the height of the stool, for I suppose she had not sat upon it since my lesson the previous afternoon, and Francine, Algeria, and I stood behind her as she played for us Beethoven's "Für Elise," a piece so common that I was at first disappointed at her selection. Because it is not a technically advanced piece (I myself have begun playing it this summer with some success), it is often played sloppily or with a glib facility that renders it trite, as if trilled out by the mechanical gears of a music box.

Birdie, however, performed the piece for us that day with a simple grace that evidenced her respect for both the art and form of the piece itself and for music as a whole. I shall never again hear "Für Elise" without imagining the small, agile fingers of Birdie Freeman upon the keyboard. And I shall never hear its final chord without remembering Francine's vapid exclamation, accompanied by an awkward parody of a ballroom waltz, during which she bumped against the serving cart and nearly upset it, thus shattering the mood of silent beauty. "Man alive, that makes me want to dance!" she cried. "You can really tear it up to beat the band, Birdie!"

Birdie laughed at Francine's antics and waved off her praise with a motion as if swatting at flies. "Oh, honey," she said, "my playing is nothing compared to somebody who's really good. I sure do like music, but I didn't take lessons very long." I had not known this. Although she had once told me that she wished she could take her students "further along," it was my assumption that Birdie had studied piano at some length in her past.

"Huh!" said Algeria. "Sounds like to me you plenty good." She raised her own broad hands and studied them with a scowl. "Couldn't never get *my* old fingers to learn somethin' like that."

Pointing to the wall above the piano, Francine asked suddenly, "Do you cross-stitch, Birdie?" She indicated the cross-stitched poem titled "Gifts from the Wildwood," which I mentioned in an earlier chapter.

"Well, you're not going to believe it," Birdie said, "but Mickey did that one. He's got a real eye for art, Mickey does." She had told us this before. "A couple of years ago," she continued, "a friend of mine at church —

he's our choir director, actually — gave me a book of poems by a Carolina poet. That's his name there at the bottom of the poem — Archibald Rutledge. Doesn't that sound like a real gentleman? Anyway, I didn't know much about poetry, and I still don't, but I just fell in love with this little poem and showed it to Mickey, and we talked about it and read it out loud and what have you, and then the next thing I know he's gone and started working it up and adding the trees and flowers and all that without a pattern or anything! I guess it's not a real masculine thing to do, but it doesn't bother Mickey. He's got a real artistic streak in him. People kid him about it, but he just lets it roll right off."

She motioned to the recliners and added, "Sometimes the two of us sit here in the evenings and do needlepoint or cross-stitch together." Frankly, although Francine and Algeria seemed to lap up every detail about the multitudinous quirks of Birdie's husband, I had long since begun to weary of them. The little man seemed far too jaunty and unconventional, and Birdie's undisguised fondness for him grated upon my nerves. We all studied the cross-stitched picture quietly before Algeria released what I took to be a disbelieving grunt. "Mmm, mmm! Can't feature no man doin' that," she said.

As it was almost three o'clock, I moved

toward the door, and Algeria followed me. Francine said, "Fiddlesticks, I guess this means the party's done!" and followed Algeria out the door, jabbering as if inebriated. "A tea party! I can't believe it! This was something else! I can't remember the last time I was at a tea party — probably when I was about eight years old! My cousin Rhonda Jo used to have a little set of dishes, and we'd spend all day dressin' up in our mamas' high heels and earbobs and playin' like we were grown-ups! And now me and Rhonda Jo are real grown-ups, and she even had a hysterectomy last year — a *complete* one." And so forth.

Birdie trailed along at the rear of our line, following us down the sidewalk to our cars, offering snippets of conversation when Francine's flood tide of words at last subsided. I heard her tell Francine that Mickey helped to take care of the cemetery, trimming around the headstones with his weed-eater and discarding wilted flowers. She had never told me this. I heard her tell Algeria that she'd be praying for her brother Sahara. By this I surmised that Sahara was once again in jail. His intermittent incarceration was, I believe, a chief source of Algeria's grievances against government and society in general, for she had charged upon more than one occasion that Sahara had never been "given a chance" in life.

As I opened the door of my car, I glanced across to where Birdie stood at the edge of the sidewalk, nodded my head, and said stiffly, "Thank you for the refreshments."

She waved at me most enthusiastically across the gravel driveway, as if my thanks had given rise within her to a great swell of emotion, and her mouth gaped with a sudden smile of immodest proportions. "Oh, I meant to tell you, Margaret, I'm going to bring you a book tomorrow!" she called. "I plan to finish it tonight, and I want to see how you like it. Thank you for coming! I sure do value your friendship."

Suddenly resentful and perhaps fearful of her friendly, grasping manner, I got into my car and, with a violent twist of my key in the ignition, started the engine. After backing into the turn space, I depressed the accelerator and shot off down the driveway as though eager to remove myself to a far country. I decreased my speed almost immediately, however, when gravel began spewing from beneath the tires of my car. I could well imagine Francine in a fit of giggles behind me saying, "Man alive, look at Margaret put the pedal to the metal, would you?"

An Expected End
16

It was only two days after Birdie's tea party that Thomas offered a startling proposition. At half past four on Friday afternoon, November 18, I heard Thomas enter the kitchen door. He was whistling "Careless Love," a mountain folk song of which he is fond. At the time I was kneeling beside the bathtub, scrubbing a panel of Venetian blinds. Though I dust my Venetian blinds each week, I feel it is important to wash them thoroughly at least twice a year. A solution of vinegar and ammonia works well. I was almost finished with the panel, lacking only two more slats.

I heard him stop at the bathroom door and heard his customary intake of air before broaching a matter of import. "Rosie," he said, "we're going to eat supper over at the Field Pea tonight."

I replied without turning my head. "I have made vegetable soup for our supper. It is simmering in the Crockpot."

"I know it," he said. "I saw it in the kitchen.

Smells good, too. But it'll keep. We can have it tomorrow."

I raised the intensity of my voice slightly. "There is no reason to waste money when our supper is already prepared for us here at home," I said. I readjusted the towels that I had laid beneath the blinds in the bathtub so as not to scratch the porcelain.

"Joan called me at the hardware store a little bit ago," Thomas said, "and she wants us to meet her at the Field Pea at six. Says she's bringin' a friend. I told her we'd do it."

I set my sponge down, turned off the trickle of water, and stood up to face Thomas. "You accepted an invitation for us to eat at a restaurant without taking into consideration my wishes?" I asked. I cradled one upturned palm in the other, holding them close to my apron so that the water from my rubber gloves would not drip onto the bathroom floor.

"Aw, now, *considerin' you* is just exactly what I *was* doin', Rosie — thinkin' of all the cookin' you do day after day and decidin' you was due a treat," Thomas said, averting his eyes from mine and craning his neck to see into the bathtub. "What's that you're cleanin' now? The inside of the furnace? Next thing I know, you'll be takin' my truck apart and totin' the pieces in here to scrub."

This was typical of Thomas. When calculating himself to be at a disadvantage in a confrontation, he will try to divert his opponent's attention and leaven the mood with humor. His humor is of a lowly form, however, most often relying upon exaggeration for its effect. He is also fond of the pun.

"You know that I detest eating in public restaurants," I said.

He laughed inanely and smote his thigh. "Well, then, just make believe it's a *private* restaurant, and you'll be okay!"

"I will not allow you to evade my objections with your juvenile retorts," I said.

There was a lengthy pause while his face took on an expression of mock wonder. "Well, I'll be John Brown," he said at last. "Is *that* what I was doin'? I just thought I was cuttin' up. I had no idea I was invadin' your objects with . . . whatever it was you said." Clad in a pair of faded denim jeans and a blue flannel shirt, the hem of which was untucked on one side, his eyes wide with feigned incredulity, Thomas looked like a grown Tom Sawyer hearing of some new superstition.

When especially infuriated by Thomas's circumlocution in the rare instances that we have what is termed a face-off, I have been driven to draw unflattering comparisons, and I did so now. "Someday you must come to Emma Weldy and engage in a conversation with Francine Perkins," I said. "The two of you could amuse each other for hours."

Though he knew Francine's identity, hav-

314

ing observed her and even spoken casually to her when he had come by the school cafeteria on some small errand, he pretended to have a lapse of memory. "Let's see . . . Francine — ain't she that *real smart* gal that's real nice and real funny that everybody likes so much? And I remind you of her, huh? Well, I'm real flattered, Rosie."

My neck muscles were so taut I could almost feel them quivering. I turned around and once again knelt beside the bathtub. "I am not going to the Field Pea for supper tonight or any night," I said, picking up the sponge and attacking with fresh vigor a slat of the blinds, a slat I had already cleaned thoroughly.

Thomas's answer came promptly. He had dropped his jocular tone. "Well, then, you'll have to call Joan and tell her yourself 'cause I told her we'd be there at six, and she's expectin' us and has it all set with her friend. I don't aim to be the one to spoil it for her, so you do the callin'. Tell her *you* ain't comin'." I heard him turn to exit, then pause to add, "She might be wantin' to know why you're backin' out, so maybe you better think up what excuse to tell her." I heard him walk through the kitchen and close the back door behind him, then the thud of his work boots as he descended the steps to the yard.

I took his remarks to mean that he intended to be present at the Field Pea at six o'clock regardless of my decision. I believe it is accurate to say that in that moment I became unreasoning in my anger. For the next thirty or forty minutes, I crashed about, first hanging the blinds with a great clatter to drip-dry over the bathtub, then dragging the vacuum cleaner out of the hall closet and yanking it along behind me as I furiously guided the power nozzle over the carpet in violent thrusts, stopping periodically to pull pieces of furniture away from the walls.

Part of my turmoil, I could not deny, was due to the fact that Joan had telephoned Thomas instead of me, an act that I knew not quite how to interpret. I suspected, however, that she had anticipated my dissent and had wanted to relieve herself of the business of countering my protests. The thought of being considered predictably prickly rankled me somewhat, I suppose.

In addition, what I viewed as Thomas's burgeoning assertiveness vexed me further. As I have said, ever since my frightened dash to the hospital emergency room in October, a subtle change had crept into our interaction with each other. Perhaps he had detected a shift of attitude on my part, though I toiled diligently, and I believe successfully, to conceal any trace of the self-consciousness arising from the awareness of my feelings on that day. Nevertheless, since that time he had gradually begun in his dealings with me to put himself and his ideas forward with more confidence. Whereas once he had been reliably timid in the face of my displeasure, he now varied in his responses from teasing parries to earnest expostulations to near reproofs. I felt as though I were being driven into corners on a fairly regular basis. This, of course, called for new reactions on my part. I was not accustomed to backing down.

The ritual of vacuuming at last worked its steadying influence upon my composure so that by the time I was ready to begin on the kitchen floor, I was reconsidering my course of action concerning the appointment with Joan at the Field Pea.

As I was disengaging the power nozzle to attach the brush for hard surfaces, Thomas reentered the kitchen through the back door. By now it was twenty minutes past five o'clock. I suppose that during his absence he had been puttering in the storage shed in the backyard, for his truck had never left the driveway. Without speaking, he stepped over the vacuum cleaner in the doorway and proceeded into his bedroom, most likely to change his clothes. I noted that his blue flannel shirt was now completely untucked.

I had not telephoned Joan, nor did I mean to, for I would not be coerced into declining an invitation that I had not accepted. If I stayed home, Thomas would have to inform Joan of the fact upon his arrival at the restaurant. Two ideas had already begun to stir within me, however, that would eventually lead to my relenting in the matter of accompanying Thomas to the Field Pea. First was the thought of Joan's disappointment, for I believed that she truly desired my presence, and I further knew that I cared enough for her to weigh solemnly the matter of disrupting her plans, and second was a swelling curiosity concerning the friend who was to be her escort for the evening. Was this the other man, besides her father, to whom she had referred earlier?

In the end, of course, I went. I vacuumed the kitchen speedily and returned the machine to the hall closet. Though I usually mop the kitchen floor immediately after vacuuming it, I decided to postpone the task until the following day. As I closed the door of the hall closet, Thomas emerged from his bedroom, wearing only his loose undershorts and a clean undershirt, and made for the bathroom. After he had closed the bathroom door, I stood outside it and spoke firmly. "Though I do not *wish* to do so, I have decided to go with you."

I heard Thomas suck in his breath, but he did not speak at once. As I turned toward my own bedroom, however, I heard the sound of water filling the bathroom sink and Thomas's voice above it. "I'll be done in just a minute so you can get in here." His tone was neutral, neither overly eager nor smug.

At ten minutes before six o'clock we were en route. Thomas was driving my Ford since I will not ride in his pickup truck, which is always liberally cluttered with the appurtenances of his vacuum repair business. We spoke very little as we drove toward the Field Pea, located along Highway 11 between Filbert and Derby — barely a mile, in fact, past Shepherd's Valley Cemetery and Birdie's house.

My aversion to eating in restaurants is long-standing. On *each* of the few occasions of public dining in which I have personally engaged, I have seen overwhelming evidence of a careless disregard for decent standards, both in the handling and preparing of the food itself and in the general upkeep of the establishment. As I told Thomas the last time we patronized a restaurant, which I believe occurred some seven or eight years ago, no one should have to *pay* to be disgusted, as that experience generally comes free of charge. On that occasion, I recall that I ate only a minuscule portion of my dinner and even then suffered from indigestion. The fiasco had been set into motion when I noticed a fly — a common, filthy housefly rubbing its legs together — atop the broccoli florets at the salad bar.

As we passed the cemetery, I glanced toward Birdie's house. There appeared to be no one at home, for there was no car in the driveway and only the porch light was burning. Birdie and Mickey were most likely attending yet another church activity, I thought, such as those that I frequently overheard Birdie describing to Francine and Algeria in the school kitchen.

Only days earlier Birdie had given a detailed account of an upcoming event that she had called "the annual Soupfest" to be held on the Sunday evening following Thanksgiving. "Everybody's going to bring a big pot of soup," she had said, "and after church we'll have us a soup supper back in Fellowship Hall. Lots of people bring muffin tins to eat out of so they can fill up all the little cups with samples of the different soups."

She had gone on to invite Francine and Algeria to visit her church that night, with their families, of course. Algeria had mutely declined with a shake of her head, but Francine said she would "think it over," expressing doubt, however, that she could "drag Champ away from the TV set on a Sunday night, 'specially not to go to *church!*" Then she had laughed with a high-pitched whinny and said, "I betcha everybody makes *turkey* soup from their leftover Thanksgiving dinner, don't they?" Birdie had replied that she was not roasting a turkey this year, for she and Mickey had been invited to their neighbors' home for dinner, and that she was planning instead to make chili for the Soupfest.

Birdie had turned only seconds later to see me standing in the doorway of my office, my clipboard in hand. I was notating the location of two fluorescent lighting panels, which, due to their dimness, I was certain were in need of replacement tubes. Having asked Ed Silvester, the janitor, to check one of them a week earlier and having seen no evidence of his attending to the matter, I was now in the process of composing a rather pointed written reminder. Seeing me, Birdie had called, "Oh, Margaret, you're welcome to come, too! I was just telling them about a soup supper at our —"

I interrupted her with a curt "I will save you the effort of repeating it, for I will not be able to attend."

I recalled the brief, stricken look upon her face and her brave recovery as she called out, "Oh, I understand perfectly! Maybe some other time."

About a half mile past Birdie's house, Thomas pointed to a collection of deserted wooden tables arranged in three long rows beside the highway. "Keep aimin' to come out here one of these Saturdays and see if that feller from Derby's got his pecans and hickories ready yet. I could sure use a pie." One of Thomas's favorite desserts is hickory nut pie, which he likes even more than my pecan pie. He is faithful to keep my supply of both of these nuts replenished. "Maybe I'll drive out tomorrow and check," he added.

We passed a series of hand-lettered neon green signs that were displayed year round: *Peach's! Firework's! Boiled P'nut's! Canalope's! Sno-Cone's!* Only a dilapidated roadside produce stand, empty on this November Friday, appeared at the end of this bannered trail — "a real letdown after all that rah-rah," as Thomas described it.

Farther on, we passed a Texaco station and a small clapboard house, which was painted the blue of a robin's egg. A sign reading *Dottie's Be-Beautiful Style Shoppe* stood beside the mailbox.

We soon drew within sight of the Field Pea Restaurant, an unassuming structure with all the architectural grace of a warehouse. Having been in operation less than a year, the restaurant had earned for itself a modest but respectable reputation among the folk of Derby, Filbert, and Berea. This had been my impression from overheard conversations at school and recent newspaper advertisements that boldly declared *We Promise Big and Always Deliver,* which seemed to me a slogan more suited to a furniture or appliance store than to a restaurant. I saw that the parking lot was crowded, bringing to mind a simile in one of Josephine Humphreys' novels — *Rich in Love,* I believe — in which she likens the cars pulled up around a diner to creatures at a water hole.

"I certainly hope we will not have to *wait* to be served," I said to Thomas, and when he did not answer, I added, "I cannot abide waiting in lines."

"Sometimes there just ain't a choice 'bout it," Thomas said calmly. I could have argued that indeed we *did* have a choice in this case, but I held my tongue. We pulled up behind a family of seven or eight who had exited the restaurant and appeared to be heading toward their car. There were several boisterously hyperactive children in the family who were darting about and squealing, flailing their arms in a great release of energy. The mother was attempting to shepherd them with the laying on of her hands, but they were far too quick for her. We crept along behind the incontinent horde and stopped when they dashed toward a large and decrepit automobile, an Oldsmobile I believe, of the approximate vintage of my 1967 Ford Fairlane but far more flamboyant in the design of its tail fins.

Thomas waited patiently as the family flung open the doors and piled into their car, a process fraught with noisy delays. I heard them, for I had lowered my window ever so slightly. One of the young children, a little boy, released his hold on a paper that he was flourishing above his head — perhaps a disposable place mat — at which point the wind caught it. The child began to chase it across the parking lot, pointing and shrieking, in spite of his mother's ineffectual pleas of "Here, Davey! Leave it alone! We'll get another one next time! We'll get you *ten* of 'em if you want 'em! Come on back here, Davey! *Watch out for that car!*"

An older child followed to assist Davey, and presently the father of the brood emerged from the car and stood to bellow, "I'm countin' to three, and then we're leavin' ya both here!" When someone inside the car sounded the horn, he stooped down and yelled, "Stop that, you little numskull! Do it again and I'll break your kneecaps!" The world is full of unrestrained parents; balance and dignity are in great want. Apparently, the children, accustomed to their father's idle threats, saw opportunity for sport, and once again the horn emitted a series of low, hooty blasts as the car rocked — I could actually see it *sway* — with small bodies throwing themselves over the front seat to have a turn at the horn.

Though I was transfixed by the spectacle and filled with horror at the thought of what it would be like to spend an hour in the home of this family, Thomas watched it all without expression except to cock his head to one side and state, "Motor on your car's idlin' fast, Rosie. How long's she been soundin' this way?"

324

Moments later as Thomas at last eased my Ford into the vacated parking space, we watched the Oldsmobile creep toward the exit, small heads bobbing in the backseat like corks upon a turbulent sea. "Right lively bunch goin' there," he said. Though he never spoke of the matter, I had begun to wonder of late whether Thomas felt the void of children in his life, his sole offspring not having survived infancy. In the traditional sense, he would have made a splendid father and grandfather, his gentleness and good humor sufficient for the many inconveniences attendant with the rearing of small children. At the Tuttle family's summer reunions, numerous young children invariably attach themselves to Thomas, screeching with laughter at his foolishness.

Making our way toward the entrance of the Field Pea, I saw Joan through the glass doors waving at us over the heads of other people inside the small lobby, which appeared to be bloated with a great congregation of diners waiting to be seated. Actually, I suppose that what I took to be a "great congregation" was perhaps no more than twenty persons. My heart sank. Delay of any sort has always annoyed me. As we entered through the glass doors, I was relieved to hear Joan call to us from her position near the front of the crowded lobby. "We're next, I think!"

" 'Scuse us, please," Thomas said as he

tapped a white-haired man on the shoulder. "Our party's up here waitin' for us."

The man turned on him with a glint of challenge in his eyes, then relaxed and smiled. "Well, if it's not Thomas Tuttle, my old pal from the hardware store!"

Thomas punched him in the arm playfully. "Hey there, Dayton, better watch out who you're callin' *old*," he said, and they both laughed heartily. Thomas opened up a path before us, although one woman whose hair was dyed an unusual shade of pinkish peach, the color of shrimp, and whose gaudy garb and artificially enhanced features gave her the aspect of a strumpet, complained loudly to her companion, "They shouldn't let people get in line if their whole group's not here!" Slowly we threaded our way through the small crowd toward Joan.

The restaurant boasted no elegant decor, but being relatively new, it appeared to be clean. In fact, I noted that the small individual bulbs in the inexpensive chandelier above our head sparkled as if recently polished. A low brick partition separated the lobby from the dining area, and carved posts of dark wood extended between the brick wall and ceiling. If one listened, the clink of dinnerware could be faintly heard beyond the dividing wall. Soft music — a guitar rendition of "Greensleeves" — was playing over the intercom.

Beside Joan stood a middle-aged man of

medium height — in fact, certainly no taller than Joan herself and perhaps even shorter — who was watching our approach; at least I believed he was doing so, although his eyes were all but lost in what appeared to be a myopic squint. He had reddish blond hair that "was goin' through a recession," as Thomas was fond of saying, thus exposing his entire forehead and a great deal more.

He was not a handsome man, though his looks certainly improved as we drew nearer and his squint relaxed. His skin had the raw, scrubbed look typical of persons with his color of hair, and a pronounced cleft was centered upon his chin. The cleft was the type of conspicuous feature, on the order of a scar or birthmark, that would be cited first were one to describe this man's appearance. In fact, he could very well be reduced to that single characteristic. I could imagine Thomas referring to him later as "that man with the hole in his chin."

Had I been choosing a mate for Joan according to physical charm alone, I certainly would have set my sights higher than this man. Since it was not my assignment, however, I could muster no regrets over his looks. Besides, one does not live for fifty years without learning to exercise caution when it comes to the relationship between physical appearance and character. I recall that my grandfather, though overweight, was sometimes spoken of as a handsome man.

Joan introduced the man to us as Virgil Dunlop, and he extended his hand to Thomas almost shyly. "Joan's given me good cause to look forward to meeting you folks," he said. He had a pleasingly deep voice and a drawl that marked him as a native southerner, most likely from a coastal region — Savannah perhaps, or Charleston, or even as far north as a Virginia port. Turning his attention to me, he said, "And you must be Margaret. Joan informs me that you know more about literature than anyone she's ever met. In fact, she says you'd wipe out the bank if you ever got on *Jeopardy.*"

I could think of no reply to this remark and so offered none but turned my shoulder slightly so that I was no longer facing Virgil Dunlop. Joan was speaking now with the hostess of the Field Pea, who was pointing to the steno pad in her hand and explaining something with a great show of earnestness and much gesticulation. A teenager behind me stepped on my heel, and though she instantly apologized — albeit in such a careless, insincere tone that she might have saved herself the trouble — I cast her a reproving glance. "I said I was sorry!" I heard her hiss to her mother behind me. I suppose, since I had so few pairs as a child, that I am more fastidious about the condition of my shoes than the average person. Scuffed heels are one of my particular peeves.

Virgil Dunlop asked Thomas how his vacuum cleaner sales were going. Joan had obviously tried to equip him with conversational topics for the evening.

"I don't sell 'em, just fix 'em," Thomas said, much too loudly, as men are wont to do, especially in public. "I must've put on more'n a dozen new belts this week. Seems like every woman in town had a busted belt!" Several people behind us chuckled, and I heard someone — most likely the white-haired man whom we had passed earlier — say, "You won't find a nicer man than Thomas Tuttle." Spurred on by what he sensed to be an audience, Thomas raised his voice another level and said, "From what I hear about the food here, that's what we all might have when we get finished eatin' tonight — busted belts!" There was more laughter, though I distinctly heard the teenager behind me mutter, "Oh, *please!*"

Virgil Dunlop smiled and shook his head. "It's curious how things go in runs like that, isn't it? My father used to be manager of a marina outside Charleston, and I remember him telling about one week in December — this was back in the sixties — when fourteen people came in asking for new oars."

"How 'bout that!" Thomas said. "Fourteen oars in a week. And in December, did you say? Funny time for a rowboat convention." I

329

attempted to catch Thomas's eye; it was imperative that he settle down. He had moved away from me, however, and was telling Virgil Dunlop about using a wooden oar as a makeshift splint when he had broken his leg as a boy.

Joan turned now from speaking with the hostess, a faint line of worry creasing her brow. "She said they probably won't have a table for four in non-smoking for at least another ten or fifteen minutes. They just seated a big group of twelve by moving some tables together, and all they have now is a table for two. She said we could have that one now and they could put two more chairs at it, but it would be pretty crowded for four. Or they could give it to somebody else and we could wait. She's gone to check on extra chairs. I told her we'd give her an answer when she comes back."

Virgil Dunlop rubbed his hands together. "Well, ten minutes goes by fast, and anyway, waiting generally makes food taste all the better. But why don't we let our guests decide?" He directed a deferential smile toward Thomas and me. Thomas had not told me that we were to be Joan's guests for the meal. Perhaps he had not considered it important, or perhaps Joan had failed to tell him. Or, most likely, Thomas knew that I would staunchly refuse to come if I felt that we were in any way being the recipients of someone else's hospitality. Receiving favors is something I have always found difficult.

Thomas looked at me and raised his eyebrows as if asking my preference. It was not a choice that I cared to make. I knew not which form of discomfort was most desirable, to be jammed together at a small table or to stand and wait for an additional ten minutes.

From somewhere behind us, a woman's voice suddenly penetrated the heavy murmur of talk around us. "*Nothin'* can be worth waitin' this long for! Let's go, and for pete's sake call for reservations next time you get the bright idea of takin' me out!" Though I did not turn to see who was speaking, I was quite sure it was the same woman who had earlier complained about our moving forward to join Joan.

All talk subsided so that the reply, an immediate remonstrance from a male voice, was clearly audible. "Hey, remember it was *you* who wanted to go out tonight!"

Their quarrel continued as they made their way to the exit. "Anyway, they don't even take reservations here, and you knew that before we came!"

"Yeah, and you knew it was Friday night, so why'd you drag me to a little two-bit place like this to stand like packed sardines for . . ."

The hostess was returning, apparently having heard the altercation, for her eyes were wide and her lips a thin, tight seam.

"Man alive, the things some people'll do right out in public," Thomas said to Virgil Dunlop, who merely shook his head and cast his gaze upward.

And, the thought sprang to my mind at once, *the things some men do in private.* The woman was offensive, certainly, but I would not judge her outright without knowledge of the man's daily conduct behind closed doors.

It was at that moment that I heard my name being called, an urgent piping as if in a troubled dream. "Margaret! Margaret!" And then there before me appeared Birdie Freeman, scuttling behind the hostess waving both of her small hands in a crisscrossing motion as if trying to arouse someone from a trance. The puzzled hostess glanced behind her and stepped aside to make way for Birdie, who approached our party and immediately touched my wrist. "Margaret, it *is* you! I was fixing to take the first bite of my salad when I looked up and saw you standing out here, and I told Mickey I was going to come out here and see if you needed a place to sit. We've got a whole table for four, and there's just the two of us. We'd love to have you join us!"

"There are four in our party." I spoke firmly though not unkindly, grateful that I could so easily reject her offer.

"Oh! I see," Birdie said, still smiling but lifting her hand from my wrist. Before she could say more, however, the hostess spoke up, a hopeful light in her eyes. "We could move the table for two over by theirs and seat the six of you together." She looked at me and her smile faded as she added, "If that would suit . . . everybody, that is."

It was an uncomfortable moment. Joan shifted uneasily, shrugged, and looked at Virgil. Her lips formed a smile of sorts, but it was not the type of smile that signifies pleasure. Indeed, it was evident that her plan for the evening did not include two strangers. Thomas pursed his lips as if to whistle and studied the floor.

In the moment of hesitation, Birdie must have sensed our collective reluctance, for she patted my arm lightly and, taking in all four of us with the sweep of her glance, hastened to assure us that she did not mean to intrude. "I can *sure* understand if you want a private table," she said, her face flushing.

If Virgil Dunlop had not taken matters in hand, we may have stood there indefinitely, testing even further the patience of those waiting behind us as we filled time with all the typical sounds of embarrassment — the clearing of throats, the shuffling of feet, the falsely cheerful stammers of "Well . . ." "Uh . . ." "What do you . . . ?"

Smiling at me, Virgil broke the awkward spell. "We'd be honored to make the acquaintance of your friends over a good dinner,

Margaret," he said decisively. "You can introduce us all at the table." Joan, the odd smile still congealed upon her face, closed her eyes for an instant and then shifted her gaze upward to the gleaming chandelier of which I spoke earlier. I am quite certain, however, that she was not admiring the twinkle of its lights.

As if he had in view an expected end of delightful proportions, Virgil thanked Birdie for her offer, nodded cordially to all of us, and said, "Well, let's follow this kind lady to her table and get this show on the road!" When he smiled, I saw that the cleft in his chin became less pronounced.

DEEPNESS OF EARTH
17

Joan telephoned me the following morning at nine o'clock. "I didn't wake you up, did I?" she asked.

"You did not," I replied. On weekdays I generally rise at a quarter past five, and on Saturdays and Sundays at eight.

She released a long, breathy sigh, ending with a humorless laugh. "Okay, tell me what you think," she said. She attempted a resigned tone, but a certain tightness and alert concern were unmistakable. "Let me warn you," she said, "I've got my note pad here just like when we go to concerts. I might even write up a report later so I can study all the angles."

I had suspected, of course, that Joan would exact a return for the price of our dinner at the Field Pea and that my payment would most likely come in the form of a critique such as she was now requesting. Though I had sensed this was coming, I felt completely unprepared. How I wished that my appraisal of Friday evening's dinner engagement were as instantly and confidently formed as that of a concert or play in a performance hall.

I felt that my impressions of the previous evening were unsubstantiated, that my thoughts had been twisted awry. I had fallen asleep the night before trying to straighten and flatten the experience, had labored through a series of bunched and wrinkled dreams, and had awakened to find no smoothness of fabric upon which to pin a pattern.

"Margaret, are you there?" Joan asked. "I need to talk about all this."

"Yes, I am here," I said. "What is it that you want of me?" I was stalling, for I knew that what Joan wanted primarily was my unvarnished evaluation of Virgil Dunlop, and that furthermore she desperately wanted it to confirm her own favorable judgment of the man.

"Please don't put me off," Joan said. "I'm as nervous as a cat. I mean, I know what *I* think, but I've got to hear what somebody else thinks. I just don't know that I can trust myself right now. I'm afraid what I'm *feeling* might be interfering with the truth. I want you to tell me your honest opinion of Virgil without even stopping to think about how it sounds. Just give me your impression of him, Margaret — everything. I'm ready."

Thus, with no chart for my course and no shore in sight, I pulled up anchor and filled my sails. "Very well, Joan, I shall tell you what I think. It is only what I *think,* however, as it is impossible ever to *know* the heart of any man. It is clear to me that you are seeking an authority who will stamp Virgil with an unqualified seal of approval. I am no authority but I will give you my opinion, though I cannot give you what you really want. You want indemnity against spurious character, a guarantee in the event of defective parts, a warranty for lifelong unimpeachability. These, however, cannot be given, Joan. As I have said before, I do not generally trust men to be virtuous in private; therefore I certainly cannot trust their public image. Granted, Virgil Dunlop seems upon casual acquaintance to be of sound character — considerate, steadfast, decent, and reliable. That he is intelligent, socially adept, and amiable there can be no question. You ask of me what is not mine to give, however, and that is assurance that this man will serve you well all the days of your life." Though I felt the gale force of many words still driving me forward, I paused.

" 'And I shall dwell in the house of the Lord forever,' " Joan said after a moment of silence. I could not easily read her tone. Frankly, I was surprised that she had tossed off a biblical quotation so spontaneously, albeit irreverently. I had never known her to cite the Bible. She spoke almost flippantly, yet I sensed that she was in a most serious frame of mind and that she wished me to continue.

This I did. "He must have known that, for you, last night's dinner party was far more than a polite formality or leisurely entertainment," I said. "No doubt he was keenly aware that he was being pinned and mounted in a display case, so to speak, and that we were all peering through the glass at him in order to classify him and to determine whether he warranted our admiration. Only a fool would fail to exhibit himself to his best advantage under such circumstances, Joan, to pass himself off as a rare specimen. It is human nature, when one knows that he is being observed and examined, to . . . well, to borrow from an old song, to accentuate the positive."

I halted my speech, and during the interval that followed before she spoke, Joan hummed a few measures of the song to which I had just referred. "Well, I asked you for your opinion, didn't I?" she said at last, and I heard a rustling sound as of sheets of paper. I wondered if she were indeed taking notes or if perhaps she were scanning the morning newspaper. "So I sure can't . . . blame you for telling me." She spoke hesitantly, as if testing the weight of her words. "And I appreciate your honesty, Margaret, I really do. I guess I should've expected as much. You're not the kind to be won over right off the bat, and that's good — I mean, if you . . . *raved* about how wonderful you thought he was, I guess I'd be . . . suspicious." Though attempting a light note, she sounded somewhat downcast.

For a brief while neither of us spoke, and then she said, "It's funny, isn't it, to think of how much difference a split second can make?" She was, I assumed, speaking of the way that she and Virgil had met.

Joan had told all of us the story at the Field Pea the night before. Two months earlier she had stopped at the Food Giant in Berea one night after working late and had turned her shopping cart sharply at the end of an aisle, around a large display of pickles in glass jars, only to collide with Virgil Dunlop, balancing in one arm three boxes of cereal, a package of paper napkins, a bag of Fritos, and a half-gallon of ice cream while carrying a loaf of bread and a gallon of milk in the other hand. In my opinion, Joan should have taken careful note of the quantity that he carried, not as evidence of his physical coordination, of course, but of his lack of foresight. Clearly, the man needed a shopping cart, or a basket at the least.

Virgil had managed to maintain his balance without dropping anything, but Joan's cart had been knocked off course into the pickle display, dislodging two large jars and leaving a mess of kosher dills, pickle juice, and shards of glass all over the floor. "I was mortified at my reaction," Virgil had interjected. "I couldn't believe what came out of my mouth. I actually said, *'Oops.'*" He had been on his way to the check-out line, he explained, but had remembered at the last minute that he needed shaving cream and was trying to locate the aisle of toiletries at the moment of collision.

Joan sighed into the telephone receiver. "It's one of those things you wonder about," she said, "the timing of it, I mean. If either one of us had been a few seconds earlier or later, or if Virgil's shaving cream hadn't run out that morning . . . well, I wouldn't be sitting here asking you what you thought of him. I wouldn't even *know* him, and maybe that would be better all the way around. All this sure has thrown me for a loop."

As mentioned earlier, I myself have mused upon the import of small fractions of time in the course of life. Had I not entered the doors of Emma Weldy Elementary School and offered myself to Mrs. Edgecombe at that precise moment in the fall of 1973, I would not, in all likelihood, be employed today as a school lunchroom supervisor. Nor would I have made the acquaintance of Birdie Freeman, nor would I be spending my summer vacation recording my recollections of her.

"I cannot tell you what to do, Joan," I said.

"It is your life. You must make your own choices and live with those choices. I only want you to be exceedingly cautious. My opinion applies not only to Virgil Dunlop but to every man, living or dead. As I said, one can never know the heart of another. You solicited my opinion, and I gave it. You are, of course, at liberty to form your own. You *must* form your own."

"Don't you think he's interesting to talk to?" she asked.

"He is knowledgeable and articulate," I said. Indeed, his intelligence seemed to be of the broad and natural sort, no doubt owing its versatility to the early introduction and lifelong attraction to books of which he had spoken.

A lengthy, though incomplete, list of topics that had been discussed around the dinner table the night before sprang at once to my mind — an amazing smorgasbord of shared knowledge and opinions to which Virgil Dunlop had been a ready, agreeably confident, and substantial contributor: the new BMW plant outside Greenville; the baseball strike during the past summer; the difference between lunar and solar eclipses — which Virgil had illustrated with the aid of a packet of sugar and the salt and pepper shakers; haiku poetry; the expedition of Meriwether Lewis and William Clark to the Northwest Territory in 1803; methods of storing solar heat; Chinese porcelain; several recent Halloween pranks in Filbert and Berea; rock formations called hoodoos; the deteriorating condition of Highway 11; the sudden death of a city councilman in Derby; nationwide jewelry fraud; a recent fire at the nearby Lena Lansford Home for Girls in Mount Chesney; General Stonewall Jackson; beach erosion; the new windows in the Presbyterian church in Filbert; and the properties of rayon fabric, among others.

And, of course, the final disturbing question that Virgil had posed over dessert. Thomas and I had shared a slice of coconut cream pie, though I am not overly fond of coconut as a rule, often because it is too coarsely ground. It pleased me to find that whoever had made this pie — the Field Pea boasted that its desserts were "homemade from scratch" — had used finely shredded coconut in moderation.

Let me pause at this point to explain why I am not reporting our dinner at the Field Pea, which lasted for nearly two hours, as a detailed chronological narrative, but rather through the vague and haphazard means of summary. The reason is quite simple: I cannot. Though I remember vividly the moments in the restaurant lobby leading up to our promenade through the dining room to the table where Mickey Freeman waited, his face alight with welcome, I cannot begin to place in order the minutes that followed.

Images of us around the table arise in sharp focus. I could draw a precise diagram of our seating arrangement, of the location of our table in relation to the others in the room, of the pale taupe and moss green floral design of the wallpaper. I can see Birdie's yellow blouse, a hue so intensely bright that one might expect it to cast a phosphorescent glow in the dark. I can see the small black combs in her hair that night, the touch of pink lipstick, the tiny pearl earrings that I had never before seen her wear.

But the exact course of the events that followed our arrival at the table is impossible to recall. The rapid whirlpool of talk, the waves of activity (Mickey tipped over a glass of iced tea, for example, as he attempted unsuccessfully to perform a sleight of hand that he had learned as a boy), and the great swells of laughter all but drowned me.

When I find it difficult to fall asleep at night, I choose among three mental exercises. First, I may envision in exact sequence the plot of a favorite book or of one of the few movies that I have seen in my lifetime — for example, *Sergeant York* or *The African Queen.* Second, I may stroll in my mind through one of the neighborhoods in which were located the various apartments that my mother and I considered home during my childhood, passing a dry cleaner here, a park bench there, and so on. Or third, I may put in order the minutes and hours of a particular day in my life, most often the very one that I am at the time attempting to bring to a close — calling to mind each specific word spoken, each observation noted, and so forth. In the process of layering detail upon detail in one of these three exercises, I most often succeed in conquering sleeplessness.

I remember quite clearly, however, my failed efforts that night after our dinner at the Field Pea to summon sleep by the third means: that of reconstructing the events of the evening. I could not begin to grasp them all and set them to rights. I could not recall, for example, whether Birdie had admired Joan's garnet ring before or after Mickey had given Thomas the black ball-point pen inscribed with *Barker Bag Co.* in an incongruously fancy gold script.

I had no idea whether Virgil had told the story about his father's hiding in a German barn during World War II before or after the waitress had mispronounced *parmigiana,* or whether Joan had teased Mickey about his bow tie — a large, flashy affair dotted with tiny colorful flags and contrasting ridiculously with his unfashionable, brown acrylic cardigan — before or after Thomas had given his silly recital of knock-knock jokes. I did recall perfectly the last thing Birdie had said that evening as she stood beside our car. "I sure liked that knock-knock joke you told about the Mona Lisa, Thomas!" Then she had shot me a teasing look and said, "You never told me your husband was such a card, Margaret. I don't know if we could stand much more of him and Mickey together!"

Aside from the flammable combination of Thomas's and Mickey's silliness, the mix of personalities in our sixsome had been diverse but compatible. Birdie and Mickey had been ebullient upon learning that Joan had visited the Church of the Open Door, where they attended, and from the expression upon their faces when they discovered that Joan's father and Thomas's uncle had been none other than Mayfield Spalding, a former church member and friend, one would have thought that they had just viewed the Seven Wonders in close succession. "Well, it's a small world, as they say in Outer Mongolia!" Mickey exclaimed. Both Mickey and Birdie had lavished liberal praise upon Mayfield for his generosity and "all the nice things he did behind the scenes," as Birdie put it. Joan had fastened upon their every word, I noted, though she said very little.

Virgil Dunlop informed Birdie and Mickey that he, too, had recently visited the Church of the Open Door, though not in Joan's company but rather during Jesse Goodyear's revival campaign. It also came to light that Virgil Dunlop, though his residence was in

Berea, was actively involved in the Community Baptist Church of Filbert, a small, yellow brick establishment only five blocks from our duplex on Cadbury Street. This news was greeted by Birdie with cries of joy. "Why, one of my dearest friends used to go there!" she said.

Joan's quandary concerning Virgil Dunlop became clear to me as the evening progressed. The expression upon her face throughout the dinner was one of war — between honest and open esteem on the one hand and heartsick dismay on the other. Though he was personally engaging, neither too brash and self-consumed nor too meek and flaccid, Virgil was unreservedly ardent concerning his religion. With no hint of apology, he made frequent reference to "God's will" for his life, "answered prayer," and "the Lord's direction." For a woman like Joan — independent, nontraditional, and quick to doubt and criticize — to be attracted to a man with strong church ties defied logic. Though we had never discussed the subject, I believe I can assert with confidence that at this point in her life Joan Spalding considered churches to be on the same level with institutions for the mentally incompetent.

Though the order of events during the course of the dinner is largely a jumble in my memory, I do recall the exact point at which Virgil made his most startling statement. We had all finished our respective dinners (I had ordered an entree called Grilled Polynesian Chicken, served with rice and steamed vegetables, all of which proved to be surprisingly satisfactory for restaurant fare) and were in the process of being served our desserts — in the case of Thomas and me, the coconut cream pie of which I spoke earlier — when Virgil put to the rest of us a question that was, I suppose, actually an extrapolation from an earlier interrupted discourse concerning the free will of man.

Sometime earlier — it could have been four or twenty-four topics removed — we had discussed briefly a book that, as it turned out, four of the six of us had read. It was a book Birdie had brought to school only the day before, on November 17, and given to me. "I told you yesterday I had a book to give you, and I just finished it last night," she had told me upon handing it to me that morning. "I know you like to read, but this might not be the kind of book you'd normally pick. I think you'll like it, though. Mickey and I think he's a real good writer."

It was a hardback book bound in dark blue cloth. Though it was upside down as she extended it to me, I had read its title — *Stage Right* — and subtitle, written in smaller letters — *The Drama of a Fundamentalist Christian Church*. "I think it's real interesting, of course," she had said, smiling. "But, then, it's about our church, so I guess I could be just the least bit prejudiced." She had gone on to explain that the Church of the Open Door had been the subject of a sociological research, an "ethnography," conducted over the course of a year by a respected writer in the field, a man named Perry Warren, who had moved to Derby for a year and had attended the church. I remembered reading an article in the Filbert *Nutshell* some months before about the research of this man and his book-in-the-making, but I was surprised now to find that the project had already been completed.

I cannot say why I accepted such a gift, given my extreme aversion toward religion as a whole, nor why I opened it to the first chapter later at home, but I had received it from Birdie's hands with a short nod, taken it home with me when my work was finished, and read it that same day, beginning shortly after two-thirty and stopping only for supper, which time came sooner than I had expected.

When Thomas had come home, I had risen from my chair quickly and set about frying two lean ground beef patties, after which I hastily prepared some frozen vegetables and sweet muffins. It was not a well-planned meal, but I do not believe Thomas took note. I delayed my bedtime by half an hour that night, and by ten-thirty I had finished the book. Birdie had written an inscription in the flyleaf — *To Margaret from Birdie, You're a new friend, but I feel like I've always known you and want to know you even better* — which I did not notice until I picked it up to resume my reading after the supper dishes were put away.

At the Field Pea, Virgil had mentioned the book as we ate, for he had read it also. "It interested me," he said, "to see an outsider's perspective of Christianity all neatly laid out and reduced to its component parts. I thought the writer did a remarkable job of maintaining an objective tone all the way through."

"But did you know he got saved?" Mickey asked. "I mean Perry Warren, the man who wrote the book. He went home a different man than when he came. That's what made it all so exciting for us."

"*And* he got back together with his wife," Birdie said. "They'd been ready to get a divorce. She and his little boy came down once to meet everybody before Perry moved back home to Illinois." She nodded and paused as if reveling in a private memory. "He still writes to some of the people at church," she added. Then motioning to me, she said, "I gave my copy of the book to Margaret, but I know she probably hasn't had a chance to look at it yet."

"I read it yesterday," I said.

"You did?" cried Birdie. "My, that was fast!"

"What did you think of it?" Virgil asked me.

"Mr. Warren is a skilled writer," I said, "with an enviable talent for turning the tedious details of a dull subject into a compelling story."

The others looked at me with expressions registering varying degrees of confusion. It was evident that Birdie did not know whether to interpret my comment as praise or censure.

Virgil replied first, easily and calmly. "That's an interesting way to put it," he said. "I believe I heard that the man is both a fiction writer and a social researcher, so what you say makes sense." Then addressing all of us, he continued. "I can see how skeptical a guy like Perry Warren would be stepping into a church like that for the first time. For one thing, here's a group of people who claim to believe in the free will of man yet at the same time believe that God ordains and controls everything that happens. One minute they're saying, 'I have decided to follow Jesus,' and the next minute 'I couldn't resist God's call.' So what kind of free will is that? We decide to give in, yet we're too weak to put up a fight? And what kind of God is that? He drags us to him bound and gagged?"

The waiter had come at that moment, I believe, and Joan had quickly asked for more rolls and butter. I had asked for a refill of *unsweetened* tea, advising the waiter to inform those in the kitchen that the taste of tea in the sweetened tea was overpowered by that of sugar. "Tell them," I said, "that a good rule of thumb is a cup of sugar per gallon of tea."

"We like ours just a little sweeter than that," Mickey interjected. "I think Birdie uses a cup and a fourth per gallon, don't you, sweetcake?" During the evening I counted seven different pet appellations that Mickey Freeman used to address Birdie: treasure, dumpling, pumpkin, precious, sugar, sweetcake, and honeybun.

By the time the waiter had taken his leave, Virgil's remarks concerning the free will of man had been buried beneath the rubble of a dozen verbal romps concerning sugar. Birdie had even joined in, playfully slapping Mickey's hand when he puckered his lips and asked if she'd like some sugar. "Yes, but I want the *refined* kind!" she said.

From there the conversation had somehow veered into the subject of prison reform, I believe — or perhaps it was an upcoming concert in Greenville by an eleven-year-old Korean violinist or the new billboard advertisement on the interstate, promoting an internationally acclaimed circus and containing a glaring spelling error: *See Amazing Acrobatic Feets.* "Yeah, they should've taken off the *s*," Mickey had said. "Everybody knows more than one foot is *feet*," to which Thomas had responded, "Or a yard if it's three feet," to which Virgil had added his own droll remark. "I never saw a three-footed acrobat." Even Joan had laughed.

The waiter returned with the rolls and tea, and at some point Joan told about a woman with whom she worked whose first name was Laureth. "She said her mother took all the names of her children off the back of a shampoo bottle," Joan said. "She's got two brothers named Keratin and Amino and two sisters named Glycerin and Xylene." Virgil commented that Laureth had come out the best in that deal, and Mickey had begun a rapid monologue of other names the mother could have selected: Purified Water, Sulfate, Hydrolyzed Protein, Citric Acid, and Yellow Dye Number Seven. Once more, Thomas had laughed with gusto at the little man's quick though adolescent wit. Birdie had laid her hands on either side of her face and exclaimed, "Why, Mickey, you're a nut! So that's why you take so long in the shower — you're reading the back of the shampoo bottle!"

Somehow dessert had been ordered and our dinner plates removed, and in the lull, during which the waiter placed our slices of pie before us, Virgil spoke with thoughtful deliberation, once again turning to serious matters. "And just what kind of God do we have anyway? If a person believes in God — in a God of love, that is — how can he reconcile all the suffering that goes on in the world? Or in his own life, for that matter?"

He went on to explain that he had been debating this very issue with a fellow teacher. Early in the evening, most likely during the introductions around the table, it was revealed that Virgil Dunlop was a teacher at Berea Middle School, instructing seventh graders in world history and eighth graders in American history. "That's Bruce's big hang-up," Virgil said. "He says he could never get into religion because any God who would let somebody go through what his father suffered before he died of cancer wasn't anybody he cared to get mixed up with." I saw the waiter studying Virgil with a look of repugnance, as though he had stumbled upon a nest of vipers. He set the last dish of pie upon our table and interrupted tersely with a promise to return with coffee for those who wanted it.

"So what did you tell Bruce?" Birdie asked, her brown eyes glowing with interest.

"Oh, what haven't I told him?" Virgil said. "We go around and around, but he doesn't even half listen to what I say before he's off on his same old line: If God is so good, he says, then why doesn't he do something about all the hunger and pain and all the *ugliness*. That's his favorite word when he's talking about life's bad side — *ugliness*. If there is a God, he says, then it's pretty clear that he doesn't care the least about people. And if he doesn't care about people, he says, then I don't want to have anything to do with him. And then he always adds, 'But I'm sure there's *not* a God.' "

Virgil let his head fall backward as he released a sigh of frustration. "There's no easy answer," he said. "It's not something you can figure out like a math problem. Do I believe that God *directs* our suffering? Bruce asked me that the other day. Does he have a big chart he marks it down on? Or is it like a lottery where your number suddenly comes up at random and it's your turn? How does God go about divvying it all up so everybody gets a share?"

For a long moment we all fell silent. I am quite certain that three of us — Joan, Thomas, and I — sincerely wished that the conversation could in some way be relieved of its heavy weight. Did it not occur to Virgil Dunlop, I wondered, that there might be those of us who preferred not to sit in a public restaurant among people we barely knew and discuss the attributes of God and the mysteries of human suffering?

It may surprise the reader to learn that the unleashing of vituperative condemnations upon God, such as those of Virgil's colleague, bestir within me a sensation akin to fear. While I truly felt that God had deserted me those many years ago in my grandfather's house, I had seen it as an oversight — an inexcusable oversight of awful consequence, to be sure, but an oversight nevertheless rather than an intentional and treacherous act against me. God had simply turned his back upon me for some reason that I could not fathom, and in so doing he had demonstrated his fallibility. I could have no part in a system of belief presided over by an irresponsible and careless deity, one who showed obvious favoritism or lapses of attention. To vilify God publicly, however, was not something I could ever find within my power to do.

At the Field Pea Restaurant over seven months ago, on the evening of November 18, a sudden curiosity welled up within me, and I believe I am correct in stating that I surprised everyone at the table, perhaps myself most of all, by turning abruptly to Birdie and addressing her boldly and directly.

"And were the opportunity to come to *you*," I said, "what would you say in response to Bruce's views? Why does God allow humans to suffer?"

The fact that the seed of Birdie's faith had grown hardy roots in a rich deepness of earth had been abundantly yet quietly manifest in her daily conduct in the lunchroom of Emma Weldy, of course, but at no time was the genuineness of her heart more powerfully demonstrated to me than by her simple answer to my question that night at the restaurant.

I believe that had she answered in any other way — had she attempted, for example, to foist upon me some pat piety, some fraudulent platitude, had she recited a list of reasons for suffering (oh, yes, as a teenager I had heard such sermons, with their trite illustrations about the tangled yarns on the undersides of tapestries), had she tried, in Milton's words, "to justify the ways of God to man," — I would have rejected her soundly, once and for all.

She grimaced, however, and shook her head sadly. "Oh, Margaret, honey, I don't know exactly how to answer that," she said. "I don't know why he lets us suffer — I just know he does. It's just part of life, and we all have our share sooner or later. And we can spend our whole life saying it's not fair that we have to pay for something Adam did, but it doesn't change a thing. I wish I had a mind that could figure it all out, but I don't. I just know two things for sure, and they don't seem to go together — God is good and we all have to suffer."

That she was honest and simple pleased me. Had she begun quoting lengthy passages from the Bible, I would have recoiled from her in a lasting way. Had she tossed off some literary quip, such as Shakespeare's "Sweet are the uses of adversity," I should have scorned her openly. Of a certainty I would not be writing a book about her.

A TIME APPOINTED
18

When I think of Birdie Freeman today, my mind is often filled with analogies from the world of science. I envision a microscopic organism surrounding and engulfing another. I imagine the slow seepage of colorless gases into what was once a vacuum. I think of the laws of thermodynamics concerning actions and reactions, of the effect of heat upon ingots of metal, of the principle of water displacement. I am reminded of the productive work of sunlight within green plants, of the irrepressible power of seeds, of the springing forth of flowers in the most hostile of soils — in the forest gloom, in the desert, upon a rocky mountainside. I see purple and yellow crocuses bursting through the crust of snow.

And without fail, when I think of Birdie, my thoughts turn to the wildflower. I have in my possession a book titled *Wild Flowers in South Carolina* by a botanist named Wade Batson. Within its pages, the edges of which begin to give evidence of many turnings, are pictures and descriptions of over two hundred wildflowers native to our state, including those with euphonious names such as Star of Bethlehem, Honey-cup, and Fairy Lily, as well as those of harsher designation: Wild-Man-of-the-Earth, Devil's Darning Needle, and Beggar's Lice. I bought the book at the Derby Public Library Used Book Sale after the incident that I shall now set down in writing.

It occurred on the Tuesday before Thanksgiving as I was gathering my books after my piano lesson with Birdie. By this time I was playing songs in the third book of THE MUSIC TREE series. Though Birdie had suggested from time to time that we omit certain songs, for it was her opinion that I could move far more quickly into more difficult music, I insisted upon studying the books methodically, page by page, even writing in my answers for every notation review, clapping out the practice rhythms, and playing each warm-up exercise on my piano at home. On this particular Tuesday I had performed four simple numbers: "Irish Tune," "If Kangaroos Danced," "Grasshoppers," and "Cobbler, Cobbler." As always, Birdie had poured upon me undiluted praise. "You've got so much talent!" she told me. "And what's more, you *practice!* I wish all my other pupils were as faithful as you."

No doubt Birdie had observed me at each

piano lesson studying the cross-stitched poem on the wall, and very likely she understood that my interest was in the poem itself, or perhaps in poetry in general, more than in the design and craftsmanship of Mickey's handiwork. As she had informed us earlier, Mickey had used no pattern but had merely begun stitching the poem in a script of his own devising, after which he had begun creating a border and a complementary scene of trees and flowers. Although neatly — perhaps even admirably — executed, it was no artistic masterpiece. The poem was not a profound statement nor a lengthy one:

Gifts From the Wildwood

I know not how to capture
This fragrant wildwood's rapture,
The magic of these dells
Where silent beauty dwells,
Where noble strength and power
In oak and pine tree tower.
But when from these I come,
I hope to carry home
Some spirit not yet had
To keep me strong and glad,
Something from oak and pine
To be forever mine;
When from these woods I part,
Some wildflower in my heart.

I was taken by the poem. Beneath its measured plainness vibrated something that struck me as intimately *familiar,* as if I had read it before, although I knew that I had never in my reading so much as come across the name of the poet, Archibald Rutledge, much less the poem itself. By now I had come to believe that it was a simple thought dwelling within the quiet center of the lines, perhaps concealed from the casual eye, that drew from me such a convincing sensation of having known the poem from an earlier time.

I have often over the course of my fifty-one years felt impressed with an idea that I do not recall putting into words. The idea is this: *Something within me cannot die.* This *something,* I have always known, is positive and strong, far bigger than the bitterness, fear, and hatred that thrives so rampantly in the human heart. Life for me, then, was not disposable. Though I did not give verbal expression to the idea, I know now that I have always felt it at the core of my soul, even during the years I was so mercilessly trodden upon by my grandfather.

I suppose this is the reason that I was never tempted to take my life and end my misery. Life simply was not expendable. If taken, it would resume somehow, for there was *something within me that could not die.* Perhaps it was this belief in the immortal — the conviction that there was something inextinguishable within all human life from inception — that emboldened me to protect the life of the only child I ever carried within me, even when my love for it was uncertain. In short, then, I have always held a deep respect for life.

My mother, of course, had spoken often of eternal life and had guided me in my youth to embrace the concept on a spiritual plane. As a child I considered the idea of a heaven and a hell to be a reasonable and fair conclusion to life on earth. The fact that my mother believed in such made it irrefutable, that is until the four-year interlude in my grandfather's house when all of my mother's well-laid theories of life and its orderliness were reduced in my mind to religious flimflam.

Within a short while, during my early teens, I had chopped and winnowed the fields of my mother's religion. Carried away as chaff was the simple belief in a divine God who arranged with loving attention to detail each step of my destiny. The sole surviving seed of my mother's crop of ideals, I suppose, was the irradicable belief that I have alluded to: Something within me cannot die.

As I read the poem above Birdie's piano each week, I began to delve into another level of meaning besides that of a visitor who fondly remembers a literal wildwood. Whether the poet intended this alternate message I know not. My condensed paraphrase of the lines might read thus: *I cannot express what resides within the deepest recesses of my soul, but I know that it is beautiful and enduring, and when I emerge from the dimness of temporal sight, I shall look within and behold a lovely, imperishable bloom.*

Though vague and incipient, the thought took root, and something began to stir within me. I began to wonder whether the concept of eternality might be a promise rather than a threat, whether it might be more than an extended period during which to suffer. The idea of the *bloom* being that of a wildflower — that hardy, widespread diversity of species that springs up uncultivated — appealed to me, for it meant that the seed could be largely ignored and yet in its time bring forth life.

I cannot call the poem a true sonnet, for in spite of its fourteen lines, its truncated meter renders it technically ineligible. Nevertheless, its form is appealing, and it was because of this simple poem by a South Carolinian poet, of whom I knew nothing at the time, that I began to hope once again. Perhaps that was the name of the wildflower within my heart: Hope. And perhaps the flower of hope may yield the fruit of faith and love.

On that Tuesday before Thanksgiving, Birdie laid a hand upon my shoulder while I was still seated upon the piano stool and said to me, "You must like poetry, Margaret.

Every week I see you reading that poem on the wall. Do you? Like poetry, I mean?"

I did not answer at once. "I find that it incites deep thought," I said at last.

"He's written lots of poems," she said, by whom she meant, I assumed, Archibald Rutledge.

"Most poets have written many poems," I replied.

"Well, that's true enough," she said pleasantly, then added, "I wish I knew more about poetry. So much of it seems so hard to understand — at least the kind that sounds worthwhile. And then the poems that are clear as day a lot of times just sound too . . . well, *shallow,* I guess I'd call it." She removed her hand from my shoulder as I rose from the stool. "Not that I'm a great thinker by any stretch!" she said, laughing.

"I, too, wish that I knew more about poetry," I said, looking down into her brown eyes. "I do read a great deal of it, but I feel that my understanding of poetry as an artistic discipline is tangential at best. At times it is as though I hear the engine running and observe that I am being transported, yet I cannot describe how the vehicle operates."

Birdie sighed as I moved toward the door. "You sure have a way with words, Margaret. I just love to hear you talk." She paused a moment, then laid her hand upon my arm as if to stay me. Though I still flinched inwardly at these uninvited advances, I was becoming somewhat accustomed to her touch.

"You remind me of a wildflower in a lot of ways yourself, did you know that, Margaret?" she asked, and when I did not answer, she continued. "I read once, or maybe Mickey told me, that when a wildflower's natural home gets destroyed, maybe by fire or by bulldozers coming through and tearing everything up — no, I think Mervin Lackey told me this — anyway, the plant will die out unless one of the seeds happens to be carried to a place that's *like* the other place that got ruined. Say if it's a marshy area that gets drained and dried out and turned into a shopping center — if they'd ever pick a place like that for a shopping center — then a wildflower seed from the marsh might get picked up by the wind or get stuck in a dog's fur or on somebody's jacket and then maybe get dropped next to a pond miles away and start up a whole new patch of flowers there. But if that same seed got dropped in a dry spot somewhere, it would just die because the conditions wouldn't be right for it to grow."

The principle was simple enough that it could have come from the mouth of a first grader; however, I saw in the body of Birdie's little speech no connection to her introduction: *"You remind me of a wildflower in a lot of ways yourself, did you know that, Margaret?"*

"I must go," I said. Her hand fell from my arm as I bent to retrieve my purse from the rocking chair. Slipping the wide strap across my shoulder, I walked toward the door. I was beginning to weary of the thought of flowers, seeds, and the like. I had business to get about. I wanted to drive to the library in Derby and then stop at a grocery store on the way home to buy a turkey for our Thanksgiving dinner on Thursday.

"I think your natural home inside you must have somehow been destroyed by something a long time ago," Birdie said behind me.

I grasped the doorknob and turned it.

"But there's a seed sticking in your heart just waiting for the right time and place to start growing again," she added.

I pulled the doorknob so forcefully that I lost my grip on it; the door flew open, swinging one hundred eighty degrees and hitting the wall with a dull heavy thump. I must have looked surprised, perhaps verging on apologetic, for she said, "Oh, don't worry about that old door. It has a mind of its own sometimes. Mickey put a little stopper down by the baseboard so it wouldn't hurt itself. See?" And she closed the door partway to point it out to me.

I proceeded forward, opening the screen door and stepping outside. As I descended the steps and walked quickly down the sidewalk, it came to me that my trek from

Birdie's living room to my car was most often marked by a feeling of relief on my part, as if I were escaping a painful examination under a light of powerful wattage. I knew that Birdie was behind me, although her canvas-soled shoes made no sound.

"Margaret, if you ever want to talk about . . ."

At that moment an airplane passed overhead at an inordinately low altitude, it seemed to me, and her words were lost in the roar. As I turned abruptly to face her, she shaded her eyes and looked up.

"I have no idea how you completed that sentence." I spoke with steady deliberation, clutching my piano books before me as a shield. Her gaze fell from the sky until it met my own. "But I assure you," I continued, "that in the event I should want to talk with you about anything, I will be the one to initiate the conversation. Until I do, therefore, you may cease your ruminations concerning the *state of my heart*."

The expression upon Birdie's face could not have been more injured had she been driven through the heart by a stake. She caught her breath and held it; her eyes grew wide as if feeling a sudden, shocking flash of intense pain; her lips opened in a soundless cry. She lifted a hand and laid it across her mouth.

I wheeled and marched toward my Ford, at

which time I saw that another car, a station wagon, had pulled into the gravel driveway and was slowly approaching Birdie's house. The window on the passenger's side began to lower and a hand emerged. "Looka who's come to bring you something!" a voice called, a deep, thick, resonant voice clearly audible above the grinding of the gravel beneath the tires.

The car came to a rest directly behind my Ford, thus blocking my exit. Birdie had trailed me to the end of the sidewalk, one hand still covering her mouth, her eyes still filled with distress. "Oh, Margaret!" was all that she had managed — in a pitiful, kittenish tone — in reply to my rebuff.

Our conversation now terminated by the arrival of the visitor, we watched as the door of the station wagon slowly opened and two large feet, clad in a pair of exceedingly bright red sneakers, appeared beneath the door and tamped the gravel for a secure placement. The woman to whom they belonged was talking the entire time. "Just keep it idlin', Joe Leonard, just keep it idlin'," she said, addressing the driver, I assumed. "I'm not stayin' but a minute."

Pitching her voice louder, she called in our direction. "Soon as I can feel solid ground underneath me, I'll get myself on up and outta here! You and Mickey ever think of pavin' your drive, Birdie? Isn't it a blessin' and a half that they finally got the parking lot at church fixed up so everybody's not always afraid of hurting theirself anymore? Bernie Paulson says his ankle still aches like all get-out on rainy days from that time he twisted it on that real windy day last March when he was carryin' his tuna fish salad out back to Fellowship Hall for the Sunday School social. He stepped on a chunk of rock that wasn't level and whoopsy . . . down he went!" She clapped her hands together with a resounding thwack.

Birdie came to herself and hastened forward to assist the woman, crying, "Here, honey, let me help you out!" The woman, however, had already found a handhold against the side of the car and was hauling herself upward. As she rose from behind the car door, I saw that she was of uncommon height and bulk. By the time Birdie reached her side, the woman was already on her feet, still talking. She had a voice unique in its timbre, low and honking like that of a bassoon. Though Birdie made a great pretense of aiding her as she stepped from behind the car door, it was plain to me that, given the vast difference in the sizes of the two women, Birdie's attentions were merely tokens of politeness.

"Marvella Gowdy was close by when he fell," the woman was saying, reaching back to close the door with a mighty slam. "But she'd been havin' one of her spells with her back so she knew better than to try to help him up. She did holler at Harvey Gill, though, and got his attention to come tend to Bernie. Bernie dropped his Bible when he fell, too, and little pieces of scratch paper was just whippin' around in the wind like it was that stuff that floats around in parades. Bernie was laughin' about it later, after he got calmed down from the spill he took, and said he lost all his sermon notes to the four winds that day and that was what made him get hisself a regular notebook to write down his notes in instead of puttin' 'em on all those little bits of paper and stickin' 'em in his Bible that-away."

It came to me while the woman's deluge of words continued that I had seen and heard her at an earlier time. Looking over at me on the sidewalk, she raised her voice and said, "It's sure a good thing he had that tuna fish in a Tupperware bowl or it might of ended up scrambled all in amongst that gravel. Them Tupperware lids seal up real tight! And if it'd been in a *glass* bowl, why, can you just imagine — it could of broke and made a real hazard!"

All at once I seized the memory. She had delivered a speech at Mayfield's funeral in January — the first time that I had seen Birdie. I recalled now her story of Mayfield's anonymous monetary gift to her family and of her attempt to thank him after she had discovered him to be the source. She had introduced herself by name before she told her story, and I was on the brink of recalling it now — I remembered that it was a somewhat peculiar name of two syllables — when I heard Birdie say, "Let's go over here, Eldeen, so I can introduce you to a good friend of mine."

Eldeen, that was the name. A woman of considerable size, as I have said, she lumbered toward me, smiling a most singular smile. In truth, she appeared to have sustained a severe wound from the expression on her wrinkled face. Something about her eyes, however, and a great deal about her speech, made me understand that the expression was intended for joy. She had short, nickel gray hair, as stiff as the bristles of a brush and somewhat ragged like the plumage of a fledgling. Her eyebrows were a thick hedge. She wore a skirt the color of pale spring grass, reaching nearly to the tops of her white socks, and a long, shapeless black tunic-style top with a large, gold heart-shaped brooch pinned askew and off center near the neck. Though it was warm for November, a dark green wool muffler was wrapped about her neck.

As I was absorbing the details of her ensemble, her words swarmed about me noisily. ". . . and *that* stuff leaked all over the place 'cause the lid didn't fit good and tight. It was so provoking! But I took it back to the store and explained the whole thing to the lady, how it made such a mess on our clean floor right before time for company to get there for supper, and she didn't say a word, just gave me my money back, which let me know I probably wasn't the first one to return one of them cheap containers. Anyway, I made up my mind then and there to splurge and spend a little extra to get Tupperware from then on and play it safe."

She and Birdie were standing directly in front of me by now. Though I am considered a tall woman, this woman was taller yet. I took a step backward, for I felt a want of oxygen.

With hardly a pause for breath, the woman continued to speak in a copious outpouring of words. "Jewel went to a Tupperware party last month and ordered us the nicest little Jell-O mold. It's got this extra part you can clamp on top to make it taller, in case you got more folks to feed. 'Course when it's firmin' up in the icebox, *that* part's on the bottom instead of the top, but then when you take it out and get it loose and turn it upside down on your servin' plate, that little extra layer is settin' up on top so pretty and fancy. Makes it look like a little weddin' cake made out of Jell-O!"

Before Birdie could interject her speech of introduction, the woman fixed me with a penetrating look and demanded, "What *is* that stuff called, anyway?"

"I beg your pardon?" I replied.

She lifted a large forefinger and scratched vigorously above her ear. "All I can think of is *spaghetti,*" she said, "and I know that's not it!" She gave a throaty bark of laughter.

I was mystified, finding no link between her question and her treatise concerning the virtues of Tupperware.

Birdie must have been likewise stymied, for she said, "What stuff are you talking about, Eldeen, honey?"

"What *is* it called?" said Eldeen. "I get so irked when I'm thinkin' of a word and it just won't come! The word *graffiti* just popped into my head, but of course that's not it. That's them bad things that teenagers scribble real big with a can of spray paint." She paused to cluck her tongue and shake her head. "I saw where somebody had written them filthy, dirty words all over the concrete wall behind the football field at the high school."

Birdie smiled and patted the back of Eldeen's broad, thick-veined hand. "I'm afraid we're not following you, Eldeen." Glancing at me, she added fondly, "A person has to get up pretty early in the morning to keep up with Eldeen."

"Well, now, I *do* like to get up early, that's for sure!" Eldeen said. "You can get so much more done that way." I could easily imagine the woman opening her mouth the moment she swung her feet out of bed and never closing it until the night was far spent. "And speakin' of spray paint," she resumed. "Libby Vanderhoff told me the funniest thing on the telephone yesterday! She had her a can of this stuff they been advertisin' in all the papers called Ex-Static that you spray on your knits and petticoats and what have you so's they won't cling. Well, she was in a hurry yesterday morning to get over to her daughter's so she could take care of her little grandbaby — the one that was born on July the Fourth, can you beat that? — and she had gone and put on a dress that was just *bristlin'* with static. So she reached up on the shelf up above her washing machine —" Here Eldeen clapped her hands together and broke off to emit an enormous, resounding quack of laughter. "And lo and behold if she didn't grab a can of yellow *spray paint* by accident! She'd been aiming for months to spray-paint an old stool with that yellow paint, and there it still sat. So she yanked off the lid, not dreamin' what she was holdin' in her hand, and went to sprayin' her dress up and down, up and down, up and down. She said she *saw* it comin' out yellow, but by the time her mind had put two and two together, she had a real mess on her hands — on her dress, too!"

Birdie laughed along with Eldeen, who was now dabbing at her eyes with the tasseled end of her neck scarf. She stopped laughing suddenly and said, "But it's that stuff I was talkin' about a little while ago when I mentioned Bernie Paulson's Bible notes scatterin', don't you know," she continued. "Them bits of colored paper that's dumped out from a window high up so's they can float around in the air during a parade."

"Oh, you mean confetti?" Birdie asked.

"That's it! That's it! *Confetti!* Don't you just hate it when a word's settin' right there on the tip of your tongue but you just can't coax it to come on out?" She pointed to the tip of her tongue, then inhaled for another verbal marathon. She would have found a congressional filibuster mere child's play.

I was most grateful that Birdie broke in at this point. She spoke quickly as if knowing that the opportunity might not repeat itself. "Eldeen, I want you to meet Margaret Tuttle, my good friend from the grade school lunchroom where I work. Margaret, this is Eldeen Rafferty. We go to the same church, and we've been friends for over twenty years, haven't we, Eldeen?"

Eldeen threw her head back and laughed loudly. "I guess we have, Birdie! Years and years and years! But I remember clear as a picture the day you and Mickey first moved here from Tuscaloosa and me and Jewel met you at the check-out in the Woolworth store downtown and invited you to come to church with us the next day. And you *did,* too! I got such a kick out of finding out your name was Birdie 'cause I had thought to myself the minute I laid eyes on you, 'Why she's no bigger'n a little chickadee!' "

"Yes, we came to church that first Sunday and never even wanted to visit another church after that," said Birdie.

Eldeen leaned forward and embraced Birdie, talking and laughing at the same time. "Oh, you sweet little thing! You just tickle me to death. I sure am glad the Lord Jesus led us to the same check-out line that day. I sure am!"

She released Birdie and stopped laughing abruptly. She gazed at me intently, her lips pursed as if in thought, her shaggy eyebrows partially lowered as a shade. "Margaret Tuttle, now if that's not a nice name," she said. "I once knew a little girl named Jamesetta Tuttle, back in Arkansas. She was named after her daddy, James, and both of 'em had hair the color of black licorice. Fact is, Jamesetta wore hers in long twirly springs that kind of looked like them licorice twists. You don't have any kin in Arkansas, do you, Margaret?"

"I do not," I replied, adding quickly, "and neither do I have time to stand here any longer. If you will instruct the driver of your car to back up, I will be able to leave."

Casting a look behind her, Eldeen smiled

happily and said, "Oh, that's my grandson Joe Leonard. He just took the test to get his driver's license this summer. *Passed* it, too. The man that gave him the test used to go to school with my daughter Jewel. Used to have a head full of red hair, but he started goin' bald before he turned thirty. Now he's just got a tuft or two."

"Yes, well, I assume that your grandson knows how to put the car in reverse," I said.

"Why, he sure does! He had to do that and lots of other things when he went for the test. He did his parallel parkin' perfect right off, the first try! The man that gave him the test said that —"

"I think Margaret does need to leave, El-deen," Birdie interrupted. "Could you get Joe Leonard to back up and let her out? Then you could stay and visit longer."

Eldeen shook her head briskly. "No, no, no! I'm leavin' myself! I told Joe Leonard we'd just stop by for a minute to see if you could use — now, looka there, I almost forgot. It's back there in the front seat of the car. Here, let's go get it." She included me in her beseeching gesture. "Come on, Margaret, you come see, too."

It was a frozen turkey, double-bagged in brown Thrifty-Mart sacks. As Eldeen told it (I will condense her verbose explanation), her son-in-law had brought home a turkey for Thanksgiving the day before, on Monday, having received it from a patron of his place of employment, which, in a coincidental development, turned out to be the Derby Public Library, the parking lot of which I probably would have been entering at that very moment had I not been delayed in Birdie's driveway.

On that same day, Monday, Eldeen's daughter had also arrived home with a turkey after stopping by the grocery store, which was to be my next item of business this afternoon if I ever managed to get past the blockade. To cap off the story, Eldeen reported with great geyserlike eruptions of wonder that she herself had been the awestruck recipient of a telephone call today, Tuesday, a few minutes past noon informing her that her name had been drawn at Thrifty-Mart as the winner of none other than a twelve-pound turkey.

"Three turkeys in two days!" Eldeen cried. "Can you feature that? Seems like the Lord just opened up the gates of heaven on us, doesn't it?" Though perhaps the thought of three turkeys tumbling out of the rich blue of the November sky could have been amusing at another time, I did not join in the laughter. "Now, we'd already made up our minds to use one turkey and save the other one for Christmas," she said, "but when I got this call today, I just threw up my hands and said, 'All right, Lord, who do you want me to give

378

this feller to?' And quick as a twinkle, I thought of you, Birdie. The Lord just seemed to say to me" — she pitched her voice even lower — " 'Drive on out to Birdie's house, Eldeen. Go on, drive on out there to Filbert.' " This brought to my mind the lines from the poem by James Weldon Johnson that read: "And the Lord said, 'Go down, Death, go down to Sister Caroline's house in Yamacraw, Georgia.' "

This, then, is how it was that I became the possessor of a free twelve-pound turkey two days before Thanksgiving. Birdie told Eldeen that Mickey had already brought a turkey home and put it in the freezer two weeks ago, and then the Lackeys, their "neighbors through the woods," had invited them a few days later to be their guests for Thanksgiving dinner.

"So we've got a turkey saved up for Christmas, too," said Birdie gently. "And our freezer is so cramped we wouldn't have room for another one."

For the briefest of moments both women had stared at each other in confusion, their kindly urges sadly thwarted, before Eldeen raised her finger, pointed it directly at me, and stated, "Then it must be *you,* Margaret Tuttle! You must be the one the Lord had in mind for me to give it to. No sir, no sir, don't you go arguin' about it. I found out a long, long time ago that God doesn't get things mixed up, and when he tells you to do somethin', he *means* it, and there's not a bit of use tryin' to talk your way out of it." She opened the car door and said, "Here, Joe Leonard, shove it over here. Old Mister Tom Turkey's goin' home with this pretty lady!"

When I turned onto Highway 11 ten minutes later, the turkey beside me on the front seat of my car, I heard Eldeen's last words fired upon me as from a blunderbuss at close range. "You're the one! You're the one God's got his eye on! I knew he wanted me to come out here to Birdie's!" A great restlessness overtook my spirit, for I felt that by some divine trick I had been present against my will at a time appointed.

And I saw Birdie's imploring eyes as she lifted the bag from Eldeen's car. "Margaret," she said, walking with me to my car, "it's nice of you to take this. It means a lot to Eldeen, bless her heart." Setting the bag in my car, she smiled at me. "And I sure didn't mean to pry earlier," she said. "I hope you'll forgive me, honey."

Everlasting Covenant

19

___

I thought it most ironic, given my recent interest in the poem by Archibald Rutledge and Birdie's remarks concerning certain characteristics of the wildflower, that Thomas arrived home that very afternoon, Tuesday, with a book newly purchased from a music store in Greenville. He had negotiated a contract with three hotels in Greenville to service their vacuum cleaners and periodically drove over in his pickup truck for this purpose. I was in the kitchen chopping a green pepper on a small cutting board when he came home. The book, which he proudly displayed to me, was a large hard-cover volume, quite thick, that bore the presumptuous title *The Three Hundred Favorite Songs of America.*

"I told the folks at the store," Thomas said, "that I wanted somethin' with lots of different songs in it that wasn't too hard to play on the piano, and they went and got this off the shelf. Said it was real popular."

As he flipped through its pages, I saw that it did indeed contain a wide variety of songs, from "Swing Low, Sweet Chariot" to "Home on the Range" to "Seventy-Six Trombones." Though I did not say so, I was pleased to note that the piano parts were simple enough that I could play many of them now and many more in the coming weeks as my lessons with Birdie continued. At once I made plans to work on some of the songs during my practice time the next afternoon.

"But look here, this is what made me buy it," Thomas said, turning to a page that he had dog-eared. Though I deplored his abuse of the corner of the page, I said nothing. "See this song here?" he said, pointing. "This used to be my aunt Prissy's favorite song in the world. She'd sing it over and over when I was a youngster."

Though I am certain that I must have stared at the title of the song as if beholding a freak of nature, I forced myself to ask calmly, "She was the aunt who read aloud *David Copperfield,* was she not?"

"Sure as shootin'!" Thomas said. "How'd you ever remember that?" Not waiting for a response, he rushed on. "The rumor amongst us kids was that Aunt Prissy had been dumped by a beau when she was a girl. But my mother never would talk about it, and 'course none of us dared ask Aunt Prissy if it was true. But many's the day I heard her out on the porch in the summertime or settin' in her rockin' chair by the coal stove when nobody was around singin' this very song right here. Funny thing was, even though it's a right sad song, she always sang it real cheerful. And I've never heard of it before or since. Fact is, I'd almost forgot all about it till I was flippin' through the book and ran across it."

Here follows the irony: The song was titled "Wildwood Flower." Labeled simply "Folk Song," with no credit given to either composer or lyricist, its words were those of a melancholy young girl twining flowers into her raven black hair. And with the more cultivated varieties of flora, such as roses, lilies, and myrtle, she was weaving "a pale wildwood flower with petals light blue." As I read the second stanza, I was taken back as if from a dashing of cold water.

Oh, he taught me to love him, he promised
    to love,
And to cherish me always all others above.
I woke from my dream and my idol was clay,
All my passion for loving had vanished
    away.

And the ending lines of the third stanza further caused my mind to reel.

I will live yet to see him regret this dark hour

When he won and neglected this frail wildwood flower.

Tell me, reader, that I am not stretching for
parallels, that you, too, see the analogy that
came upon me with such force, though your
failure to grasp it would make no less powerful its impact upon me. Surely the unknown
composer of this folk song telling of a girl's
betrayal at the hands of a trusted suitor — a
simple tune sung for many years by many
people, including Thomas's spinster aunt,
and now found notated within a book in the
1990s — had given no thought to the meaning that now leapt at me from the page,
compressing into its lines, in a sense, my
entire life: Had I not been badly used, and,
upon awaking as if from a dream, had I not
discovered an idol of clay and had not my
heart ceased to love?

I speak not of my grandfather, but of him
whom my mother had proclaimed faithful
and almighty, ready to deliver. I speak of
God. He had proven as traitorous as my
grandfather — no, more so by far. He had
won me as a child but had heartlessly rejected
me. He had taken my mother — my father,
also, if one were keeping strict account —
and had replaced her with my grandfather.
He had taken my son and replaced him with
nothing. He had made of my life an unend-
ing tragedy.

Recalling Birdie's words *"You remind me of a wildflower in a lot of ways yourself, did you know that, Margaret?"* my eyes once again sought out the line that encapsulated what I thought to be God's offense toward me: *He won and neglected this frail wildwood flower.* Had I been honest with myself at that moment, I would have acknowledged, as I do now, that like the young woman in the song I had for many years nursed a spirit of vengeance, longing to "see him regret" my "dark hour." The word *grudge* is too mild a word for what I had felt against God since the age of thirteen. And part of my anger was that I knew my own powerlessness to do battle with him.

At some point I was aware that Thomas had begun singing the song for me, tracing his long forefinger under the words as he did so, but his voice was as a strong, aimless wind swirling about me, and the words and notes upon the page were as dust being carried far away. He must have stopped when I turned and fled the room, but I cannot recall. In my bedroom I regained my composure and emerged some short time later to resume supper preparations. Thomas had set the book of songs, closed, upon the piano by this time. Later, he observed me surreptitiously as we ate, and though he talked at great length, he did not trouble me with questions.

Perhaps you will see why I felt as though I were suddenly being smothered in a great drift of wildflowers, for in addition to the preying of the poem of Archibald Rutledge upon my mind, Birdie's remarks to me concerning wildflowers, and my husband's serendipitous discovery of an old familiar song about a wildwood flower, I further espied as I drove to school the next morning, the Wednesday before Thanksgiving, something of which I had taken no previous note, though I am certain it must have been clearly visible at other times as I had driven this route over the years.

No doubt you sense what is coming, ironies piling upon one another as they are. Here is what I saw alongside the road on the bank of a shallow ditch early one November morning: a stand of wildflowers with pale lavender-tinged petals.

While I consider myself an astute observer, I did not recall having seen these clusters of flowers before this day, though I could only assume that they had been growing there for some time. My initial response was of irritation. It was November, well past the time for the blooming of flowers! Yet there they grew, visible to all who traveled that way.

I am not a superstitious person, nor a believer in signs and wonders. I knew that there was no sinister force at work bent upon driving me mad. However, though I straightway attributed to coincidence the repeated encounters with wildflowers, I nevertheless felt an involuntary shiver pass over me as I continued on my way to school that morning. I stopped as I drove home that afternoon and picked one of the roadside flowers — stem, leaves, and all. In the book of wildflowers that I acquired a short time later, I found its scientific name: *Gentiana villosa.* Its common name is the pale gentian, and it blooms in the Carolinas, Georgia, Tennessee, and West Virginia from September through November.

Enough of wildflowers. I determined to put them from my mind. The atmosphere in the school kitchen that day, the day before Thanksgiving, was festive. Though the entire morning was one of unceasing effort — the kind of day that Francine called "hairy" — yet there was a nearly tangible spirit of comradeship among Algeria, Francine, and Birdie.

The menu called for turkey, of course, with rice, gravy, applesauce, rolls, and pumpkin pie. Although I had often pointed out to the regional ARA office that the serving of turkey on the day prior to Thanksgiving evidenced poor planning in that we were duplicating the exact meal that would be spread before the great majority of our schoolchildren the very next day, the tradition nevertheless continued, those in the ARA office obviously unconcerned with such details. Too, I suppose the point could be made that a number of our students would not sit down to a turkey dinner on Thanksgiving Day. Many would be fortunate to eat hot dogs.

Throughout the morning the merry crash and bang of pots and pans could be heard in the kitchen, bringing to mind a phrase from Anna Quindlen's second novel, *One True Thing,* in which the narrator refers to the similar metallic clanks of her mother's kitchen activities as "the tympani of my childhood." I, too, can still hear the percussion of my mother's cooking utensils in the early morning, for this was the sound to which I awoke each day for the first thirteen years of my life. My mother was fond of breakfast, routinely preparing eggs, bacon, toast, and pancakes before leaving our apartment for her job.

Intermingled with the cymbals of the pots and pans in the school kitchen that morning was Birdie's flutelike laughter. At one point I heard her exclaim, "Oh, I just *love* this time of year!" Because of her affection for the season and for the schoolchildren, I suppose, she had brought to school, unbeknownst to me until later, five large bags of what I believe are called gummy worms — soft, brightly-hued candies shaped like worms and of a rubbery texture.

"Won't they get a kick out of finding these

little worms in their applesauce?" I heard her say to Algeria as I exited my office to take my place at the cash register before the first class filed through. Her remark alarmed me, of course, for I feared at first that the worms of which she spoke were real ones she had found inside our jars of applesauce — the result of careless processing — and I was ready to investigate the matter and to rebuke Birdie for treating such a circumstance so lightly.

I stopped abruptly just outside my office door upon hearing Birdie's jolly talk of worms, and from my vantage I observed her as she extracted from a cellophane bag a handful of the soft candies and held them up, separating them like thick yarns from a matted skein, and began placing them, one by one, onto the five empty trays set before her. I then watched her drop a large spoonful of applesauce upon each worm and push the trays one at a time to Algeria on her left, who added a serving of rice and gravy. Francine was just bringing over an enormous tray of sliced turkey from the warming oven, calling out as she did so, "Gobble, gobble, gobble. Here comes old Tom!"

It was too late to halt Birdie's plan, but I was greatly disturbed that I had not been consulted. Although I am permitted by the regional office to make slight alterations in the menus — as in the substituting of light bread for biscuits, for example — such changes are to be carried out at my discretion and in strict moderation. I would never have approved of the sugary treats.

I could not let the offense pass. With a squaring of my shoulders, I approached Birdie just as the first child — an unkempt boy by the name of Roscoe Stokes — led the second graders into the serving line. When I appeared at Birdie's right side, slightly behind her, Francine was just sliding a full tray toward Roscoe. With a soft chirrup of laughter, Birdie addressed Roscoe. "Why, hello there, Roscoe, honey, if it's not one of my favorite little boys in the world. I sure did like that story you wrote about the chipmunk named Spike." Birdie had distributed to all the classes the second issue of *Sheep Tales* the day before.

Roscoe grinned and wiped his nose against the cuff of his faded red shirt, which was not only too small but also noticeably soiled. As he moved his tray along the silver rails toward the unmanned cash register, I spoke Birdie's name.

She turned with a start. "Why, hello, Margaret, I didn't see you walk up!" she said.

"I cannot fully discuss the violation at present," I said sternly, "but you have flagrantly disregarded an official policy by distributing unauthorized sweets to the children. I do not recall your seeking my approval for this." I cast a severe glance at the bag of gummy worms lying open before her but hidden from the children's view by a stack of empty trays. "And furthermore," I added, "Algeria and Francine should have dissuaded you." I cast a reproving look toward Algeria.

Birdie's hand, inside its overlarge plastic disposable glove, reached out as if to touch my arm, but I stepped back. "Oh, Margaret," she said, "I thought . . . well, I sure didn't mean to . . ."

Algeria glared at me combatively and uttered a defiant grunt as I turned away and stalked toward the cash register where Roscoe and two other children stood waiting for me. The grin had faded from Roscoe's face, and he stared up at me in fright as if viewing a dangerous animal at close proximity. For the next hour and a half, I tore off ticket stubs with a mighty vigor, furiously flattened wadded bills, and all but threw coins into the proper slots.

Positioned as I was at the end of the serving line, I heard Birdie's voice continually, as I did every day. "Oh, look at Vicky's pretty pink hair bow!" and "Here, Jason, honey, do you think this'll get you through the rest of the day?" and "Mrs. Lucas, I can tell you're a good teacher by the way your children always look so bright and happy!" And I heard the children's greetings to her. "Hey, Miz Birdie! My cousin's comin' from Beaufort today!"

and "Can I come back for seconds on rice, Miss Birdie?" and "We gonna sing that song about the cat again?" Miss Grissom, the music teacher, had attended a funeral on Monday and had asked Birdie to direct the afternoon choir rehearsal by herself that day, during which Birdie had taught them a song about a cat called "Don Gato."

All of the teachers had a kind word for her also. Miss Partridge, a slip of a girl who was a first-year teacher in the fourth grade, said, "The children just *loved* the pilgrim cupcakes, Birdie! They're writing you thank-you notes this afternoon." Evidently the gummy worms were not Birdie's only donation of sweets that day. I discovered later, as I inquired into Miss Partridge's comment, that once a week since September Birdie had been baking treats at home and leaving them early in the morning on a teacher's desk with a note, such as "To all my little friends in Room 3-C — Guess Who?"

As the children discovered the worms in their applesauce, they set up a clamor in the lunchroom. One entire class of third graders, laying the treat immediately to Birdie's account, called out in unison, "Thank you for the worms, Miz Birdie!"

Jasmine Finney, the sulky child for whom Birdie had bought a pair of sneakers two months earlier, came back through the line holding her worm by the tail. "You give us these?" she asked Birdie, and Birdie opened her eyes wide in mock surprise. "Me? Now, whatever gave you such an idea, Jasmine?" Jasmine pointed her finger straight at Birdie and said, "You did it. I can *tell*." Then she threw her head back and dropped the whole worm into her mouth. Before she left, Jasmine said something else to Birdie that I could not understand because she was chewing at the same time. Evidently her words were not lost on Birdie, however, for she leaned forward and said, "Jasmine, you're a dear to say that. Now, you go on back to your teacher and be a star pupil this afternoon, you hear?"

Birdie had brought about a marked difference in the entire lunchroom. In past years, while Vonnie Lee was full of quick, foolish talk, at which Francine endlessly giggled, and while Algeria occasionally engaged in lively conversation once the early morning was past and the day was underway, I would not have characterized our kitchen as a happy place. Each of us had her own private sorrows, which, though temporarily set aside each day, nevertheless seemed to seep into the corners of the room like a fetid vapor. Birdie's coming had cleared the air. Teachers and pupils alike were won by her smallness, her deftness, her gentleness. Even Mr. Solomon, the principal, had begun visiting the kitchen and lingering to chat. He and Birdie discovered that both of them had lived in Tuscaloosa, Alabama, during a three-year period in the early seventies.

On this particular day Mr. Solomon came into the kitchen as the fifth graders were filing through the line, and his laugh resonated loudly as he observed Birdie's placement of a gummy worm upon each tray before serving the applesauce. "Whose clever idea was that?" I heard him say, whereupon Algeria and Francine cast self-vindicating glances in my direction as if to say, "There now, see? Mr. Solomon thinks it's clever."

After the last class had been served, I returned to my office to count the day's cash and prepare it for deposit. Before I could seat myself, however, Birdie appeared in the doorway.

"I know you have your schedule, Margaret," she said, "and I don't like to be the one to interrupt it, but I just have to talk to you before another minute passes. I feel so awful about upsetting you with the gummy worms. I always seem to be stepping out of line!"

I sat down, and she advanced closer toward my desk. "I was planning to resume our conversation in greater detail after completing my paper work," I said, not looking directly into her eyes. About her neck she wore an old-fashioned pendant of silver that I had noticed earlier that morning — an oval bearing a small pale green stone, a peridot, I believe it is called, in its center. The silver oval appeared to be a locket, and I knew that I had only to ask and she would eagerly open it to show me what was inside. I did not intend to ask, however. The pendant provided a convenient focal point as I spoke to Birdie, and staring at it, I measured my words. "I am willing to overlook your impulsive violation of policy today, but you must understand that the menus are carefully planned and regulated and are not to be changed in the slightest degree without my authorization."

The face of the locket, I saw now, was worked about with a fancy scrolled engraving, worn practically smooth. Its surface area was approximately that of a quarter, though, as I have said, the shape of the pendant was elliptic. It was suspended from a short chain of poor quality, most of which was concealed beneath the collar of her white blouse. I suppose my scrutiny of the necklace had reminded her of it, for in the pause that followed my statement, Birdie lifted a hand and pressed lightly upon the locket with two fingers as if assuring herself that it was still in place.

"Oh, Margaret, I'm ashamed that it never dawned on me to ask you." I still did not lift my gaze to her eyes, but I knew that her eyes were fixed upon my face. "I see now that I was wrong," she continued gravely, "but of course now it's too late. I'm not trying to be stubborn and change the way things are done around here, I'm really not. I just wasn't thinking — or I guess I *was* thinking but not about following the right steps. I was only thinking of how exciting it would be for the boys and girls. Will you forgive me, Margaret?"

I had no heart for scolding her, I realized now. My earlier anger had been spent, and I believe it was at that moment that I understood the exact nature of my feelings for Birdie Freeman. For three months I had felt within me the warring factions of love and hatred toward her. It was not Birdie herself whom I hated, of course, but rather the softening of my heart, the stirring up of old remembrances, the gradual opening of gateways.

I did not want to love again, I told myself; indeed, I had vowed not to do so. Yet each contact with Birdie further eroded my defenses. I felt increasingly vulnerable, and this was what I hated. As I looked steadfastly upon the glint of the pale green stone in the center of her locket, I knew that I was guilty of fakery. As other women put on airs of various kinds, a behavior that I self-righteously denounced, I saw clearly my own falseness, for I had been pretending, quite convincingly, to despise someone whom I had grown to love.

Such knowledge could not be made public,

however. Certain things were expected of me. I could not at the age of fifty become a different person. Or could I? Only recently had I finished a book — *Stone Diaries* by Carol Shields — in which a character named Alice made the following claim: "The self is not a thing carved on entablature." Her point was that one can, by a force of the will, change himself in extreme, fundamental ways. For example, whereas Alice had lived for nineteen years as a contentious, domineering fault-finder, she decided after her first year of college to become a kind person and set about to do so. But I did not want to change! Or did I?

I felt that my course was set, but I saw trouble ahead. Thomas, for example, had for the fifteen years of our marriage allowed me my idiosyncrasies to an extent that others would certainly deem incredible. Ours was a symbiotic relationship, an exchange of goods and services, a business arrangement without physical union, yet I have already set down for you the slow changes at work between the two of us of late.

Though I still conducted myself in a brusque manner toward him, Thomas had begun in recent weeks, as reported in an earlier chapter, to approach me more directly and with less reserve. I know not to what cause to lay this change, although, as intimated previously, I believe that Birdie's coming into my arena, so to speak, had distracted me. Sensing a shift — though I doubt that he could have defined it in words — Thomas had begun venturing closer. As proof, that very morning he had said to me as I opened the door to leave for work, "Margaret, *I'm* gonna cook our Thanksgiving turkey tomorrow." I had set my lips and closed the door firmly without reply, as if angry, though in truth only mystified.

To return to Birdie, however, I cannot tell how long we remained silent following her request for forgiveness. I continued to gaze at the silver pendant about her neck, as if held by a hypnotist's power, and she began to toy with it, tapping upon the peridot lightly, then running her finger around it in a tiny circle. I wanted to tell her to stop, to point out that the engraving was nearly invisible as it was and that she would erase it altogether if she did not take care, that her tampering with the stone could loosen it. But I said nothing.

A phrase from Willa Cather's *My Ántonia* kept repeating itself in my mind as I watched the tiny clockwise motion of her finger: "What a little circle man's existence is." At length — most likely it was only seconds of time that had passed — she leaned forward, braced her hands upon my desk as she had done upon previous occasions, and repeated her question. "Will you please forgive me, Margaret? I'll be sure to ask next time."

I lifted my eyes to hers and spoke, my voice much louder than I had intended. "As I said, I will overlook the incident today, and it would be better for all if there were no next time."

For an instant before she smiled and replied pleasantly "Thank you, Margaret," I tried to imagine what she would have said had I opened my heart to her at that moment, had I said something like this: *"Birdie, of course I forgive you. My anger is but an act, a poor attempt to cover my pride and fear. Please be patient with me and continue to be my friend, for I need your help."*

I permitted myself a brief interval of wishing — that my soul were as unobstructed as Birdie's, that I could reach forward and touch others unabashedly, that I could speak with her simple honesty, that I were not so trussed with doubts and seasoned rage. I had read a book some months earlier called *The Weight of Winter* by Cathy Pelletier — not a riveting book, for I felt that the author's style was still in its formative stages, yet compelling enough that I would not abandon the story midway — in which one of the characters resigns herself to remaining in the town where she grew up, reminding herself that if she were to grow restive she could always retreat to "that gauzy realm of wishing." This seems to me, upon reflection, a most unsatisfactory way to live one's life.

I realized as Birdie turned and left my office that I would never be content merely to wish or to imagine myself more like her. What I was beginning to desire earnestly, I knew, was actually *to be* more like her. The truth could not be denied: I wanted to change. Yet I did not know how.

At the same time, however, the perfidy of my past rose up before me like a spectacular monster, and I heard its evil laugh, as if confirming an everlasting covenant with doom and damnation. I longed to call out to Birdie, to summon her back, to seek her help in exorcising the demon of my past, but I sat silently at my desk and watched her return to the kitchen. I saw Algeria and Francine move toward her as if ready to offer comfort. I saw Birdie smile and shake her head, and I remembered a curious thing I had once read in a magazine: that in certain eastern European countries when a man shook his head, he was signifying "yes," and when he nodded, he meant "no."

A MORE EXCELLENT
WAY
20

As I reported earlier, events unfolded so rapidly during the months of October and November that I began to feel quite a stranger to myself at times. On the day before Thanksgiving, the truth had stirred within my heart that I cared for Birdie Freeman to a degree surpassing the ordinary. I was not prepared, however, to act upon the realization openly, primarily, I suppose, because affectionate behavior was foreign to me.

You can imagine the emotional rearrangement necessitated by such developments, one upon the heels of the other, so to speak, for only a few weeks prior I had suddenly come to see that I cared for Thomas in a way I had thought impossible. Truly, my feelings for both Thomas and Birdie were *developments,* for they had taken root imperceptibly and had bloomed quietly.

Looking back upon those months of awakening, I feel a pang of sadness that I continued to conceal from Thomas and Birdie for weeks to come such knowledge of my fondness for them. In fact, I believe that immediately upon understanding the altered state of my emotions, I assumed an even more severe behavior toward both. I am quite certain that my hardness of manner was grounded in uncertainty, in timidity, in distrust — in short, in fear. Most likely my sternness was not altogether convincing, however, for as I have said, Thomas had begun to deal with me more confidently, yet still with gentle forbearance and an underlying respect.

Upon a number of occasions, beginning with the week of Thanksgiving, the phrase *too late* haunted my mind. I could not rid myself of the conviction that an individual's opportunity to make known his tender feelings to another could not last indefinitely, that doors forced open did not remain so permanently, that once a prime moment had passed it could seldom be retrieved. What's more, I knew that a man or woman who failed to act upon the truth of his affections was forfeiting the joy of what I had begun to think of as "living honestly."

Pressing upon me daily was the memory of two books in particular: *Remains of the Day* and *84 Charing Cross Road.* In the first, the author, Kazuo Ishiguro, illustrates the failure to seize love, letting it wash away through one's fingers like fine sand to be carried to the ocean depths. The story of the butler and the housekeeper is one of lost opportunity, of failure to speak openly and thus penetrate the barrier between them. Likewise, Helen Hanff, in her fine epistolary work *84 Charing Cross Road,* tells of a friendship that, though charming and satisfying on one level, nevertheless falls short of complete fruition because of procrastination. I began to feel an increasing burden to ventilate my soul, to fling open windows and breathe deeply before it was too late.

It is of some interest to me that much, perhaps most, of what I have learned about human interaction has come through books. While I believe that most people turn to fiction in order to confirm what they know of life, for most of my fifty-one years I have reversed the act — judging and validating life by the books I have read. "Yes," I may say to myself, "what I overheard between the mother and her adult daughter in the parking lot of the library is realistic because I read a conversation similar in many regards in Alice McDermott's novel *The Bigamist's Daughter.*" Of physical, romantic relationships built upon love, my only knowledge is that which I have gleaned from fiction, for as of yet I have not experienced such union firsthand. If ever I do — and I have found myself wondering of late if such could ever come to pass — will I not say to myself, "This is what I have read in books"?

Thanksgiving Day dawned sunny and mild for November. Thomas set about early in the day cleaning his outdoor grill — a brick affair that he had erected in the backyard shortly after our marriage but had put to use only rarely, due to the fact, I suppose, that I did not care to relinquish my control over the cooking of the meat, preferring instead to start supper before he returned home from the hardware store. After scrubbing and hosing the metal rack, he began laying charcoal and hickory chips in the lower part of the grill. I watched him for a while through my bedroom window, which faces the backyard.

I had washed and thawed the turkey, given to us, you recall, by Birdie's incurably talkative friend, Eldeen Rafferty, and it sat now in the refrigerator awaiting further attention. As I watched Thomas preparing the grill, I knew that I could choose one of two courses: I could obstruct his plans by hastily setting the turkey in the oven to bake, or I could allow him to grill the turkey uncontested.

I saw him check his watch and disappear into the storage shed. He emerged a few seconds later bearing a large sheet of metal that he placed over the top of the pit, turning it twice to determine the best fit. He had equipped the sheet with a wooden handle for lifting, for it was intended as a lid. This sheet of metal he then removed, sprayed with water, and wiped with paper towels. I saw that he had apparently taken a new roll of paper towels from the kitchen pantry and was using them quite profligately, as is usually the manner of men with disposable goods.

I reached my decision. I would leave the cooking of the turkey to Thomas. I dimly recalled a pheasant he had grilled some fourteen or fifteen years earlier, and I suddenly craved the taste of smoked fowl. In addition, I thought of the other dishes I planned to prepare for our dinner and realized that I could devote more of my time and oven space to those if I were not continually marking the progress of the turkey.

I spent the morning and early afternoon in the assembly of a yam casserole, shoepeg corn pudding, green bean bake, creamed broccoli, cranberry salad, yeast rolls, and a pecan pie. I am not given to cooking dishes in advance and freezing them. I prefer to eat my food on the same day that it is prepared. I had brewed tea the night before, however, and had set it in a sealed pitcher in the refrigerator.

We generally eat our Thanksgiving meal at two o'clock in the afternoon, but it was almost three o'clock when we finally sat down that day. Thomas had spoken very little during his comings and goings from yard to kitchen, but it was plain that he considered the grilling of the turkey to be not only a matter of great import but also an adventure he relished. When he finally brought the turkey into the kitchen on a platter, he carried it before him solemnly and set it upon the counter with the attitude of one presenting a sacrifice. We both studied it silently. It was fit to be pictured in a magazine.

"Ain't he a dandy?" Thomas said at length.

"I hope the meat is not dry," I said. "Grilled meat often is."

"Depends on the meat *and* on the one doin' the grillin'," Thomas said. "You must've forgot what a hand I always was at outdoor cookin'."

"Well, we shall see," I said. "It *looks* satisfactory."

Thomas loosened up and laughed with his usual abandon. "Yep, like my pop always used to say ever' time we'd sit down at the table, 'Looks good enough to eat!' "

Though I saw nothing humorous in the remark, I smiled slightly and turned again to the kitchen table, upon which I had laid a white tablecloth and our white dishes, our only set at the time. I had placed a neatly ironed green napkin beside the forks at each setting. Now I set a small dish of cranberry salad to the left of the forks at each place.

Thomas walked to the stove and lifted the lids of the casserole dishes one at a time. This is generally an act I greatly dislike. I had communicated to him early in our marriage that he could view the food when it was set upon the table and not before, for there is nothing more annoying when one is working in the kitchen than to have someone underfoot, especially a man who is only meddling and has no intention of volunteering his help. I let it go for the moment, however, with only a brief word. "Dinner will be on the table in five minutes. No doubt you will want to wash your hands."

Thomas tested me further by turning on the faucet at the kitchen sink in order to wash his hands. I have told him repeatedly of my aversion to hand washing within splashing distance of food being prepared for consumption. The first time I told him this, some sixteen years ago, he grinned and said, "Prepared for consumption? Does that mean for *eatin'*? Now what else would you be preparin' food for, Rosie?" He understood my point, however, and only rarely failed to go to the bathroom sink.

I set trivets upon the table and transferred the casserole dishes from the stove, then placed the turkey in the center of the table. After putting ice in the glasses, I poured the tea, checked on the rolls in the oven, and announced to Thomas that everything was ready. A few minutes later we sat down to our Thanksgiving dinner.

The evening we had eaten at the Field Pea Restaurant, Virgil Dunlop had asked if he might "bless the food," as he termed it. We had acquiesced, of course, not caring to argue the matter publicly, and he had prayed quite without inhibition, only barely lowering the volume at which he spoke. It was a custom that I had been familiar with as a girl; both my mother and my grandparents had said grace before meals. I had ceased private prayers some years before fleeing from my grandparents' home, having seen the inefficacy of prayer in general and of my prayers in particular, and I had not heard a prayer uttered at mealtime since the age of seventeen. Thomas had never given any indication to me of having prayed in his lifetime.

You may imagine my astonishment, then, when upon sitting down for our Thanksgiving dinner, Thomas cleared his throat, inhaled deeply, and said to me, "Rosie, it's such a pretty table you've gone and fixed up that I think it deserves somethin' special. Is it all right with you if I . . . well, I thought I might . . . you know, just say a little somethin' before we eat."

"What do you propose to say?" I asked as if confused, though in truth I suspected his meaning.

He did not answer but instead bowed his head and recited the following: "For this food we give thanks and ask . . . and ask to be fed and filled with . . . with plenty." He paused a moment, seeming unsure of the next step, and then said, "Amen." Neither of us looked at the other while we unfolded our napkins and placed them upon our laps. Thomas took a noisy drink from his glass of iced tea and said, "Now I'll cut the turkey," and he picked up the carving knife and proceeded to do so rather expertly. I had all but forgotten that during the months before we were married and for some time thereafter, he had demonstrated his meat-carving skill quite regularly. I cannot say why he had ceased the practice over the years, but most likely it was again my own impatience to get a job done that led me to take over not only the preparing of the meat but the slicing as well.

Thomas has large and powerful hands. As he carved the turkey, the thought came to me that they were also capable. I believe that one's character in many ways is imprinted upon his hands. Though I often avoid looking into a person's eyes, I most often study his hands closely. I have a vast mental catalog of them. I remember my mother's hands as if they were my own. As I grew to adulthood, in fact, one small pleasure to me amid the abundance of pain was the recognition as I looked upon my own hands that they were becoming very like what I remembered my mother's to have been. If I have "set a store," as Thomas would say it, upon any of my physical attributes, it would, I suppose, be my hands. This is one way that Birdie had first wedged a crack in the door of my heart, for you may recall that she had more than once spoken of them in favorable terms.

"That is certainly more than enough turkey for the present," I said, realizing that Thomas had now sliced a sixth piece. He laid the carving knife alongside the platter and reached for my plate, upon which he placed a slice of breast meat. I rose at the sound of the oven timer and removed the rolls from the baking sheet to a serving basket. Excluding Thomas's repeated murmurs of "Mmm-mmm," we spoke very little as we served our plates from the casserole dishes, buttered our rolls, and so forth.

Something must have sparked within Thomas an urge to reminisce, however, for once his plate was full, he began talking of Thanksgivings past. In most families I believe it is the wife whose words weave colorful, unbroken monologues of repeating patterns; if not the woman, then certainly the children. Thomas, residing in a home with a silent wife and without children, had, I suppose, taken to talking in order to fill the emptiness, at times conversing more or less to himself, although I was almost always listening even when it may have appeared otherwise.

His memories this day spanned many decades, mingling stories from his boyhood with those of recent years, including even the Thanksgiving dinner of a year ago, when I had baked a huckleberry pie from berries that I had frozen during the summer and Thomas himself had made vanilla ice cream in our wooden churn to serve with the warm pie. I recalled my threefold irritation over the homemade ice cream: first, that he had set the churn in the bathtub without a protective cloth beneath it to prevent scratches, of which several resulted; second, that the expenditure of time and ingredients was completely unnecessary, considering the fact that I had bought a half-gallon of Sealtest vanilla ice cream two days before for the express purpose of complementing the huckleberry pie; and third, the season seemed inappropriate for homemade ice cream. I am sure that there are those, however, who would say the same about grilling a turkey outdoors on Thanksgiving Day.

We continued in this manner — Thomas talking and I listening — until he stopped abruptly and asked, "What do you remember about your Thanksgivings, Rosie?" Glancing at me innocently, he took a sizable bite from his roll and then, chewing, shifted his gaze to the soft inside of the roll, cocking his head as if looking upon a strange and wonderful thing. I could not remember the last time he had attempted to probe into my past, and I bristled at once at his question. I felt a sudden corrugation in what had been a smooth and peaceful day.

"For the past fifteen years I have eaten Thanksgiving dinner at the very table at which we are now seated," I said. "I am sure that your memories of those occasions are as clear as mine."

This last utterance had slipped out. I did not for a moment believe it. Over the years I had often noted with amazement the considerable mutation that took place between an actual event and Thomas's subsequent recollection of it. I am speaking not only of a man's tendency to exaggerate in reporting matters such as his height, the length of a fish that he caught, or the number of attendees at a rally, but also of the total transformation of simple facts. In the retelling of a story, Thomas often altered it to an astonishing extent, although the original story was itself sufficiently unbelievable. I had never been able to determine whether his modifications were intentional — for the purpose of embellishment — or whether he simply extemporized as his memory failed him.

"But what about all the years before those?" Thomas asked me now, holding his roll as one would hold a small sponge; he pushed it about at the edges of his serving of corn pudding as if tidying it up. Looking up, he smiled at me. "Don't you remember any Thanksgivin's from when you were little, Rosie? Did your mother fix a turkey? Did you go to a parade?"

I could, of course, have written a book about the Thanksgivings of my girlhood. The day was always a grand occasion for my mother, and therefore for me, too. My mother was a splendid cook, and though our fare was generally limited in quantity, it was sumptuously prepared and served. I always helped in the kitchen, learning many of the culinary skills I employ yet today — for instance, the making of perfect giblet gravy, pie crust, and corn bread. The day was filled with laughter, I recall, and the two of us took walks, listened to music, and read. Often my mother recited lines of plays that she had memorized and entire poems, such as "The White Cliffs of Dover" and "Fern Hill," and selections from Masters' *Spoon River Anthology*.

I did not care to lay out such details for Thomas, however, for I feared that once I began I would not be able to stop. Remembering my mother's love of poetry, I had wondered since my recent discovery of Archibald Rutledge whether she had known of him. I believe she had studied poetry at some point in her life, either during her years of college before leaving her parents' home or during subsequent correspondence courses and independent reading. Since she had lived and studied in New York and the Midwest, however, her poetry courses most likely would not have included a Carolina poet whose name is not even listed in Merriam Webster's *Encyclopedia of Literature.*

"Here, I'll tell you what — let me prime the pump," Thomas said, filling his fork with yam casserole and lifting it toward his mouth, studying it with a brief, ceremonial seriousness. "I'll tell you about something that happened the Thanksgiving I was thirteen, then you can see if you can remember that same Thanksgiving." I felt as if a lead weight had suddenly plummeted to the pit of my stomach.

Thomas opened his mouth wide and inserted the forkful of yam casserole. After chewing a moment, he said, " 'Course, that won't work, will it? I don't mean that *same* Thanksgiving 'cause you wouldn't've even been alive yet, but maybe you can try to think of how you spent the Thanksgiving you was thirteen." He did not know what he was asking!

He launched into a twisted tale of the Thanksgiving of 1938, when he had lived in Kilgore Cave, North Carolina, and his father's four brothers had come with their families a day early so that the men could go hunting, the purpose being to provide a variety of meat for the Thanksgiving table.

"The rule was you couldn't go huntin' with the grown-ups until you was thirteen, so that's how come I remember which year it was 'cause it was my first time to go out with the men," Thomas said.

The last thing I heard Thomas say before I was swallowed by the cold, black memory of my thirteenth Thanksgiving was this: "And they had to stay for six whole days 'cause that snowstorm was the worst in fifty years — twenty-three people in a five-room house for six days!" I remember wondering vaguely whether these were accurate numbers.

In 1957, when I was thirteen, I had been at my grandparents' house in Marshland, New York, only a few months when Thanksgiving arrived. It was an icy day. My grandmother had banned me from the kitchen, claiming that I made her nervous. The truth was, I believe, that she could brook no competition in her domain, especially from a child. When I had made corn bread for supper only days after coming to live with them that summer, my grandfather had pronounced it a triumph, exclaiming overmuch concerning its superiority to the corn bread he was accustomed to eating. I had observed my grandmother's expression upon this occasion. It was not one of pleasure.

My grandfather had at that time a small room in the basement that he referred to as his "darkroom." Oh, how incredibly dark it was! In those days he took many photographs with a Kodak camera — a black rectangular apparatus the size of a large file box — and most of these were mounted in a series of green albums arranged on the bookshelf in the living room. Others, I found later, were kept in a small box in a locked drawer in his darkroom. If given a set of watercolors today, I could, by mixing, duplicate precisely the color of the box. It was dark rust red, the color of dried bloodstains. That Thanksgiving Day in 1957 was the first time my grandfather acquainted me with his darkroom. As I heard my grandmother overhead plodding about in the kitchen, as I heard water coursing through the pipes of the old house, as I heard the violent thunks of the ancient furnace churning out hot air, I was silently plunged into a pit of evil from which I have never escaped.

When later that day the three of us sat together upstairs at the kitchen table for our Thanksgiving dinner — a great undercooked turkey occupying a large serving plate in the center of the table — I remember staring at the tabletop during my grandfather's lengthy prayer. Hearing his deep voice quiver with emotion as he began "O dear God, we are so unworthy to partake of thy abundant goodness," I traced my finger in tiny loops over the bright yellow Formica and took quiet, shallow breaths.

I looked about the kitchen, still pressing my fingertip upon the yellow tabletop, and was stabbed by one of those mad, brilliant thrusts of consciousness — of self-consciousness, it could be called — during which one doubts whether he really exists at that moment yet simultaneously knows and marvels that he does. Only a year ago I had been warmly havened with my mother, and now I was lost in "a hideous and desolate wilderness," to borrow William Bradford's words. All I could say when each dish was passed to me was "No, thank you, I am not hungry." In my grandmother's eyes I saw fury, and in my grandfather's, warning.

During my silent yet intense recollection of this terrible event, Thomas pushed his chair back suddenly and walked to the refrigerator. "Here, have some more ice," he said, dropping several cubes into my glass of tea. I could not even rouse myself to object to his handling the ice with his fingers instead of using the tongs. A few amber drops of tea splashed out onto the white tablecloth, but Thomas did not notice. When he again seated himself across from me, his face bore an uneasy expression — the solidified, uncomfortable, waiting look of a newscaster during a delay between a scripted cue and the shift to an auxiliary field report.

"Can't come up with anything?" he asked at last.

I became the field reporter caught off guard, having missed the cue; for an instant I could not connect his question with its meaning. When I did, I merely shook my head and said, "Not at the moment, no." It was then that I noticed my plate. It appeared that I had cut only a thin strip from my slice of turkey, and though a few green beans lay speared upon my fork, I could not recall having eaten any. A small bite was missing from my cranberry salad. Thomas, meanwhile, was refilling his plate with second helpings.

Picking up my fork, I set about to eat. The grilled meat was delicious.

All was quiet for a while until Thomas cleared his throat. "It's all a choice, you know, Margaret," he said. He was serving himself creamed broccoli, messily, so that it spilled over into the green bean casserole beside it on his plate.

"I beg your pardon," I said, though not in a challenging tone, for this time indeed I did not know what he meant.

"Puttin' things behind you," he said. "It's a choice a person's got to make. Either you forgive and forget or you don't. Sometimes it's mighty hard to put things behind you and move on ahead — I know it is, believe me." He spoke kindly, neither lightly nor didactically. His words, in my opinion, were nevertheless too glib, too easy.

"I'm sorry if I opened up somethin' you don't like to think about," he added. "I shouldn't go pokin' my nose around, and I try not to, you know I do. But I believe what I said, Rosie, and I'll say it again. It's all a choice. You either cut it off and leave it behind you or you drag it along like a dead weight everywhere you go. You get to pick. I know what I'm talkin' about, Rosie."

He paused a moment, then continued. "Forgiveness — it's a big part of living a good life. That's what my aunt Prissy always used to tell me. And I always suspected she'd had to do a lot of forgivin' in her lifetime." He leaned forward and spoke gently. "It helps to wipe the slate clean, Rosie. It's something you can *choose* to do."

I could not speak for several moments, and when I did my voice sounded distant and hollow, as if emerging from a great cavity. "Please do not lecture me about choices," I said. "I know more about choices than I ever care to know."

We sat in an edgy silence for some time, the only sounds being those of our silverware scraping our plates and of the ice clinking in our glasses. Something struck me during this interval that, though I had not suspected it heretofore, I realized now with an unquestioning certainty. *Joan must have spoken to Thomas in private concerning me.* I knew it was so. Joan had strongly intimated to Thomas, if not openly revealed, what she had discovered of my troubled past.

The choice to forgive was not a new idea to me, of course. I had read Jane Hamilton's novel *A Map of the World,* a remarkably

419

conceived piece of fiction with two central ideas at its core: first, that the briefest carelessness may bear permanent and insufferable consequences, also the premise of many other books, among them Donna Tartt's lengthy and breathtaking novel, *The Secret History,* and second, that an individual chooses his response to those consequences — in short, that he may choose to forgive those responsible for his pain or, of course, he may choose not to forgive.

On Thanksgiving Day I knew that were I ever to emerge from my darkness to seek a more excellent way of living, perhaps even to explore for myself the path that Birdie Freeman had taken, this must be my first step: to choose to forgive. It was a dangerous and desperate step, but how I yearned for the respite it could afford — if indeed there were any respite to be had.

A few minutes later I cut into the pecan pie and lifted out the pieces to place them upon two white dessert plates. The secret of my pecan pie, as well as of my hickory nut pie, is in the preparation of the nuts. They must be lightly toasted before the pie is baked. As I served the pie I thought of Birdie's honest brown eyes. I thought of her contentment and of her homely radiance, and I knew that I wanted what she possessed *to be forever mine.*

■ ■ ■ ■

PART THREE:
WHEN FROM THESE
WOODS I PART

■ ■ ■ ■

A Little Oil in a Cruse

21

But forgive whom? The thought of forgiving my grandfather was unthinkable, for to my mind *forgiveness* carried with it an absolving of responsibility and a willingness on my part to forget the crimes, to put them behind my back and never again to look or reflect upon them. On the one hand, I felt that such complete remission for such grievous acts of horror was humanly impossible, while on the other I suspected that I had grown so attached to my bitterness that I could not bear to give it up, for its amputation would utterly disable me.

Like inhabitants of war-torn countries who refuse to flee their homes, unable to imagine life in any other place, I had grown to depend upon my wrath. It was my homeland. Though its hills and valleys were deeply marred and though the view from all sides was bleak, it was nevertheless familiar to me.

While I wanted to believe that my grandfather's sins exceeded the act of redemption, something told me that it was I and not he who stood in the way of forgiveness. For he *had* most urgently requested my forgiveness. I will tell of this later.

After we finished our Thanksgiving dinner, Thomas helped me clear the table. He sliced the rest of the turkey, and I wrapped it in packages for later use — some for sandwiches, some for casseroles, soups, and so forth. The smoked flavor would alter the taste of my usual post-Thanksgiving dishes, such as turkey divan, turkey and rice soup, and turkey tetrazzini, but perhaps the change would not be unpleasant. Thomas also set aside a number of entire slices to take to our duplex neighbors, the Purdues, next door. He said that Nick Purdue had shown an ardent interest in his backyard grilling earlier in the day, hobbling down the steps a number of times to look on and offer comments.

"I'll be switched if he didn't almost start *droolin'* one time when I lifted up the lid so's he could see," Thomas said. "I mean it, Rosie, he had to lick the corners of his mouth where it was startin' to collect!" He chuckled. "Guess what Thelma was throwin' together inside didn't hold a candle to what he was smellin' from our side."

While we had eaten our servings of pecan pie earlier, Thomas had not entreated me further to talk about my past. We had eaten in silence for several minutes before he had begun telling a story he had heard from a customer at the hardware store the day before. Having finished a thousand-piece jigsaw puzzle, the woman, Betty Earle Fosdick by name, had carefully slid it onto a sturdy board, loaded it into the back of her station wagon, and taken it to a framing shop to have it dry-mounted and framed for display. As she was turning into the parking lot of the framing store, her station wagon was rear-ended by a Jeep. "The tailgate flew up and them puzzle pieces ended up all over the inside of her car and out on the pavement," Thomas said, "and Betty Earle said some of 'em even landed on the hood of that cotton-pickin' Jeep! Can't you just see it — all that work right down the drain!" Though I did not join in his laughter, I was nevertheless relieved that he had turned his conversation from me to the misadventures of others.

But to return to the matter of forgiveness, the idea pushed itself into my mind as I moved about the kitchen storing leftovers, scraping plates, and brushing crumbs from the tablecloth that perhaps it was God whom I must forgive. No sooner had the thought shaped itself, however, than I dismissed it. Though it was true I had long borne a grudge against God for what I considered his thoughtless dealings with me in my youth, I knew in that moment that for me to grant forgiveness to God was a presumption past imagining.

I had not thought of it until then, but it came to me now while I filled the sink with hot water, that my very anger against God was testimony to my belief in his existence. Were I an atheist, I would never give form to so many thoughts of God, ill thoughts though they were. No hazy mental ramblings were mine but oftentimes direct conversations along this order: *"You left me alone. You turned your back upon me when I was most helpless. When I was smitten with fear and pain, you were not there."* Often my questions were spoken in mockery, as the words of Elijah to the prophets of Baal on Mount Carmel: *"Were you in a conference with the other members of the Trinity discussing your plans for the universe? Had you embarked upon a journey far from heaven, perhaps to renumber the stars? Or perhaps you were exhausted from cosmic concerns and were taking a rest?"*

I remember well the aftermath of guilt in my earliest rantings against God, though over time I became inured to such stirrings of the conscience and closed my mind to the verses from the Book of Job that sprang forth in refutation of my charges against God — questions put to man by God, such as "Where wast thou when I laid the foundations of the earth?" and "Knowest thou the ordinances of heaven?"

Now, on Thanksgiving Day, the thought of

forgiving God was set aside as quickly as it offered itself for consideration. Over and over the following words, again from the Book of Job, repeated themselves to me: "Shall he that contendeth with the Almighty instruct him?" To my knowledge I had neither read nor heard these words since I was a teenager.

I found myself, therefore, in a peculiar dilemma. How could there be healing without the cleansing act of forgiveness? I was angry with both my grandfather and with God yet could forgive neither. I could not forgive my grandfather, for besides the fact that I was as yet unwilling to liberate him, he was dead. Furthermore, I had now discovered that I could not forgive God, for to do so would denigrate his deity. If he were God, he did not stand in need of man's pardon. The knowledge that I still believed in the existence of God, even defended him against myself, was curious indeed, unsettling in one sense yet strangely comforting in another.

When Thomas left to take the slices of turkey next door, I washed the dishes and pondered my predicament. Through our poorly insulated interior walls, I heard Thomas knock on the Purdues' front door, and I heard Nick's uneven gait as he stumped slowly into their living room, calling in feigned irritation, "Hang on, for cryin' out loud, I'm comin'!" Nick was in the habit of shouting because of Thelma's partial deafness, and he never adjusted his volume when speaking to others.

I knew that Nick would engage Thomas in a conversation, most likely repeating himself numerous times, and that Thomas would be drawn into the Purdues' living room, quite compliantly, to seat himself on the sofa cushion, of which there was only one. The other two cushions had been shredded to ribbons by an enormous stray cat Thelma had imprudently taken in for a day some months earlier, and according to Thelma it had suddenly turned wild during the night for no apparent reason, though I stoutly believe he must have had some provocation. The sounds that we heard through our shared walls that night were unearthly. Nick had managed to encage the animal in the laundry hamper, had driven it to the Saluda River at two o'clock in the morning, and had upended the hamper, depositing the cat into the water.

I heard Thomas knock again, and I heard Nick shout, "I *said* I'm comin', by gum! Can't you hold on?"

While slowly wiping a white dinner plate with my soapy dishcloth, I remembered emerging from a taxi in Marshland, New York, in the early summer of 1973, wondering whether my grandfather was still clinging to life inside the house at the end of the sidewalk. I had turned twenty-nine the week before. As I stepped out of the taxi, my thoughts were a battleground. Though berating myself for returning to the scene of my wretched childhood, I hotly defended my right to do so and was inexplicably drawn toward the front door. I carried with me the same large suitcase that I had watched my mother pack so often when I was a little girl. The taxi driver called something to me, but not understanding his words, I merely said, "No," and the cab lurched away from the curb with a squeal of tires.

My return to Marshland had been precipitated by a most unusual occurrence. To celebrate my twenty-ninth birthday the week before, I had attended an outdoor summer concert by the University of Illinois Symphonic Band in Urbana, Illinois. At this time I was residing in a small town in Illinois called Monticello, where I was employed as a companion and domestic for an elderly woman of considerable means though limited wits.

On my birthday that year, Mrs. DuBois had given me the day off. Her niece, who lived in Tolono, was to spend the day with her. I do not believe she knew it was my birthday. I certainly did not tell her, and I know of no way that she could have had access to any of my personal records. She was an eccentric woman, however, and often behaved unpredictably. She had merely called me in the night before and dictated that I was to go somewhere the next day — she did not care how I chose to spend my time — for her niece was coming for a visit and would see to her needs. As I left the room, I had felt something hit my back; she had thrown her car keys at me. "Bring it back in one piece," she had said as I stooped to pick them up.

The concert took place in the University quadrangle, and I sat on a low stone bench off to one side and behind the other listeners. It was early evening by this time, and I had spent my day pleasantly, first in the public library for two hours, then in a shopping center called Lincoln Square for one hour, where I had purchased a hairbrush and a fountain pen. Next I spent an hour in a park, where I had eaten the chicken salad sandwich that I had brought with me and read several chapters of Sinclair Lewis's *Arrowsmith,* the last of which was chapter sixteen, in which Martin Arrowsmith begins to chafe under the tedium of looking down throats and writing prescriptions and in which his wife, Leora, delivers a dead child.

It was after I read Leora Arrowsmith's mournful words "He would have been such a sweet baby" that I stood abruptly, swept the bread crumbs from my lap, and prepared to leave the park. This is the danger of reading. One never knows what will be stumbled upon, what old embers may leap again to flame.

From there I had walked to a bookshop only a block from the campus and, though my powers of concentration were not at their peak, spent the better part of another hour reading the poetry of Edna St. Vincent Millay and snatches of Joseph Conrad's *Typhoon*. I left the bookshop around four o'clock, having purchased a collection of short stories by Sarah Orne Jewett. Before the concert I had also visited the Museum of Natural History on the campus, had eaten a bowl of soup in the cafeteria, and had read the most recent issue of the *Atlantic Monthly* in the University library.

"He would have been such a sweet baby." The words had intruded upon my heart more than I would have liked. As I left the library and made my way to the quadrangle, I heard clearly the last words spoken to me by my son: *"I do not want a nap, Mommy."* He had repeated them four times, each time more slowly, and I had sat on the bed beside him stroking his brow and watching him surrender to sleep.

It was the last time that I saw him outside the throes of physical pain, for when he awoke from his nap that day, he went to the kitchen where a large pot of water was coming to a boil. I was preparing to make applesauce. Though I did not witness the accident itself, it is my belief that Tyndall, having often watched as I adjusted the heat controls under

431

boiling liquids, wanted to help by lowering the flame. He was only four years old. It was in 1966.

I was in the living room at my typewriter when I had a momentary but stunning presentiment of danger. I was transcribing medical records at the time and had just typed the word *lacerations* when suddenly I froze and a blinding terror overwhelmed me. Perhaps it was some small sound that I heard or the shadow of a movement through the doorway, but remembering all at once the water that I had set to boil, the thought gripped me: *Tyndall is in peril.* At the same moment that I bolted from my chair, I heard the screams that I shall never forget. Of course I blamed myself fully. Is there a mother reading this who would not do the same?

I said earlier that when I arrived at the site of the outdoor band concert, I had spent a pleasant day. This is true aside from the troubling thoughts of my son. I was quite accustomed by now to the torment of my memories. They were as much a part of my day as the putting on of clothing. They rushed upon me continually, often triggered by a single word or act, or more often arising spontaneously with no stimulus.

Sometimes it was simply the sight of something as common as a full trash can that brought them on. I still recall as if it were yesterday the first time I noticed that all the trash cans in our apartment were full. It had been Tyndall's responsibility, one of his "chores" as we called them, to empty the smaller cans into the large one in the kitchen, and he had been very proud of the carrying out of this lowly duty. He had been dead for many days when I opened my eyes and saw the trash cans brimming over with wadded balls of tissue. My loss struck me afresh, so deeply that I could weep no more. My tears somehow seemed now but a shallow manifestation of a sorrow too deep to release. I would not weep again, for to do so was too easy an outlet. I would gather and hold my grief within me as a great reservoir.

On the day of the band concert, almost seven years had passed since Tyndall's death. I sat on the stone bench watching the other listeners, most of whom sat or sprawled upon the grass in front of me. The band members were assembling unhurriedly, removing their instruments from their cases, talking briefly in small groups before finding their seats and beginning their disharmonious warm-up preliminaries.

I recall only the first number of the concert — a stirring composition titled *Fanfare and Allegro* — for it was during the applause following the opening piece that the most unusual occurrence took place. My life seems to have been built upon coincidences. I was aware that someone had joined me on the stone bench, but I had not looked at the person. I knew that it was a man, however. As the applause subsided, I felt his eyes upon me. I turned my head away from him, but when I looked again I could see that he was still studying me. The conductor had by this time raised his arms to begin the next number. I rose and began walking away from the bench, intending to find another place to sit. When I did so, I heard from behind me a low, urgent call.

"Margaret? Margaret?"

Though I had almost forgotten the old fear of hearing my name called in this manner, as from one who recognized me, my heart was instantly constricted with dread. I walked faster, turning my steps toward the Student Union, but the voice followed.

"Margaret, is that you? Wait, Margaret!"

I began running, but still he came.

"Stop, Margaret, I want to talk to you!" He drew beside me and touched my arm. "Margaret! It's me — Lester Kirby. Remember me?"

I stopped running and faced him. We were both breathing heavily. "You are mistaken," I said. "I do not know you."

But I did. You may remember my mentioning in a previous chapter the youth director at my grandparents' church in Marshland, New York, who had reported to my grandparents that I did not mingle well with my peers at the youth activities I was required to attend. I would have recognized him at once, I believe, had I looked at him when he sat down beside me on the bench, for he had not changed considerably since I last saw him some twelve or thirteen years earlier, except in his manner of dress. Whereas he had always worn a necktie when I knew him in Marshland, even to Saturday youth activities, he was dressed now in a pair of khaki trousers and a navy T-shirt.

He was a fair-skinned man with the soft, rounded features of a child and a mottled flush upon his cheeks. His brown hair, finely textured, curled slightly above his ears. When speaking before a group, I recalled, he had always talked too loudly, in a strained pitch, and had fidgeted nervously with his fingers, intertwining them and clicking his thumbnails together. This he did now as he stood before me.

"Lester Kirby," he repeated as if to prod my memory. "From Marshland."

We stared at each other while the band behind us played something slow and stately. It may have been "Elsa's Procession to the Cathedral" by Richard Wagner, but I cannot be certain.

"Leave me alone," I said, then repeated, "I do not know you."

"I knew it was you as soon as I saw you," Lester said.

"Please go away," I said.

"Look, Margaret, I don't want to bother you. I just wanted to . . . well, I don't know. I just saw you and recognized you. Listen, I . . . I don't even live in Marshland anymore. Haven't for over three years now. I haven't even been back to visit since I left. I still get a letter from Pastor Gibson every now and then, but I don't write back. I just wanted to . . . to say hello to you. I'm not trying to scare you."

Lester Kirby's eyes were searching mine, but I read no censure.

"Why are you here in Urbana, Illinois?" I asked.

"Graduate work," he said, then shook his head. "Yeah, I know, I am sort of old for this kind of thing. Seems like I've been in school all my life."

I recalled now that while he had served in an associate capacity at the church in Marshland he had been commuting to a college near New York City. I believe that he was studying at the time for a master's degree in some field related to history. Many of the illustrations that he had used in what were called "challenges" at the end of every youth activity were from history, and he was particularly fond of the American Civil War era.

He had somehow come into possession of an authentic uniform of a Union commander and had brought it to church one day, along with a bayonet and bullet casings. He felt strongly that men of ungovernable passions had stirred the nation to a precipitous war, that had men of reason prevailed, there never would have been a War Between the States. This was a view I found to be of interest, though, of course, there is never proof to be had for such conjecture. I wondered now what Lester Kirby's response would have been had I chosen at some point during those Marshland years to confide in him concerning my grandfather's unspeakable brutalities against me.

We must have stood in silence for some time, for when he spoke again, I realized that far behind us the band had ended its second number and a pattering of applause could be heard. "I never knew why you ran away, Margaret," he said now, "but . . . after it happened and all the talk died down, I started wondering if maybe you didn't have a good reason. I . . . I never knew, though." He suddenly stopped fidgeting and buried both hands inside his pockets. He glanced down at his feet and then once again looked earnestly upon my face.

"What field are you studying?" I asked him.

"Historiography," he said. "I'm working on a doctoral degree." He laughed somewhat self-deprecatingly. "Who knows if I'll ever finish? I'm almost forty and still going to school."

"One should never be done with learning," I said.

He asked me whether I too was enrolled in a course of graduate study at the University and seemed almost disappointed when I answered that I was not. I told him that I did not live in Urbana but had come only for the day. Again, the expression in his eyes gave me reason to believe that he wished otherwise. I suppose he was lonely; he did not seem to be the type of man to attract friends easily. He was nervous and retiring. I cannot imagine why he would have taken the position in Marshland as associate pastor and youth director, for he had never seemed comfortable in the role. Even to me as a teenager, he had given the impression of trying too hard to do something for which he was ill suited.

I had always wondered if my grandfather had invented a plausible story to explain my absence after I disappeared from Marshland. It would have been difficult, though not impossible, for my grandparents to disguise the fact that mine was a sudden and unexpected departure. To set the matter to rest, I asked Lester before we went our separate ways whether my grandfather had ever spoken of me after I left Marshland.

Lester grew thoughtful. Once again he removed his hands from his pockets and began interlacing his fingers. "No, at least not that I ever heard," he said. "It always seemed . . . odd to me, really, but then your grandfather wasn't the kind of man to say much about anything, if you know what I mean. He sort of kept to himself."

"Yes," I said.

"Of course, I don't mean . . . well, he was always ready to share his ideas at church business meetings or with the deacon board, and he always got things done, that's for sure. Most organized man I ever saw. His notes at deacons' meetings included everything down to the last detail. Had a real head for money, too. Pastor Gibson used to call him his right-hand man."

"A pillar of the church," I said. Lester looked at me quickly as if searching for a concealed interpretation, but I returned his gaze without expression.

"Would you . . . I mean, I don't know what you've got planned, but I just thought maybe you'd like some coffee," he said. "Or there's a good place for ice cream a couple of blocks from here. We could talk if you wanted to."

"I do not drink coffee, and talk is something I generally avoid," I said, though not unkindly.

"Well, now, I can understand that, I guess," Lester replied. "Maybe you'd just rather go back and finish listening to the concert," he said with a slight swivel of his head. When I did not answer, he added, "I won't bother you. I could sit somewhere else."

When first I had set eyes upon Lester Kirby just minutes earlier, my heart was filled with fear and dread at the thought of his offering me unsolicited information about my grandparents. How was it then that I suddenly opened my own lips and voluntarily asked, "Is my grandfather still alive?" I can truthfully say that I had no intention of asking such a question, and after the words fell from my lips I fervently hoped that they had been only imagined and not uttered aloud. I knew in an instant that I had indeed spoken, however, for Lester answered promptly.

"Yes, but he was very sick the last I heard."

Somehow I had expected this news. I had been awakened three or four times in recent months by troubling dreams, during which I heard my name called in a voice I both knew and hated. I had set it down to the power of suggestion, however — to the strange origin of dreams in the distortion of common occurrences — for I had recently sat with Mrs. DuBois as she watched a filmed version of *Jane Eyre* on a televised matinee and had heard, with Jane, the calling of her name across many miles by Mr. Rochester following his unfortunate accident. Whereas Jane responded with warm and ready sympathy to Mr. Rochester's call, however, I shrank from the memory of my grandfather's voice and had awakened each time with a cold stab of panic.

"When did you last hear this?" I asked.

"Pastor Gibson sends me a packet of bulletins every couple of months and writes a note sometimes," he said. "I think it was probably back in January or February when he mentioned your grandfather being sick."

Neither of us spoke for a long moment, and I remember two distinct sensory impressions during this interval: First, the band began another piece with a decided Latino flavor; between the notes of a pulsating bass figure I heard the chattering of tambourines. Second, I saw a green oak leaf float from a low-hanging branch behind Lester and land upon the sidewalk two feet from him. I remember wondering why a green leaf would fall.

I took my leave of Lester Kirby only minutes later and have not seen him again since that time. We did not go together to buy ice cream, nor did I return to the band concert. I walked about the streets for over an hour after our encounter, taking careful note of the way the roots of great trees caused the sidewalks to heave and crack. I did not stumble, however, for I kept my eyes upon my feet. I was filled with amazement at the knowledge of my grandfather's illness. My thoughts scattered, I recall, and I even found myself at one point reviewing Lester's question concerning graduate study and musing over what he might have said had I told him that I had not graduated from high school, let alone college.

I cannot deny that among the many regrets of my life is that of not completing my formal education. I am quite sure that I could have lost myself as an academic, not in the sense of escaping my past but perhaps of pushing beyond it by way of scholarly achievement. Even as I write this, however, I doubt its truth, for one is forever inextricably linked to his past. Any "pushing beyond" is only fleeting. Always he must be ensnared and dragged back by the insidious tentacles of memory.

The idea of a college education, however, consumed only a very small portion of my thoughts during that hour. My mind was awhirl with the revelation that my grandfather was at last reaping his well-earned harvest. Before I reached the place where I had parked Mrs. DuBois' car, I knew that I must go to Marshland. As I drove from Urbana back to Monticello, I began to lay my plans for the upcoming journey to New York, a journey that, at the time, seemed to me imperative. I nevertheless felt a brewing uneasiness at the thought of looking once more upon my grandfather's face. What purpose would be served by doing so? Would it not be safer and wiser to keep my distance?

I cannot explain why I felt impelled to travel to Marshland. I would not like to think that I wanted to see for myself that my grandfather had at last been made to suffer for his sins upon me, but I can think of no other reason that I should wish to see the man who had destroyed my innocence and had plunged me into hell. Indeed, I must be honest; to say that "I cannot explain why I felt impelled to travel to Marshland" is dissemblance, to put it gently — or falsehood, to state it frankly.

Thus it was that I found myself five days later, in June of 1973, making my way slowly yet inexorably toward the front door of my grandparents' house. I had told Mrs. DuBois that a family emergency necessitated a hasty journey eastward, that I had been summoned quite unexpectedly. In the strictest sense, I suppose my words held some grain of truth.

I have read of the returning of victims to the scenes of their misfortunes as a stepping-stone to restoration. Facing one's persecutor and revisiting the venue of crime are said by some to be essential components of emotional healing. I was not concerned with healing at this time, however, at least not consciously. Whether one can be unconsciously working out a means of healing I do not know. I know only that my desire in the summer of 1973 was to see with my eyes the physical wreckage of my grandfather.

And this I did. I had not counted on double vengeance, for I saw not only my grandfather, wasted to a shell of suffering, but also my grandmother, teetering on the rim of insanity. A licensed practical nurse had been employed to care for them; she came for eight hours each day. It is a marvel to me now that my grandmother had labored so arduously to follow the nurse's instructions for the dispensing of medication during the night, for my grandfather's bed care, and so forth — it must have taken unimaginable effort — when ending his life, and her own, might have been so easy for her to accomplish. Whether the thought never crossed her mind or whether her scruples would not allow such speedy delivery, I shall never know.

By my reckoning, my grandfather was at this time around eighty years of age. I wondered, as I gazed upon him for the first time in more than twelve years, what name to put to my feelings for this man, once so strong and hardy, now eaten from within by cancer. It was not pity, yet it was not the hatred that I had so long nurtured. I had no word for what I felt.

My arrival was fortuitously — if such a word may be used in such a circumstance — timed, for my grandfather could still recognize faces and speak intelligibly, though only in weak gasps. A week later he had lost these powers. The first words that he spoke when I stood above his bed that day were these: "Is it you, Margaret? Is it?" And when I affirmed that it was, he closed his eyes and cried out hoarsely in anguished tones, "Oh, Margaret, forgive me."

I did not reply, and the nurse, whose face went slack with incredulity, suggested that I let him rest. I turned to leave, but he opened his eyes and cried out again, reaching toward me with one hand. I could not bear the thought of his skeletal hand upon mine and did not step nearer. "Will you . . . will you forgive me, Margaret?" he gasped. But I did not answer. My grandmother, hunched in fright outside the bedroom door, fled from me as I exited, casting fearful glances at me over her shoulder and pronouncing curious curses, or so I supposed they were, upon me. "The devil and beast!" she said. "The seven vials of wrath poured out . . . the harlot of Babylon!"

I stayed in my grandparents' house for almost three months. My grandfather died one morning between midnight and six o'clock ten days after my arrival. My grandmother awakened me by pounding and shouting upon the door of the bedroom where I slept. I could not distinguish her words, but I guessed their import. A week later, three days after my grandfather's funeral, she, too, was dead. In September I boarded a Greyhound bus and journeyed from New York to Filbert, South Carolina, having chosen it at random from an atlas, as I mentioned in an earlier chapter.

This, then, is the foundation upon which Thomas let fall his well-intended words on

Thanksgiving Day concerning choices, for-giveness, and the like. In reporting what hap-pened to me these many years ago, I have aimed at a neutral tone. It strikes me now, however, that I may have erred in the includ-ing of so many details concerning my grand-father's death. Perhaps I have imposed upon my narrative an emotional heaviness. I can-not recall what I felt upon his death and that of my grandmother's only days later. It certainly was not sadness, nor was it relief. Again, I have no word for what I felt. Perhaps if the truth be known, I felt nothing. I read recently the words of Elie Wiesel, winner of the Nobel Peace Prize, in his book *All Rivers Run to the Sea.* He explained why he could not cry when his father died at the hands of the Nazis at Buchenwald: "I had taken leave of myself." I understood what he meant, for this had also happened to me many years ago when I had closed my heart.

This, then, is another chapter, to put it tritely, in the life of the woman named Mar-garet Bryce Tuttle, upon whom Birdie Free-man, many years later, began administering the ointment of her kindness. She came into my life bearing a little oil in a cruse and set about quietly sprinkling it upon me, then rubbing it gently. And like the widow of Za-rephath, her oil was never depleted; rather, it appeared to replenish itself daily.

Returning to my grandparents' house had

wrought no healing; indeed, it had likely opened my wounds anew. I certainly felt no sense of closure upon my misery, for I had seen, like the speaker in William Blake's poem "The Poison Tree," my own moral perversion in viewing the ruin of those who had done me harm.

A Table in the Wilderness

22

The summer days are passing more swiftly than my story is progressing. Already it is July 15. I cannot consider my life of a year ago, before the advent of Birdie Freeman, without great wonder at the many changes that have taken place. Even now, during this summer of recollection, I am seeing more changes. Last week, for instance, Thomas and I impulsively set off on a day trip to Hampton, north of Charleston, something that we had never before done. I will speak more of this later.

I made the journey to Marshland, then, and saw what I went to see. It is a strange irony to me that though I witnessed the death of my tormentor, his stranglehold on me did not diminish. The moderate sum of money to which I fell heir in no way mitigated my anger. I was still gripped by bitter memories, and futile regrets preyed upon me.

But enough of regrets, at least of mine. Birdie Freeman had regrets of her own, two of which I came to know shortly before what I have labeled "The Beginning of Our Friendship." This turning point occurred in December of last year. I shall continue my progress toward it by resuming my earlier narrative.

On the Friday after Thanksgiving Birdie and I were not yet truly friends, not even after Thomas and I spent four hours that evening with Mickey and her in their home beside the Shepherd's Valley Cemetery. School was not in session on that Friday, but Birdie had told me on the previous Tuesday that she would be happy to continue our piano lessons uninterrupted if I would drive to her house on Friday.

By now I had finished the entire MUSIC TREE series and was making my way through a book from the Frances Clark Library for Piano Students called *An Introduction to Piano Literature,* which included a number of folk songs and singing games such as "Clapping Song," "Pop! Goes the Weasel," "A-Hunting We Will Go," and the like. After this I was to move to the second book in the series, which contained a selection of short pieces by master composers — simple minuets by Bach and Mozart, dances by Haydn, a sonatina by Beethoven, and a march by Schumann. I practiced diligently each afternoon, for I was most eager to advance to this book, as well as to a companion volume of short pieces by contemporary composers such as Bartok and

Kabalevsky.

At noon on that Friday the telephone rang. Thomas answered it, for I was working in the kitchen. I had just prepared a gelatin salad for that night and was setting it in the refrigerator. This is another way in which Thomas is still a young boy. He likes Jell-O, chocolate pudding, and peanut butter sandwiches.

From the tone of Thomas's voice and his playful ripostes, I believed the caller to be Norman Lang at the hardware store. Thomas had planned not to open his vacuum repair shop for the day, but I supposed that a customer had appeared, claiming to need immediate service, and knowing Thomas's inability to refuse a request for help, I expected him to be on his way to the store within minutes.

I was greatly surprised, therefore, to hear him say, "Yep, she sure is. She's right in here in the kitchen just bustlin' around busy as can be. Well, actually, she's stooped down in front of the icebox right now. Just a second and I'll get her on the phone for you." He stepped toward me, extending the receiver and stretching the telephone cord from the hallway off the living room. "Here ya go, Rosie. It's for you." I could not imagine why Norman Lang should want to speak with me. I moved through the kitchen doorway to relax the taut cord.

"This is Margaret speaking," I said. I heard Thomas step out the back door to the washing machine, which had just begun to thump clamorously — its signal that the weight of the clothes was unevenly distributed or "out of whack," as Thomas called it.

And then instead of Norman Lang's voice, I heard Birdie's. "That husband of yours is the biggest tease," she said. "I couldn't stop laughing!" To illustrate her point, she broke off to laugh breathlessly, apparently remembering something foolish he had said. I did not reply, and she soon stopped laughing and stated her business. "I was just thinking," she said. "Why don't you and Thomas come over around five o'clock this afternoon? You can have your piano lesson then, and after that you and Thomas could stay and eat supper with us."

I objected to the thought of our husbands' presence at my piano lesson, and I said so.

"Oh no, they wouldn't be up here with us," Birdie said. "Mickey's going to take Thomas downstairs to the basement and show him his workshop and all his little trinkets and things. They won't bother us one bit. The fact is, they won't even be able to hear us down there." Thomas returned to the kitchen, and I heard a brief gush of water from the sink faucet.

I paused. Birdie's plan did not suit me, yet I did not care to voice my protest within

451

Thomas's earshot.

"I'm not going to go to a lot of trouble for supper," Birdie added, as if this additional information might win me over.

"I have just made a gelatin salad for our supper tonight," I said. I meant this as an introduction for the declining of her invitation.

As in past instances, however, she misunderstood my meaning. "Oh, that'll be fine!" she said brightly. "Bring it along! I was going to have ham and macaroni and cheese. A Jell-O salad will be just the thing!"

I wondered in the brief moment that followed whether she had intentionally turned my words, whether she did so regularly, reading their true meaning but quickly manipulating them to her purpose. Was Birdie Freeman capable, I wondered, of manipulation? Or was she so guileless that she attributed to the speech of others her own innocent motives? Was her blindness due to deficiency or design? Could it be that she *chose* to think only the best of others, or was it an unconscious act?

Even as I pondered these questions, I heard myself say, though somewhat flatly, in a tone of resignation, "I will bring corn bread also."

Like our dinner at the Field Pea, the evening at Birdie and Mickey's home does not remain in my memory as a neatly sequenced occasion. I cannot understand why this is so, for it seems that such out-of-the-ordinary experiences should be recalled with great clarity of detail, in thorough and well-ordered outline form, rather than as a vast honeycomb of disparate images. For aside from the occasional one-day family reunions with Thomas's relatives in North Carolina, we had not been invited to someone's home for supper during the entire fifteen years of our marriage. Likewise, we never invited guests to our home.

The evening with Birdie and Mickey consisted of a variety of activities, my piano lesson occurring at the outset, followed at some point by the meal, which we took in the kitchen at a white enamel table such as those associated with Depression-era diners. The chairs, though similar in style, were unmatched. They were all painted glossy black, however.

Birdie was a proficient cook, though her dishes were unpretentious. Besides ham, macaroni and cheese, gelatin salad, and corn bread, our supper also included speckled butter beans, baked squash, iced tea, and a custard pie. Birdie informed us that Mickey had made the piecrust. He had learned the art early in their marriage and by now "could do it blindfolded," Birdie told us fondly. We did not eat the pie, however, immediately following the meal but rather waited, as Mickey put it, "for the sediment to settle." Birdie praised my corn bread and gelatin salad, declaring them to be "the finishing touches" to the meal, and at great length she admired the serving dish that held the gelatin.

Before leaving home, I had transferred the salad from its mold into a large round ceramic dish with a lid, which was actually intended as a vegetable casserole, so that it could be easily transported. Though the full effect of the molded design could not be seen, concealed as it was within an enclosed dish, I preferred this arrangement to the prospect of an accident such as the one Francine had reported at work one day several years ago.

En route to her mother's apartment for supper one night, Francine had swerved suddenly to miss an animal — "I *think* it was a dog," she had said, "but it sure was movin' slow, and Watts and Gala both said it looked to them like a raccoon" — and the cherry Jell-O salad that Champ was holding in his lap had slid right off the plate onto the front seat of the car. "It scooted across the seat like it was *waxed,*" Francine had said, "and it landed right smack up against me." She had acted out the rest of the story, balancing her bulk upon one of the kitchen stools, her hands clutching an imaginary steering wheel. "When I looked down and saw that big red quivering blob of I-didn't-know-what up aside of me, I *screamed.* It looked like a blood clot! All I heard was Champ yellin', 'I didn't do it, Mama! I didn't do it!' Anyway, I jerked that steering wheel so hard the other way that we left the road and plowed through a bob-wire fence, then took off across that piece of farmland out there past the Sunny Dale Feed and Seed. By the time it was over, the ones of us that wasn't screaming was crying." At the telling of it, of course, she was laughing and gasping for air as if floridly maniacal, and she ended the tale with her customary summation: "That was sure something else!"

"What's that pattern called?" Birdie asked now, gesturing toward the serving dish.

"I believe the name printed on the bottom of the dish is Morning Glory," I said.

"Well, it's just beautiful," she said, then asked, "Do you have a whole set of dishes like that?"

"No."

"She oughta," Thomas said. "I keep tellin' her we need us a new set. Those old white ones we got has missin' pieces and some of 'em's chipped. They —"

"They do not seem to affect your appetite," I said.

Mickey laughed and pointed a finger at Thomas as if shooting a gun. "She got you!" he cried. To me he said, "I know what you're saying, Margaret. I don't like to spend money on things like that, either. It's the same with our silverware here. See, they don't all quite match, but they're decent and clean — well, at least they *were*." He held up his knife, which was coated with butter and corn bread crumbs.

Birdie had lifted the gelatin dish above her head and was looking at its underside. "I don't think I've ever seen this pattern in the stores," she said.

"They probably don't carry it at Wal-Mart, puddin'," Mickey said.

"Oh, stop it," she said, laughing. "I don't do all my shopping there, and you know it."

"Oh, that's right, I forgot," Mickey said. "You go to Big Lots, too."

"I told you to behave tonight," she told him. Setting the dish down, she leaned forward and addressed Thomas, tilting her face up at him. "I think it's real sweet of you to want to get Margaret a new set of dishes." She smiled approvingly.

"I'm kinda afraid to," Thomas said, winking at me. "She might throw 'em at me, one at a time." He never would have spoken to me in this manner a month ago, I thought, and I could not recall his ever *winking* at me before.

I recount this portion of our dinner conversation only because it touches upon what happened later, in December, at the metamorphosis of my relationship with Birdie from acquaintance to friendship.

At some point during the evening all four of us descended to the basement. Since my years in Marshland, I have always felt un-settled in basement rooms. I once rented a basement apartment in Vincennes, Indiana, but moved after only three days, forfeiting a month's rent. I have no doubt as to the source of my unease concerning basements. Had Mickey and Birdie Freeman had a darkroom in their basement, I may very well have become physically ill. Birdie and Mick-ey's basement, however, was full of light and color. It would most likely be possible for the average person to forget that he was in a base-ment.

Mickey had converted the area into a multipurpose room — a study, a den, a laundry and sewing room, a walk-in pantry, a workshop, and what he called his "recreation corner," which was merely a card table and Ping-Pong table both pushed against the wall. Though the room was not divided in any way by partitions, the effect was not one of chaos. Everything was in its place. The visual impact, though powerful in its diversity, was what some might call "domestically cheerful."

In his workshop area Mickey created "little nut people," as Birdie referred to them, from the shells of pecans, black walnuts, acorns, peanuts, and chestnuts. Eyes, noses, and mouths were painted onto the tiny faces, and hair was simulated with a variety of botanical materials from pine needles to dried grass to strings of pollen, all of which were trimmed, sprayed with preservative, and glued upon the little heads of the nut folk. The bodies were also made of shells; an acorn head, for example, might have a pecan shell for its body. Each finished figure was glued onto a thick strip of bark. Samples of his workmanship were displayed upon a long shelf.

Most recently he had been experimenting with what he called a "career line," and he pointed to these with particular fondness. "This little guy here's a doctor — see what he's got around his neck?" Around the shell man's neck hung what could have been taken for a wire necklace, some sort of tribal talisman perhaps, but apparently was intended by Mickey to be a stethoscope. The figure wore a tiny white lab coat, which, Birdie interjected, Mickey had made out of some scraps from old pillowcases.

One shell man in a black robe had a beard and wore a mortar board upon his head. He was a professor, Mickey explained. He had also made a figure skater with paper clip skates and a blue velvet costume, this one mounted upon a small hand mirror to signify an ice rink, and a butcher, who wore a white apron smeared with small streaks of blood. Mickey had pricked his own finger to achieve the effect, Birdie told us.

After Mickey showed us his miniature handicrafts, he urged us to sit down on the couch and watch a video of *Funniest Football*

Fumbles, which Birdie had bought him for his last birthday. As the video played, he and Thomas held their sides and hooted as if they had lost their senses. Birdie, seated upon the arm of the sofa beside Mickey, joined in also, laughing freely and adding comments such as "Oh, this is one of my favorites coming up!" Above the vivid green of her blouse, her small face glowed. Aside from her white uniforms and the brown dress she had worn the first time I saw her, at Mayfield's funeral, Birdie's closet must have irradiated with the hues of tropical birds. Francine had reported having seen Birdie one weekend at the BP gas station "wearin' a dress the color of a tangerine!"

As I consider the sport of football to be on an even lower plane than that of boxing and of World Federation Wrestling matches between outlandish, moronic men — which Thomas watches from time to time, claiming to find them funnier than *Hee Haw* reruns — I chose instead to look about the basement room, taking in the details of its furnishings. Of special interest to me was a bookcase beside an old oak desk. By squinting I could make out several titles: *Adam Bede, Middlemarch, The Three Musketeers,* and *The Robe.* I could not help wondering if Birdie had read all, or any, of them.

"Did you see that one, Margaret?" Mickey

asked, leaning forward and grinning at me from the opposite end of the couch. "Here, let me rewind it. You don't want to miss this one. It's a real doozy, as they say in Madagascar." He replayed the fumble.

Thomas slapped both knees and laughed as though demented. "Did you see that?" he asked me.

"Yes, I saw it," I replied. There are rare times when, with only the barest of motivations, I feel myself propelled headlong into a speech. This was one of those times. It was as if I were observing the launching of a rocket, knowing that I possessed no power to recall it. My lips parted, and once begun, the words flowed with a forceful freedom, as if from an arterial wound. "Yes, I saw it. I saw an adult man in a padded suit move backward and sideways down a rain-slicked field, stretch out his arms to catch a slippery ball, seize the ball, and tuck it under his arm. I then saw him reverse the direction in which he was running, plunge mindlessly past seven or eight opposing players — all of whom failed to halt his progress — and raise the ball above his head in an immature taunting fashion as he neared the end line, at which point I saw him, as I could have predicted, lose his balance on the wet ground and flail about in an awkward dance before dropping the ball and collapsing upon one of his own teammates, another man whose IQ most likely does not exceed the speed limit."

The laughter had died midway through my speech, and no one spoke for a moment when I finished. Then Mickey sat forward farther and said to me seriously, "You talking about the speed limit in town or on the freeway?"

Birdie swatted at his arm and said, "Oh, hush, you silly thing," and the three of them erupted again into laughter.

"I'll have to say you summed it up pretty well, Margaret," Mickey said, wiping his eyes. Turning to Thomas, he asked, "Your wife can sure tell it like it is, can't she?" Thomas raised his eyebrows and emitted a low whistle, but said nothing. Perhaps I had embarrassed him by my speech.

"She's a walking dictionary," Birdie said, shaking her head. "Didn't I tell you she had a way with words, Mickey? Didn't I?"

Before we left, Mickey and Thomas unfolded the Ping-Pong table. Birdie and I sat on the sofa and watched the two of them play three games. I recalled Thomas's skill at the game, as displayed at his cousin Spade Littleton's house in North Carolina at family reunions, but Mickey was a far better player than Thomas's relatives. Small and quick, he was an indefatigable opponent. Thomas, on the other hand, though taller and at least a decade older, was shrewd in his placement of shots and returned each ball with a deceptive spin, thus winning two of the three games.

Mickey demanded a rematch at a later date and informed Birdie and me that "next time we'll make you ladies play, too."

Later we all returned upstairs. I mounted the twelve steps quite rapidly and immediately began to breathe more easily with the knowledge that I was again above ground level. As we ate our slices of custard pie in the living room, I discovered two facts about Birdie Freeman. These are the regrets of which I previously made mention.

One came as the result of a question posed by Thomas to Mickey. "You folks have any children?"

"No, we don't," Mickey said. You may recall that I had suspected such to be the case from my first meeting with Birdie. Furthermore, I had never heard her speak of children or grandchildren. Mickey pointed to a collection of photographs on a small table; the picture of Birdie and him on their wedding day was the largest and most centrally positioned. "The two little boys over there are my nephews," he said. "Two of the finest children you ever met. Smart, handsome, talented — all of it inherited from their uncle, of course." He crossed his eyes and let his tongue loll.

To write that "a shadow passed across Birdie's face" at the mention of children would sound banal and sentimental. I will therefore say simply that the expression upon her face altered from contentment to studied cheerfulness. And when she asked suddenly, "Does anybody want anything else to drink?" her voice sounded like glass, bright and fragile.

As she left the living room with Mickey's and Thomas's cups, Mickey said, "Of course, I've tried my best to fill in for children by acting like one, haven't I, precious?" and she laughed gaily but without conviction. I could not help wondering if she had spoken openly with Algeria and Francine of her childlessness. I must admit that though I overheard much of their talk, there were times when they fell silent at my approach. From my kitchen cubicle I could see the three of them conversing as they worked, and I often wondered what they were saying.

"And what about you?" Mickey asked. "Any kids?"

"Nope," Thomas replied. "We don't have any, either." I kept my eyes on the doorway through which Birdie had disappeared, watching for her return.

As Thomas and I stood beside the front door around nine o'clock that evening, Birdie candidly acknowledged another regret of her life. We were in the midst of exchanging polite farewells. Birdie and Mickey had begun the ceremony by pressing themselves upon us in a great rush of feelings. "We are just *so* glad you could come over!" "We'll have to do this again!" "Thank you for the delicious Jell-O!"

"And the corn bread!" "We'll break out the Ping-Pong paddles again next time and have another go at it!" "Y'all just drop by and visit us *anytime!*" and so forth.

For guidance through the mechanics of taking one's leave, I found myself reviewing scenes from novels that I had read, and after Thomas had offered his thanks in some detail, I briefly declared my own. "Your gracious hospitality has exceeded mere courtesy." Though of my own invention, I do not deny that I composed the statement by imagining what one of Jane Austen's characters might have said after having dined at a neighboring country estate.

Turning to Mickey, Birdie raised both hands and placed her fingers lightly upon her temples. "Did you hear that?" she said to Mickey. "Isn't it just like listening to music to hear Margaret talk?" Then to me she said, "Oh, Margaret, I wish I'd been as smart in school as I know you must have been. I count it a real privilege to work at Emma Weldy with somebody like you! If I'd ever gone back to school, maybe I could have ended up a tenth as smart as you. I sure wish I had. I sure do." Had it not occurred to her, I wondered, to question why someone as highly educated as she assumed me to be was working in a public school lunchroom?

No one spoke for a moment, but Mickey put an arm around Birdie and pulled her close to his side. "If you were any smarter, treasure, you wouldn't be able to stand living with a slowpoke like me!"

The two of them laughed, and Thomas and I stepped across the threshold into the chill of the November night. Looking toward the cemetery, I could see the faint outlines of white headstones luminous under the moon. Birdie and Mickey followed us onto the porch, and Mickey called out to us as we made our way to the car.

"Watch out for the loose gravel! Take her arm, Thomas!" Thomas did so, and I did not pull away. "Go slow down the driveway — you turn too soon and it'll be a *grave* mistake! You'll run into a *dead* end! Y'all come back! Next time maybe we can play some Rook!"

They continued to stand on the porch, waving at us while Thomas turned the Ford around to head down the driveway. Then as we slowly drove away, Mickey stepped to the door, reached inside, and began flipping the switch to the porch light. It was not until later that I thought of the evening as what it was in a metaphorical sense: a table in the wilderness. Even today I can still see the blinking of the porch light and the small figures of Mickey and Birdie side by side upon the top step spreading for us the bounty of their kindness even as we departed.

A WATERED GARDEN
23

As the days passed and Christmas neared, I braced myself. I clearly saw the danger of Birdie's daily favors and tokens, knowing that such gifts, though of little extrinsic value individually, would collect into a great debt, and that debt would surely exact a personal commitment. I feared such a commitment, yet I knew that Birdie was winning my heart, and even as I prepared to deny her entrance, I knew furthermore that she was already well within the portals.

I dreamed one night of a large bud, the size of a man's fist, tightly sealed against springtime yet powerless to withstand its quiet force, yielding at last to open with time-lapse acceleration into a startling, symmetrical bloom of unearthly beauty, an enormous Georgia O'Keeffe flower. When I awoke, it was, of course, still winter; nature's spring would not come for months. Another spring was astir, however, and its harbinger was about her business.

Birdie's gifts were many and unceasing, and not only to me but also to Algeria and Francine — no, truly, to everyone at Emma Weldy. Her liberality of spirit was a steady, gentle rain. For many weeks my response to her offerings had been one of outward annoyance. Often I discarded the trifles, thus offending my highly refined sense of thrift, not because I could find no use for them but because it was my way of rebelling against the incursion of the giver into my life.

Throughout September and October I had disposed of a considerable assortment of small gifts: a bookmark; a plastic shower cap; a pencil; a packet of herbal seasoning; a pocket calendar; a small note pad; a card of buttons; a spool of turquoise ribbon; a miniature book bearing the ostentatious title *Meditations of Tranquillity for the Contemporary Life;* and a photograph of Algeria, Francine, and me — a candid snapshot that Birdie herself had taken one morning in October as the children were filing through for breakfast. Algeria, wearing her usual morning scowl, was dispensing a dipperful of cream of wheat into a bowl. Francine, her head ducked, appeared to be stifling a sneeze. From my post at the cash register, I was studying Francine over the heads of several children, an expression of rebuke upon my face.

Other gifts I had kept for one reason or another: a Level One piano book of hymn duets, an embroidered dish towel, and a small tin of lemon drops. The bonsai, of course, was still thriving. I watered it daily. It was a living thing. There was no question of my discarding it. Even these latter gifts, however, I held to some degree in contempt, aggrieved by their encroachment, their flagrant disregard for boundaries, their implication of restorative powers.

How could a scrap of fabric or a miniature potted tree balance the weight of my past pain? What right had Birdie Freeman to ply me with frivolous odds and ends, to burden me with her generosity, to clutter my life with *things?* Had she been moody, quickly offended, or tiresomely pedantic, I could have dealt with her more easily; indeed, any number of personality defects would have sufficed. She was, however, inexhaustibly cheerful and good-hearted, and it was, of course, her kindness of soul more than the gifts themselves that opened up the way before her into my life.

I had always despised the character of Melanie Wilkes in the novel *Gone With the Wind,* for I felt that she was a goody-goody without the affectation that makes such a character comical. She was a woman devoid of faults, and herein lay her flaw as a fictional character. Her portrayal on screen by the actress Olivia de Havilland, however, displeased me less, for it brought a measure of realism to the flat depiction upon the printed page, and I found myself wishing that such a woman could exist, though I knew it to be impossible. Even in my mother, whose seraphic smile and nobility of heart set her above common mortals, were certain manifestations of humanness. For example, to outsiders — which included the great majority of living persons — she could speak with a sharpness bordering on rudeness, though at other times she could be a charming conversationalist.

When Birdie Freeman had first appeared in the lunchroom of Emma Weldy Elementary School in August, I had begun to observe her closely, guardedly, for I knew that, given enough time, whatever appeared to be pure would prove itself an alloy. By December, however, the imperfections that I had uncovered were few: a childlike gullibility and naïveté resulting in broad misconceptions about the fundamental nature of life itself; the tendency at times to misinterpret even the plainest and most direct language; an irritating habit of referring to Mickey at every turn; a nature marked by such extreme deference to others that she ingloriously offered herself, to use a slang term, as a "doormat"; and, of course, her physical abnormalities. Besides her projecting front teeth, she was as flat-chested as an eight-year-old. I had to concede, however, that she wore her defects bravely. One had to admire her lack of subterfuge in smiling, for instance. Never did she attempt concealment of her teeth by closed lips or an artful placement of the hand. Neither did she resort to padding her bosom.

It was on the seventeenth day of December, a Saturday, that I ceased looking for Birdie's faults, knowing that even if, or rather *when,* they appeared, they would be of no consequence. In short, this is the day that I realized she was truly my friend — not only that she wanted to be my friend but that I likewise wanted to be hers. At the age of fifty, I at last acquired a friend.

She called me that Saturday afternoon in December, all aflutter, and asked if she and Mickey could stop by our house later that day to deliver something. "It'll probably be another hour or so," she said, "sometime around four I'm guessing." When I paused, she said, "We won't stay long." I heard Mickey say something in the background, and she laughed and said, "Oh, stop that!" quickly adding, "I wasn't talking to you, Margaret. Mickey is acting up again." Still, I did not reply at once, and she continued. "I know I ought to wait for this, but I just can't. There are just some days when an idea hits you, Margaret, and nothing will do but to carry through and do it right then! You know how impulsive you get at Christmastime." I knew no such thing.

But she sounded so youthfully exuberant, so eager and hopeful that to gainsay her assertion was unthinkable. "Do you know where we live?" I asked her.

"Not really," she said. "I think Thomas gave Mickey a general idea of where it was that night you came to our house for supper, but he's not sure if you turn before or after Pate's Barber Shop once you get off the highway."

I proceeded to give her directions, which she repeated aloud to Mickey, who must have been standing by with paper and pencil. I had realized by this time that she was not calling from her home, for there were other noises in the background. At one point an electronic beep sounded, and I heard a woman's voice cry, "What am I doing wrong? Why won't it ring up?" I concluded, of course, that she was telephoning from a store. When I hung up the receiver, I said to Thomas, who was sitting in his recliner watching a fishing program on SC-ETV, "The Freemans will be coming by in an hour."

"That so?" he said. I could tell that he was trying to mute his interest. "How come?"

I said simply, "Birdie said that they have something to deliver."

In the kitchen I checked the bread I had set to rise, pressing two fingers into the doughy dome. Finding it ready, I punched it down

471

with great force, deposited the lump upon my cutting board, and proceeded to wield my rolling pin as if it were an instrument of torture. My thoughts were a jumble. I did not want Birdie Freeman to come to my house. I had not invited her. I did not want to see her shining eyes and ready smile, her tightly braided hair, her small hands extending to me yet another bagatelle, for surely gift-giving was her purpose in coming.

Then the thought came to me — from where I cannot say: *I will parry her thrust with a gift of my own.* I would not stand by. I would meet her head on. I would not be obliged forever. But what was my gift to be? To cancel my debt, it must be of substance and quality.

As I opened a cupboard to remove the bread pan, my eyes lighted upon the ceramic casserole dish that Birdie had admired. I lifted it out and examined it. Neither chipped nor discolored, it looked new. Its bowl was rather shallow yet round and wide. I had learned that it was able to accommodate a larger quantity than one would estimate upon first glance. The lid, also of ceramic, was fitted with a knob for grasping, this knob being molded and painted to look like a purple flower bud. On opposite sides of the bowl were two handles designed to simulate twisted vines. I had used the dish only rarely, for its size was larger than I generally needed, and it seemed impractically showy for our table. Most often I use my one-quart Corningware dishes.

To be truthful, I did not know from where the dish had originally come, although it had fallen to me secondhand by way of Norman Lang's wife, an inveterate frequenter of yard sales who regularly cleared her shelves to make room for more of the cast-offs of other people. Edith Lang had set up a table in Norm's hardware store and displayed a number of items with a sign that read *Make an offer.* Thomas had paid two dollars for the ceramic dish and brought it home.

The decision was made in a trice. I would give Birdie the casserole dish as a Christmas gift. Of no matter that it was used merchandise. Indeed, the fact that it had been my own could serve, I suppose, to increase its value by the suggestion of sacrifice.

I quickly greased the bread pan, rolled up the rectangle of dough, folded its ends, and placed it in the pan to rise again. After cleaning up and putting things away, I took the casserole dish into my bedroom and set about finding a suitable box and wrapping paper.

The doorbell sounded at 4:02, a single, feeble chime. Thomas opened the door and welcomed Birdie and Mickey with a great display of cordiality, as if greeting old comrades. I came into the living room from the kitchen and stood on the far side next to the piano. The gift, which I had wrapped in glossy green paper and adorned with a large bow of white crinkle-ribbon, sat in full view upon the wooden chair beside the telephone. Thomas had seen it, I was quite sure, but had not inquired about it.

Birdie stepped inside first, looked around, and emitted a sigh of admiration. "Oh, I just knew your house would be neat as a pin! Look, Mickey, there's the bonsai I gave her. Why, look at the buds! It's getting ready to bloom again, isn't it? Everything sure is trim and pretty, Margaret." If the truth were told, I had begun to view the interior of our duplex as empty and lackluster in comparison to the occupied corners and vivid colors of Birdie's house. Our home appeared to be constructed of logic, whereas hers vibrated with imagination.

Mickey was bearing a large box wrapped in gold foil. From his posture and the strain of his smile, it appeared to be quite heavy. I was suspicious, however, for Mickey Freeman was capable of elaborate playacting. He could very well have persuaded Birdie to wrap one of his nut figurines in the enormous box as a joke.

"Got a match?" Thomas asked him.

"Sure, both my shoes are just alike!" Mickey said, and the two of them laughed, though Mickey's laugh broke off as he shifted the weight of the box.

"Here, let's put that thing down," Thomas

said, and he helped Mickey set the box gently beside the couch. A moment of awkward silence followed, during which the four of us stared at one another by turns.

Then, "Here, here, take a load off your feet." This was from Thomas, who motioned to the couch.

"Take their coats," I said, and he made a gesture as if aiming a firearm at his head.

"What am I thinking of?" he said. "You can tell I'm out of practice at this, can't you? Here, let me have your coats." I sincerely hoped that they would refuse to relinquish their coats and be on their way. After all, Birdie had stated that their visit would be short. My wish was not to be granted, however, for Mickey helped Birdie remove her coat — not the short blue one she wore to school but a longer, fuller one, a nubby tan tweed in an old-fashioned flared cut with enormous brown buttons — and then took off his own light blue jacket, which could scarcely have afforded sufficient protection against the December cold.

Birdie was wearing a royal blue sweater with a cowl neck. The fabric had a furry loose pile like mohair. She looked misplaced inside the large, fussy garment, though she seemed unaware of its ill fit. I noticed also at this point that the bottoms of her two front teeth were smeared with orange lipstick. I glanced impatiently at Mickey. He should have told her of this. Husbands could perform so many useful services if only they were more alert.

Thomas disappeared into his bedroom with the coats, and Mickey and Birdie sat down tentatively upon the edge of the couch. Birdie told me later that she was quite nervous at this point. "You were standing there so still and *solemn* by the piano," she said.

"Getting a lot colder than the forecast said it would," Mickey said to me, rubbing his hands together in what I considered a womanish sort of way.

"Yes," I said.

From next door there was a sudden blast of sound from the television, then Nick Purdue's voice rising in protest. "Turn that cotton-pickin' thing down, Thelma!" Then came the heavy tread of footsteps crossing the floor, followed by a decrease in the volume of the television. "What's it gonna take to make you wear that hearing aid I bought you?" Nick shouted.

Thomas reentered, grinning. "See what you're missing out on livin' way out there by that graveyard?" he said. "Bet *your* neighbors don't carry on like ours."

Birdie laughed politely, and Mickey shook his head. "You kidding? The folks in that lot next to ours are a noisy bunch — always croaking, kicking buckets, and what have you." Again, he and Thomas laughed with gusto.

"Actually, we do hear the Lackeys who live back behind us a little ways," Birdie said when their laughter had subsided. "When Delores goes shopping, Mervin turns up his stereo full blast. He likes big band music from the forties mostly, so it gets real lively out at our place sometimes."

"Yep, it's enough to wake the dead," Mickey said. Thomas laughed so hard that he began coughing. After several hacks, he cleared his throat and sat down in his recliner, swiveling it to face Mickey and Birdie.

Before the tasteless humor could proceed, I picked up the gift on the chair beside me and took it to Birdie. I would be first, and I would dispatch the business quickly. I wanted nothing more than to see Birdie and Mickey on their way. "This is for you," I said.

She looked up at me stunned. "For me? Oh, Margaret, whatever . . . ? I sure didn't come over here expecting you to give me anything!" Her expression of bewilderment turned to one of great delight as she studied the package. "Why, isn't that the prettiest thing? I always did love that kind of ribbon. Mickey used to call it corduroy ribbon, didn't you, Mickey? I used to buy it in all different colors."

Mickey nodded and smiled at Birdie. "I don't imagine Margaret meant for you to just sit there and look at it, honey bun. Go ahead and open it. I can't stand the suspenders, I

477

mean suspense."

I retreated to sit on the small chair beside the telephone table, a distance from the others. Birdie began to unwrap the present, first unwinding the length of white ribbon, then removing the bow itself, then slowly prying the cellophane tape from one end of the package.

Mickey picked up the bow and began pulling at the ringlets of ribbon. "I used to love to watch Birdie make these little curlicues on the ends," he said. "She'd just whip out her scissors, zip, zip, zip, and presto . . . she had her a whole bunch of little Shirley Temple curls."

I frowned at Mickey. The thought of a husband finding pleasure in watching his wife curl ribbon seemed to me an aberrant form of behavior. Meanwhile, Birdie was making headway with the unwrapping.

"I just don't know *what* this could be," she kept saying. "What did you go and do this for, Margaret? Here, Mickey, hold the paper while I pull the box out." Together the two of them succeeded. Mickey was left with a cocoon of glossy green wrapping paper while Birdie, a look of awe upon her face, held the white box.

"Just like always," Thomas said, looking at me and jerking a thumb at Mickey. "The men get left holding the bag!" This was not the first time in recent days that Thomas had said something to me in a teasing manner concerning differences between men and women — things that he never would have said a year ago.

"Knowing Birdie, she'll probably want to save the paper, won't you, plumcake?" Mickey said, and Birdie nodded. Mickey began flattening the paper.

Birdie closed her eyes as if steeling herself for a breath-stopping surprise, then slowly removed the box lid and handed it to Mickey. She opened her eyes, and for several moments she gazed down into the box, her face filled with wonder. She lifted her hands and poised them midair as if preparing to clap them together, but then she brought them slowly to rest upon her cheeks. I had wrapped the dish in a deep square box that I had found in the hall closet and had set the lid upside down in the bowl, cushioning it well with tissue paper.

With great care Birdie at last reached into the box and lifted out the casserole dish, emitting cheeping cries that could have been interpreted as signifying either extreme pain or speechless joy. Her words settled the question, however. "Oh, Margaret! This is . . . oh, I just can't believe you've given me this . . . this exquisite piece of — oh, Mickey, *look,* it's a serving dish in the Morning Glory pattern just exactly like . . . well, just like the one she brought to our house that night,

remember? Look at the cunning little handles
— and the lid!"

She broke off effervescing to gaze at me
rapturously, her eyes shimmering. "Margaret,
I know I carried on over yours, but I sure
didn't mean for you to go and *give* me one of
my own. But I'm just so . . . oh, so deeply
grateful! And really, it's all so *funny* when you
think about it." I saw nothing funny whatsoever and was bewildered at the expressions
on their faces as she and Mickey exchanged
glances.

She held the bowl up like a trophy. "Won't
my friends at church think I'm the fancy one
at our next covered-dish supper?" She smiled
at each of us in turn.

Then, handing the dish to Mickey, she rose
from the couch and with an almost reverential
timidity, as if approaching a shrine, moved
toward the chair where I sat. Before I could
ready myself, she had thrown her arms about
my neck and resumed her speech of thanksgiving. "What a dear, dear thing for you to
do! You just don't know how much this
means to me, Margaret! Why, that dish cost a
lot of money! I'll think of you every time I
use it, and believe me, I'll use it over and
over and over! Thank you, Margaret, oh,
thank you for your gift!"

As soon as I could gather my wits, I stood
up, thus stanching her words of gratitude and
forcing her to release her hold upon my neck.

Smoothing my skirt, I spoke briskly. "Yes, well, you are most welcome. And as for the cost, it was nothing — literally. The dish is not only exactly like the dish I took to your house, it is the very dish itself."

To which she promptly replied, "Well, then it's all the more special to me! Yes, all the more special." Looking back at Mickey, she beamed. "And isn't she going to be surprised when she opens our present?" she said.

"Maybe so if she ever gets a chance to," he said, smiling. Assuming a comical grimace, he addressed Thomas. "Women can drag out the simplest things, can't they? Now, if you and me were the ones giving each other presents, it'd be over and done with by now." But to me he said, "That's a mighty nice dish you gave Birdie, Margaret. She'll sure enjoy using it, and I'll sure enjoy eating whatever she puts in it!"

Birdie gestured to me. "Come on over here and sit on the couch, Margaret," she said. "Here, Mickey, can you put the present up here beside her?" As Mickey feigned great physical exertion and asked Thomas if he knew of a good doctor for hernia operations, Birdie grasped my hand and led me across the room.

Seated upon the couch, I felt as though I had been shoved onto stage without knowing my lines. The three pairs of eyes watching me might have been three thousand for the discomfort they caused me.

"Go on, open it," Birdie said. She took a seat on the couch also, on the other side of the gift. Mickey sat on the edge of the rocking chair where I often read at night. He leaned forward expectantly, his hands clasped together. Thomas watched me from his recliner with a sympathetic cast of eye, his head to one side as if trying to judge my frame of mind, a cautionary crease in his brow, probably hoping that I would behave courteously.

I am certain that by now my reader has seen where this gift exchange was leading. I, however, was altogether oblivious to the O. Henry-like twist of events preparing to spring itself upon me. Somehow I managed to unpeel the yards of gold foil paper from around the box. It was a thick cardboard box approximately the size of a large microwave oven, and I found that it was indeed very heavy. Mickey had not been playing a prank after all.

Outcomes are always more easily foretold by the spectator than by the participant, you must remember. Though the reader has undoubtedly divined the contents of the box, for my part I was utterly incredulous when I lifted the cardboard flaps and saw what was inside.

I do not know what expression finally settled upon my face, but I clearly remember the turmoil of confusion and disbelief within me. Without speaking, I lifted the dishes from the box one by one, unwrapping them from their foam protectors, and gingerly setting each cup, each saucer, plate, and bowl upon the piano bench Thomas had placed in front of me.

As I emptied the box, never taking my eyes from the dishes, Mickey was the first to speak. "Well, she hasn't thrown any of them yet," he said gravely, no hint of mischief in his voice.

Silence for several more moments, then from Thomas, "Maybe she's waitin' till she's got all her ammunition out of the case and stacked up ready to use."

"If I was you, I'd get down on the floor behind your chair before she gets through unwrapping them," Mickey said.

"Can you stay and help bandage me up after it's all over?" asked Thomas.

They continued in this vein for the duration.

As I proceeded with the unwrapping of the dishes, Birdie took each foam pad from me, laying them in her lap one atop the other. She said nothing, nor did she give any sign of hearing our husbands' words of jest.

At last an entire eight-place setting of Morning Glory dinnerware was neatly displayed before me. The men had fallen silent. Only the muffled sounds of the Purdues' television set and the sporadic yipping of the Jansens' dog, Pedro, from across the street could be heard. Still I had not spoken, yet I knew that the moment could be delayed no longer.

I picked up a cup and held it in the palm of my hand, tracing my finger around its smooth, hard rim. I turned my head and looked at Birdie, whose body inclined toward me, whose eyes shone like brown quartz, whose lips were parted as if wanting to speak yet knowing not what to say. I glanced down at the cup again, then back at Birdie, and at last I spoke. "Why are you doing this?" We both knew, I am certain, that my question encompassed more than this culminating act of generosity. It included the entire three and a half months of our acquaintance.

Her answer was swift and unflinching. "Because I love you, Margaret. That's why."

I made no reply, yet, at the risk of sounding melodramatic, I must report that at the sound of her words I felt a sudden wrenching within my heart, a nearly visceral sensation, like a great healing stab of pain that brings long-awaited relief. And I knew that, were I given to displays of emotion, I could at this moment fill the cup I held in my hands with tears — tears of sorrow that a friend had been so long denied me and tears of joy that she had at last arrived. I did not weep, however; I merely stared into the cup.

I saw no vision, I heard no voice from heaven, I spoke not in tongues; yet in that instant I recalled a verse from the Bible, a promise I had thought broken, along with others, many years ago: "And thou shalt be like a watered garden."

Birdie had reached across the now-empty box and laid her hand upon my shoulder. "Oh, I'm so happy, Margaret. I hoped so much you'd like them. I was so glad Thomas talked about your dishes that night you ate supper with us. I'd been trying to think of something to get you, and that gave me the idea. Of course, I got this pattern because I knew you already had one of the extra serving dishes, but now you've gone and given *that* to me. Isn't it funny?"

It was not a question that needed an answer, and she did not pause to receive one. "You really bought them yourself, though, did you know that?" When I knit my brow in puzzlement, she laughed. "Oh, yes, you did! I just put aside the money you kept leaving on my piano after every lesson and saved it all up till I found something I thought you'd like — you *do* like them, don't you?"

"Yes," I said, turning my face to hers. "Yes, I like them very much, Birdie."

December 17 was pivotal, therefore, because on that afternoon I was washed ashore, so to speak, by the tide of Birdie's goodness. It was not so much the magnitude of this latest gift, though its cost and size, in truth, very nearly overcame me, but it was Birdie's perseverance. She had worn me down. I knew that I could withstand the floodwaters of kindness no longer.

After emptying the large box in the living room, Thomas and Mickey transported the stacks of dishes into the kitchen and set them upon the counter. I then filled one side of my kitchen sink with hot suds and the other with clear, scalding water, and Birdie and I stood side by side. I washed each dish and handed it to Birdie, who first dipped it into the clear water for rinsing and then wiped it dry with a large white dish towel, the very dish towel, in fact, she had given to me. It was made of flour sacking and bore in one corner an embroidered assortment of colorful vegetables: carrots, corn, tomatoes, and the like. After drying each dish, she placed it upon the countertop. We proceeded at a leisurely pace.

"I hope I haven't complicated things for you," she said at one point. "Do you even have room to store all these dishes in your cupboards?"

I had already considered the matter, of course, and told her of my plans, nodding toward each cupboard as I explained the necessary adjustments to be made. I have never been one for accumulating items or for retaining ones that have fallen into disuse, so my few kitchen cupboards afford adequate space.

"I will donate our old set of dishes to the Salvation Army," I said, and Birdie nodded approvingly.

"That's a real thoughtful thing to do, Margaret," she said. "Not everybody would do that." She paused and then added, "I sure hope it won't be hard to give away your old ones, though. I'd feel bad if I knew you were attached to them."

"I do not attach myself to things," I said at once, then lest I seem ungrateful for her gift, I attempted a qualification. "Of course," I said, handing her a plate to rinse and dry, "I have never owned a set of dishes to equal these." I lifted my eyes briefly to meet hers, then turned aside quickly.

In the living room our husbands were keeping up a continuous flow of talk. It appeared that they had discovered a mutual interest in the old *Andy Griffith Show* and were testing each other's knowledge of characters and plots. Mickey called into the kitchen, "Birdie, you'll never guess. Thomas here knew the answer to the pretzel question!"

"Well, almost," Thomas called. "I knew it was pretzels, and I knew it was Lydia somebody, but I couldn't remember her last name." The question, Birdie explained to me, concerned a character on an episode of the *Andy Griffith Show,* whose excuse when declining the offer of a pretzel was "They lay on my chest." Lydia was Goober's date in one episode, Birdie went on to say, and her last name, which Thomas could not remember, was Crosswaithe. Though I was tempted to point out Lydia's confusion between the verbs "lie" and "lay" and, furthermore, to ask of what possible use was such inconsequential knowledge of obscure television characters, I said nothing.

"Ask him the one about the Smithsonian!" Birdie called back.

In the living room we heard Mickey pose the question to Thomas. "Okay, okay, here's a good one. You know how Barney always gets words mixed up — well, what did he call the Smithsonian Institute in that episode where he bought the motorcycle and sidecar?"

"Easy," Thomas said. "The Smith Brothers Institution."

"Oh, he's good, he is. Yes, he's *really* good," Mickey said, to which Thomas replied, "That's the best imitation of Floyd Lawson I ever heard!"

"Listen to them in there," Birdie said to me. "In lots of ways those two are like peas in a pod, aren't they?" Indeed, it had already occurred to me that, were our lives a work of fiction, Mickey and Thomas could never reside as primary characters in a single plot for this very reason: They were too much alike. There was a want of conflict between them, which would render their coexistence bland and static or, rather, redundant. Many physical differences separated them, of course, as well as a wide gulf in matters of religion. In temperament and personality, however, they were cut from the same bolt.

"They do seem to have a great deal in common," I said, easing the rest of the plates into the sudsy water. Neither one of us spoke for several moments as we listened to Mickey and Thomas quiz each other on Mayberry trivia. "Who taught Aunt Bee how to drive?" "What did Andy call his best fishing rod?" "What brand of gas did they sell at Wally's station?" "Who was Barney's favorite waitress at the diner?" "What was Mayberry's largest department store?" "What three things did Opie wish for from the fortune-telling cards?"

and the like.

"Mickey just loves that show," Birdie said at last. "He used to watch the reruns every evening when they came on at 6:30. They moved things around, though, and now I think it comes on in the morning sometime. When he thinks of it, he'll set the machine to record it, and then we'll both watch it after supper. I like it a lot, too. Do you?"

"It is better than some programs," I said. I imagined Birdie and Mickey sitting side by side on the couch in the basement watching *Andy Griffith* reruns, laughing together. I wondered briefly if Mickey worked on his latest cross-stitch pattern as he watched; then I remembered that Birdie had once said they sat upstairs in their recliners when they did needlework. Perhaps, instead, he put the finishing touches on his nut people while keeping one eye on the television. Or perhaps he did nothing else as he watched. It was not difficult to picture him mesmerized by the antics of the Mayberry hayseeds, leaning forward to catch every word and gesture, storing away questions to share with other fans.

". . . and I told him I didn't know," Birdie was saying.

Not having heard what preceded this, I did not respond. I immersed a small stack of fruit bowls beneath the soapy water and then stirred the water a bit with my dishcloth.

After a pause, during which Birdie hummed

lightly as if to cover an awkward silence, she said, "It doesn't really matter, though, and I can sure understand if you'd rather not talk about it. We all have things we don't like to discuss."

Though I had not heard her question, I felt sure that she was correct, that indeed I would rather not discuss whatever it was, and so I said, "I would prefer not to." I did not speak brusquely, however, and she smiled as she took a bowl from me with no sign of having been affronted.

"Wasn't that what that man in the story always said?" she asked, drying the inside of the bowl with great concentration.

"I beg your pardon?" I said.

"The man who always said he'd prefer not to do whatever anybody asked him to do? Mickey and I read that story together a while back, but now I can't remember the man's name. It was a funny name. I keep thinking of Barney, but that's probably because I keep hearing the men in there talking about Barney Fife. It's not Barney, but . . ." She raised her voice and called to the next room. "Mickey, what was —"

"Are you referring to Bartleby the Scrivener?" I asked.

"That's it! Bartleby! Never mind, Mickey, Margaret answered my question." She looked up at me with the admiring eyes of a child. "I should've known you'd come up with it, Margaret. I bet you could really help us out with our reading. We're just —" She broke off abruptly and lowered her eyes as if from sudden shame.

"With your reading?" I asked, puzzled. Frankly, it surprised me to find that Birdie was acquainted with Melville's tale of Bartleby.

She fluttered her fingers. "Oh, you'll probably think it's silly, and it probably is, but we've been trying to read different books and stories and things together for the past few years. . . ." She paused, emitting a nervous glissando of laughter. "And then we talk about them. It's just a little project we thought might . . ." She did not finish the sentence but shook her head and clamped her teeth upon her lower lip as if wishing she had not spoken of the matter.

Was there nothing that Birdie and Mickey Freeman did not do together? I wondered. It struck me as a severely confining way of life.

"It is a commendable project," I said. "I do not think it silly."

Birdie laughed again. "Oh, heavens, I'd be embarrassed for you to hear us talk. We know so little about what's really good. But still, it stretches us and makes us think, I guess. We didn't do a whole lot of reading as children, neither one of us, so we've got a lot to make up for." She stepped back, opened up her dish towel, and waved it about as if to dry it out. "We've started taking turns picking what we'll read next," she continued, "and we try to have a little variety. When we first started, I think we read three books in a row by Louis L'Amour until I finally told Mickey I was ready for a change!" She stepped forward and took another bowl from me. "I need to ask you sometime for a list of things you'd recommend. We're trying to raise our level a little bit as time goes along."

She went on to extol the virtues of a novel that they had recently finished, a book that I myself had read ten years earlier, shortly after its publication in 1984: *Cold Sassy Tree* by Olive Ann Burns. "Oh, but I was so upset at the ending!" she exclaimed. "Why that author had to go and make Mr. Blakeslee die I'll never understand. That was the most disappointing way for things to turn out just when everything looked so hopeful!" We worked in silence for a while, and then she said, "But, really, I guess that's the way it goes in real life, too, lots of times. Things are going along just fine and then all of a sudden they turn upside down."

"That is true," I said. I could not help thinking of a book I had begun reading to Tyndall on his fourth birthday, a book that, because it was too advanced for him to grasp with full appreciation, I had paraphrased for him. In an early chapter of the book — *The Wind in the Willows* by Kenneth Grahame —

Mole, Rat, and Toad ventured from the narrow country lanes onto the highroad, where "disaster, fleet and unforeseen, sprang out on them." I have never forgotten the words. I have reminded myself of them often, for they have so aptly described my life.

"Mickey thought it was funny the way I took it so to heart," Birdie continued. "He tried to make me laugh and get over it, but I wouldn't listen. He kept saying, 'It's just a made-up story! It's not real!' But I just pulled the covers over my head and, like I said, wouldn't listen." By this I surmised that their reading sessions must take place at bedtime.

She went on to discuss another book they had read earlier: *Selected Short Stories of O. Henry.* I was somewhat taken back, in a pleasant sense, by her assessment of the writer, whose given name, as the reader knows, was William Sidney Porter: "He could tell a good story, all right," she said, "but for some reason I got a little tired of them before we were done. They all had a funny little twist at the end, and none of them seemed very *natural* somehow." I would have expected her to adore O. Henry's gimmicks.

"Of course," she added, "I guess things like that happen in real life, too, don't they? Take what just happened right here in your house, for example. Who would ever have thought that we'd both give each other dishes in the very same pattern?" This remark sent a small tingle through me, for had I not, upon opening Birdie's gift some thirty minutes earlier, seen certain comparisons to O. Henry's "Gift of the Magi"?

From the living room came the sounds of sustained laughter. "And the one where he gets Gomer to go with him to the haunted house!" we heard Mickey say. "Oh, and the Fun Girls — you ever see that one?"

"Yep, that's a good one all right," Thomas said. "And the one where he joins the choir — that's my all-time favorite I think."

Birdie smiled. "Mickey sure gets a kick out of Barney Fife. You know, there used to be a man who went to our church who looked just like — but what am I thinking of? You would know all about that, I guess, seeing he was related to you. It's sure been nice to see his daughter at our church a couple of times lately." I did not know that Joan had attended the church more than once. "Tell me," Birdie went on, "did other people see the resemblance or just us?"

I knew of course that she was speaking of Thomas's uncle Mayfield Spalding. "It was a fact that attracted frequent notice," I said. Indeed, Mayfield had often complained about the number of people who regularly accosted him with inquiries: Was he related to Don Knotts? Was he Don Knotts's father? Was he Don Knotts's brother? Was he Don Knotts?

One time, when Mayfield was younger, he was waiting to cross a street and a man had leaned out a car window and yelled, "Hey, Barney, where's Andy and Opie?" I decided to tell Birdie this and did so. She laughed with delight.

By now I had begun washing the cups and saucers. We would soon be finished with the set of dishes.

"You know, people looking like other people reminds me of something," Birdie said. "Maybe I shouldn't tell you this because some people don't like to be told that they favor somebody else, but I said to Mickey the first time I met you that I thought you looked like that actress . . . you know, the one who's had all those husbands. What's her name — Elizabeth something or other. Her name's on some kind of perfume, too. I sprayed some on once in Belk Simpson, but it's way too strong for me."

I pretended that I did not recognize the woman's identity. "Well, anyway," Birdie said after I shook my head and assumed a blank expression, "she used to be a real pretty woman when she was younger, so it was meant as a compliment."

I handed her a cup, which she rinsed and began to dry. "High praise indeed," I said, "to be likened to someone who used to be young and attractive, who cannot keep a husband, and with whom you associate an overpowering odor." I suppose I meant these words, which were spoken without a trace of levity, to be a test of sorts. If Birdie read them one way, our friendship would remain as it was now — tentative and polite; that is, if she hastened to clarify and apologize, I could keep her at arm's length. Had I been permitted at the time to choose her response, I would perhaps have preferred this one. By reading my words in another light, however, she could nudge our relationship into something closer to sisterhood.

There was the briefest of pauses, and then she spoke without looking up, continuing to wipe the cup, which was already so dry that the dish towel made small squeaking sounds against it. "Of course," she said, "she's overweight, too. Did I mention that? Yes, she's gone downhill something awful. In fact," and here she broke off, frowning slightly as if searching her memory, then opening her mouth in feigned dismay, "now that I think about it, that woman might even be *dead* by now."

Neither of us laughed outright, but as our husbands began whistling the theme song of the *Andy Griffith Show* in the next room, we exchanged the smallest of smiles.

It was a few minutes after five o'clock when we finished with the dishes. Thomas had turned on the television, and he and Mickey were chuckling over a ridiculous program of which Thomas was fond, a program called *Mystery Science Theater 3000*. He had tried to entice me to watch it one day by telling me that it was too funny to try to explain, and I had replied that as soon as my hands fell idle on a Saturday I would accept the invitation. By this I meant, of course, that I would never watch the program.

"Well, I guess we're all through," Birdie said with satisfaction, hanging the damp dish towel on the metal rod from which she had taken it earlier. "Could I help you switch your dishes around and get these up in your cupboards?"

"No," I said. "I will do that myself." I had loosened the stoppers in both sides of the sink, and the water drained out with great sucking noises. With my dishcloth I was wiping down the porcelain.

Birdie nodded at me. "I understand perfectly. There are just some things nobody can help you with, and I guess rearranging your kitchen cupboards is one of them." She put a hand to the top of her head and patted in a small circle as if checking for loose hairpins. "My, we've got to get on home," she said, looking at the clock on the stove. "I never dreamed it was already five. Oh, and look at your bread," she said, pointing to the stovetop. "I hope I haven't thrown your baking schedule off."

I could not remember a time when I had

left a loaf of bread to rise too long. I quickly twisted the oven knob to "Bake" and set the temperature at 400 degrees.

We heard Mickey from the living room. "Birdie, mousekin, you've got to see this!"

"I wonder what they're up to now," she said cheerfully. "Can I help you with anything else in here, Margaret?" When I shook my head, she turned and exited the kitchen. "Well, let's go see what our men are laughing about now," she said. But I stayed behind to remove the wet dish towel from the rod and take it to the back porch, where I spread it across the top of the washing machine. I finished wiping out the sink, selected a clean dish towel from a drawer and laid it across the rod, and then set the bread in the oven to bake. An idea had suddenly taken shape in my mind, but it unnerved me to think of carrying it out. My heart had begun to pound at the very thought of it.

When I stepped into the living room moments later, Birdie was sitting on Thomas's green ottoman next to Mickey, who was seated in my rocking chair, which he had turned and pulled closer to the television. I stood for a moment surveying the scene. The three of them were watching the television screen, upon which a ghastly, moaning figure draped in white appeared to be stumbling toward a precipice; tremulous violin strains accompanied his melodramatic progress toward doom. "Okay, okay, if you're going to get that upset about it, I'll raise your allowance!" quipped a tiny voice. Thomas, Mickey, and Birdie laughed in unison.

"Shhh!" Mickey tapped Birdie's arm. "You'll miss what they say next." The camera panned down the side of the cliff to a rocky shore, where a dark-haired young woman in a bathing suit stood scanning the coastline anxiously. "Hey, Annette!" called the little voice. "What's the matter? Did you lose your beach blanket?" Thomas, Birdie, and Mickey laughed again.

The concept of the program, I soon understood, was to exploit outdated substandard movies for a bit of fatuous entertainment — or put another way, to generate from inanity yet more inanity. As the original movie played itself out, a trio of mockers posing as theatergoers were silhouetted in the corner of the screen, and from this vantage offered sarcastic witticisms and droll comments concerning the action and dialogue upon the screen.

At the commercial break, Thomas looked back at me and grinned. "They like my program, Rosie. See? I been telling you how funny it is." Mickey and Birdie looked at me also, both of them smiling. "Come on in and set yourself down," Thomas said, waving toward the couch.

"We've got to get going," Mickey said, springing to his feet. I had seen Birdie tap the face of her watch. "We didn't mean to stay but a few minutes, and here it's already been an hour. I don't have a very good sense of time. Seems like Birdie's always having to tug my leash and drag me away from places, aren't you, dumplin'?" Birdie rose to stand beside him.

This is when the idea that I mentioned earlier made itself known. When I spoke, my voice sounded serrated and metallic, like a rusted saw. "Will you stay for supper?" I asked from the doorway, my heart still thudding within me. What if they accepted my invitation? While I earnestly hoped that they would not, I felt my heart filling with a curious sense of adventure. Thomas swung his chair around and gaped at me, making no attempt to disguise his shock.

Birdie was making signs of protest, shaking her head and moving one hand rapidly from side to side, palm down, as if brushing crumbs from a tablecloth. "Oh no, Margaret, no, that's sweet of you, but I don't want you to feel obligated to feed us just because we don't know when to leave. We'll just take our coats and get on our way."

Looking at Mickey, she added, "We still need to stop by Marvella's, you know, and pick up those cupcakes she wants me to decorate for the fellowship tomorrow night. I told her we'd come by sometime late this afternoon." She tilted her head in thought.

"And if we wait till later, she won't be home." Birdie glanced at me and, as though I cared about a total stranger named Marvella, offered, "Marvella's going over to Harvey and Trudy Gill's tonight to help them make a Christmas wreath for their front door."

"It will be a simple meal," I said. "Should you want something more substantial than roast beef sandwiches and potato soup, our supper would be unsatisfactory. Should you choose to join us, however, we will eat at six o'clock."

Mickey and Birdie turned to each other for help in deciding the matter. Thomas still sat in his chair as if thunderstruck. Whispering loudly, Mickey jerked a thumb toward me as he addressed Birdie. "Do you think there's any chance she'd let us break in the new dishes if we did stay to eat?"

" 'Break' is an unfortunate word choice when speaking of my new dishes," I said, and Birdie and Mickey both laughed.

"Oh, now, she's a quick one, isn't she?" Mickey said. "Yes, a really *quick* one, she is." Though by no means a devotee of the *Andy Griffith Show* myself, I could nevertheless tell that Mickey's imitation of Floyd Lawson, the barber, was indeed quite good. Thomas still appeared to be disoriented. He did not speak but gazed first at Mickey and Birdie, then at me, then back at Mickey and Birdie, then again at me.

It was decided that Birdie and Mickey would drive to the home of their friend Marvella, who lived midway between Filbert and Derby — "right under the shadow of the water tower," Mickey said — and then return to our duplex by six o'clock to be our guests for supper. Now that it was settled, I found it difficult to believe that I had actually extended the invitation, that it had been accepted, and that, barring unforeseen conflicts, we would be seated at our kitchen table with Birdie and Mickey Freeman within the next hour.

"Could I stay and help you with the meal?" Birdie asked. "Mickey could go get the cupcakes by himself."

"No," I said. "I will see to everything myself."

"You'll help her, won't you, Thomas?" Birdie said, and Thomas smiled distractedly.

"I will get your coats for you," I said, since Thomas had made no move to do so. Walking into Thomas's bedroom, I heard him emerge from his trance at last to say, "Well, now, we'll sure look forward to seeing you folks back in a little bit."

As I gathered Birdie's coat and Mickey's jacket into my arms, my gaze fell upon Thomas's blue chenille bedspread. I paused briefly and looked at his bed. Though of only a moment's duration, I was suddenly and unaccountably pierced with a feeling that I knew to be pity, though I had not felt it for many years.

The headboard and footboard of the bed were of oak. The design had a certain sturdy elegance, as if crafted by a colonial cabinet-maker. The bed had belonged to Thomas before we married. Very possibly it was the bed he had shared with his first wife, Rita, though I had never asked about its history. Thomas kept a tidy bed. The bedspread was drawn up and snugly tucked beneath the pillows, its nubby geometric design precisely centered, the fringed edge clearing the floor by an even inch. He had never been one to leave his bed unmade nor to toss articles of clothing upon it.

I looked at the bed now as if for the first time. "This," I said to myself, "is where my husband" — I rarely thought of him in this way: as my husband — "has lain every night for the fifteen years of our marriage; this is where he has lain alone." I came into the room only to vacuum the carpet on Fridays, to dust the furniture on Tuesdays, to return clean laundry to his bureau drawers on Mondays and Thursdays, and to hang freshly ironed shirts in his closet on Wednesdays. Since the day of our marriage, he had changed the sheets on his bed each Saturday, though I, of course, had always washed, folded, and stored them on the shelves of the linen closet.

I knew that if I sat down upon the mattress now, the box springs would squeak, for I heard them from my room each night. The thought of Thomas sitting upon the edge of the bed in his nightclothes and then slipping his feet beneath the sheets and the blue bedspread descended upon me now as a frail mist of sorrow.

The feeling of pity had its source, I suppose, in an image registered only minutes earlier but now permanently lodged within my mind. I envisioned Birdie and Mickey Freeman side by side in their own bed, propped with pillows and furnished with mugs of cocoa and a gooseneck lamp. I heard their voices reading aloud and saw their eyes focused intently upon the printed page. I wondered briefly whether they shared a single book or secured two copies. This picture of conjugal harmony stung me, contrasting as it did with the present thought of Thomas lying in silence and solitude.

When one clutches his past bitterness like a prized gem, it numbs him to a great many things; it blinds and deafens him. His thoughts are concentered in self. Though it may seem beyond belief, I had never before this moment given thought to Thomas's life as the husband of a woman like myself. Perhaps this was one of Birdie's most valuable roles as my friend: Besides giving me cause to trust and hope again, she demonstrated to me the ballast provided a man by his wife's open and steady love.

Without intending to do so, I raised Birdie's tweed coat to my face, then immediately felt foolish. I must lay aside my weak sentiments, I told myself. Birdie and Mickey were waiting for their coats, and I had a meal to complete. I removed my face quickly from the folds of Birdie's coat, but not before I had caught its scent, a faintly spicy odor as of woodsmoke and crushed bayberry.

The thought crossed my mind that the garments of the Old Testament priests, as they prepared sweet incense for the holy place, must have smelled like this. As I turned to leave Thomas's bedroom, I heard Mickey say, "Maybe she decided to take a nap in there," and I noted that the aroma of baking bread was beginning to fill the house.

An Enduring
Substance
25

It is no great wonder to me that Leo Tolstoy could write so long a book as *War and Peace;* rather, I marvel that it is so short. I had hoped by the end of this month, July, to have completed my story, but I feel that it has scarcely begun. In the writing of each chapter, I find myself engaged in a battle. Perhaps other writers struggle similarly. I do not know. It is as though my heart is swollen with my story. I feel that I must set it down upon paper, and quickly, or I will surely break open and fly apart. Curiously, I imagine my heart as a fordhook lima bean allowed to soak too long and thus bursting its jacket. The metaphor perplexes me, for I do not like fordhooks. They are too large and lack the flavor of the baby lima. Furthermore, I see no relationship between a bean and the composing of a manuscript.

My battle is this: As I tell my story, I am impeded, first, by the sheer magnitude of material I wish to record and, second, by a proclivity for detail. No sooner do I set about to describe a simple interaction between Birdie Freeman and me than I realize it is not at all simple. Each incident is rich and expansive, teeming with sensory impressions and intersecting my life at many points. It cannot be condensed; or perhaps I mean that to condense it would minimize its role in my life, would blur the story, would verge on desecration. Yet I fight within myself. *I must include this fact. No, it is of no ultimate consequence in the larger story. But it is, for it is as a subtle shading in a fine painting. No, you must omit it. I cannot, for it adorns the whole.*

Moreover, I have woven other stories into my story of Birdie, and those, too, must be told. My path has diverged into many. In rereading parts of my manuscript, for example, I see that I have abandoned Thomas's cousin Joan for many pages, leaving unresolved her dilemma concerning Virgil Dunlop, the teacher at Berea Middle School with whom she had developed a friendship; indeed, I see that I carelessly failed even to complete the account of our telephone conversation in which she asked my opinion of him.

I clearly recall Joan's final remarks in that conversation: "Of course, I could never *marry* someone with a name like Virgil Dunlop. Can't you just imagine it? Joan Spalding Dunlop. People would think I was a sporting goods heiress or something. Everybody would expect me to be an expert at all the racket sports." She had attempted a laugh, but it had punctured and gone flat. "Besides," she had said, trying for an offhanded manner, "he wouldn't have me. He already as much as told me that. 'I'm looking for somebody who knows the Lord' is how he put it." When I did not reply, she had concluded our conversation with a tone of false brightness. "And we all know I don't qualify in that category!"

Between the time of our dinner at the Field Pea Restaurant in November and Birdie's coming to my house with a new set of dishes in December, I had spoken to Joan by telephone one other time and had accompanied her only a week earlier, on December 10, to a concert in Greenville by a touring brass quintet from New England who called themselves the Gateway Five.

As after any other performance, we went to the Second Cup Coffee Shop, where she composed her newspaper critique. My contribution, as with all musical concerts, was largely confined to suggestions concerning diction, for she possessed a broad understanding of music.

Though disinclined to ready displays of affection, Mayfield Spalding had given his daughter something of value, something that she had never interpreted as an act of love, though I have attempted from time to time to instruct her in this matter. From the time Joan was six years old, her father had engaged teachers for her in piano and later violin. He had monitored her practice sessions in the evenings and had attended every recital in which Joan had played, though, according to her, he had always sat in the back row and then, after she played, had left and waited for her in the car. She continued her study of piano and violin through college. Even now she plays in the community orchestra in Greenville and has a standing invitation as guest soloist at the Fiddlin' Fair, which closes the annual Hayride Festival in Clinton.

The Gateway Five performed a repertoire astounding, I thought, in its variety, especially considering the fact that the concert was in December, thereby leading one to believe that the program would consist of Christmas music. This was not the case; the pieces ranged from Baroque fugues to transcriptions of standard orchestral works to ethnic dances. In her description of a stunningly discordant passage in a twentieth-century piece, Joan used the word *rambunctious,* for which I recommended a more aurally precise substitution: *bellicose.* She nodded as she made the change. In another sentence I suggested that she utilize the adjective *confluent* to describe the merging of two melodies in counterpoint. Again, she did so.

Though Joan made mention of Virgil Dunlop only once during the evening, I knew that she still thought of him often. As we sat at the Second Cup after the concert, she asked if I thought the trombonist of the Gateway Five was as technically proficient as the other four players. In fact, I did not. Though my ear is not trained in the finer aspects of brass instrumental techniques, I believe that I possess a keen sense of hearing and a naturally discriminating ear for musical quality. I had detected a want of facility and crispness in certain exposed passages by the trombonist, who was a rather gaunt man with a beaklike nose and long wisps of wiry gray hair that fanned out stiffly behind his ears as if from an electrical charge. He looked to me like a character from Washington Irving's imagination, a kinsman of Rip Van Winkle, perhaps.

Joan scribbled a sentence or two, then paused to stare at the plastic cap of her Bic ball-point pen. "Virgil said he used to play the trombone in high school," she said. She wrote two or three more words and then looked up again, pressing the knuckle of her forefinger into the center of her chin. I wondered if she was perhaps thinking of the cleft in Virgil Dunlop's chin. "He said every instrument had its own personality," she continued, "or I mean the people who played them." I must have looked puzzled, for she began to explain. "All the trumpet players in his band were these feisty, fast talking show-offs, he said, and the clarinets were these odd little fastidious kids, and the —"

She broke off as if suddenly losing interest in the whole business. Running a finger across her brow to straighten her bangs, she returned her attention to the sheet of paper before her. As she bent her head to write, her black hair fell about her face like a dark silk veil.

I will continue the story of Joan and Virgil as my narrative moves forward, but as Christmas neared, this is how the relationship stood: Joan's interest in Virgil Dunlop had not waned but had apparently grown warmer. The fact still amazed me, knowing Joan as I did. That Virgil seemed unwilling to pursue a deeper friendship could be seen as one of his chief attractions, I suppose, although I am in no way suggesting that Joan was drawn to him only as a teenager, adoring one who appears inaccessible, who "plays hard to get," as the saying goes. Since Joan is sensible, intelligent, and mature, I do not believe this was the case.

To return to December 17, Birdie and Mickey reappeared upon our doorstep within an hour of departing, Mickey now wearing a ball cap to the back of which was affixed an imitation ponytail. Thomas, whose display of mirth once again exceeded proper boundaries, reacted with great hilarity and asked

Mickey where he had bought the cap, after which he declared his intention of buying one for himself. "That'll really go over big in the hardware store," he said.

Birdie shook her head and said to me, "Margaret, I think we've got a couple of little boys on our hands." She meant it in fun, of course, but I knew it to be true.

Between the time that Birdie and Mickey had left and returned, I had completed the making of a large pot of potato soup. I had already peeled and diced the potatoes earlier in the day as well as fried, drained, and crumbled six strips of lean bacon. The actual assembling of the soup was no difficult task. I always use one can of evaporated milk to one cup of two-percent milk and one-half cup of water for the soup base. On this day I quadrupled the amounts designated on my recipe, also adding increased portions of chopped onion, parsley, salt, and pepper for flavor. The roast beef had only to be sliced and arranged upon a plate. I had cooked it for our supper on the previous night and, as is my custom, had wrapped part of what was left to use for sandwiches. I had baked a chocolate cream pie that morning and set it in the refrigerator to chill.

We sat down to supper at half past six. At my direction Thomas had inserted several compact discs into the player so that the music of Strauss, and later of Mozart, could be heard from the living room. I had laid the table with a blue-checked cotton tablecloth and blue napkins, both of which complemented the blue violet of the morning glory design on the dishes. Both Birdie and Mickey ascended into ecstasies over the table setting. "It belongs in a magazine!" Birdie kept repeating.

Although I ate only a small serving of soup and half a sandwich, the others took seconds. The kitchen seemed to me a contracted version of itself that night, as if the ceiling and four walls had shifted inward. The effect for me was as of finding myself suddenly hedged about in a thick fog, hearing sounds that were at the same time muffled yet amplified. And though on the one hand I felt adrift in my own home, ill suited for my role as hostess, I felt on the other a deep satisfaction, as of setting one's craft upon a straight course. In spite of limited visibility, my chart was reliable. Hospitality was good, and the laughter and talk around our table seemed a fitting thing.

The evening of December 17 is engraved upon my memory. I could write an epic titled "December 17: Six Hours of Time." Someday perhaps I will do so, but at present I feel that I must pass over many of the particulars of the evening in order to reveal a discovery that came to my attention as Birdie and Mickey were taking their leave a few minutes past ten o'clock.

The evening had been a success. Though my nerves were somewhat frayed from the strain of navigating through unfamiliar waters, it had surprised me to find that Thomas was a comfortable and genial host. Had he been as awkward as I, our venture into entertaining would surely have capsized.

We had talked of many things both during and following our meal. Mickey had spoken at length of kite flying, a lifelong hobby, and of purple martins, which flocked to his gourd birdhouses in great numbers each spring. Birdie had told amusing stories about former neighbors of theirs in Tuscaloosa, one of whom discovered in an attic trunk a genuine Stradivarius violin. Another neighbor, by the name of Oliver Malone, had been extremely fond of turnips and had planted turnip seeds each spring. "Imagine everybody's surprise," Birdie said, "when a new family moved in right next door to the Malones with the last name of — you won't believe this," and together Birdie and Mickey had cried, "Turnipseed!"

Thomas had slapped his knee and interjected, "I once knew a Turnipseed! Dewey Turnipseed. I'd almost forgot about him. That was the name of a boy I knew in the war, from Mississippi I believe it was. Nicest fellow you'd ever want to meet, except he had an odd habit of suckin' on his teeth like he had food caught in 'em."

This led to a discussion of other curious names we recalled: Walteretta Pimento, Chickie Roast, Quince Pickle, Daphne Smallmouth, Bingo Mush, and so forth. I told of a girl who had attended Latham County High School in Marshland, New York, at the same time as I: Zinnia Greyhound. This in turn opened the subject of nicknames, and Thomas reeled off the nicknames of some of his kinfolk in North Carolina: Grease, Longlegs, Trout, Gypsy, Spade, Link, Barley, Gnat, Largo, Moonbeam, and Sled. Oddly, Thomas is one of the few in his family who is called by his given name. Granted, he is also one of the few in possession of what could be considered a common name, other Tuttle men bearing inconvenient, unwieldy names such as Barksdale, Hathaway, Ephraim, Ballenger, and Chrysler, to name several.

Mickey volunteered that his own nickname had been "Mouse" as a boy and explained it thus: "My ears stuck straight out when I was a kid, even more than they do now, believe it or not. It was a big old fellow in seventh grade by the name of Scofield Purvy who first called me Mickey Mouse, and it caught on real fast and finally got shortened to Mouse. 'Course I got even by calling *him* Scurvy, for which I paid dearly." Mickey groaned and held his jaw as if having received a blow. "Old

Scurvy sure had a mean left jab!"

Thomas chuckled and remarked that his nickname in school had been "Tattle," suggested both by his initials T. A. T. and by his last name. He had never before told me this, and I could not imagine that the nickname had in any way described his behavior, for Thomas would hardly have been the type, even as a child, to make public the indiscretions of others. "I used to just hate it like the John-Brown dickens," he said, "but I knew better than to let on. It kinda died out after I got on up past fourteen, fifteen."

Birdie had smiled and remarked, "Nicknames can be real cruel sometimes. I guess I could have ended up with something a lot worse than Birdie!" Indeed, it was easy to see how she could have suffered at the hands of other children, given her plainness and her large, protruding teeth.

"So, Margaret, 'fess up," Mickey had said at last. "You know all about our nicknames. What's yours?"

When I did not answer at once, Thomas spoke up. "Tell 'em, Rosie."

"Rosie?" Mickey and Birdie cried in unison.

"Where did that come from?" Mickey asked.

"Is your middle name Rose?" asked Birdie. "Or is it because of her pretty complexion?" she asked Thomas.

Thomas then recounted in grandly embel-

517

lished fashion the story of our first meeting at the hardware store and his facetious references to Rosie the Riveter. He composed and delivered a dialogue script between the two of us that, though it did not take place as he claimed, nonetheless provided great entertainment for Mickey and Birdie.

"What a sweet story!" Birdie exclaimed, laying a hand upon one cheek and beaming at me. "And to think the two of you got married as a result of you buying a hammer at the hardware store. Do Algeria and Francine know about this, Margaret?"

"No, they do not," I said quickly. "Nor do they need to." I could not bear the thought of Francine and Algeria calling me Rosie behind my back and snickering over the details of my personal life as they performed their kitchen work.

"She sure was a catch, wasn't she, Thomas?" said Birdie.

"Oh, yesiree," Thomas replied. "Took me forever to get her in the boat! Snapped my line and lost a couple of my best lures 'fore I landed her!" He laughed briefly, as did Birdie and Mickey, but seeing that I was not smiling, he quickly said to Mickey, "And how did you two meet?"

"Oh, we lived next door to each other," Mickey replied, patting Birdie's hand. "The day after my family moved to Dothan, Alabama, I looked out my bedroom window and saw Birdie hanging out the wash."

"And I've been hanging out the wash ever since," Birdie said, laughing. "Mickey loves line-dried sheets." Then, turning to me suddenly, she said, "Margaret, I wonder if you'd let me copy your recipe for the potato soup. I believe it was the best I've ever had. I have trouble getting mine seasoned just right."

Later we watched the *Lawrence Welk Show* on television from eight o'clock until nine. The program, which was a rerun from years past, featured selections from Broadway musicals. For example, Myron Floren played "The Wells Fargo Wagon" on the accordion, Barbara and Bobby danced to a medley of *West Side Story* tunes, Norma Zimmer sang "Some Enchanted Evening," and a men's chorus, clad in wide-lapeled sport coats in a bold navy-and-red plaid, sang "The Surrey with the Fringe on Top."

Following that, at Mickey's suggestion, we played a single round of what he called the "Dictionary Game," which required inventing and writing down definitions for unusual words found in the dictionary, after which we all voted for the definition that sounded like the correct one. The four words that night were *honan, rathe, peplos,* and *yapok,* two of which I already knew.

By the time Mickey and Birdie stood to leave at ten o'clock, I was both physically and emotionally spent. Though Thomas urged them with great sincerity to stay longer, I said nothing.

"Oh no, we've got to get on home," Mickey said. "We don't usually stay up this late on Saturdays. Birdie likes for us to get to church on Sunday morning a half hour before folks start arriving so she can run through her music on the organ one more time." There was a momentary pause, during which I held my breath to prepare for what I knew was coming. Thomas must have sensed it also, for he cleared his throat and dropped his gaze to the floor. "We'd love to have you two visit our church tomorrow morning," Mickey said. "We're having a special Christmas program."

"I will get your coats," I said and turned to exit the living room. Behind me I heard Thomas clear his throat again at great length and finally say, "No, no, I think we'll have to pass this time."

"Well, some other time maybe," Mickey said. "I think you'd like our people a lot, and we've got the finest preacher in these parts. Not to mention lots of good music, and . . ."

"And there's even a fellowship after church tomorrow night," I heard Birdie say. "Maybe it would suit your schedule better to come to the evening service. Our young people always take charge of the evening service on the Sunday before Christmas."

"Naw," said Thomas slowly. "I don't reckon night would be any better'n morning as far as church goes. But we're obliged to you for askin' us just the same. . . ." He pretended to be interrupted by a spate of coughing.

As I reentered carrying Mickey's jacket and Birdie's coat, I saw Birdie put her hand to her mouth. "Oh, I almost forgot about the cupcakes, Mickey! I've got to frost them tonight before bed."

"She-zam!" cried Mickey, lapsing into an imitation of Gomer Pyle. "Now see what you did," he said to Thomas. "We've gone and had such a good time that we forgot all our responsibilities." To Birdie he said, "Don't worry, angel, I'll help you get it done." Then he struck an actor's pose, one hand extended and, still speaking with a countrified drawl, said, "Can't stay in the woods no more 'cause I got promises to keep, not to mention the miles I gotta truck 'fore I lay down to sleep."

I did not respond to his egregious miswording of Frost's poem, though I was somewhat surprised that he knew the lines well enough to demolish them so neatly. I could not hold myself back, however, at his next words. As I laid his jacket over his outstretched arm, he yawned elaborately and said to Birdie, "Well, buttercup, I guess it only goes to prove what it says in Isaiah — 'There's no rest for the wicked.' "

"Peace," I said.

"What's that?" Mickey said, looking at me quizzically.

"The verse says that there is no *peace* for the wicked," I said, wishing that I could stamp out my words like a small fire.

Mickey zipped up his jacket and reached to take Birdie's coat from me. "That'll teach me to try to quote things around smart people," he said pleasantly. I saw that Birdie was studying me as Mickey helped her into her coat. She did not button her coat but stood very still, an expression of somber contemplation upon her face.

Then she stepped forward and took my right hand in both of hers. Though I should have been prepared for this gesture by now, I was not. I must have winced, but she did not release her hold. "We can't begin to tell you how much we've enjoyed ourselves," she said. "It's been an evening we'll always remember, Margaret." Still holding my hand — in fact, applying additional pressure upon it — she looked back over her shoulder at Thomas. "It sure was a happy day when I started to work at Emma Weldy and met your lovely wife. And then we had a bonus when we got to meet you!" Thomas opened his mouth as if to reply but merely smiled and said nothing.

Addressing me again, Birdie said, "Thank you, Margaret, for the good supper and for my nice casserole dish. You don't know what it all means to me." How effortless her pretty actions and words seemed! For an instant I tried to imagine myself uttering courtesies with such grace, but the picture did not take shape. I was most desirous of one thing: to extract my hand from hers. She was my friend now, true, but I was by no means initiated so suddenly into the ease of physical contact.

Without warning she stepped even closer, let go of my hand, stood upon her tiptoes, and embraced me for the second time that day. In so doing, one of her earrings, a silver disk, became dislodged and fell, clattering against a small maple end table and then bouncing to the floor. I was grateful for the distraction, for she immediately sprang back and put a hand to her earlobe.

And this is when I made the discovery that I referred to earlier. Before Mickey could respond, she bent quickly before me to retrieve the earring, which had landed a few inches from my feet. As she did so, the cowl neck of her royal blue sweater fell loosely from around her neck. Beneath her sweater she wore a white nylon slip, which also drooped as she bent forward, and before I could look away, I saw Birdie Freeman's chest. There is no way to put this delicately. I do not say that I saw her breasts, for I did not. She had no breasts. I saw her chest, scarred and flat. Too late her hand flew to her neck to press her sweater against her.

I believe I maintained my composure at the time, taking care not to alter the arrangement of my features, and I do not believe Birdie suspected anything. I lifted my chin slightly, I recall, and fixed my gaze upon the upper frame of the front door. My thoughts ran to confusion. Disconnected phrases of many things I had read whirled about in my mind, three of which were these: "When he seeth the blood upon the lintel" from the book of Exodus in the Bible; "Love's austere and lonely offices" from Robert Hayden's poem "Those Winter Sundays"; and "If I moved to Tashkent and lived in a yurt," the only memorable line from a tediously introspective novel titled *Shine On, Bright and Dangerous Object* by Laurie Colwin.

I saw no immediate relevance between the strange convergence of these quotations and what I had just seen, but this had happened before. I knew it to be my method of coping with shock, of delaying the absorption of disagreeable knowledge. Upon reflection, however, it would be possible, I suppose, to force a linkage between each of the phrases and the situation at hand, though I will not at this point take the time to put it in writing, except to say in the words of Laurie Colwin that "if I moved to Tashkent and lived in a yurt," I could never escape the memory of what I saw that night in my living room.

The moment is of considerable import because it modified my perception of Birdie. Before this time I had imagined her past, when I thought of it at all, as a level, straight road between green pastures. I now knew that she had suffered, at least in a physical sense. Perhaps she had made her peace about it long ago, accepting it cheerfully as her lot in life, but the fact that she had never spoken of it led me to think that deep within her was sheltered a very private grief.

Even as I underwent this adjustment of mind, however, I felt within me the conflict of ambivalence. On the one hand, I felt a twinge of what I knew to be sympathy, yet on the other, a flare of anger. I did not want the burden of this new knowledge. Why had she had no corrective surgery? Had she never heard of prosthetics? Why did she not take greater care to clutch her garments to her to spare others the sight of what I had seen?

"They're sure nice people, aren't they?" Thomas said a few minutes later as he stood at the front door watching the Freemans back out of our driveway. He expected no answer from me, or so I thought. When I said nothing, however, he recouched his question. "What do you think it is about 'em, Rosie? Why is it they're so different from us yet I still can't help likin' 'em so much — both of 'em?"

My answer fell from my lips unbidden. "They seem to possess an enduring substance, I suppose."

Thomas nodded. "An endurin' substance

. . . I guess that's one way of puttin' it." Then he laughed as he slowly closed the door. "I'm gonna get me one of them ball caps next week," he said.

SURE MERCIES
26

The next day I was beset with worry. I rose from my bed, dressed, tidied my bedroom, and went into the bathroom to splash cold water upon my face. As I looked at myself in the bathroom mirror, I wondered, first of all, what had come over me to invite Birdie and Mickey to such a meal as I had prepared the night before. Why, when I could make the most succulent chicken and dumplings, pepper steak, or pork tenderloin, had I chosen to serve as my first meal for guests *potato soup and cold beef sandwiches?*

When I was a girl, my mother had always made an occasion of dinner. We ate our evening meal late, around eight o'clock, and we sat down to a table laid with silver table service, linen napkins, and a finely crocheted tablecloth. Often a candle and fresh flowers adorned the center of the table. At the time, this daily ritual was in no way extraordinary to me, for it was all that I had known. Reflecting upon it now, however, it is a marvel to me that my mother had possessed the energy to keep at it.

After she arrived home from work between half past five and six o'clock, the two of us looked over the schoolwork my mother had assigned me that morning and discussed any questions that had arisen. I wrote my questions in a notebook throughout the day. Some were the result of genuine puzzlement, such as "Was Lycidas somebody John Milton knew, or was he a mythical character?" Other questions were for clarification: "What kind of gene mutations will always be passed on to an offspring, and what kind will not?" Others were slant thoughts that crossed my mind as I read: "How is cellophane wrap made?" or "Who invented the first stapler?" or "Why is Easter always on a different date?"

Once my school books were set aside and my questions discussed, my mother and I began preparing our dinner together. On certain days she had left instructions with me in the morning concerning the meat: to brown the cube steak at four o'clock, for example, and then to make gravy, pour it over the meat, and place it in a covered dish in the oven on low heat. By the age of ten, due to my mother's excellent instruction, I could cook quite well. My mother considered cooking to be an art. She eschewed abominations such as cake mixes, "instant" potatoes, or imitation vanilla. "A skilled workman does not take shortcuts," she often said.

The dreadful years that I spent with my grandparents were only more so because of my grandmother's culinary incompetence. Her watery sauces, her dry meats, her flavorless and undercooked vegetables, her heavy breads — all were a miserable contrast to what I had known. I could only wonder how my mother had developed her cooking skills, having grown up on my grandmother's fare. I could have been of service in the kitchen had my grandmother let me, but it soon became apparent that she viewed my help with a heart of jealousy. When my grandfather spoke highly of my biscuits or requested second portions of my chicken pot pie, my grandmother left the table like a sulky child.

Once, when I watched her flatten a ball of pie crust dough with her hands and then mash it haphazardly into the pie pan, I said, without thinking, "Would it not be better to use your rolling pin for a more uniform crust?"

She shot me a look of what I interpreted as intense animosity and ordered me to leave the kitchen. "I'll not have an impudent child telling me how to do things I've done all my life!" she called after me. Another time when she told me that I was kneading the bread dough far too long, I answered in the words of my mother, again without pausing to consider the effect. "A skilled workman does not take shortcuts."

She laughed derisively and replied, "And how would a thirteen-year-old know anything about a skilled workman?"

Presently I was banned from all kitchen work on the pretext that I jangled her nerves with my slow, methodical movements. My grandparents ate their evening meal at half past five, and if the food itself had not been enough to suppress my appetite, the early hour would have been. "Eat!" my grandmother would cry. "Don't think you'll snack later on. You'll not get another bite until morning!"

My grandfather would lower his eyelids and study me with a sinister gaze, his great jaws masticating ponderously. "You eat now or go hungry," he would say. Each evening I felt as if I were being pulled asunder, longing on the one hand for the unpalatable food to be swept away and the meal ended, yet on the other wishing that I could remain permanently adhered to my chair at the table so as to be spared the darker hours of the night to come.

Whereas my mother and I had talked happily as we ate our dinner, my grandparents' table was for the most part silent and hostile. When my grandmother ventured a timid observation, my grandfather either ignored her or denounced the remark as vacuous. My only conversation consisted of monosyllabic answers to my grandfather's direct questions: "Does your science teacher ever talk about the time he had to answer to the school board for allowing students to experiment with chemicals unsupervised?" *No.* "Is that Benchley boy in any of your classes — the one whose mother is a barmaid at the Taboo Lounge?" *Yes.* "Did you sit out of the dancing lesson in gym class like I told you to?" *Yes.* "Did you read that dirty novel your English teacher assigned for class?" *No.*

This last answer, however, was an untruth, though not strictly so. The book in question was *The Scarlet Letter,* which I had already read chapter by chapter with my mother only months before she died. When I was assigned to read the book in my tenth-grade English class, over two years later, I found that I remembered it with such clarity that I could yet quote brief passages from it. I felt that I knew the characters intimately. Under my mother's guidance I had extracted literary symbols, had dissected conflict and motive, had traced the three-part structure of the novel.

I did not read the book again, as I was afraid to do what my grandfather had expressly forbidden, but I performed so well on the test and essay at the end of our study of the novel that my English teacher suspected me of having received assistance from a student in another class who had taken the test earlier in the school day. I found her suspicions to be laughable, although I displayed no outward sign of this, for I had no friends who would have extended to me such aid had I been in need of it, which I was not. Though my teacher did not pursue the charges, she reassigned me to a desk in the front row, so as to squelch any further ideas of cheating, I suppose.

After I ran away from my grandparents' home, I determined to elevate the quality of my evening meal to what I had known as a child, to regain a vestige of lost refinement and pay tribute to my mother's memory. Though my income was minimal, I purchased my produce and meats carefully and prepared for myself wholesome, well-seasoned dinners. The first boardinghouse where I roomed had a large kitchen, and each renter was allowed use of it. I cooked my meals after the others had vacated the kitchen but carried them on a tray to my room instead of eating at the communal table. To my dismay, however, my cooking habits seemed to arouse a great deal of interest. Other boarders began to wander into the kitchen and exhibit an overbearing curiosity in my menu. I was forced at times to be blatantly rude.

After my son was born, therefore, I took care to find an apartment with its own stove and refrigerator. As Tyndall grew past babyhood, I began to introduce to him the niceties of proper dining, showing him how to hold his spoon, to take small bites, to wipe his mouth, and so forth. By the age of four, he was quite a gentleman at the table and would politely offer this speech after our evening meal: "Thank you, Mother, for my dinner. May I please be excused to help you clear the dishes?"

He begged to help me in all aspects of my kitchen work, often slowing my progress, of course. He took seriously his small duties, and I yet remember his earnest sobs upon dropping a saucer one night and seeing it shatter. "Oh, look, Mother! Oh, look!" he kept repeating as he pointed in horror at the broken pieces. I comforted him and swept away the fragments, but later at bedtime he wept afresh. "I broke the pretty dish, Mother! I broke it!" I have not permitted myself to think of these things for many years.

After Tyndall's death, I could hardly bear the sight of a stove or a boiling pot for many months, yet gradually as I returned to life, though a soiled and ragged remnant of it, I began once more to turn to cooking for myself in the evenings, more as an antidote for loneliness than for any concern over nourishment. In addition, I often cooked for my elderly clients when employed as a domestic.

When I arrived in Filbert and applied for employment at Emma Weldy, I was pleased to find that the kitchen staff prepared the dishes "from scratch," as the supervisor at that time, Lola Tyler, boasted to me repeatedly. I soon discovered, however, that her claim was overstated, for a number of corners were cut, as they say. Pudding and gravy mixes were commonly used, as were instant potato flakes and Bisquick. The dessert known as cherry crisp was nothing more than canned pie filling topped with prepackaged graham cracker crumbs.

Once again I fear that I am straying from the center of my narrative, although my history pertaining to the subject of cooking perhaps helps to explain my fretful afterthoughts concerning the inelegance of the meal that I had served to Birdie and Mickey. A drought demands a proper end, I reasoned. To depict a bountiful downpour of cool rain after a dry season, that is to celebrate my acquisition of a friend after years of solitude, I should have served a banquet. My potato soup and roast beef sandwiches were as insubstantial as a trickle of rain in an arid land. I chided myself that surely the laws of hospitality had not been fulfilled.

On the day after Birdie and Mickey ate supper with us, I worried about more than potato soup and sandwiches, however. Uppermost in my mind as the morning wore on was the thought of Birdie's past suffering. An image of her disfigurement was deeply engraved upon my mind, and a simple, irrefutable truth presented itself to me. Having borne a great weight of pain in my own past, I had become impervious to that of others, always assuming that mine was worse. In all honesty, an insidious form of pride had crept into my heart and taken up residence: the pride of suffering.

The pride of suffering is ancient, I suppose. I think it likely that Job of old felt a peculiar satisfaction when, passing among his fellowmen, he overheard someone say, "There goes Job. He was the man sorely buffeted by Satan." I can imagine him straightening his shoulders and lifting his chin as he felt a certain celebrity status. "My loss has been of such historic proportions that it will be recorded for posterity," he may have thought.

While comparing wartime injuries, two of Thomas's cousins, both in their sixties at the time, almost came to blows at a family reunion one summer several years ago. One of them, whose nickname was Gnat, had begun bragging about the wounds he had sustained as a ball turret gunner in World War II. The other, a stout man of acerbic tongue, dubbed Gypsy, had served as navigator on a B-29 and had spent the last six months of the war in a German prison camp. Gypsy had hotly objected to Gnat's glorification of gunners in general and ball turret gunners in particular.

"So you came out of it with a little limp," he said to Gnat. "And how many meals did you have to miss while you was laid up in the field hospital? How many times did you fight somebody for a scrap of wormy bread? Did you ever know what it was like to feel like pukin' but there wasn't nothin' to puke up?" The two of them were bellowing like rabid bulls before the contest came to an end. Thomas and his cousin Spade actually had to restrain the two of them from fisticuffs. It was perhaps one of the clearest demonstrations I have ever witnessed of the kind of pride of which I am speaking, though at the time I could not see its relation to me. I had never participated in such a debate concerning my own degree of suffering, yet I know that my pride was considerable and that over the years it had multiplied as if permeated with a potent yeast.

The sight of Birdie's scars led me to consider her loss. I was forced to reconstruct my picture of her past, which I had invented as an idyll of rural simplicity: a sun-drenched childhood; a close-knit family gathered about the hearth reading the Bible and uttering treacly sentiments, protected from life's injustices by the whim of the same God who willed that I should experience them fully; a joyous, innocent courtship; a warm and loving marriage.

I knew now that at some point a grim

intermission had interrupted this charmed play. That she had done battle with cancer was evident. I knew also by now that she had borne no children, and I suspected that this too had caused her great pain. Which is worse — to have lost a child or never to have had one? I could not say.

The realization that Birdie Freeman had suffered gave me cause to worry, for it disarmed me in a sense. I saw Birdie and myself in sharp relief as two sides of a coin: peace and strife. We had both been damaged yet had emerged as opposite as heads and tails.

There is a certain confidence, an unhealthy superiority I suppose, spawned by the attitude that one's own suffering exceeds that of others. I recall watching an old television program in a neighbor's apartment one day as a child. When my mother played Scrabble in Mrs. Gault's apartment, I was permitted at times to turn on the television. As I remember it, the program, which was called *Queen for a Day,* consisted of a parade of downtrodden women who, one by one, tearfully confided to the world at large the miseries of their lives.

While I deplored their private distresses and their public humiliation (it did not occur to me at the time that their televised confessions were voluntary), I was filled with admiration at the efficiency of the Applause

Meter in determining which woman's suffering was greatest and therefore deserving of relief in the form of a new washing machine, refrigerator, and the like. I have often wondered since that time if any of the winners ever lorded their victories over the other women backstage after the program, flaunting their armfuls of red roses, then patting their "Queen for a Day" crown and boasting, "My misfortunes are the grandest of all!"

How was I to approach Birdie now that I knew her secret? A single inadvertent glance as she had bent to retrieve an earring had narrowed my edge over her. For many years I had used my suffering as a wedge between others and myself. I was excused from the requirements of friendly social interaction because my past had taught me to trust neither God nor man. Though I still felt assured, I suppose, that my suffering would register far higher on the Applause Meter than Birdie's, her scars had nonetheless taken me back. She had suffered, yet she had not withdrawn. Rather, she reached out to others with eager hands, giving, helping, and always, always touching. I knew that my friendship with Birdie would force me to recast my life in drastic ways, in ways that I thought of as disruptive.

And not only were my worries that day confined to the inappropriate meal I had served and to the disturbing discovery about

Birdie, but as I moved about our duplex that Sunday, looking for things to set right — adjusting a lampshade, straightening an antimacassar, moving a footstool — my thoughts turned to Thomas. Without his noticing that I was doing so, I observed him as he read the newspaper and then turned on the television, first watching the conclusion of an old movie titled *The Mask of Fu Manchu* and later changing the channel to watch WWF Wrestling at noon.

He exercised no restraint in the expression of his enjoyment over the wrestlers. I was accustomed to his laughter and to his frequent entreaties as I passed through the room. "Look at this'n, Rosie! Ain't he a beefy thing? Watch 'im now; he's gittin' ready to pounce! Whoa! Right in the solar plexus! Don't you know that's gotta hurt like all get-out?" Of course, he was fully aware that each bout was a staged affair, that the blows were neither delivered nor received, yet he found great humor in the entire production.

I have never deluded myself as to Thomas's earliest and strongest attraction to me. To assert that it was anything other than my cooking would, I believe, be falsehood. Thomas had lived alone for over ten years. There is no need to elaborate upon what a hearty meal will do for such a man, what visions of future meals he may conjure up. The first meat I cooked for him was oven-barbecued chicken;

I make my own barbecue sauce. When he took his first bite, the expression upon his face was one of bliss long deferred.

Though I was by no means actively searching for a husband at the time, given my vitriolic distrust of men, it came to me, as I said in an earlier chapter, that the two of us could cohabit to the mutual benefit of the other, and when Thomas proposed marriage, I agreed. After our marriage was made legal and Thomas moved into my duplex, we took upon ourselves traditional roles. I was cook, laundress, and housekeeper. Thomas proved himself most useful in a multitude of capacities: general repairman, auto mechanic, house painter, plumber, electrician, errand boy, gardener, and so forth. Indeed, he was a factotum of home maintenance.

Whether Thomas was resigned from the outset to the terms of our marriage — that is to the absence of a physical union as I had specified — or whether he hoped that I would relent over the course of time, I do not know. Though at first I regarded him with wariness, he never trespassed the boundaries that I had specified nor requested, by word or act, a renegotiation of the spoken contract.

On the day after the Freemans ate supper with us, as I watched Thomas sitting in his recliner before the television, strange, unsettling thoughts suffused my mind. It was astonishing to me, when I paused to think of it, that in all of my reading of contemporary fiction, I could not recall such a marriage as ours. I had read, of course, of spouses who over the passage of difficult years had become alienated from each other and had ceased all physical relations, but of marriages initiated as business partnerships and thereafter conducted as such, I could call to mind none. Nor was I aware of any such marriages outside the world of fiction — in "real life," as they say — although I suspect that a great many do exist.

Since my fright en route to the emergency room in October, on the day when Nick Purdue had suffered a stroke, I had become increasingly aware of my — I can think of no better word — *dependence* upon Thomas. It had happened without my taking note. I inventoried his contributions to my life and found them to be many.

On the morning of December 18, I began to wonder how Thomas felt about our marriage. I began to wonder whether he ever imagined the two of us engaged in easy banter, whether he ever wished to touch me. I worried that our friendship with Birdie and Mickey would only serve to engender within him a longing for what he did not possess, that is, the unreserved devotion and cheerful camaraderie of his wife. I worried that already he had wistfully observed Birdie and Mickey's relationship and had wished for the same.

As Thomas watched two professional wrestlers pretend to pummel each other, I prepared for myself a cup of tea and sat in my rocking chair to read the Filbert *Nutshell.* We sat scarcely three feet apart, each absorbed in his own diversion. After several minutes I turned to the obituary page and saw that a former member of the school board had died: Ross Bertram Honeycutt. His age was reported as seventy. My immediate thought was *Thomas is seventy.*

I glanced across at Thomas, but his attention was riveted upon the television screen. Though I had read the obituary page countless times before this and had taken regular note of the ages of the deceased, I had never before felt such a shudder of apprehension descend upon me as I made the transfer between such information and my own husband. It was as though I heard a pronouncement of doom — *"Thomas will die"* — followed by another — *"You will die."* Though I tried to lay it to the account of my pessimistic bent, I was nevertheless distraught. The thought of losing Thomas troubled me deeply. I raised the newspaper higher so that I could not see him. But I found myself once again staring at the picture of Ross Bertram Honeycutt on the obituary page of the Filbert *Nutshell* and heard once more the whispered judgment: *"Thomas will die."*

By this time, Thomas had stirred from his

recliner. He turned off the television and walked to the front door, turning back to say, as was his Sunday custom, "I'll be back in time for dinner." Then he closed the door, descended the front steps, and backed out of the driveway in his truck. Almost every Sunday afternoon since we were married he has gone to the hardware store to play cards in the stock room with Norm and two other cronies. I do not pry into his business and have never had cause to suspect him of gambling or drinking during these interludes. I have never smelled anything stronger than peanuts on his breath when he comes home.

I laid the newspaper on the footstool in the living room, and for the first time in the fifteen years of our marriage I walked into Thomas's bedroom with no specific mission in mind. I was not fetching coats for guests; I had no shirts to hang in his closet, no clothes to put away in his bureau drawers, no dust rag in my hand.

The thought came to me that perhaps worrying was an auspicious sign, for in my lifetime I had worried only when buoyed by hope. When one's existence is without hope, there is little cause to worry. I had worried as a child, for my mother had instilled within me a sense of apprehension concerning strangers. I flinched at every knock upon the door and clasped my mother's hand fearfully when we moved about the city.

On the other hand, I had not worried when living in my grandfather's house. I came to see his abuses as inevitable. Worrying about them made no difference in their regularity. I existed as if drugged.

When I ran away from Marshland, I worried obsessively, constantly looking backward over my shoulder, walking stealthily even across the floor of my own apartment. Later, as I moved from town to town with Tyndall, I continued to worry lest my grandfather should track us down.

After I lost Tyndall, I no longer worried. Hope had vanished. I ceased to care whether my grandfather traced my whereabouts. Neither did I worry when I returned to my grandparents' house and attended them upon their deathbeds, nor when I moved to Filbert and took up my life there. I did not worry what others thought of me nor of what would become of me. I simply lived from day to day, performing my work and fending off the advances of others with the skill of long practice. I rebuffed even the schoolchildren of Emma Weldy, who soon gave up their efforts at friendliness.

But now I had arrived at this point: I found myself once again fraught with worries. As I stood in the doorway of Thomas's bedroom and looked about, I felt oddly comforted by my worries, as if they were sure mercies that had been awaiting the easement of austere penalties. I stepped into his bedroom and, not knowing what else to do, sat upon the edge of his bed.

I do not know how long it was that I sat upon Thomas's bed that Sunday afternoon and studied every aspect of his bedroom as if for the first time. Though I dusted and vacuumed the room according to an unvarying schedule, I had never remained within its four walls longer than necessary. As I sat upon the blue bedspread that day, I noted signs of wear that had escaped my eye during my cleaning sorties.

The bedspread itself was growing thin from use. The looped fringe along the edges looked ragged as if frequently snagged. The gold braided rug beside the bed had begun to unstitch near the center, and I saw a corkscrew of transparent nylon thread lying loose atop it. The plain dark blue curtains at the windows looked listless from repeated washings. They were the same curtains that I had hung in the room when I first moved into my duplex. The bedside lamp, with its stout wooden base, was purely functional. It had never possessed aesthetic appeal even when new. The lampshade, once a creamy white, had darkened to the color of scorched parchment.

Having no eye for decorating, Thomas had never expressed discontent with his bedroom or its spartan furnishings, although it was he, strangely, who over the years had brought home a number of accessories for other rooms of our duplex: an oak magazine rack, a ceramic urn, a rattan wall shelf, and an Oriental umbrella intended for ornament.

Thomas's bedroom was clean and tidy, for there were no knickknacks to clutter it. As I scanned its length and breadth, however, it came to me that it was a cheerless place to spend one's private hours. There was but a single picture in the room, a large framed print of a Carolina wren upon a dogwood branch, and above the bed hung a gun rack displaying one rifle, which I believe was in working order though, of course, unloaded.

I ran my hand across the raised geometric pattern of the chenille bedspread and wondered whether Thomas had a bedtime ritual. Did he look through back issues of *Field and Stream* before turning out his light? Several were stacked neatly upon his bedside table. Did he plump his pillow? Did he pull the bed covers snugly to his chin, or did he fling them back to sleep unfettered? It struck me that I did not even know whether my husband customarily slept on his back or on his side. Furthermore, it had never occurred to me to *wonder.* Did Thomas fall asleep immediately upon lying down, I wondered now, or did he remain awake, tossing restlessly? If so, what did he think about during the night hours? On the chair beside his bureau I saw the electric heating pad, its cord wrapped neatly around it. Thomas must have used it recently, but why? I wondered whether he had ever gone into my bedroom when I was not at home and sat musing upon my bed as I was doing upon his.

By the time Thomas returned home later that afternoon, I had collected my wits enough to have our Sunday meal ready to serve. Though it had not taken a great deal of effort, the food was tasty and received Thomas's verbal approbation. I had saved the gravy I had served with the pot roast a few days earlier, and to that I had added the roast beef that still remained from what we had used for sandwiches the previous night. I had cut the meat into chunks, stirred it into the gravy, and simmered it slowly. This I spooned over beds of rice as a rich, savory sauce. To complement the main dish, I also served purple hull peas, creamed corn, julienne carrots, baked zucchini sprinkled with basil and parmesan cheese, and sweet muffins.

I attended to Thomas's talk at dinner that day more closely than usual, and I observed him when he was not looking at me. As I have said in an earlier chapter, Thomas is not an unattractive man. He looks a decade younger than his seventy years, carries his height with a natural dignity, and has what has been called a photogenic smile. If he did not speak aloud and if he dressed the part, I suppose he could pass for a veteran politician, even a former president perhaps. He is more handsome than Lyndon Johnson, Jimmy Carter, or Richard Nixon but lacks the youthful lines of John Kennedy or Bill Clinton. His looks run more toward those of Ronald Reagan, I suppose, although during the Reagan era Thomas could never reconcile himself to the fact that "a movie actor was runnin' the whole John-Brown country."

Early in the meal he launched into a tale related to him that afternoon by Ned Boswell, one of his card-playing foursome. It was a farfetched story, a "humdinger" as Thomas called it, involving a dead cat and a shopping bag, and I interrupted him midway, asking, "Did Ned Boswell witness this incident first-hand?"

"Naw, but his next door neighbor said she knew the woman's best friend who it happened to over near Pelzer," Thomas said. He resumed the story, and I listened to its conclusion, in which an ambulance figured.

"I believe Ned has been taken in by what is known as an urban legend," I said when

Thomas had finished the story.

"A what?" he asked. "What's that supposed to mean? You don't think it's true?"

"I heard Francine tell the same story to Algeria and Birdie two months ago in the school kitchen," I said. "The only variation in her version was that the final scene took place in a doughnut shop instead of a Chick-Fil-A. According to Francine, her mother heard the story from a man who used to live in Powdersville, whose brother knew the ambulance driver. Moreover," I added, "after Francine recovered from her fit of giggles at the end of the story, Algeria informed her that her mother had heard the story a year ago from her mailman, who said that his chiropractor told it to him. According to the chiropractor, he saw it happen outside a McDonald's next to a mall. In Francine's story the victim was a white woman, and in Algeria's it was a black man."

Thomas gaped at me for a brief time and then threw back his head and laughed robustly. "Wait'll I tell Ned!" He laughed again, thumping the table, and then asked, "What's that you call it again?"

"An urban legend." I then told him in abbreviated form another such story about a man, a cigarette, and a can of hair spray that had been passed around as fact in the Midwest many years ago. It, too, ended with ambulance attendees bearing the hapless man away upon a stretcher. When I was a girl, my mother had told me of hearing the story upon five different occasions, each time in slightly altered form, from persons claiming to have close ties to someone who knew the man.

Thomas pondered this silently for some time. " 'Course stories like that could've started out true, you know," he said. He was slowly peeling the paper from around another muffin, handling it gently, almost admiringly, as if fearful of doing it harm. "It could be a case of passin' somethin' around so much that it just keeps gettin' a little bigger. And then so's he won't sound like a total fool, the feller tellin' it says he heard it from so 'n so, who knew the person — had him over for supper ever' Tuesday or played checkers with him or somethin'."

I conceded that such might be the case, that were it possible to trace an urban legend to its source, there very likely could be an original anecdote of valid credentials bearing some slight resemblance to the augmented public rendition. "But mankind is seldom satisfied with the plain truth," I said, and Thomas nodded gravely.

The rest of the meal passed in a routine manner. At five o'clock, after the dishes were washed and put away, Thomas said to me, "Come go with me, Rosie. I want to run over to Derby for just a minute. We won't be gone long." He was standing in the kitchen doorway, retucking his flannel shirt inside his trousers.

"I have things to do here at home," I said, and picking up the dishcloth, I wiped the countertop again, although I had already done so three times. The truth was this: Though pleased at the invitation — for Thomas seldom asked me to accompany him anywhere — replying negatively had become such a habit that the words had fallen as if of their own accord.

"Aw, come on, Rosie. You'll like this. It's a new county flea market Norm told me about. They're doin' it just one weekend a month through the winter, but it closes down at six on Sundays. It's indoors at the old fiber mill in Derby. He told me today there's some feller's got a booth with all kinds of tools and car parts for sale."

"Flea markets are a blight on society," I replied. "They are often nothing but dens of thieves peddling their stolen wares."

"You know good and well that's not always the case," Thomas remonstrated teasingly. Then his eyes brightened. "Say, I'll tell you what, though. You ride along with me, and I'll drop you off at that library in Derby you like so much, and then I'll go and hobnob with the thieves and robbers all by myself."

"Some of the vendors have been arrested and their goods confiscated," I said with asperity. The mention of the library made the offer tempting, however. I generally visited the Derby Public Library on Tuesdays after my piano lesson at Birdie's house, but if I went today I could return the books that I had already finished and check out more. I was particularly wanting to look for a copy of a book by Tobias Wolff called *This Boy's Life,* of which I had read several favorable reviews. I had known of the book for perhaps four years but for some reason had never secured a copy. Only recently I had once again seen it cited on a list of "Contemporary Memoirs Worth Reading." Though I prefer novels, I also read biographies, historical works, adventure sagas, and collections of essays. In this way I am able to mollify my literary conscience. *I do not live altogether in a fantasy world,* I can tell myself. *I have one foot firmly planted in reality.*

"The library closes at six on Sundays," I said, with a glance at the clock upon the wall.

"Well, then, that's perfect," said Thomas. "It's all set. We can be there in twelve minutes, and that'll leave us both forty-five minutes or so to look around. Let's go!" He bowed in the kitchen doorway with an absurdly exaggerated flourish of the hand toward the front door, in the fashion of an Elizabethan courtier.

Without reply I hastened to gather my library books and purse from my bedroom, then put on my coat and followed Thomas to the car. The trip to Derby passed quickly, with Thomas telling me a story I had heard before. It was a story his aunt Prissy had loved to recite concerning her father, who had purportedly driven his 1928 Ford down into the Grand Canyon on a mule trail and forded the Colorado River in the car.

"Come to think of it, betcha that was one of them urban legends, too!" he said when he finished. "Nobody could've done that. Betcha there's grown people all over the country claimin' their uncles and grandpas did the same thing." A few moments later, as we passed Shepherd's Valley Cemetery and the Freemans' house, Thomas chuckled. "I'll have to ask Mickey if he's ever heard any of these crazy stories. He'll get a kick out of 'em."

I found myself wondering, as I cast my gaze upon Birdie's house, how the icing of the cupcakes had gone the night before. Had Mickey helped her as he had promised? And in spite of myself, another thought crossed my mind. I wondered if the Christmas program at their church had been well received that morning. Had Birdie played an organ solo at some point? It came to me that Birdie and Mickey would soon be preparing to leave their house, frosted cupcakes in hand, for the Sunday evening service and the fellowship of which they had spoken.

I did, in fact, find *This Boy's Life* at the library that day, along with several other books that interested me, and as I stood in the glass-enclosed lobby a few minutes before six o'clock waiting for Thomas to return for me, I riffled through the pages of Tobias Wolff's book, sensing the familiar swell of anticipation that every avid reader knows. My eyes lighted upon an account of Tobias Wolff's mother, who was an active listener to the woes of others, responding readily, as he described it, "with intense concentration and partisan outbursts of sympathy." A picture of Birdie sprang to my mind. I saw her brown eyes agleam with feeling as she listened to a stranger in a supermarket line. I heard her prompt words of comfort, of encouragement, of goodwill. And, oddly, I felt the touch of her hand, as if I were the stranger.

It was at this juncture that a most unexpected encounter occurred. A station wagon pulled to a stop in front of the entrance. Behind me I heard a voice from inside the library. "Here's our ride, Willard! I'll go on out and tell Jewel you'll be along directly, soon as you get all the lights out and things locked up nice and tight." Even though spoken from the other side of the glass door, I heard the words distinctly.

The door behind me opened, and I heard the voice again. "Oh, my stars, I didn't know somebody was out here waiting in the vestibule!" I believe it was at that instant that I identified the woman's voice, though I did not turn around. Deep and throaty with a muffled resonance, it was not a voice that one could easily forget. "Just set your mind at ease, honey," she said, and as I heard her slow steps shuffling toward me from behind, I stiffened with dread. "We won't go off and leave you all by your lonesome. No, sir, not a bit of it! Willard and me will wait right here with you till your ride shows up."

By this time she had reached my side. As she turned slowly to face me, a most peculiar smile transformed her features into an expression of luminous pain, although, given her words, I was quite certain, as I had been upon our first meeting in Birdie's driveway, that she meant it for joy. Her face was prominently presented to the world with no softening frame of hair, for she wore a dark green woolen scarf wound and cinched tightly about her head, well off her brow. Indeed, she could have passed for an old Russian grandmother. Her eyebrows, extraordinarily thick, hung down over her eyes like bushy visors. She was a large woman, you may remember, and the copious gray cape that she wore today amplified her size.

"Why, I'll be if it's not Margaret Tuttle!" she cried. "Remember me — Eldeen Rafferty? I met you at Birdie's that day when the Lord sent me out there to give away my prize turkey. And there you were in Birdie's driveway, just standin' there waitin' like you are right now! My, my, my. I'm glad I decided to come to the library today, else I wouldn't of seen you!" She laughed with delight and clapped her large, gloved hands together. Then she leaned forward a bit and raised the volume of her voice, as if my hearing were impaired. "Did he bake up nice and juicy and golden brown for you?"

I looked quickly toward the station wagon outside and saw that a woman had emerged from it and was hurrying toward the entrance with an umbrella, for a light pattering of rain had commenced. I wished earnestly for Thomas's arrival. My mind suddenly filled with uncharitable thoughts as I imagined him engaged in price haggling with some shady huckster at the flea market while I was forced to wait in the company of this woman of unparalleled verbosity.

Turning back to Eldeen Rafferty, I nodded. "Yes, the turkey was most satisfactory."

"Oh, now, that tickles me good to hear that!" she said. "I keep asking Birdie about you every week at church. 'How's your pretty friend Margaret Tuttle?' I say to her, and she says, 'Oh, just as pretty as ever.' I told her there was something about you that I just couldn't put my finger on" — she lifted a large forefinger and glared at it fiercely — "but it was something I liked, something I liked a *whole lot.*" With the last two words she jabbed her finger toward me and bestowed upon me another of her tortured smiles.

The other woman had made her way from outdoors into the lobby by now. "That's my daughter Jewel," Eldeen said proudly, and the woman smiled cordially. "This here's my friend Margaret Tuttle," Eldeen said to Jewel. "We're just waitin' till her ride comes." Before I could assure her that I would wait outside alone, she cried out, "Oh, good, and here comes Willard now! You can meet him, too!" She pointed to the man now locking the interior door and said, as if announcing a dignitary, "That's my son-in-law, Willard Scoggins. He's Jewel's husband." I knew the man by sight, of course, having frequented the Derby Public Library for many years. He looked up and spoke a friendly word of greeting.

"He works here," Eldeen continued, "and I've spent the afternoon today with him here at the library like I do sometimes, and now we're on our way to church. Normally he doesn't work till closing time on Sundays because of choir practice — he leads the choir, you see — but there isn't any choir practice tonight. And even at that, he'd normally ride to church in his own car, except that it's in the shop gettin' the brakes fixed, so we're havin' to double up. He's felt the brakes slippin' for a while now. The pedal would go all the way to the floor!" She extended one arm, pressing the heel of her hand forward as if to demonstrate the faulty pedal. I was astounded, as I had been at our previous meeting, that the woman took for granted my interest in the mundane details of her life.

As Jewel turned to speak to Willard, Eldeen moved closer to me and said in a confiding tone, "Willard just got promoted to head librarian a little over two months ago. He moved into a new office, the one right off the big check-out desk, you know. That's where Miss Mabel Weatherby's office used to be. It has the big plaster of Paris penguin sittin' by the door and that great big globe clock on the wall, which is sure a sight to behold except that most all the countries of Africa has different names now, but I say hang on to it 'cause someday it'll be an antique!"

With barely a pause for breath, the woman pressed forward. "Miss Weatherby left lots of her things for Willard to use since she doesn't have any place for them at home in her little apartment, which to hear her tell it is no bigger'n a doll's house. You ought to see this pair of bookends she left Willard that's two halves of a unicorn. They're *heavy,* too — made out of real cast iron. I told him he sure better not drop the front half on his toe 'cause that horn could poke a hole right through a body's shoe, not to mention their foot! She's retired now, you know — Miss Weatherby, that is. They gave her a going-away party back in September and had it right here in the library with streamers and party hats and whistles and all kinds of folderol. Had lots of refreshments, too. Jewel made some of the best little cream cheese cakes with a little dollop of raspberry sauce plopped on top and some pretty little rolled-up ham salad sandwiches and deviled eggs and this punch that had dabs of orange sherbet floatin' around in it and . . ."

"Mama, your friend might not be interested in the whole menu," Jewel said, smiling at me from behind Eldeen. Her husband, I noticed, was moving about the small lobby, retrieving bits of paper and depositing them into the trash receptacle. He picked up two soft drink cans against the wall and shook them slightly.

At this point I saw Thomas pull up behind the station wagon, and with great relief I made ready to move toward the door.

"Oh, this must be your ride!" Eldeen said happily. "Be sure before you get in, though! I read in the paper about that woman over in Honea Path who jumped in the backseat of a car at a stoplight without lookin' good at the driver, and she was a'diggin' round in her pocketbook lookin' for some Rolaids and talkin' so much that she didn't find out till six blocks later that it wasn't her son at all but some man from Greenwood on his way home from a huntin' trip! Now, if that doesn't beat all! They reported it in the 'Funny Tidbits' column, but nowadays it could of turned out to be a tragedy instead of a funny tidbit if that driver'd had the devil in his heart. You just know if he was out huntin', he must of had all kinds of guns and weapons with him that he could of put to evil use!"

Willard Scoggins was holding the door open for me, and Jewel came to my side to escort me to my car with her umbrella. I was suddenly reminded of a lovely poem by Archibald Rutledge in which the central image is that of a man walking his friend to the car in the rain. I had found a large volume of Mr. Rutledge's poems in the library a month earlier and had read many of them by now.

Thomas was leaning across the front seat, I noticed, and in a moment the passenger door swung open for me.

"I sure hope we get to see each other again sometime, Margaret!" Eldeen called after me. "The Lord's brought you to my mind over and over and over since I met you! I almost didn't come to the library with Willard this afternoon, but I'm sure thankful I did, else I would of missed you!" She was still talking when I closed the car door. Jewel stepped back from the curb and waved good-bye to me as Thomas pulled around the station wagon, behind the steering wheel of which sat a teenaged boy. As I recalled from our first meeting, Eldeen had a grandson with a driver's license.

"Who was that hollerin' at you?" Thomas asked.

"A woman who gives tongue to every thought that passes through her mind," I said.

Thomas chuckled and said, "Sure sounded like she could talk the hind leg off a donkey."

Had I known that more surprises were to be unfolded before we arrived home that Sunday evening, I might not have felt so grateful to be rescued from Eldeen Rafferty. Thomas took it into his mind to stop for a banana split at a place called Darlene's Kreamy Kones next to the Wal-Mart in Derby. He insisted that I choose something also and would not be persuaded otherwise. At last I told him that I would take a small dish of vanilla ice cream, and though he snorted with contempt, he ordered it for me.

We settled into a booth with our dishes before us. I recall the discomfort that I felt at sitting directly across from Thomas with a bright fluorescent light directly overhead. At home we took our meals at adjacent sides of the kitchen table rather than opposite each other, so when I raised my eyes and looked straight ahead, I saw the back door, and Thomas, when he did the same, saw a wall calendar from Norm's Hardware Store.

As we ate our ice cream in the red vinyl booth at Darlene's Kreamy Kones, Thomas talked of what he had seen at the flea market, concluding that "there sure was a bunch of junk for sale." His only purchase had been a burlap bag of roasted peanuts, about which he now expressed doubts. "At that price, half of 'em's prob'ly rotten in the shell."

For some reason Thomas seemed suddenly to slip into a morose frame of mind and grew uncharacteristically quiet. Perhaps it was due to the lingering memory of the dingy stalls and shoddy merchandise of the flea market combined with his suspicions concerning the bargain price of the bag of peanuts, or perhaps it was the onset of the winter rain outdoors contrasting with the false brightness of the ice cream shop, which, except for the two of us and a frowzy gray-haired woman behind the counter, was deserted. Perhaps it was the tardy realization that this was an inappropriate time of year to be eating a cold dessert and that three dollars and fifty cents was an excessive amount to pay for so little.

Or perhaps it was the music that began playing over the speakers soon after we were seated: a recording of the Andrews Sisters. The woman behind the counter was mouthing the words along with the recording, I noticed, and while we ate she sat slouched upon a stool casting surly glances in our direction, as if wishing that we would leave so that she could have the place to herself once again. Perhaps she wanted to sing aloud and bring back the days of the forties and fifties when life had been full of promise. Indeed, it seemed to be the music that played upon Thomas's mood, for I saw his jaw tighten as he scanned the ceiling for the audio speakers.

"You know, Rosie," Thomas said as if trying to dredge up a small measure of cheer, "I keep thinkin' about them crazy stories and all the people that believe they're true." He was speaking quite loudly, his voice pitched higher than usual. "People'll believe anything, won't they? The world's full of suckers!" He shook his head, then smiled halfheartedly and sighed, as if finding the subject depleted and himself too exhausted to speak in competition with the music.

He took several large bites of his banana split in swift succession. A new song was playing now, one that my mother had sung to me a number of times: "I'll Be Seeing You in Apple Blossom Time." After it ended, the sisters launched into a livelier song: "The Boogie Woogie Bugle Boy of Company B." Thomas glared up at the corner where one of the speakers was mounted and swallowed as if with great difficulty.

"Let's go," Thomas said abruptly. He slid across the seat of the booth and stood up.

His plastic ice cream dish was nearly empty, but I had taken only a few token bites from around the perimeter of my single scoop. I followed his lead, however, and we left together, dropping our dishes into the trash bin beside the door and hurrying through the rain to the car.

Thomas started the car but did not put it into gear. He inhaled deeply and closed his eyes. Then he opened them and shook his head as if to clear his thoughts.

"Are you ill?" I asked. "Or do you dislike the music of the Andrews Sisters for some particular reason?"

I had guessed correctly. He turned to look at me for a long moment and then offered a faint, sickly smile. "I guess I can't hide things very well, can I?" Instead of putting the car into motion, he reached forward and turned off the ignition. The rain splattered against the windshield. I followed the path of a single droplet as it slid downward, gathering into itself other droplets.

"Who was the fool who said music could soothe the savage beast?" Thomas asked quietly.

And though I do not think he expected an answer, I said, "I believe it was an English playwright after the time of Shakespeare, and the phrase is 'savage *breast*,' not beast."

"Couldn't prove it by me," he said, then added, "But whoever it was, he didn't tell the whole story, 'cause music can sure rile up a body, too." He mindlessly ran a finger around the steering wheel for a few moments, and presently he stopped, then looked at me and asked, "Do you ever wish you could wipe things out of your mind, Rosie?"

I did not reply, for I was certain he knew the answer I would give. Had he not recently delivered to me a lecture about the virtues of one's putting the past behind him?

"I mean, it's kinda like those crazy stories we were talkin' about," he said. "You start out with somethin' that happened to you one time, and you run it back and forth in your mind over and over, tear it apart and put it back together, add a little bit to it here and take away a little bit there until it might end up a different story from the way it really was." He stopped and sighed. "Then again, it might stay the same, and sometimes that's worse. But whichever way it goes, you let it haunt you and torment you, and you just can't get past it."

I sat very still, my lips pressed in a firm line. Whereas Thomas had begun by speaking about himself, his words now seemed to be aimed at me. Or could it be that he, too, carried within his soul some secret torment?

When he spoke again, it was a half whisper. "I killed a man once, Rosie."

I shot him a look of surprise at the sudden divulging of this news, though it came to me almost at once that since he had served in the armed forces during World War II, the incident must have occurred then. My words came quickly, almost impatiently. "Many men have done the same in wartime," I said.

"It didn't happen in the war," he said. "I ran over a man with a tractor, and he died."

I sought his eyes and saw that his words were true. "It was an accident," I ventured.

"Yes," he said.

"Then you are not to blame," I said, though I knew that my words were empty.

"I was daydreamin'," he said. "It was my carelessness that killed him."

"It was not intentional," I said, regretting my words at once, for I understood that this fact, rather than assuaging one's feelings of guilt, could only exacerbate them. Over the course of time, I suppose, one could pardon himself for bringing about another's death in self-defense, as a duty of war, or for the sake of honor, but to snuff out a life because of momentary inattention or youthful negligence would be personally and permanently irremissible.

Questions flooded my mind: When had this happened? Who was the man who had been killed? How could Thomas have failed to see him in time? Why had the man not simply moved out of the way? How fast could a tractor move? Had death come instantaneously? Had Thomas been charged with manslaughter? I knew that he would tell me anything that I asked, but I found that I could not bear to ply him with my questions, to probe into the particulars.

I cannot even guess how long we looked at each other, scarcely breathing. The rain increased, drumming upon the roof of the car for a furious minute and then subsiding all at once into a steady drizzle again.

Thomas at last broke the spell. "The man was dirt poor," he said. "Little old farm that never put out anything, had maybe a dozen scrawny chickens, a bony horse or two. Wife had died. Didn't have a family, just a little bean pole of a girl twelve years old, nobody else. We took the girl in to live with us, and when I came back from fightin' in the war I was expected to marry her and provide for her."

"Her name was Rita," I said.

"Yep, it was," he said. "She was sixteen when we married, and I was twenty-two." The rain had abated more, as if someone were shutting it off slowly by means of a faucet. It was cold in the car. Thomas must have seen me shiver, for he turned on the ignition, adjusted the heater, and pulled out of the parking lot slowly.

I felt the tension within me both heightened and alleviated by the interruption, for though I longed for Thomas to continue talking, I also wanted to cover my ears. My husband's past, of which I knew so little, had a sudden and powerful hold over me. I wanted to learn it in one sitting. At the same time, it frightened me to face the specter of his first wife, for I shrank from the comparison with a sixteen-year-old bride.

"She hated me," he said presently as we passed through the outskirts of Derby. I felt a collision within me. "I think she'd always hated me for what I did to her pa," he said, "but she was the real quiet type and wouldn't talk hardly at all. You couldn't ever tell what was goin' on inside of her. My folks said I owed it to her to give her a home and make it up to her for losin' her daddy, and so my daddy told her the plan, and she told him to tell me she'd marry me." We were on Highway 11 now, headed back toward Filbert. "I remember the night before the weddin' wishin' I could run away," Thomas said.

The rain had stopped completely, and the sky was clearing. I gazed up into the night and was astonished to see how quickly the clouds had parted, how brightly the stars behind them were glittering. I saw Orion spread-eagled against the blackness.

I thought suddenly of the words in *Kon-Tiki,* which my mother and I had read when I was a child of ten. Thor Heyerdahl described the nighttime view of life on a raft in the Pacific Ocean thus: "The world was simple — stars in the darkness." As it had come to

Mr. Heyerdahl that life, when distilled to its essentials, was the same for man in A.D. 1947 as it was in 1947 B.C., so it came to me that night that my life was only one of countless stories of human pain; that though I had considered myself the prima donna of sufferers, I was simply one of a vast troupe; that darkness indeed descends upon every man and woman, but that moon and stars also shine down upon all.

"After we was married, she opened up and started talkin'," Thomas was saying now. "Oh, did she ever. She talked plenty. Nobody would've believed me if I'd have told 'em the things she said. Some days I couldn't believe my ears. She hated me, like I said, but she was real jealous at the same time. Always accused me of havin' girlfriends behind her back. Would slap me one minute and throw herself all over me the next."

I could not form a picture of these things; indeed, I did not want to! Thomas was talking faster now, spitting his words out as if they were sour fruit. "Nagged at me to move away from my kin in North Carolina. She said things'd be better and we'd be happier. So we did. We packed up and moved down here, only it didn't get better — just worse. When she wasn't complainin', she was listenin' to her phonograph records. The Andrews Sisters — it was always them. Used to make me sick at my stomach hearin' their perky singin' when I was livin' in hell."

Thomas had reached a speed of sixty miles per hour by this time but suddenly glanced at the speedometer and decelerated. "When our baby died," he said after a heavy pause, "she said it was my fault. Said the baby was puny 'cause I kept her all tore up inside the whole time she was carryin' it."

Thomas did not speak again until we pulled into our driveway. "I lived with that woman over twenty years," he said. "When she took sick and died, it was like I'd been let out of jail." He looked straight ahead as he spoke. "I told my family not to ever say her name in front of me again."

I felt as if my sense of order had been upended, as if every fenced city within my kingdom had been battered and despoiled, as if I had been swept away in a mighty whirlwind. Yet for all the violence within me, I sensed that there was to be a propitious end, that thrust forth from my confining province, my view of the landscape was to be much improved.

Though the question was inappropriate for the time, I could not stop myself from posing it. "Why did you marry me?" I asked.

Thomas took the key from the ignition and, still without looking at me, said, "Oh, somehow I knew you'd be . . . safe and . . . well, *steady,* Rosie. I could tell you were a good woman. I'd had a bad one, and I wanted a good one. I wanted to forget." He sucked in his breath and added, "I guess we spend our life tryin' to forget things, don't we?"

Repairer of the Breach

28

I mean to cover much ground in the chapter at hand. Unlike the last five chapters, which belabored the passing of only two days in December, this chapter will traverse swiftly over time. By the end of it, I plan to have progressed through the end of February. As the summer days are waning, so my stamina is flagging. August is rapidly advancing upon me, and I must complete my tale.

Though I have no doubt that I could write at least one chapter for every day of my friendship with Birdie from December forward, I have calculated that to do so, an additional one hundred chapters would be required; thus a single volume could not contain the whole. Too, I am postponing a number of weighty actions until the close of my story, and while I feel a foreshock of terror at the thought of what I must do, I nevertheless find my heart straining toward the finish.

I was fifty years old, then, when I crept

forth from my hiding place, my eyes blinking in the strong light. It is a strange phenomenon of life that one can see a thing many times but never observe it, that he can hear yet not attend, that he may be fully sentient yet lacking in perception, understanding, and feeling.

I had known on a rational level, of course, of suffering in the lives of others, but I had never allowed the knowledge to penetrate my heart. For many years I had seen the children of Emma Weldy Elementary School file through the lunchroom. Upon many occasions I had looked into hollow eyes bespeaking lost innocence and betrayed trust and had taken note of ragged clothing and ill grooming, yet I had never allowed myself to be touched by these outward signs of inner wounds. I had read extensively. My books, magazines, and newspapers spared no details in the reporting of injuries both physical and emotional. When one is in bondage to his own brand of hurt, however, that of others is easily forgotten, if dwelt upon at all. It is discounted as second-rate.

Within twenty-four hours, on December 17 and 18, I had been unexpectedly made aware of personal suffering in the lives of both Birdie and Thomas, the two people who had demonstrated toward me what I knew to be a genuine constancy of love. For once I made no attempt to measure their suffering by the yardstick of my own past. Because I cared for them — more deeply, I knew, than I could bring myself to confess — the knowledge of their past suffering carved a tunnel through my wall of pride and pain. And not merely a tunnel; no, it was as if a stick of dynamite had cleared out a wide cave within me, had opened up outlets for sunlight and air.

In the days that followed, I emerged as if from a trance, the scales falling from my eyes so that I saw the many sorrows of others outside my small circle. And just as one first becomes aware of a thing and then sees examples of it upon every hand, so I began to observe evidence of great misfortunes in the lives of others and to contemplate the weight of them.

In the kitchen of Emma Weldy the following Wednesday, the day school was to be dismissed for the Christmas holidays, I saw a remarkable and unprecedented sight. Algeria came into the kitchen that morning upon arrival and without speaking approached Birdie and enfolded her in an enormous embrace, which was returned with great warmth. Though Algeria could have picked Birdie up and cradled her like a baby, it was not the embrace of mother to child but rather one between equals. The fact that they were of different race, temperament, and size was of no consequence.

At the time, I was counting the cartons of

milk in the cooler. With the holidays approaching, I wanted no surplus. While I did not gawk unabashedly at the two of them as did Francine, I could not help wondering why Algeria, who, like me, generally bristled when touched, had conducted herself in this manner.

"Hey, hey, you two, what's going on?" Francine asked but received no answer.

At last Algeria released Birdie, held her by the shoulders, and said gruffly, "Bless you, Birdie."

"Oh, honey, you're as welcome as can be," Birdie said, and though they both laughed, I believe they could as easily have wept.

That afternoon the mystery was brought to light. I stayed later than usual, busying myself in my office and the pantry, and then I drove to the bank to make the day's deposit, after which I returned to the school, for I meant to speak with Birdie privately. By this time she had settled herself at the desk in my office cubicle with a stack of papers before her, assuming that I was gone for the day.

She had typed and duplicated a Christmas issue of *Sheep Tales* a week earlier but was reading through poems and stories on the subject of winter fun in preparation for the January publication. She remained charmed by the samples submitted to her by the teachers, although my assessment of the children's writing skills was considerably less glowing.

In comparing their facility with language to my own as a child, I felt that our schools were falling far short of the mark. There were, of course, isolated examples of clean and unspoiled writing. One child, for example, had written "I shook the burned-out light bulb and heard jingle bells far away." This, I thought, was a felicitous metaphor. Another child wrote that "the brook rushed and swirled over the rocks like foamy milk," and another wrote about a fairy who "had little yellow wings the size of a flower petal" and lived inside a cookie jar.

When I walked into my office, Birdie leapt to her feet. "Oh, Margaret, I'm sorry! I thought you had already left. Here, do you need your desk back?"

I told her that I did not and went to my filing cabinet as if searching for something. I removed a folder, of which I had no need, and, after closing the drawer, asked Birdie whether she would be traveling during the Christmas holidays. She looked surprised but not displeased that I had questioned her thus and answered that their plans were to stay at home. We talked in this manner for several minutes, she turning the same question upon me and proposing in dulcet tones that we "get together again over the holidays."

My primary aim in seeing her after hours was to satisfy my curiosity concerning the incident between Algeria and herself that morning. I was hoping that she would talk of the incident unprodded, but when she did not, I asked her forthrightly, and she willingly explained the matter.

On Monday of the same week, only two days earlier, Birdie had invited Algeria to her home for supper the following night, but Algeria had declined, saying that she could not leave her mother. When urged to bring her mother, Birdie said that she had again refused, at last explaining that her mother was bedridden.

"Come to find out," Birdie said, "Algeria never goes *anywhere* at night because she's always taking care of her mother. During the day while she's here at work, she pays a neighbor to go over a couple of times to check on her, and of course she has brothers and sisters coming in and out, but they're grown and have families of their own, some of them. There's two brothers that still live at home, I believe, but one of them's had a lot of trouble with the law and that's really on Algeria's mind a lot. And there's an elderly uncle who lives next door who can hardly walk, so Algeria helps him out when she can, and she's always baby-sitting for her nieces and nephews, too — or maybe it's *great*-nieces and nephews. Anyway, she's the main-stay for the whole family! If she decided to think about just herself and go off somewhere for supper, there'd be nobody to look after her mother and her uncle and her brothers and everybody else."

To think that I had worked with Algeria for over ten years and had never known these facts about her life, except that her brother Sahara had been in jail, caused me to feel a twinge of shame. I wondered whether she had ever told Francine about her family.

"But if she declined your invitation, what prompted the display of emotion toward you this morning?" I asked.

Birdie shook her head as if discounting a minor point. "Oh, well, when we found out what the situation was, we decided to take supper over *to her.* Mickey was such a big help. He got off work early and fixed some of his soda biscuits and roasted a whole chicken and made the best glaze for it! I made this mashed potato casserole that everybody seems to like and some crowder peas and other things. Mickey helped me make a pie — just a plain old apple pie, but it turned out pretty."

"Had you told Algeria that you were bringing a meal?" I said.

"I told her not to cook anything that night," Birdie said, "so she had to know what we were up to. But we didn't get there till after six-thirty, and I was afraid she was going to think I wasn't coming even though I told her it might be after six. It turned out that when we got there, she had run next door to her uncle's, and it was one of her brothers that let us in. Cairo, I think he said his name was. We took everything to the kitchen and then said hello to her mother — oh, Margaret, she's the pitifulest sight — and then we scooted away before Algeria got back from next door. It was such fun!"

I realized then that this mission of hospitality must have been executed the day before, on Tuesday, the afternoon of my piano lesson. Yet Birdie had spoken not a word to me of her plan on Tuesday, and I had sensed no anxiety in her manner, no attempts to cut short my lesson so that she could be busy about her work. She had walked with me to the driveway, as was her custom, and had stood waving while I maneuvered my Ford onto Highway 11. By my estimation she had been left with only three hours to assemble and deliver the meal for Algeria and her family.

It came to me as I stood in my office that afternoon that Birdie Freeman considered the feeding of others her ministry. She took to heart the injunction "Feed the hungry." Food was her craft, her defining grace, her gift to the world. It is perhaps surprising that I felt no pangs of jealousy upon hearing of her labor on Algeria's behalf. Now that she was my friend, I could have clamped down upon her in an emotional sense, becoming possessive and resentful of her overtures to others. That I did not do so is a credit to Birdie, not to myself. Though her service to others never slackened after we became friends, I nevertheless felt that she extended to me a double portion of her generosity, the cream of her love. Perhaps others felt the same way, that she was their special friend. If so, it was because of her great supple heart, capable both of absorbing all and of wringing itself dry.

Concerning her relationship with Algeria, another notable interchange occurred later, in January, when emotions nationwide were flaring over the courtroom drama involving the former black football hero accused of murder.

On the day after the verdict had been made public, Francine and Algeria had engaged in a brief but acrimonious row, after which each had gone about her work sullenly for some time. Francine, of course, hotly maintained that "O. J. Simpson was guilty as a dirty rag," that "he blew a gasket and killed those two people, then tried to cover his tracks." She was enraged that he had "gotten off scot-free" and attributed his acquittal to "money and power, pure and simple." Algeria, on the other hand, held that "a bunch of bigoted police" had "set 'im up" and "they was so blind with hate they didn't even see their own stupid mistakes."

Birdie winced visibly over the heated altercation and, after a long interlude of rancorous silence, set about making peace. "Oh, let's don't quarrel like this," she said, flashing appealing looks to both Algeria and Francine, though they pointedly avoided her eyes. It was already late morning by now, and most of the preparations for lunch had been completed. Birdie sat down on a stool at the large steel table with a slice of cheese pizza — the main selection for the day — on a napkin before her. When no one responded to her plea, she bowed her head and closed her eyes for what seemed to be several minutes. She always prayed before eating her lunch but seldom at such length.

I was standing in the kitchen at the time, replenishing the stock of disposable tableware at the serving line. I saw first Algeria and then Francine cast watchful glances toward Birdie. Generally, the three of them sat down together for an early lunch sometime before eleven o'clock, but today Francine and Algeria had stationed themselves in opposing corners of the kitchen, like boxers between rounds. Each was eating pizza, Francine sulking at a smaller worktable beside the large sink and Algeria leaning against the ice machine, almost hidden from Francine's view. Thus positioned, Algeria was only a few steps from Birdie whereas Francine was perhaps twenty feet away.

Birdie at last opened her eyes and looked

up, first at Algeria, then at Francine. She had to speak quite loudly to be heard over the hum of the ventilators. "Nobody's asked me," she said, "but I'm going to tell you what I think about all this O. J. business anyway." She took a small bite of pizza and chewed with great deliberation. "There's probably no way we're ever going to know the truth," she said at last, "but I think you're both right."

Algeria and Francine looked at her suspiciously but said nothing, and she continued. "Yes, I do. I think you're both right. My first reaction, when I heard the earliest reports, was that he probably did it." She looked directly at Algeria, who grunted and jerked her head to the side. "And I still think there's a good chance that he did," Birdie said. "But . . ." she paused and addressed Francine across the room. "I also think it's the lowest and most despicable thing in the world when men who've sworn to uphold the law are shown to have mean, lying spirits. That detective lied on the witness stand, and I wouldn't put it past somebody like that to plant false evidence just to be spiteful."

Algeria was looking at her again, studying her from grim, narrowed eyes. "It seems to me," Birdie said, "that half the people are saying *he's* guilty and the other half are saying the *police* are guilty, but I think — and Mickey says the same thing — that *both sides* could be guilty. Maybe O. J. *did* kill those people, and maybe the police *did* tamper with things."

As I headed toward the pantry, I said curtly, "The first class will be arriving soon. I trust that things are in order."

"Yes, they are, Margaret," Birdie replied firmly, then closed her argument with Algeria and Francine thus: "A lot of bad, bad things were aired in public through all this. It's hard to believe the ugly things human beings will do. Some days I tell Mickey I don't want to even watch the news or read the paper, and lots of days I don't! But there's somebody who knows what the whole truth is about all this O. J. business, and that's God. It's all over now, at least the trial is, and we've got to go on living and working together. We've got to leave it behind us and just do our part to be good and honest and . . . well, just treat people the way we want to be treated. I say we lay it all aside and be friends like we've always been."

She lifted her carton of milk and sipped through the straw, then set it down and smiled in turn at Francine and Algeria. Raising both hands as if in surrender, she said, "I'm done now! That's all I'm going to say." Very meticulously she wiped her mouth with a paper napkin and added, "Well, then, I guess we'd better get ready for the children!"

Though Francine and Algeria did not give voice to their reconciliation, I heard Francine say later, after the last class had been served, "Oh, good grief, I just slopped peach juice all over the floor here," and I saw Algeria make her way at once to the janitor's closet and return to mop it up.

Sometime in January I discovered that Mickey Freeman had upon more than one occasion visited Algeria's brother Sahara in the county jail. This came about when I overheard Birdie and Algeria talking in the kitchen one day. "Mickey says he thinks Sahara's making a real turnaround," Birdie said. Her back was toward me. Algeria's reply was indecipherable. "Well, the last couple of times Mickey's talked to him," Birdie replied, "he said Sahara's really listened. And he's been reading the Bible Mickey brought him, too."

Likewise, Birdie became a participant in Francine's life. I learned from overheard conversations, for example, that Francine's son Champ had attended a bowling activity with one of the teens from Birdie's church, and that Francine and her children had gone to a Sunday morning service at the Church of the Open Door and stayed for a potluck dinner afterward. Also, Birdie and Mickey had kept Francine's two youngest children, BoBo and Watts, overnight when Francine and her mother had driven to Aiken to visit Francine's sister following an emergency operation for a ruptured spleen, which Francine had described in minute detail to Algeria and Birdie as they prepared macaroni and cheese in the lunchroom kitchen the day after she returned.

At last Algeria had said, "Shut up, you makin' me sick!" and Francine had concluded her remarks with "Well, anyway, she's gonna have a scar that's something else." Within minutes she had begun telling of a woman she had met in the hospital waiting room whose husband had lost a foot to gangrene and stopped only when Birdie patted her shoulder and said, "Well, Francine, I'm going to be praying for both your sister and that poor man on a regular basis. Now, honey, will you help me get these pinto beans heated up?"

It was from Birdie that I learned of Francine's failure to collect child support from her former husband, who had left for work one morning two weeks after Watts was born and had never returned home. I had known none of this. "She sure is plucky to be raising those four children all by herself without a bit of help!" Birdie had said.

As for Thomas and me, Mickey and Birdie continued indefatigably to seek our company. As the new year began, scarcely a week went by without our taking a meal together. We frequently played Rook, table tennis, and the Dictionary Game, and on an unseasonably warm Saturday in February we even played croquet on the expansive lawn in front of Birdie and Mickey's house. After our croquet game, Mickey grilled hamburgers on their patio in the backyard, and with her hand mixer Birdie made chocolate milk shakes, which we drank out of root beer mugs. In the months that followed, Birdie taught me the joy of laughter. "You've changed so much since I first met you, Margaret!" she often said. Whenever we talked of our first two months together as co-workers, she always exclaimed, "I was just convinced that you couldn't stand the sight of me!"

Thomas took to dropping by the Freemans' house whenever he drove to Greenville on Saturdays, and he and Mickey often played checkers on these occasions and watched an *Andy Griffith* rerun. One day Mickey took Thomas to the Lackeys' house through the stand of pine trees and introduced him to Mervin Lackey, who owned a fishing boat, and one Saturday the three men drove to Lake Jocassee to fish for trout.

My piano lessons continued on Tuesdays and Fridays, with the issuance in February of an unexpected proposal from Birdie.

"Margaret," she said to me one Friday afternoon as we drove to her home, "how would you like to play the organ?" It was a chilly day, and she wore a tartan muffler about her neck.

"Have you given up on my learning to play

the piano?" I asked.

"Given up?" she cried, throwing her hands in the air and laughing. "Why, I've taught you practically everything I know. In another year you'll be way ahead of me, and I'm not just saying that." She grew somber. "I was thinking," she continued, fingering the fringe of her muffler, "you're going to need somebody one of these days who really has some training to take you further in piano. I'm sure you could find somebody qualified over in Greenville. But here's my idea for now — I was thinking it might be fun for you to try your hand at the organ."

She pointed suddenly to a car coming toward us on the other side of the road. "I think that's Dottie Puckett! She and Sid live up on the highway a little past us. Sid runs the Texaco, and Dottie has a beauty shop — you've probably seen the sign for it." She leaned forward and waved with vigor, though, of course, the other woman could not have recognized her. Settling back, she continued laying out her plan. "I don't mean give up the piano but just branch out and take on another challenge. The organ's got a different touch from the piano, but I think you'd like it real well. How would you like to try it?"

The proposition provoked my interest, although I wondered whether professional keyboard pedagogues would have endorsed the plan. It does not strike me as an ideal instructional tactic to introduce two different instruments in so short a time to a novice musician. Even as I considered the idea with piquant regard, however, I saw an immediate obstacle. "Neither of us has an organ," I said.

Birdie had foreseen both the impediment and a solution. "Oh, but we do!" she said. "You see, I checked with our pastor, and he said we could use the church organ. I usually drive over sometime on Saturday anyway to practice my songs for Sunday, so we could set up a time and you could meet me there — if you could spare the extra time, of course. I know Saturday's a busy day for catching up at home."

Like Pharaoh of old, I felt my heart harden. "Have you not invited me without ceasing to your church functions, and have I not repeatedly declined?" I said stiffly. "Do you think that you can now resort to inveiglement to lure me inside your church?"

She appeared to be both puzzled and mildly insulted. "We would be the only ones in the church, Margaret," she said, "except maybe Brother Hawthorne, but he would be in his office if he was there at all. We'd just be using the organ, and it would only be one time a week for an hour or less. I don't know what that word *inveiglement* means, but I'm sure not going to try to force you to do anything. I just thought you might like to try something new is all."

We were on Highway 11 now, passing the feed store and a defunct gas station with a faded sign: Buster's Food & Gas. A wondrously gnarled tree stood beside the sign, and for a moment I marveled at the sinister energy suggested by its upraised tangle of black boughs. One could almost imagine that it had been frozen by still photography in the midst of a frenzied dance.

Neither of us spoke for a brief interval, and then Birdie said, "Nothing would please me more — and I mean this — than for you and Thomas to visit our church some Sunday. And while I'm on the subject, I'll go ahead and tell you that I pray for it every day, and I mean to keep on. I'd give anything, Margaret, for you to turn your heart to God, and I'm not ever going to give up hoping you will. From the little bit you've told me about your background, I know you've got some things festering in your heart, and I pray about that, too. But I want you to know something — I'm going to love you till I die, no matter what, even if you never step foot inside my church." She turned to her right and directed her gaze out the passenger window. In her lap her small hands were clasped tightly, her knuckles peaked like tiny whitecaps.

The next week I told Birdie that I would like to start the organ lessons as soon as it could be arranged, and on February 25 I found myself seated for the first time at the organ console in the sanctuary of the Church of the Open Door in Derby. I had not been inside a church for over thirty-three years. By a stroke of ill fate, the elementary organ books that Birdie had ordered had not yet arrived, so the only printed music available at my first lesson was the hymnbook, from which Birdie selected four hymns for our use.

It struck me as grossly ironic that my first hearing of these hymns in over three decades was by my own hands, fumbling at the keys of an unfamiliar instrument in the very place that I had vowed never to enter. The experience of my first organ lesson was bittersweet. I was powerfully drawn to the instrument itself, though sorely vexed by the environment and the music. As would be expected, Birdie heaped upon me enthusiastic acclamation for my first halting performance, declaring me once again "a natural," and in subsequent lessons I began to exercise with greater artistic sensitivity the touch essential for proficiency on the organ. Following our lessons I would generally remain at the church for an hour, sometimes longer, to practice.

The following Tuesday, February 28, was Birdie's birthday. Merle Cameron, the secretary at Emma Weldy, had circulated the news to the classrooms, and all day the children showered Birdie with cards and handmade trifles. Many of the teachers also favored her with small gifts — candles, decorative tins, note paper, and the like. Algeria gave her a shiny billfold of candy apple red, and Francine gave her a box of Russell Stover chocolates.

It is my belief that a gift, while it may please the recipient mightily, nevertheless reveals the preferences of the giver as much as, or perhaps more than, those of the receiver. I have no doubt that Algeria imagined herself the proud possessor of a red billfold and that Francine coveted the chocolates for her own enjoyment.

I gave much thought to a gift for Birdie's birthday, and in so doing was guided in my selection by my aforementioned theory of gift giving. Remembering the Christmas gift that she had given to me, it came to me that her motive for buying the set of dishes, though unquestionably reflective of her good heart, perhaps also testified of a desire on her part. For this reason, my gift to Birdie on February 28 was a set of Morning Glory dinnerware, which she opened that afternoon when I accompanied her to her home for my Tuesday piano lesson. Mickey had left a house key under the mat at the back door, and Thomas had taken the gift over during the day and set it on the kitchen table. From her response upon seeing the dishes, one might have thought that I had deeded to her a diamond mine.

When her gasping and exclaiming had

begun to subside, I said to her, "You bought them yourself, you know," at which she chortled briefly, almost mindlessly, before breaking off to look at me questioningly. She tilted her head to the side and contorted her face as if having ingested a bitter herb.

"Why do I get the feeling you're throwing my words back in my face?" she said, shaking a finger at me. "Now, Margaret, if you mean what I think you mean, I'm going to just —"

Pitching my voice higher, I said, "Oh, yes, you did. I just put aside the money I would have left on your piano after every lesson and saved it all up until I found something that I thought you would like. You do like them, do you not?" Together we laughed as she threw her arms about me. Since Christmas I had left off payment for my piano lessons, an act which Birdie took, I believe, as a sign that our friendship had been sealed.

As she walked me to my car after my lesson that afternoon, thanking me repeatedly for the set of dishes, a thought came to me, and when she paused during her redundant expressions of gratitude, I said to her, "I have not heard you say how old you are today. Are you sensitive about your age?"

"Oh, my lands, no!" she replied, laughing. "I'm fifty-two. Although now that I think about it, I don't remember you ever telling your age, either." This was an example of something that I had noted with great frequency; that is, Birdie's penchant for turning the topic of a conversation from herself to another.

"I am fifty," I said.

"Oh, your year of jubilee!" she cried.

"Yes, well, when it is past," I said, "I shall try to recover from the immense thrill of it all."

Birdie laughed and shook her head. "There you go making fun of me again." We were standing beside my Ford by now.

I knew of the ancient Levitical law of the land regarding the fiftieth year to which she was referring, of course: the proclaiming of liberty to bondmen, the restoring of property, the ceasing from planting and harvesting. My grandfather had been curiously fond of the book of Leviticus and had drilled me at length concerning the burnt offering, the meal offering, the peace offering, and so forth. Even today I can recite the instructions for the cleansing of a leprous house, the baking of shewbread, and the stoning of a blasphemer.

"Now that I think about it, however," I said, "if I understand the law correctly, the year of jubilee actually commenced at the close of the forty-ninth year and extended through the end of the fiftieth year. Because we number our birthdays following each year of life, therefore, my fiftieth year concluded on the day before my fiftieth birthday. My year of jubilee, you see, is past, and my next will not begin until the day after my ninety-ninth birthday. I shall have to be more watchful when that one arrives so that I may celebrate appropriately."

Birdie lifted her face and laughed gaily as if sharing a joke with the gray February sky. "I can't keep up with you!" she said when her laughter died. "You can be a real tease sometimes, you know it?" Her smile fading, she grew reflective. "I don't care what you say, Margaret. You're a different person from when I first met you back in August, and I think you know it even if you won't admit it." I did not reply but opened my car door. "Don't you think it's interesting," Birdie continued, "that God *wanted* his people to be happy and even wrote laws requiring them to take rests and have special feasts?"

I could not stop the words which sprang from my mouth. "It appears to me that God put a great deal more thought into providing for the suffering of his creatures than he did for their rejoicing."

Seated behind the steering wheel, I inserted my key into the ignition and turned it. The door was still open, however, and Birdie, no trace of playfulness upon her face now, put her hands on her knees and leaned toward me, raising the volume of her words above the engine and speaking distinctly. "We can't do anything about suffering, Margaret," she

595

said. "It's been around forever, and we're all going to have our share. Just because somebody's had a hard life doesn't mean they've got a right to take it out on other people — or on God, either. Especially on God. He knows all about it. It's part of his big plan somehow — and don't ask me how."

Her words seemed to be pouring forth with increased velocity, and I was aware that I was staring at her in unveiled surprise. "We're all responsible for how we act, Margaret," she went on, "and there are a million ways to be mean. We can be mean in big ways by killing people or stealing or cheating, or we can be mean in little ways by being rude and snapping at everybody. A murderer is guilty in a big way, but all of us are guilty when we wrap ourselves up in our own little world and don't think about how we treat others."

No immediate reply came to my mind in response to this amazing and disjointed retort, and I suddenly felt mentally enfeebled. I could not begin to construct an argument to attack her logic. I suppose her boldness struck me with greater force than did her actual words. I had never before experienced difficulty in tearing apart mere words and divesting them of their sting, of separating the veneer of style from the underlying content, of exposing fallacious reasoning. Yet for the moment I was speechless. I, the great upholder of judgment for all miscreants, could find no words for my own defense. For all of my adult life I had granted myself clemency, but here stood Birdie Freeman pointing the finger of blame at me. For there could be no mistake that she was referring to me, that she judged me "mean in little ways."

I depressed the accelerator and raced the engine of my car, then reached out to close the door, thus constraining Birdie to take a step backward. I did not lower my window but merely nodded good-bye to her as I put my car into gear.

"Thank you again for my wonderful present!" she called as I backed away. "I love you, Margaret!" And I heard her say again, "Oh, I do love you, Margaret!"

Once I had turned my car around and begun to move down the long driveway, I looked into my rearview mirror and saw her childlike figure still standing at the end of the sidewalk. What a nondescript person God had chosen for his emissary, I thought. What a small, light vessel for the vanguard of his heavenly fleet, what an obscure tinderbox for his fires of revival, what a frail repairer of the breach.

Strangely, I recalled at that moment a line from a book that I had read three times as a young child: Frank Baum's *The Wizard of Oz*. The words were those of the Cowardly Lion, who exclaimed over the fact that "such small animals as mice have saved my life."

And even as these thoughts crowded in upon my mind, I heard, as if spoken in my ear, the words of Gideon from the Bible: "Behold, my family is poor in Manasseh, and I am the least in my father's house." And I remembered that God had delivered the hosts of the Midianites into Gideon's hands.

A Cloud of Witnesses
29

In mid-March Birdie took leave of her senses and patronized a beauty shop, the very one of which she had spoken to me scarcely four weeks earlier. It was operated by Dottie Puckett, a fellow church member, who lived in a blue house on Highway 11.

When Birdie arrived at school one Monday morning with her hair cut and curled tightly about her face, I wanted to weep. It was not so much that the new style was unbecoming, for, in truth, I doubt that any hairstyle could have offset the limitations of Birdie's homely face. It was simply the advent of *change* that I opposed. I had come to love her, and my regard for her included to some extent her plainness: her unfashionable homemade or secondhand clothing, her unpretentious ways, her unadorned face, her simple plaits of hair wound atop her head. Had she appeared one day wearing elaborate makeup or a stylish and expensive garment, I would have objected as strenuously as I did to the martyrdom of her hair. I was unwilling to let go any part of her.

Upon Birdie's arrival that morning, Algeria appeared to pause only momentarily, eyeing her rather casually, in fact, with merely the slightest lifting of her eyebrows. Francine, on the other hand, responded with a great flappable show of emotion, nearly swooning with what she called "the shock of it all." She employed her favorite phrase, "something else," six times during her hypercharged display — I counted them. It was difficult to ascertain whether Francine approved of the new hairstyle or deemed it a failure, for her remarks possessed no coherence; indeed, few of them made little sense whatsoever, formed as they were of random bits of meaningless verbiage strung together. "Well, I never!" "What in the world . . . ?" "You just up and did it!" "Why, you little . . . !" "If that doesn't beat all!" "How did you ever . . . ?" "You're just something else, you know it?" and on and on.

When Birdie at last approached me, it was with an air of shyness. I had turned away from the spectacle of Francine's babbling and was opening two large boxes of paper goods that had been delivered the previous Friday and left beside my office door.

"Well, good morning, Margaret," I heard her say behind me.

"Hello," I answered without turning to face her.

"I guess you heard Francine carrying on about my new hairdo," she said, stooping beside me to gather several packages of paper napkins from the box. "You want these in the pantry with the others I guess?"

"Yes," I said, answering both questions at once.

She helped me empty the box and store the goods, neither of us speaking for several minutes. When we were finished, she carried the cardboard boxes to the delivery entrance and set them down, where Ed Silvester would pick them up later and dispose of them.

As if it were an ordinary day, Birdie then turned to me and said, "Did we decide to cut those apples into wedges for lunch or just give each child a whole apple like we did last time? I know we were talking about it yesterday before I left. They do waste a lot when they get a whole apple."

I gave her a long look, beginning with her white Keds and moving up past her white socks, her white skirt with its gathered waist, her white collarless blouse, and the silver locket around her neck.

By now I had learned of the contents of the locket: a curl of silver-white hair, which at Birdie's request the undertaker had clipped from the head of Mickey's deceased mother at a funeral home in Tuscaloosa fifteen years

601

earlier. Of Mickey's mother Birdie had said simply, "I always thought of her as my real mother." The locket had been a wedding gift to Birdie from her mother-in-law. It had been in the Freeman family for five generations. Mickey had spoken of his mother on a number of occasions, identifying her as the one from whom he had inherited his inclination for high jinks. "She used to crouch down by the window and do a great imitation of jungle birds whenever somebody walked by on the sidewalk in front of our house," he had said. "She got the biggest kick out of seeing people look up in the big sycamore tree in the front yard." In addition, she could yodel, crack her knuckles, whistle like a man, juggle dinner knives, and balance a broom on her nose.

At last I brought myself to draw my eyes upward past the locket to Birdie's face, and making a great effort at objectivity, I concluded after a few moments of silent study that the new hairstyle had the contradictory effect of making her appear both younger and older. I had seen toddlers with the same profusion of curls. To be truthful, the permanent itself had been artfully administered, without the seared and frizzed results one so often associates with such a procedure. The gray in her hair was more noticeable, however, resulting in an incongruous union of youthful curls and fading color. With her short hair, she put me in mind of a picture I had seen of Eudora Welty, whose hair at the time had been cropped and curled and whose horselike teeth precluded her being spoken of as a southern beauty, though the legacy of Miss Welty's writing certainly puts to rest any doubts concerning her interior loveliness.

"Wedges," I said at length.

Birdie smiled and replied pleasantly. "Well, now, I was about to ask you if the cat had your tongue. All right, then," she said, making ready to leave. "I think I'll wait a little while on that since we don't want them all turning brown before we serve them."

"Why did you tamper with your hair?" I asked, and she wheeled around with a mingled expression of amusement and condolence.

"Oh, Margaret, honey, is *that* what's the matter?" she said tenderly, advancing toward me and laying her hand upon mine. She smiled up at me with motherly caution as if choosing and weighing her words to soothe a child. "It's just *hair*," she said at last. "It doesn't change anything about me, except maybe my looks a little bit, and I can't go very far up or down in that department."

She smiled and placed my hand between both of hers. "I've been thinking about doing this for a while now," she said, "and Mickey told me to just go ahead and try it instead of talking about it. So I did. I went to my friend who has a shop in her house and told her what I wanted. To tell you the truth, ever since I met you I've wished I could wear my hair like yours. Of course, it turned out shorter and a whole lot curlier than yours, and I couldn't hold a candle to you anyway, but I guess I was just ready for a change. Who knows? I might get tired of it after a spell and let it get long again." She patted my hand and then stepped back once again. "Now, then, I've got to go get my hairnet on and get busy!" I watched her cross the kitchen, calling out to Algeria, "Do I need to get more syrup packets for the waffles?"

As March progressed, Birdie and I, in the company of Mickey and Thomas, spent many hours together in a variety of activities Birdie referred to as "our little excursions." To three of these, all of which occurred on successive Saturdays, I shall devote the remainder of the chapter.

The first was on March 18. Birdie and Mickey had joined Thomas and me for supper at our duplex. Since his success with the turkey at Thanksgiving, Thomas had begun to revive his forsaken talent at the grill, and on this particular night he had grilled to perfection four porterhouse steaks. Following the early meal, which we had finished by half past five, Thomas suggested taking a walk before eating dessert. We wore our jackets, for the temperature was in the low fifties.

Four blocks from our duplex is a poorly kept neighborhood park with a dirt baseball field. As we neared the park, Birdie and I walking together behind Mickey and Thomas, we saw a group of boys fanned out over the field under the supervision of a burly man who was barking orders from home plate. He was wielding a bat in his right hand, using it to point to various players as he flung out corrections. The boys looked to be between the ages of eight and ten.

"Oh, look, a ball practice!" said Birdie. Mickey started singing "Take Me Out to the Ball Game," quite loudly, and Thomas joined him. The man at home plate stopped mid-sentence and glared in our direction. Several of the boys laughed as if grateful for a break in the tension.

"Okay, now, listen up!" the man bellowed, turning back to the field. "You let your concentration down like that in a game and you're sunk! You'll be exactly the kind of players in a game that you are in practice!" Mickey and Thomas let the song die out, of course, and some of the boys cast uneasy glances toward us.

"Not exactly the Mr. Rogers type, is he?" Mickey said, and we continued along the sidewalk, Birdie never taking her eyes off the field. "Did you play ball as a kid?" Mickey asked Thomas.

"Ate, drank, and slept it," Thomas said.

"My dream was to someday break Babe Ruth's record." It was difficult to tell whether he was reporting a fact or employing hyperbole. He had never told me of harboring such a dream as a child.

"How many times do I have to tell you to get your glove down!" the man on the field yelled. "That's the worst mistake a fielder can make! Don't let me see that kind of sloppy stuff again, Porter!" The shortstop, who had let the ball roll between his legs, hung his head as the center fielder trotted forward to retrieve the missed ball. The man then hit a fly ball to right field, and a unison moan rose from the field. "Aw, no, Hawkins'll never catch that," we heard the first baseman say. All eyes turned toward the right fielder, whose head was thrown back, whose mouth hung open, whose hands dangled loosely at his side, and whose feet were firmly planted. Anyone could see that the ball was going to fall many feet behind him.

"Oh, back up, honey, back up!" Birdie was shouting, gesturing with large, sweeping motions. "You can do it! Get your glove up!"

The boy did take several timid steps backward but had waited too long to move, and the ball landed behind him.

The coach shook his head in disgust, and the boys all seemed to brace themselves for what was coming. "Hawkins! Look at me!" the man yelled, and the boy did. "Do you know what these are?" the coach said, pointing the bat to his own large feet. "They're called *feet!* And do you know what these are?" he continued, jabbing two fingers toward his own eyes. "They're called *eyes!* And this is a *hand!*" he said, waving his left hand dramatically. "The *eyes* and the *feet* and the *hands* work together, Hawkins! When your *eyes* see where the ball is going, you move your *feet* in that direction, and you raise your *hands* to catch the ball."

The coach paused and filled his cheeks with air, then expelled it slowly, shaking his head all the while. "And there's another part of you that's got to be working, too, Hawkins, and that's your *brain.*" Here he tapped his head lightly with the bat, crossed his eyes, and wagged his tongue. "I know you got feet and hands and eyes, but I got to tell you I'm starting to wonder about the brain!" The other boys laughed, though I suspected that they were doing so not purely out of cruelty but also because they knew that it was what the coach wished them to do.

Birdie stood rooted to the sidewalk for a moment. I had heard her utter a small, choked cry at the beginning of the man's speech to the hapless right fielder, and she stood now with one hand to her face. Mickey and Thomas had continued walking, talking all the while, unaware that we were not following.

All at once Birdie sprang to action. She made her way quickly to the opening in the fence and directed her steps straightway toward the man standing at home plate, calling all the while, "Excuse me, sir, excuse me! May I have a word with you?" Mickey, hearing her, turned around in alarm. By the time he had taken it in, however, the scene was underway. Birdie had stationed herself only a few inches from the man and, her head lifted upward, was earnestly but quietly conversing with him. Her hands were crossed and placed under her neck as if to shield against a draft, or perhaps a blow.

Mickey, galvanized by the sight, leapt forward and ran toward the fence, waving his hands and crying, "Hold it there, sugar cake! He's not going to let a woman on his team! It's for boys! Here, sir, I'll try to explain it to her!" It was apparent to me, and maybe to the coach also, that Mickey was speaking with irony, using humor to avert a fracas.

Birdie scarcely paused, however, but continued to address the man entreatingly, though I could not hear her words. For his part, the coach appeared to be dazed, glancing back and forth between Birdie, positioned beneath his chin and delivering a seamless monologue, and Mickey, advancing toward him with comic comportment.

The incident lasted no more than two or three minutes, but when Mickey escorted

Birdie back to the sidewalk, I saw that she was breathing hard and her mouth was set in a grim line. "Let's go on back to your house now," Mickey said to us, and we set off without delay, Thomas and I leading the way.

Ten minutes later we were seated at our kitchen table. I had filled the teakettle with water, and as we waited for it to boil, Mickey attempted to put us all at ease with a silly story about a man who worked at the Barker Bag Company with him, who supposedly had collected old crutches for years and had recently painted them all white and used them to construct a fence for his backyard. He kept looking at Birdie as he talked, and when she laughed at the conclusion of his story, he appeared to be relieved of a burden.

As I served our dessert, white cake with peppermint frosting, Birdie cleared her throat and spoke.

"I'm okay, everybody, so you can all quit walking on eggshells."

"Well, that's a load off my mind," Mickey said, pretending to wipe his brow and examine the soles of his shoes. "But it's going to take forever to clean up all the little pieces on the floor."

Birdie slapped his hand lightly and said, "Oh, stop it." Looking at Thomas and me, she said, "You must think I'm half crazy, but something just comes over me when I see a little child being mistreated. I don't know of anything that upsets me more! That poor little boy couldn't help it. He was so . . . so . . ."

"So ill equipped to do what was demanded of him," I said, and to my surprise, the others laughed in a sudden simultaneous rush, as if a valve had been turned to release pressure. Feigning more annoyance than I felt, I continued. "The boy's parents should not subject the child to such punishment. Anyone can see that he finds no joy in baseball, and he certainly has no natural gift for it. It is a parent's responsibility to provide opportunities for his child to excel in areas for which he is suited." I had never before in my life expressed such an opinion, though I do believe it to be true.

Birdie nodded emphatically. "You're absolutely right, Margaret. Absolutely." But then her eyes clouded. "So many problems with children are really the parents' fault — but, then, of course, some of these little children might not even have parents to look out for them. I wonder if that little boy does. . . . Hawkins, wasn't that what the man called him? I wonder how many Hawkinses there are in the phone book. Maybe we could . . ."

"Now, puddin', you can't solve all the problems of the world," Mickey said.

Though we eventually moved to other topics, Birdie still seemed heavy of spirit when she and Mickey wished us a good-night at half past eight. Our evenings together rarely ended so early. After they left, Thomas said, "She sure is a softhearted thing, isn't she?"

On the following Saturday, March 25, Birdie proposed a picnic. Only once, before we were married, had Thomas and I eaten a picnic lunch out of doors, and my memories of the experience were anything but agreeable. Perhaps an entomologist would have remembered the occasion with greater fondness, but as for me, we had hardly unwrapped our sandwiches before I suggested that we repack our basket and return to my duplex to eat apart from the company of flies, ants, and gnats.

We accompanied Birdie and Mickey on a picnic that March day, however, for Birdie's heart was set on it, and in Mickey's words, she would "pout and kick and scream all day if she didn't get her way," to which Birdie simply laughed and replied, "Not to mention holding my breath and biting and scratching!" Mickey urged us to wear comfortable shoes for walking and arranged to pick us up at one o'clock. It was a clear day. The sky was a rinsed blue.

It had been a mild winter, and spring had come early. We drove sixty miles to a state park called Jones Gap, and there we ate our lunch at a table beside a stream. Birdie spread a clean cloth over the table, and I can see its design yet: trellised ivy and yellow butterflies.

As it was too early in the year for insects or crowds of people, my recollection of the day is unmitigatedly happy.

We talked of many things as we ate. I recall in particular Mickey's description of a circus that he and Birdie had attended in Tuscaloosa in the early days of their marriage. "She had never been to one before," he said, "so I thought I'd better educate her." He began laughing as he continued, so much so that Birdie had to pick up the narrative and complete it.

As she told it, she had become "woozy when I saw those people up in the air," and when the trapeze artists began their routine, "I had to put my head between my knees to keep from passing out." Later, a clown had squirted a water gun into the crowd, hitting Birdie squarely between the eyes, at which she had emitted a startled shriek that "cut right through all the other noise and even made the ringmaster stop and ask if one of the monkeys had gotten loose in the crowd." When the dogs came out and started doing their tricks with hoops and balls, she said that she "laughed so hard I started crying and hiccuping at the same time." To make matters worse, Mickey had told all the people sitting around them that he was a scientist and had brought her along with him because he was doing a research project on "Schizophrenics in Highly Stimulating Environments."

What I remember most vividly about the day, however, is the walk along the trail beside the stream and into the woods off the marked path. There were, of course, many evergreens, and the early pale buds of the basswood, poplar, and river birch were abundant. Most notable, however, were the many species of herbaceous plants that Mickey pointed out as we moved along. Some time earlier I had acquired, as I related in a prior chapter, a personal copy of a field guide for wildflowers and had browsed through it at length. I had not realized before the day of our picnic, however, that one of Mickey's many interests was the study of regional flora, a hobby he had pursued with keen and assiduous enthusiasm. Indeed, he was a wealth of botanical knowledge, and though he dubbed himself "an amateur," I had every reason to trust his observations as fact.

As we hiked, Mickey pointed out and identified by name many plants, offering instruction both in simple matters such as the difference between the dicot and monocot, directing our attention to examples of each, and in finer distinctions such as petioled and sessile leaves, various blade margins such as ciliate, serrate, and dentate, and floral structures such as superior and inferior ovularies.

He was filled with delight that day, I recall, to come across a number of early blooming wildflowers: purple field pansies, which, although according to Mickey "you can find them practically anywhere there's dirt," were nevertheless a favorite of his; bluets, which grew in delicate clusters along the stream bank; bloodroot, the juice of which may be used as a dye; henbit, which Mickey called "a cute little nuisance of a weed"; and a clump of small bluish flowers newly unfolded that he conjectured to be a species of veronica called bird's-eye speedwell.

"We'll have to come back next month," he said as we turned to make our way back toward the stream. "In April you'll see a lot of Solomon's seals and wood anemone and — well, would you look at *that!*" We had come to a small clearing, and Mickey held up his hand for silence, then tiptoed in exaggerated fashion toward the base of a large rock.

"Look! It's a trillium!" Mickey said. "It must be the first one of the season. You hardly ever see them this early." He went on to name the different varieties that grew in our region: the yellow, the narrow-leaved, the nodding, Vasey's, and the rose trillium. This one was a rose trillium, although the petals were white. Mickey explained that in this species the flower bloomed white and then turned pink.

"Isn't that pretty the way the petals curve back?" said Birdie. "Oh, Mickey, let's pick it for Margaret!"

Mickey appeared to pause before reaching

down to pluck the trillium, stem and all. Handing it to me, he said, "I can pick flowers by the armload from our backyard and it doesn't bother me a bit, but it's hard for me to pick the wild ones for some reason." Looking down at the flower, he pretended to pat its head and said, "Sorry, little feller, my wife made me do it."

I have the rose trillium yet today, pressed between sheets of waxed paper in my dictionary, between pages 534 and 535, on which are printed the words beginning with *frequent* and ending with *frolic.* Between those guide words lies the word *friend.*

On the following Saturday, April 1, we pulled into the Freemans' driveway at four o'clock in the afternoon. The sky had clouded earlier that afternoon, but it had not yet stormed, though heavy rain was in the forecast.

The Freemans' front door was open, and Mickey waved to us, then disappeared briefly. Moments later Birdie emerged from the house wearing a bright salmon pink dress with a ruffled collar and a black stole of artificial fur draped about her shoulders. Mickey's dark suit was enlivened by a green and yellow polka-dot bow tie. He carried a large multicolored umbrella. "I told Mickey I'm afraid we look like a couple of April fools!" Birdie said. "I hope we won't be an embarrassment to you, but I didn't know how dressed up we should get since we've never been to something like this." She wore pendulous pearl earrings, and two rhinestone combs were nestled among her curls.

"Yep, I bet we'll turn a few heads with all our frippery," Mickey said. *Frippery* was a word that Thomas had selected for a recent round of the Dictionary Game, which the four of us continued to play from time to time. As one would imagine, Mickey's definitions were always highly preposterous, relying heavily upon wordplay. The definition he had submitted for *frippery*, for example, had been *Chinese acrobatics.*

After they had settled themselves in the backseat and Thomas had put the car into gear, Mickey said, "We've got to stop meeting like this, folks, or you're going to get sick and tired of us."

"Or the other way around," said Thomas. As we proceeded down the Freemans' driveway, I noted that there were three people standing around a grave in the cemetery. I saw one of them, a woman, kneel to lay a bouquet beside the headstone, and I wondered briefly whether she had loved the person buried there or whether she was only there out of obligation.

"Get tired of *you?* No chance of that!" cried Birdie. "I told Mickey just this week that I feel like the two of you are so deep we could never get to the bottom of you."

616

Mickey sang the first two measures of an old Sunday School chorus, "Deep and Wide," then stopped abruptly and said, "I don't guess you two know that song, though, do you? And anyway, the *wide* part might not be taken as a compliment!"

I cannot explain why I spoke aloud the remaining words of the chorus except perhaps to prove that I did know the song. I believe I must have sensed even as I spoke "There's a fountain flowing deep and wide" that something would come of my carelessness; in truth, perhaps I wanted something to come of it.

"Now, see," Mickey said to Birdie, "there she goes again." Then to me he said, "Margaret, I'm going to ask you something you might not like, but if that's the case, you can just tell me to mind my own business, and we'll talk about something else like hog-calling contests or the feeding habits of orangutans, take your pick." Mickey, seated directly behind me, paused a moment as if waiting for encouragement, but I said nothing, neither turned my head to give the appearance of receptivity.

"Now, Mickey, don't start poking your nose —" Birdie began.

"No, no, now don't you go shushing me, precious," said Mickey. "I mean to ask her. We've been friends for months now, and we've never gotten to the bottom of this. If she doesn't want to answer, she'll make it plain. She's not shy that way, you know."

We were headed south on Highway 11 by now, toward Highway 72, which would take us to Abbeville where we were to eat supper and then attend a play at the Abbeville Opera House. The meal had been Birdie's suggestion, the play mine. Thomas and Mickey had agreed to the trip because, as Mickey said, there was food involved.

"Okay, Margaret, here's my question," Mickey said, leaning forward. He took in a great breath of air and then said, "Did you know that when your car battery short-circuits it smells like rotten eggs?"

Thomas laughed a sudden explosive burst, and Birdie said, "Oh, Mickey, you're just impossible!"

"No, seriously," Mickey said, "I do have one question for you, Margaret. Here goes. We can tell from things you've said that you've been to church at some time in your life, and we can sure tell you don't want to go back — to that church or any other one. What I'm wondering is this: Do you think God is bad because a certain church was bad? Or are you coming at it from the other angle — that churches are bad because God is bad? Or . . ." He paused for a few seconds, then ended lamely, "Do you just not want to talk about it?"

I believe there is a specific point at which

one is ready to talk, when time and the totality of circumstances have coalesced into a ripeness of mind and spirit, and I believe that the trip from Filbert to Abbeville on April 1 was such a time for me. I was willing to open my heart. Seated as we were, I did not have to endure the discomfort and distraction of facing my audience. The question had been posed in the presence of sympathetic listeners, and I had ample time in which to answer it.

"You said that you had one question, but you have asked three," I replied. I heard Thomas hum a few tuneless notes, as he often does when nervous or amused.

"Okay," said Mickey boldly, "I'll take back the last two. How about just the first one?"

Without hesitation I began speaking and did so without interruption for thirty-two minutes. To my recollection I had never in my adult life talked for so long an unbroken span except when reading aloud the chapters from *Charlie and the Chocolate Factory* in the Emma Weldy library many years ago and when conducting opening staff meetings in the lunchroom each fall. Without sharing graphic specifics, I revealed the cause of my alienation from God: my grandfather's predacious acts against me in private over a period of four years while in public he served as a church elder.

I told of the two losses that flanked the casting away of my faith: The deaths of my mother and of my son. While Thomas drove, staring straight ahead and hearing for the first time many things about which he could have only wondered, and while Mickey and Birdie sat silent behind me, I abridged the story of my life into thirty-two minutes, concluding with these words: "Therefore, as I have seen no evidence of God's love to me, I can muster none for him, and as churches exist for the purpose of exalting this God, I can only avoid them."

I felt calm when I had finished, though at the same time expectant, for I knew that my words would stir a response. We must have driven for at least a mile before another word was uttered, and it was Birdie who spoke first.

"That's a sad, sad story, Margaret. I had put some of it together already from things you've told me, but hearing it all at one time almost takes my breath away. Nobody can argue that you've had a hard life and have —"

We were passing through Hodges by now, and I grasped the edge of the seat as a black dog suddenly darted across the road in front of us, though by the time Thomas had applied the brakes, the dog had vanished between two houses.

"Well, dog-gone," said Mickey, and Thomas laughed. "Now, then, go on with what you were saying, lambkin," Mickey urged.

"God doesn't let people suffer just to be mean, Margaret," said Birdie. "He's not out to get us. He loved Job, but he let him go through some awful times. We all have to go through bad times — it's the curse of sin — but the difference is that Christians have the Holy Spirit in their hearts to hold them up. God's aim for us when we suffer is to heal us and to bring us out stronger than when we went in."

Birdie leaned forward and laid her hand upon the back of the front seat as if to substitute for touching me. "Suffering is part of life just like happy times," she said, "and you *have* had some happy times, Margaret. You had four terrible years with your grandfather, and I sure don't want to make light of that, but God did give you the wits and strength to finally get away from him. And you also had four years of being a mother and having a little boy of your own, and I can't think of anything more wonderful than that! Of course, I can't imagine how painful it must have been to lose him, and your mother, too — oh, but I'm so glad you *had* them both, at least for a little while. Even if you had to lose them, you still *had* them."

She fell silent and leaned back in her seat, but Mickey picked up the theme. "You can look at suffering lots of different ways, you know. Sometimes it's the only way God can get a person's attention. Take this man who just joined our church a couple months ago. He'll be in a wheelchair the rest of his life because he picked the wrong place to dive into a lake. Young guy, not even forty yet, married, three little children, had a real active life, was a golf pro at a country club over in Athens, Georgia, and now he can't walk. You know what he does? He's started a counseling ministry for accident victims. He has an office in Greenville and Spartanburg both and visits people in hospitals all over the state. That's what I call putting your pain to good use. Now, I don't have anything against golf pros, but which job do you think does more good and helps more people — the one he used to have or the one he's got now?"

No one said anything for a short space of time, and then Mickey resumed. "And of course I don't need to remind you that you can't judge everything in a pot by what's floating on top. Seems to me like you're painting all churches black because of one bad man in one church you went to over thirty years ago."

Once again Birdie leaned forward. "You never can tell how you might use your sad past someday to help somebody else, Margaret," she said.

The words of Birdie and Mickey did not chafe. With the memory of Birdie's physical scars upon my mind and of the brittle, splintered brightness of her voice when speaking of children, I took in what she said and reserved it for further consideration.

By the time we arrived in Abbeville, the day had taken on a decidedly meditative cast, though not melancholy. The sky still lowered, and thunder rumbled in the distance. The four of us had never before sustained such a conversation; though solemn, it was strangely uplifting. We ate a most satisfying meal at a popular restaurant operated by Mennonites and later, after walking the streets surrounding the quaint town square, found our seats in the Opera House for the performance of Tennessee Williams' *The Glass Menagerie*.

Driving homeward late that night, we discussed the play. Thomas and Mickey laughed at Amanda Wingfield's nattering tirade over her son's failure to chew his food properly, but Birdie said, "It's really a sad play, though, isn't it? They all wanted something different but didn't get it."

More than any other work by Tennessee Williams, this drama had always haunted me. Perhaps I had for all of my life felt a kinship with Laura, whose hopes were dashed when her long adored savior proved unsatisfactory. As we rode in silence for a few moments, I heard again the closing lines of the play, spoken by Tom Wingfield. "Blow out your candles, Laura — and so good-bye."

I had seen the play only once before but

had read it many times, relishing the pensive gloom of the ending. Tonight, however, I felt a curious buoyancy of heart not at all in keeping with the mood of the play. Once again, and more powerfully than before, I felt the seed of hope sending down roots within me. While Laura's rescuer had been only a brief illusion, I felt that my salvation was a sure and imminent reality, that it would be no concealed and closely guarded secret, but that a cloud of witnesses, both seen and unseen, stood by awaiting the unshrouding of my buried faith.

The rain unleashed as we pulled into the Freemans' driveway late that night, escalating almost immediately into a spring hailstorm.

"Gang, gang, the hail's all here!" Mickey cried.

Joy in the Presence of Angels

30

For pure atmosphere, I do not believe that I have read a book to equal Archibald Rutledge's *Home by the River*. Birdie gave the book to me in early April, wrapped in lavender tissue paper and tied with white ribbon. "Mickey brought this home yesterday, and we thought you'd like it," she said, placing it upon my desk when she arrived at work one morning.

I removed the wrapping paper, leafed through the pages of the book, and thanked her sincerely. I had by this time read most of the poems in Rutledge's collected works, *Deep River,* and I had formed many ideas of the kind of man he must have been. This new book would verify or amend many of my assumptions, and I looked forward to reading the poet's account, in prose, of the restoration of Hampton Plantation, his ancestral home in the Low Country of South Carolina.

"Mickey said we all ought to take a trip to Hampton one of these Saturdays," Birdie said. "It's not all that far from Charleston. He said maybe we could even splurge and spend the night in a motel if you and Thomas were interested."

I did not answer but glanced back at the book and pretended to study the photograph of Rutledge on the book jacket. What would Birdie say, I wondered, were I to tell her that Thomas and I had never stayed in a motel together? What would Thomas say were I to mention Birdie's suggestion?

She took my silence for reluctance and did not press the matter. "Just ask Thomas about it sometime," she said, "and we can talk about it later. It would probably work better to wait till after school's out . . . if we decide to do it at all." She left my office, humming.

As I said, the book evoked as strong a sense of place as I have ever encountered in literature. At times when I was reading, it was as if I were breathing in the very air — the warm, damp fragrance — of the coastal country with its profusion of magnolia, dogwood, yellow jasmine, red woodbine, camellia japonica, sweet bay, myrtle, gardenia, and holly. I could close my eyes and hear with perfect clarity the shrill cry of the bobolink in the rice fields, the lapping of river water against the sides of a cypress canoe, the grunting of a foraging raccoon.

With patience and absolute cleanness of style, Rutledge instructed me in the ways of the lowlands. I learned of the transplanting of the redbud Judas tree, the unearthing of old wine bottles and Delft tiles, the mystic oneness with nature achieved by the marshland natives, unexpected clashes with bull alligators and diamondback rattlesnakes, the flight of the wild turkey, the nesting of the wood duck, the heavy flooding of the Santee River, the shadowy stealth of the gray fox, the rise of the moon above the pinelands.

And as I read the book over the course of six days in April, my soul opened wider. I wanted very much to visit this plantation, to view the majestic columned house and the massive oak upon which George Washington had gazed and pronounced his blessing, to walk through the gardens once tended by the gentle Flora, a former slave, whose magical touch with growing things included first a liberal measure of love.

You may imagine the sharp piercing of truth I felt when I read the lesson that Rutledge drew from Flora's gardening skills: "The best way to make people flower is just to love them." I paused from my reading and lifted my eyes. I was sitting in my living room at the time, in my rocking chair, and all about me I saw tangible tokens of Birdie's generosity of spirit: the tiny green leaves of the bonsai, the collection of piano duets, a crocheted doily, a cinnamon-scented candle, and the book in my lap, to name several.

From outdoors I heard the delicate tinkling of the wind chimes that Birdie and Mickey had bought for us at a craft fair in Williamston. Thomas had hung them from a branch of the pear tree in our side yard.

Had I felt that her gifts were only a ruse to ensnare me, as I had once declared though never truly believed, Birdie never would have won my heart. I am not easy prey for tricksters. By April, however, I knew that her gifts were merely an appendage of her love. They were not calculated. They had no other purpose than to please me.

How could it be, I asked myself, that in so short a time I had begun to loosen my grip upon my past suffering, to acknowledge the pain of others, to ruminate upon the long-ago teachings of my mother, wondering if perhaps the seed that she had planted in my heart and that Birdie had watered after long dormancy could indeed flower. How could it be that I had gone to the attic, unlocked my trunk, removed from it my mother's Bible, and begun reading the book of Job and the Psalms?

My question — "How could it be?" — was answered simply in a single word: love. I once again began to embrace truths that many years ago I had given over, for I saw in Birdie a trusting and selfless equanimity concerning the crooked places in her own past. She was the linchpin of my healing, the instrument of my salvation. Birdie had loved me to liberty, or at least to its brink. There were yet steps to be taken before my peace with God was secured.

School was closed for the spring break during the second week of April, prior to Easter Sunday. I met with Birdie as usual, however, for my piano lessons on Tuesday and Friday and for my organ lesson on Saturday morning. Though my ear informed me that I had much ground yet to cover in my musical training, I was progressing, in Birdie's words, "by leaps and bounds!"

Following my piano lesson on April 11, the Tuesday of our spring break, Birdie and I fell into conversation about unrealized talents. I had ended my lesson by playing "To a Wild Rose" by Edward MacDowell, and Birdie had, as always, grown immoderately laudatory in her commendation of what she referred to as my "perfect styling of each phrase."

My lesson over, she had invited me to stay for some light refreshments. "I wonder how you would've found out about your gift for music if we'd never met each other," she said as she poured for me a glass of grapefruit juice in the kitchen.

We sat down at the table together with a plate of sugar cookies between us. I ate only one, although they were delicious. "You seem to assume a false premise," I said, "namely that I *would* have discovered my ability without your aid."

"Oh, but of course you would have!" she cried. "Talent can't be buried forever."

"It can, and it often is," I stated.

"Oh no, not talent like yours. I just know that someday, somewhere you would've stumbled across a piano or some other instrument and learned it by trial and error if nothing else," she said. Still, her talk was always focused upon me. When I tried to turn it to her, as you will see in the following exchange, she resisted as she always did.

"Perhaps I would have," I said, "but the possession of potential in a given field in no way guarantees opportunity for development. None of us knows what he might have been in a different environment and under different influences. I believe, for instance, that *you* possess talents that have never been brought to fruition," and I looked at Birdie almost sternly.

"No, no," she said, laughing, "I've gone as far as I can go, but *you,* Margaret, you could really do something in music. I think you ought to look into private voice lessons, too. Why, you could get into one of the chorales over in Greenville. I'm sure of it!"

A few weeks earlier, Thomas and Mickey had begun singing "Down in the Valley" one evening after we had played a game of Rook. Thomas took the melody and Mickey harmonized. "Come on, gals, join us!" Mickey had urged, and Birdie had entered on the melody, at which point Thomas had shifted to bass. At last I filled in the alto line, and when we had finished, Birdie had turned upon me as if stunned. "I had no idea you could sing like that!" she exclaimed, to which Thomas had added, "Well, I've lived with her going on sixteen years, and I didn't know it, either!"

"You would be a better teacher than any teacher at Emma Weldy," I said to Birdie now.

"Oh, heavens!" she said, fanning her face. "I love children, but I couldn't teach! I didn't go to college a single day!"

"People of all ages pursue college degrees," I said.

"Well, I don't believe I'm up to that," she said. I detected a wistfulness of tone, however, even as she protested, but the moment passed. "Now, *you're* the one who should be looking into college courses!" she said. "You really ought to think about going further with your music, Margaret, and I mean it!" Clearly, she was determined to talk about me and not herself.

The following Saturday evening, April 15, we met Birdie and Mickey, along with Joan and Virgil, at C. C.'s Barbecue, located on the main street of Filbert between The Golden Toe Shoe Repair Shop and Sparky's Office Supply. Short on decor but long on taste, C. C.'s Barbecue attracts a multitude of customers from all parts of the state and was even featured several years ago in a regional book titled *Southern Spice: Barbecue in the Southeast.* To secure seating, it is necessary to arrive early, and this we did. By five o'clock the six of us were seated in a large booth next to the front window. I noticed that although the blinds were free from dust and the window glass was wiped to a sheen, a dead spider lay curled up in the corner of the sill.

C. C.'s was named after its original owner, a man whose full name had been Christopher Columbus Boatwright and whose recipe for barbecue had purportedly been a family secret for over one hundred years. C. C. Boatwright had moved his family to South Carolina from Kentucky in the early 1950s and had opened C. C.'s Barbecue in 1955. By all appearances no changes had been made in the furnishings of the interior since its opening. Aside from the spider, however, it was clean. The present proprietor is a grandson of C. C., with the curious name of Wooster Sneed Boatwright.

Joan and Virgil were by now seeing each other quite regularly, and together they had visited the Church of the Open Door in Derby three or four times, although Virgil was still actively involved in his own church in Filbert. Joan had attended his church several times, also.

It had been Birdie's idea to invite them to meet us at C. C.'s. She had inquired about them repeatedly since our evening at the Field Pea Restaurant in November and, according to Joan, had welcomed them enthusiastically, almost embarrassingly so, each time she had seen them together at church. Since Christmas Joan had not sought my counsel concerning her relationship with Virgil but had told me twice that "things were looking pretty good," which I took to mean either that she was moving closer to the acceptance of Virgil's theological ideals or that he was slowly removing himself from the tentacles of his religion. I felt the former to be the more likely of the two. I did not interrogate her, nor did she offer details.

As C. C.'s Barbecue offers only a buffet-style meal — serving pork, chicken, beef, mutton, and a dozen vegetables — there was considerable shuffling about and a great deal of coming and going among the six of us as we ate our dinner. Though the continuity of our conversation suffered somewhat, there was no lack of volume, both in the sense of quantity and loudness, most of it being light banter and casual observations.

I hold in my mind three memories of Birdie from this night. First, I recall that Virgil spoke at length about the mysterious stone colossi on Easter Island in the Pacific Ocean, and when he had finished, Birdie said, "How fascinating. I've never even *heard* of Easter Island before!" She shook her head and added, "Margaret's been putting ideas about college in my head, but if I ever did try to get in, I'm afraid they'd just laugh and say I had to start all over in first grade."

Mickey objected promptly and loudly, declaring Birdie to be "smarter than a whip" and telling her to remember her own advice that "you never know till you try it." She quickly tried to change the subject, but Mickey was not to be put off. Holding his napkin in front of her face as if to silence her, he held forth, his words sounding of repetition, as if he had rehearsed the matter many times to her in private. "Now that we're both working, we've got more money than we need," he said, "and I could help her study — as if *that* would do any good." Apparently, then, Birdie had kept our earlier conversation about college in her heart and had not only pondered my words but had even told Mickey about them.

Birdie swatted Mickey's napkin away and, turning to Virgil, asked, "Going back to mysteries, how do you think the Egyptians ever got those huge pyramids in place?" Mickey and I shared a look.

My second memory is a picture. Joan was telling of a man with whom she worked, describing his idiosyncratic nature, though not in a mean-spirited fashion. "At least once every half hour he combs his hair," Joan said, "and he writes everything out by longhand before he enters it in the computer, and he uses a *pencil,* never a pen. And of course the pencil has to be *sharpened* after every few sentences. Oh, and if he's in a strange room, he's got to figure out which direction north is or he can't function."

She went on to narrate the story of attending a meeting in the company of this man. "We had to go down several flights of stairs because the elevator was broken," she said, "and then we twisted around through all these hallways until we came to the conference room, which was big and well lit but didn't have any windows. So the meeting starts and Gerald is acting *so weird* — squirming around in his chair, looking up at the ceiling, then at the doors, tracing patterns in the air with his finger, sighing, and on and on. So I finally lean over to him and say, 'What in the world is the matter with you?' And do you know what he says? You won't believe this! He gives me the most desperate look and says, 'Which way is north? I've lost track.' Of course, I didn't have the foggiest idea, but I pointed immediately to the back wall, and then he settled right down."

Throughout this tale I watched Birdie. Her face was alight, her teeth clamped firmly upon her lower lip and her eyes fixed intently upon Joan. A phrase from Tracy Kidder's splendid book *Old Friends* came to my mind as I studied her. Mr. Kidder, in describing one of the residents of Linda Manor Nursing Home, wrote that the man had "a large capacity for vicarious enjoyment." If this man's capacity was large, Birdie's was immense, enormous, surpassing all limits. I can see her yet, bending toward Joan as she listened.

As I said, this memory is but a picture, for I cannot recall precisely what Birdie said following Joan's story. No doubt it ran along these lines: "Well, now, aren't people just the most interesting things? There are so many different kinds!" And had she met Gerald someday, she would have taken him under her wing with great tenderness and would have done everything within her power to ensure that he never lost his bearings.

My third memory of the evening is as a blinding white flash against which I hide my eyes. Before we parted, Birdie and Mickey walked with Thomas and me to our car, which was parked in the lot to the rear of C. C.'s. Joan and Virgil had already said good-bye and driven away.

"I wish we had time to play some Ping-Pong," said Mickey. "Or go for a walk — I'm full as a tick, as they say in Kuwait!" And he patted his stomach gently as if it were sore to the touch.

"If we get done at church at a decent time, maybe we could call you and you can come over for a little while," Birdie said with an expression in her eyes, which, as I look back upon it, seemed beseeching. Mickey had already told us before supper that they were scheduled to meet at the church at seven o'clock, along with other members of the decorating committee, to "add a few little touches" to the sanctuary for Easter Sunday.

"Or you could drop by our place," Thomas said. "Maybe we could play some Rook. Margaret and I need to get you back for last time."

"Well, we'll have to see how it goes," Mickey said good-naturedly. "Knowing some of the folks on the committee, it won't go fast. There'll be a lot more talking than decorating."

"And you'll be one of the worst!" Birdie said, laughing. Mickey pretended to be offended, pushing out his lower lip.

The two of them bade us farewell and had already moved away when Birdie appeared to think of something and swung back around. "Margaret! Thomas! Won't you . . ." She paused and contorted her face as if agonizing over what she was about to say. It was only a fraction of time, but I believe that I sensed what was coming. She took a step toward us and held out her hands, tilting her head imploringly. "Well, what I'm trying to say is

. . . would you please at least just *think* about coming . . . well, tomorrow is Easter Sunday, you know, and . . . oh, I know we've been over all this before, but . . ."

Mickey broke in, feigning a Chinese accent and holding his hands before him in a subservient, prayerlike pose, trying, I suppose, to ease the tension. "Ah-so, me translate for tongue-tied wife. Thomas and Margaret welcome to come to Church of Open Door tomorrow. We have special Easter service." Then, speaking normally, he added, "And we could probably even arrange a meal afterward, couldn't we, treasure?"

"Oh, by all means!" Birdie said. "I've got a ham I'm going to fix for our Sunday dinner, and we'd love to have you join us after church!"

"Ah-so!" said Mickey. "Eat ham with chopsticks!"

I despised myself for my response. I have relived the scene many times, wishing that I could alter my role. I was selfish and obstinate.

It is important to understand that in the past weeks, before our outing to C. C.'s Barbecue, I had actually begun to entertain the thought of visiting Birdie's church unannounced some Sunday, of arriving at the last minute and sitting in a back pew, of exiting swiftly at the conclusion of the service so as to escape the attention of church members such as Eldeen Rafferty. I had begun to feel a strong yearning to see Birdie at the organ, to hear prayers offered and hymns sung, to hear her beloved Brother Hawthorne preach, to observe firsthand the people of whom she so often spoke.

I had taken to arguing with myself over the matter. *Remember Marshland,* I warned myself. *Remember your grandfather. Remember the hypocrisy. Remember your vow never to enter another church.* I then answered my own objections. *This is not Marshland. My grandfather is dead. My vow has already been compromised by my organ lessons at the church.*

Like a petulant child, however, I opposed being led by the hand, and as we stood in the parking lot of C. C.'s Barbecue, I was filled with a perverse contrariness.

Thomas looked at me, his eyebrows raised as if in resignation. He shrugged and seemed on the verge of acquiescence when I spoke. "I thought that we had reached an understanding on the subject of your church," I said to Birdie. "Your needling and cajoling only serve to confirm our suspicions that your friendly advances are driven by ulterior motives." Like a child, I shoved away the very thing that I wanted because — oh, the shame of it — because *it was offered to me.*

Even as I spoke, fully aware of my disgraceful behavior, I was too proud, too stubborn to retract my words. The excuses that I chanted silently were feeble and altogether insubstantial. *I will not have my actions dictated. I will not surrender unless on my own terms. I will not be snared by offers of dinners,* and the like.

I whipped about and opened the car door, seated myself, and pulled the door shut with far more force than necessary. Through the closed window I heard Thomas's voice, then Mickey's in reply, but I could not distinguish their words. From Birdie I heard nothing. I was aware that the conversation had ended and that Thomas was walking around the car to the driver's side. I turned my head slightly and could see, through my peripheral vision, that Mickey and Birdie were moving away from our car toward their own.

Once seated in the car, Thomas made no move to start the engine. All was quiet except for the sound of his breathing. I have often wondered, at times with amusement, why women can breathe noiselessly, yet men must make an audible business of it. I found no amusement in the thought at this moment, however. At last Thomas spoke in a low, even tone. "That was uncalled for, Rosie. You hurt Birdie's feelings." He paused and then added, "She was cryin'." Another short interval and then, "It wouldn't hurt a thing in the world if we was to go to their church one Sunday. It'd sure mean a lot to 'em." Another pause before he inserted the key into the ignition and then, "Birdie sure sets a store by you. There was no need to answer her so rough." I said nothing, but my heart burned with shame.

I tried to telephone her later that night, but only once, at ten o'clock. To my great relief there was no answer, and I did not try again. The next morning at nine o'clock, Easter Sunday, a basket sat beside our newspaper on the front doorstep. It held freshly baked cinnamon rolls and a note in Birdie's handwriting. "We made these this morning and wondered if you were ready to eat again after that big meal last night." It was signed "Mickey and Birdie."

It did not slip my notice that they must have arisen before daybreak to bake and deliver homemade sweet rolls before going to church. I believe that I had only to say the word *church* and Thomas would have brushed off his black suit and stood ready at the door within minutes. I did not say anything, however, and when we ate our Sunday meal at two o'clock, neither of us seemed to have an appetite.

On Monday morning, April 17, I summoned Birdie to my office cubicle shortly after her arrival at school. At that time I delivered a carefully composed, pathetically inadequate apology. "My words on Saturday night were not meant to offend you. I regret having spoken hastily."

Birdie smiled at me, but it was a restrained smile. "I'll learn sooner or later, Margaret, not to push you. I'm sorry, too. I promise not to ask you again." I suppose that I should have received her pledge with gladness, but strangely, I did not. "You know, Margaret," she continued, "I was thinking, being your friend might just be the happiest and most important thing I do in my whole life. It might make you mad for me to say this, but I believe God has been getting me ready to be your friend for all these years. And I want to be a good one!"

Before I could respond, she smiled again, her face radiating with joyous purpose, and left my office. She appeared to have forgiven and forgotten my harsh words of Saturday night, for twice within the course of the morning she stopped by my office to converse briefly, once to share a story that Algeria had told her concerning a foiled burglary at a 7-11 store and later to ask for Joan's telephone number. "Mickey suggested that the six of us have a cookout at our house sometime soon," she said. "Do you think Joan and Virgil would play croquet with us?"

On Tuesday, April 18, she brought to work a tiny origami bird, which she placed upon my desk. One wing was slightly higher than the other, but as the bird was no more than two inches tall, the mild deformity resulted in only a faintly perceptible list. "There, that's the first one I've made that looks like anything," she said. "Mickey got this book at the library, and we've been trying different shapes. His are better than mine, though. You should see the grasshopper he made!" I picked up the bird and studied it at close range. It was made of pale blue paper, folded intricately. That it had taken a great deal of time was evident.

"Thank you," I said. "I shall display this beside the bonsai and figurine on my piano." One of Birdie's most recent gifts to me had been one of Mickey's "nut people." Fashioned from a small pecan shell and a large peanut shell, the figure wore a little white dress. Glued to one pipe-cleaner hand was a miniature wooden spoon and from the other dangled a red thread affixed to a dime-sized cardboard disk imprinted with tiny numbers, which was intended to represent a stopwatch. On the bark base were stenciled the words *Lunchroom Superviser.* Uncharacteristically, I smiled over the spelling error, seeing it as part of the figurine's charm.

We had our piano lesson as usual that Tuesday afternoon, and the last words I heard Birdie say before I got into my car and backed out of her driveway were these: "You know, Margaret, I think one sign of true friendship is that when you say good-bye, you're already looking forward to the next time you'll see each other." She could have said this at any number of other times during the course of our friendship, but she did not. She said it on the afternoon of April 18. This was the last time I saw her.

Sixteen hours later she was dead. Perhaps to some her death was overshadowed by another tragedy of national proportions on that day of April 19 — the bombing of the Alfred Murrah Federal Building in Oklahoma City. Surely those whose lives were directly affected by the bomb had no thought for a small, plain, obscure middle-aged woman in South Carolina whose life had suddenly ended. For my part, though I mourned with my countrymen the great magnitude of death and destruction in Oklahoma, and though I felt outrage at the cold premeditation of the act, it was but a pittance of sorrow compared to the vastness of my grief over losing Birdie.

When she had not arrived at school by seven o'clock on the morning of April 19, Francine came to my office door and asked, "Birdie didn't call in sick, did she?" I was aware of her tardiness, of course, and had already walked through the lunchroom and into the hallway twice, hoping to see her small form hurrying toward me.

"She did not," I answered. I saw Algeria glance at the large clock on the kitchen wall and then toward my office. She was in the act of arranging slices of bread on a baking sheet for the making of cinnamon toast.

" 'Cause if she did, we're in a fix," Francine said. "It's hamburgers for lunch, and Birdie always starts them fryin' while me and Algeria finish up breakfast."

"I know perfectly well what is on the menu for lunch," I said, "and as I told you already, Birdie is not ill. No doubt there is a good reason for her being late." I felt a chill of dread nevertheless, for it was now well over thirty minutes past her usual time of arrival.

Algeria joined Francine at my office door. She was shaking a large plastic jar of cinnamon and sugar. "You gonna call her house?" she asked gruffly, scowling at the telephone.

"I telephoned five minutes ago and received no answer," I said.

Francine and Algeria looked at each other without speaking and went back to their work. A few minutes later I found Mervin Lackey's telephone number in the directory and dialed it. As you may remember, the Lackeys were Mickey and Birdie's closest neighbors, or as Mickey was fond of saying, "our closest *living* neighbors," though their house was two hundred yards behind the Freemans' and through a stand of trees.

A woman answered the telephone, and it was clear to me that I had awakened her. When I identified myself and told her of my concern, she asked me to hold the line while she went to the back door, from where she could see through the trees to the Freemans' carport. She returned within seconds and said that their car was gone. I thanked her, then notified the school office of Birdie's absence, and went out into the kitchen to help Francine and Algeria.

"I don't like it," Algeria said. "Somethin's wrong." She was transferring a sheet of crisp toast from the oven to the warmer.

"Birdie's never been late a single day!" said Francine. "She'd call if something was wrong . . . unless maybe she can't get to a phone. I sure hope nothing bad's happened. Did you read about those two women in Pickens who got kidnapped by those teenagers that set fire to a church? The women came in to clean the church and caught the boys pouring gasoline all over —"

"Francine, that is totally irrelevant to Birdie," I interrupted impatiently. "Now, watch what you are doing. You have spilled sugar all over the floor."

When Mr. Solomon came into the kitchen twenty-five minutes later, I could read disaster upon his face. I did not want to hear his words. The children had begun filing through the line for breakfast by now, and I was standing at my post beside the cash register. As Mr. Solomon approached me, I heard a fourth-grade boy call out, "Hey! Where's Miz Birdie at?"

The very word *accident* implies a departure from what is expected and desirable. Most are senseless, without pattern. I know first-hand of such calamities. I suppose I should have been prepared, and perhaps to some degree I was, for I had come to think of my friendship with Birdie as a treasure highly cherished, of inestimable value, yet ephemeral. I felt as though it were — as the saying goes — too good to last. Her death completed a trinity of losses in my life. In that regard, therefore, I suppose it was not without pattern. I lost my mother. I lost my son. I lost my friend.

Driving south on Highway 11 that morning, Mickey Freeman had suffered a near fatal heart attack. His body had collapsed forward, and the car, traveling at an estimated speed of fifty miles per hour, had left the road and collided with a tree. Birdie had died instantly.

To have Birdie snatched from me could have — and perhaps only a month earlier *would* have — pushed me backward, spiraling me once again into profound darkness and railing against the God who allows those whom he claims as his own to suffer. I cannot say why her death did not send me reeling and cursing, but I know this: Though the depth of my sorrow over losing her cannot be measured, I believe that I felt it to be inevitable. I will not say *fitting,* though were she able to speak today, she would no doubt take it a step further. I can almost hear her saying: "God had it all planned out, Margaret, and he meant it for good!" I believe there is one word that Birdie would desire, could she choose a descriptor for her death. Not tragic, not disastrous, not calamitous, but *beneficial.*

A person's death forces scrutiny of his life by those left behind, and for those who knew Birdie Freeman, such examination could serve only to enlighten and uplift their hearts. In contemplating the life of Birdie, the fight has gone out of me. I have no Rosetta stone by which to decipher the meaning and purpose of suffering, but I know that its imprint upon the scroll of mankind is foreordained. I cannot understand, nor do I need to. To borrow the words of David, the thought "is high, I cannot attain unto it."

I have read that Kierkegaard, a philosopher whose ideals would hardly agree with those of Birdie and her fellow churchgoers, was obsessed with the biblical story of Abraham and Isaac, for he believed that it exemplified perhaps better than any other the divine contradiction of God's nature: He is good and he allows, even demands, suffering. That confidence in such a God requires a "leap of faith" is an understatement. The chasm is broad and dark. But Birdie had done it. She had crossed the gap and had bade me follow.

On April 22 I at last attended a service at

Birdie's church. No one played the organ at her funeral. Mickey was not present; he was still confined to the hospital. I suppose that my tale is in some way balanced by the fact that it begins and ends with a funeral, and further, that at Birdie's funeral, as at Mayfield Spalding's, tribute was publicly paid by Eldeen Rafferty. Though I groaned inwardly when the large, ungainly woman stood to speak, I was soundly instructed in the minutes that followed, and not without great surprise, as I listened to her words. As I said earlier, Birdie was not one to talk of herself. Smarting from my own past wounds, I had taken what had amounted to no more than a fleeting interest in Birdie's. Eldeen Rafferty opened my understanding.

Eldeen stood at the front of the church beside Birdie's casket, which was closed. She wore a dark navy dress that had no belt, giving her the contour of a massive pillar. Around her neck was wrapped a gaudy scarf striped with the colors of summer fruit — watermelon, raspberry, peach, lemon — bunched and fastened clumsily with a silver pin in the shape of a butterfly. Before speaking, she laid her hand upon the lid of the casket and closed her eyes briefly as if in prayer. Then lifting her face, she proclaimed, "Birdie Freeman was a saint of the Lord Jesus and a precious gem in his crown!"

She spoke with such thunderous conviction

that Thomas, seated beside me, visibly flinched. "And she was one of the sweetest, truest friends I had in this world," Eldeen continued, "and there's probably lots of other folks that says the same thing 'cause she never met a stranger. I've planned out a speech that comes from her name, Birdie, B-I-R-D-I-E, even though that wasn't her real name, which was Bernadetta, but hardly a soul ever called her that. The first letter of Birdie is *B,* and that stands for *bright,* 'cause Birdie was the brightest, cheerfulest, faithfulest Christian I ever knew. She was always smilin' and would just sparkle up a room with her pretty little laugh."

Eldeen put her head to one side and pursed her lips before resuming. "I don't know if I should even say this or not — I hadn't *counted* on sayin' it, and she probably wouldn't *want* me to — but I'm goin' to anyhow 'cause I feel like the *Lord* wants me to."

She nodded emphatically and moved her large forefinger across the audience. "Birdie's smile was a sign of the grace and goodness of Jesus in her heart," she said, nearly shouting once again, " 'cause if anybody had a right to look out-of-sorts and down-at-the-corners, it was Birdie! Some of you maybe didn't even know she never had her a real mama or daddy. She was shoved around here and there when she was a little girl, nobody really wantin' her." Here she paused and engaged in a bit of playacting, changing the timbre of her voice with each line and gesturing dramatically. "Here, you take her!" "No, I don't want her. I got enough kids of my own!" "Get a load of this little scrawny girl — probably can't even earn her keep!" "Send her back to the orphanage!" "I can't take her. What good would she do me?"

Eldeen shook her head sadly and lowered her voice. "Why, she was almost a grown-up woman 'fore anybody down here on earth loved her!" Eldeen jabbed her finger as if singling out various individuals and said, "Can you imagine bein' a little girl and not havin' a soul to love you? With some folks it would of closed 'em up tight and made 'em feel mean and sorry for theirself, but with Birdie it made her open herself up wide 'cause, you see, she had Jesus in her heart. She got saved by readin' a gospel tract when she was only a little girl, and she latched onto Jesus and lived for him the rest of her life!" Someone seated behind me blew his nose loudly.

At intervals Eldeen herself wept freely as she spoke but halted only once to wipe her eyes with a man's handkerchief that she removed from inside the cuff of her dress sleeve. "She was a little bitty thing," she said, "but she was *strong in the Lord!* She bore up! She knew about bein' sick and about doc-

651

tors' knives and such. She looked old Mr. Death in the eye nearly twenty years ago, but she asked God to heal her and he did it!"

"She knew about wantin' somethin' and not gettin' it, too," Eldeen went on. "It like to broke her heart that she couldn't ever have babies, for she did love little children, Birdie did, but then she settled her mind about it, and one day she said to me" — Eldeen pitched her voice higher, producing an odd, husky squeak — " 'Eldeen,' she said, 'I might of been too busy to help out all the folks that needs help if I'd of had children. I think God wanted me to use my spare time bein' light and salt to all the people that needs it!' Birdie was like that Shunamite woman Brother Hawthorne was preachin' about last week. *She did what she could!* And I only hope I can be a *tenth* as givin' and carin' and lovin' and faithful as she was!"

With the ease of a natural-born storyteller, Eldeen moved through her acrostic outline, and although some of her key words seemed at times to overlap with others, and although her illustrations often failed to pertain directly to the point at hand, she held her listeners entranced. The letter *I* stood for inspiring, *R* for ready, *D* for diligent, *I* for industrious, and *E* for eager. She must have spoken for twenty minutes, though I was unaware of the passage of time.

At last she appeared to be finished, moving

652

as if to sit down, but then she stopped and held up her hand. "And one more thing I just now thought of!" she said. "A bird *flies!*" Eldeen extended both arms and flapped them with large, almost graceful motions. "A bird was made with wings to push hisself up off the ground, to *mount up.* And that's how God made Birdie. She did exactly what her name says! She waited on the Lord God and trusted in him, and he renewed her strength and gave her wings like a eagle!" The fluttering of her arms had grown slower as she spoke her concluding words. "And that's what he wants every single one of us to do, too — soar up above the world with praise on our lips!" She looked across the audience and then said firmly, "That's what Birdie would want me to close with."

The funeral ended with the reading of Scripture and the singing of a congregational song, identified by the pastor as Birdie's personal favorites. As he read the third chapter of John's gospel, I felt the falling away of a doubt — not that God sent his son, not that his son must die, not that man must believe in Jesus, for indeed from childhood I had never balked at these truths, but that *God so loved the world.* Oddly, this had been my stumbling block — not God's plan for man's redemption, not the vicarious atonement itself, but the motivation behind it. Again I imagined Birdie's voice: "See, Margaret, God *planned* for his own son to suffer, but he did it out of *love* for us." When one looks at suffering with this fact in mind, it is hard to remain bitter.

And as we sang "Footprints of Jesus," I closed my eyes and saw a strange sight, one I can yet see: Birdie Freeman pausing inside the threshold of heaven, turning back to beckon to me, smiling with great joy in the presence of angels. Curiously, I see upon her shoulders wings of the finest feathers, pure white, outstretched as if in flight, though she stands at heaven's gate. I want to tell her that she may fold her wings, for she has reached her destination.

Meanwhile, I stand at the edge of a deep forest, ready to emerge from its shadows, and *when from these woods I part,* I shall, in the words of Eldeen Rafferty, push off the ground and mount up.

EPILOGUE

The epilogues that I have read at the ends of books have affected me in different ways. At times I am annoyed by them, for the story is done. Some writers, it seems, cannot bear the thought of silence and must, like Eldeen Rafferty, continue talking because after so long, I suppose, it has grown to be a habit. At other times I am gratified to find that the author has written an epilogue, because without it the story is still loose, not tamped down. The epilogue, as I understand it, should serve a purpose. It is not merely for adornment. It often reflects upon events that have occurred between the final chapter and some subsequent time.

Note to the reader: Do not deluge me with protests concerning the death of the central character, for you were amply forewarned. Did not I deplore the "pall of death" upon my story at the end of chapter one? Did not I speak of Birdie Freeman always in the past tense from her earliest appearance in the tale?

Did not I stress repeatedly her physical proximity to a cemetery? Did she not seem to belong more in heaven than on earth? Taken together, these and other signposts pointed plainly to Birdie's end.

And yet, of course, she has not ended.

Two days ago I saw Algeria in Winn Dixie. We met each other in the center of an aisle, between the paper towels on one side and the dishwashing liquid on the other. I spoke first.

"Good day, Algeria."

She nodded, without smiling, and said simply, "Margaret."

"Mickey wrote us a letter last week," I said to her. "He has found an apartment near his sister's house in Tuscaloosa."

"Uh-huh. He sent my brother a postcard," she replied.

"We have only three weeks before school starts again," I said, and she grunted and shook her head. As she reached to take a box of Brillo pads from the bottom shelf, I asked, "How is your mother?"

"Not gettin' no better," she said, straightening and tossing the box into her cart, which was quite full and poorly arranged, as if she had given no thought to organization. "But she ain't no worse off neither, I don't guess." She frowned at the shelves of paper goods behind me. "I gotta get back to her," she added, pushing her cart forward a few inches.

"Yes, well, good-bye. I hope you . . ." but I could think of no way to end the sentence.

We both moved forward, past each other, and then I heard her ask from behind me, "Margaret? You got somebody gonna take her place yet?"

I turned back. "A woman has been hired," I said. "But she will not take her place." We looked at each other for a long, silent moment.

"Nuh-uh. No way nobody could do that," Algeria said before turning once again. "No way in the whole world nobody could do that."

We never drove to Hampton Plantation, of course, at least not the four of us. As I mentioned earlier, Thomas and I took a day trip to the coast a few weeks ago. We left early one morning and visited Hampton, where the wild indigo, marsh pinks, meadowsweet, and red woodbine were in bloom. We walked to the edge of the Great Santee River, heard the drone of cicadas, and smelled the moist earth. We saw the George Washington oak festooned with moss.

We then drove south to Charleston and toured the Battery and the Market. We walked along the beach until the sun began to sink toward the horizon. Having looked past the beauties of nature during my years of isolation, I feel a great urgency to drink in forests and hills, shores and valleys, flowers and trees. "About the woodland I must go," as A. E. Housman put it. Thomas and I both removed our shoes to walk along the Charleston beach, and when he took my hand, I did not pull away. Before we left the shore, we stood and looked out toward the ocean, its waters enflamed by the sunset.

"She wanted us to come here together," I said at last. "I wish we had." And I turned to Thomas and laid my head upon his shoulder. He gathered me to himself tenderly, and I wept. "I miss her so," I said. As the waves washed over my feet, at last I opened my heart and released my great burden of sorrow. I was flooded with remorse, of course, for my many unkindnesses toward Birdie, and I was filled with wonder that she had countered each rebuff with yet more love. I know not how long I wept in Thomas's arms, but when I had emptied myself of tears, I spoke these words aloud: "Thank you for giving her to me." I was not speaking to Thomas, of course.

Later we ate dinner at a small restaurant that charged exorbitant prices and arrived home after midnight.

Whether there can be any romance for Thomas and me I do not know. I feel certain, however, that there can be, that there *is* love in plentiful supply. When we pulled into our driveway at half past twelve in the morning, I said to Thomas, "I would like to go back to

Charleston sometime." And then I added, "I would like to stay longer than a day."

He glanced at me quickly, breathed in sharply, and said, "Anytime you say, Rosie. You just name it." In the months since Birdie's death, I have begun to share small bits of my heart with Thomas and have found him to be a most gentle and ready listener.

In May, after Mickey went home to recuperate, Thomas and I visited him frequently. Mickey's recovery was slow and painful. His heart was wounded in every way. He closed his eyes when I spoke to him of Eldeen's speech at Birdie's funeral. He was sitting at home in his recliner at the time with a tray in his lap, for Thomas and I had brought supper to him. "Oh my, I don't think Birdie would've wanted everyone feeling sorry about her upbringing," he said. "I hope Eldeen didn't overdo it. That was something Birdie didn't like to dwell on. I can't figure out how Eldeen ever dragged it all out of her. I sure never heard Birdie bring up the subject." He smiled ever so slightly and added, "That Eldeen — she might be long-winded herself, but she sure has a way of getting other folks to open up and talk, too."

"People who loved Birdie should know what she overcame," I said. "It helps us to see things differently in our own lives." I wonder now at times whether Birdie could have shaken me from my stupor sooner had she taken a different course, had she looked me squarely in the eye, for instance, and said, "Quit wallowing in your past! Use it as a springboard! Move ahead! You didn't invent suffering!" Had she enumerated for me her own history of suffering — her rejection as a child, her battle with disease, the pain of barrenness — perhaps she would have disarmed me earlier. But perhaps not — who can say? It was not her way.

With his eyes still closed, Mickey told us again of standing at a window as a young man in his house in Tuscaloosa and seeing Birdie at the clothesline next door. "The wind was whipping up good that day," he said, "and she had to practically wrestle those clothes to get them on the line. I could tell she had spunk, little as she was. I yelled something foolish out the window to her, but she wouldn't hardly give me the time of day — acted like she had to get done and get back inside. We found out later she'd lived with those people next door for over a year but wasn't related to them in any way, and they let her know as soon as she came to live with them that she was there to work. They had six kids, so there was plenty to do."

Mickey went on to tell how his mother had taken an interest in Birdie and had looked into the situation next door more closely than the neighbors would have liked. "We weren't exactly their favorite people after Mother reported them," he said. "They ended up moving away, and months later Birdie came to live with us. She was seventeen, almost eighteen by that time."

Eldeen Rafferty's words came back to me. *"Why, she was almost a grown-up woman 'fore anybody loved her!"*

"The interesting thing about that family next door to us," Mickey said a few minutes later, "was that they were the ones who started Birdie in piano, even though they didn't know that's what they were doing and sure wouldn't have done it if they'd known."

One day a week, as Mickey told it, a piano teacher came to the house to instruct the oldest child, a pampered, indolent boy of ten or eleven who had not the least bit of musical inclination. Arranging to be in or near the room where the piano was located, Birdie listened with utmost attention, all the while dusting, mending, ironing, and so forth. When opportunity arose for her to be alone in the house, which was seldom, she flew to the piano to practice what she had heard. "When Mother signed her up for her own lessons after she came to live with us, Birdie *cried*," Mickey said. "I can still see it. I mean she turned on both spigots full force!"

He stopped speaking for a few minutes to finish his meal, and I removed the tray. "But she sure didn't like to talk about her past," he said at length. "Maybe it would've helped if she had — I don't know. She was a real private person in a lot of ways."

"Eldeen said that Birdie never knew her parents," I said.

Mickey shook his head. "No. I don't know the details, but from what my mother found out, I think it was one of those cases you hear about — a baby being abandoned in a public place." He laid a hand to his forehead. "The whole thing sounds made up, doesn't it?"

"She would have been a good mother," I said.

Mickey nodded. "Oh, the best. The very best." He sat forward and laid his hands on his knees. "She probably never told you we tried to adopt a baby once. Had the room all painted and a crib set up — the whole works. At the last minute the mother backed out. It was real hard on Birdie. She said she couldn't ever go through that again, so we never did."

Before Mickey moved back to Tuscaloosa at the end of May, we drove to his house on three consecutive Sundays to take him to church. Of course we attended the services with him. I could not bring myself to look at the organ on those Sundays, but I could feel its presence, cold and mute. It still sat unoccupied.

One Sunday as we were leaving his house, Mickey walked to the piano and removed the cross-stitched poem from the wall above it. "I've been meaning to give this to you," he said to me. "Birdie would want you to have it. She was always telling me I ought to do another one so she could give it to you, but I never got around to it." He advanced toward me holding the picture before him.

"It is too great a gift," I said, stepping back.

"She loved you, Margaret," Mickey said. "Think of it as a gift from her. You wouldn't refuse her the happiness of giving you something, would you? Anyway, I've got to start packing up, and this'll be one less thing to worry about." I took it, of course, and the next day Thomas hung it for me on the wall above my piano, where I see it each time I lift my eyes from the keyboard.

We were with him on the last day of May, along with other friends from the church, when the moving van drove away. The house was empty but would soon be occupied by a family with several small children. "Birdie would approve of that," Mickey had said when he told us about the sale.

Thomas and I were the last of his friends to leave. Mickey wanted to take one last walk through the house alone, and then he would follow the moving van to Tuscaloosa. He hugged Thomas first and then me. Not one of us spoke a word, for the moment was too full for words. As we got into the car, however, Mickey called out, "You haven't seen the last of me!" Thomas paused to blow his nose before starting the car, and as we pulled away Mickey stood alone on the porch, waving until we turned onto Highway 11.

Many books that I have read are clean and symmetrical, nearly seamless — Anne Tyler's *Dinner at the Homesick Restaurant,* Terry Kay's *To Dance with the White Dog,* Gail Godwin's *The Good Husband,* Shirley Abbott's *The Bookmaker's Daughter.* This is not to say that these are *perfect* works. I am reminded, for example, of a faulty assumption concerning marriage that Shirley Abbott lays down: "The gap between two bodies can never be permanently bridged" — an assumption refuted, I believe, by the marriage of Birdie and Mickey.

Other stories move in fits and starts — Mary Morris's *Songs in Ordinary Time,* Amy Tan's *The Joy Luck Club,* Laura Esquivel's *Like Water for Chocolate,* all of which are nevertheless compelling, although again not perfect, works. I do not prefer Laura Esquivel's mixing of realism with phantasmagoria, for instance.

I acknowledge that my extended tale of Birdie is patched and irregular, like a beginner's badly pieced quilt. I am loath to display it, fearing that by deficient workmanship my story is neither lovely nor serviceable.

Had I known Birdie longer, I could have presented her in a more convincing light. I would have seen her flaws of character, for undoubtedly she had them, and I would have

664

woven them into the whole. As extremes are rarely believable, there are readers who will accuse me of selective and slanted reporting, but to them I shall answer that I have told all that I have seen.

Perhaps Birdie Freeman, out of my sight and hearing, screamed with defiance at police officers, kicked small animals, and spoke ill of her fellowman. Perhaps she exceeded the speed limit, slipped merchandise unpaid for into her pocketbook, or lied on survey forms. Perhaps she answered Mickey in a waspish manner, saved the best slice of dessert for herself, or made much of minor aches. Had I observed such human frailties, I would have included them in the record. I have no stomach for Pollyannas and Little Lord Fauntleroys. I am quick to spot cheap veneer, whether in furniture, literature, or character. Therefore, to the naysayers and cynics among my readers — with whom I sympathize, for I am of the same nature — I repeat in my defense: You have seen Birdie Freeman as I saw her: gentle of spirit, high of principle, unfaltering in kindly demeanor. I have added nothing and have omitted only more of the same.

Birdie gave me much. No mortal can convict of sin, offer atoning grace, or restore the faith of another, yet God can use a man or woman to hold a lantern so that others may find the way to truth. Birdie was my lantern.

Her light shone with great conviction. That she was sent to me from God I know without question.

The best stories leave the theme unstated. A competent writer communicates through suggestion. His message rises unspoken from between the words of his narrative like music from another world. Its bold announcement would fall upon the ear as discord. As I am a novice, however, I doubt my powers, and lest I should have wasted these many pages, I must set down, for my own peace, the distillation of my tale. Herein lies the sum of my words: *"And now abideth faith, hope, love, these three; but the greatest of these is love."* Given sun and rain, a flower *will* bloom. To the human heart love is irresistible. Though I have not solved the mystery of suffering, I have felt the healing work of love.

I have rambled long past dark, and daybreak is at hand. I have before me three telephone numbers, which I shall dial after the sun is up. My decisions have been made. And after I make my three telephone calls, I will inquire at a nearby private college concerning a course of study. I will seek instruction in piano and organ, in music theory, in vocal technique. I also wish to survey the history of music. I may attend classes in the afternoons, evenings, summers. Perhaps someday before I die I may compose a sonata. I will also study poetry.

But first, my telephone calls. I have before me the telephone number of the Lena Lansford Home for Girls in Mount Chesney. I will ask the administrator whether I may serve as friend and mentor to a girl who has suffered, perhaps to several. I am ready, as Mickey expressed it, to "put my pain to good use." I have laid aside a sum of money that may serve to relieve some small burden from a troubled girl.

The second number is that of Pastor Theodore Hawthorne of the Church of the Open Door in Derby. Some weeks ago he came to our home one evening after having telephoned first. He asked Thomas and me that night if we had given any thought to the things we had heard during our visits to the church. We told him that we had. He did not push or pry but told us that he would consider it an honor to answer any of our questions or counsel us in any way. We put him off, kindly, but Thomas told him that we would "be back in touch." I shall call him, and we shall meet with him, perhaps this very night.

I find that I want very much to be among the just, who live by faith. And, though a late-blooming wish, I want also to show my faith by my works, as Birdie did. To this end, perhaps tomorrow I shall cook a dinner of fried chicken, creamed potatoes, buttered carrots, and garden peas. I shall make yeast rolls and peach cobbler, and Thomas shall drive me to Algeria's house to help me carry in the dishes. This could be a small start.

The third telephone number is Joan's. I will give her my manuscript to read, for I feel that I must not keep it. I will talk to her of her church attendance and will ask her about Virgil Dunlop. When describing Joan, I want to be able to say, "She is my friend" rather than simply "She is my husband's cousin."

After these and many other matters are settled, I shall ask Theodore Hawthorne whether I might practice the hymns for an upcoming service and sit in Birdie's place at the organ. My hands shall touch the keys that she once played, adjust the stops, and turn the pages of the same hymnal. My feet shall press the same pedals.

Strangely, it is Birdie's feet of which I have often thought of late. Her footsteps in my life were quick and soft, busy about their work, seeking direct paths yet careful to avoid treading upon new sod or trampling *some wildflower in my heart.*

I look out my window and see that the sun is rising, spreading its colors over the world. Rain has fallen during the night, the lakes are full, and the rivers flow to the sea.

ABOUT THE AUTHOR

Jamie Langston Turner has been a teacher for twenty-seven years at both the elementary and college levels, and has written extensively for a variety of periodicals, including *Faith for the Family, Moody,* and *The Christian Reader.* Her first novel, *The Suncatchers,* was published in 1995. Born in Mississippi, Jamie has lived in the South all her life and currently resides with her husband and son in South Carolina, where she teaches creative writing and poetry at a university in the Southeast.

The employees of Thorndike Press hope you have enjoyed this Large Print book. All our Thorndike and Wheeler Large Print titles are designed for easy reading, and all our books are made to last. Other Thorndike Press Large Print books are available at your library, through selected bookstores, or directly from us.

For information about titles, please call:

(800) 223-1244

or visit our Web site at:

www.gale.com/thorndike
www.gale.com/wheeler

To share your comments, please write:

Publisher
Thorndike Press
295 Kennedy Memorial Drive
Waterville, ME 04901

1-12